The Hometown Bookshop

JENNA WARREN

Fairlight Books

First published by Fairlight Books 2025

Fairlight Books
Summertown Pavilion, 18–24 Middle Way, Oxford,
OX2 7LG

A CIP catalogue record for this book is available from the British
Library.

1 2 3 4 5 6 7 8 9 10

ISBN 978-1-914148-78-1

www.fairlightbooks.com

Printed and bound in Great Britain

Cover Design © Rebecca Fish

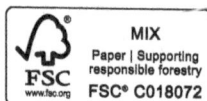

MIX
Paper | Supporting
responsible forestry
FSC
www.fsc.org   FSC® C018072

For the booksellers

I

Greg

It was a Monday morning in late May, in the middle of my twentieth year as manager of Seaswept Books. I had my morning routine down to a fine art. I got to work at 9.50am, switched on the lights and powered up the computer and till system. At 9.55, I went into the tiny stockroom, where I made myself a cup of coffee. At 9.59, I unlocked the front door and flipped the sign to *OPEN*. Then I took my place behind the counter, where I spent a blissful three minutes sipping my coffee and staring at this little place that was mine. Well, practically mine, at any rate.

From my seat, I could see the full length of the bookshop. My favourite section – Classics – was within handy reaching distance of the counter. Beyond that, there was General Fiction, Sci-Fi and Fantasy, and Crime. The opposite wall was devoted to non-fiction, mainly Local Interest. Finally, just in front of the large bay window, was the Children's section.

All of the shelves were full, and there were several teetering piles of unsorted volumes on the tables in the middle of the shop floor, and around the edges of the shop floor itself. There were a *lot* of books in Seaswept Books, and all of them had been lovingly chosen and acquired by me.

I sipped my coffee again. My mug had a slogan on it: *Employee of the Year*. This was Maria's idea of a joke, because I was the bookshop's only employee.

It was all very peaceful. Until, of course, the inevitable phone call, which came at 10.05am.

It was Mrs Johnson. Mrs Johnson called me every Monday morning. The reason for her call was always the same.

'Hello, Greg, dear. I was just wondering if Stephen King had a new book out yet?'

'Not this week,' I said. 'But I can check the publication date of his next one.'

I opened our wholesaler's website and typed in *STEPHEN KING*. While I was typing, my elbow caught my coffee mug. The mug tilted. Time seemed to slow. Then the receptacle toppled over, spilling a slow motion, cinematic flood of coffee all over my computer keyboard.

'Oh, fuuu—' I said, before realising I was still on the phone, and swallowing the remaining consonants.

'Are you all right, dear?' said Mrs Johnson.

'Yes, sorry, quite all right.' I grabbed a duster from under the desk.

'You're not busy, are you?'

'No, no.' I dabbed at the spillage, but the duster was having very little effect. I looked around for something else to use. There was a box of customer orders just behind the counter, the top stuffed with the sort of packing paper which expands to fill any available space. I picked some up and continued dabbing the keyboard.

'Have you found his next book?' said Mrs Johnson.

I peered at the computer screen. 'Yes. It's out in October.'

There was a sigh over the line. 'I wish he'd get a move on.'

'Well, he usually publishes at least one book a year,' I said, unsure why I felt the need to defend the honour of one of the world's bestselling authors.

'I suppose you're right,' said Mrs Johnson. 'I expect he's a very busy man.'

'I expect he is,' I said. The packing paper wasn't particularly absorbent. I gave up and scrunched it into a soggy ball. 'Would you like me to pre-order his new book for you?'

'Is it in paperback?'

'No, hardback. £22.'

A pause.

'I think I'll wait for the paperback, dear.'

I suppressed a sigh. 'Of course, Mrs Johnson. That's no problem.'

We said our goodbyes. When Mrs Johnson had hung up, I stared down at the keyboard. I turned once again to the duster and managed to mop up the excess coffee. Then I tipped the keyboard upside down, dislodging several brown droplets onto the counter. I cleaned this up with antibacterial spray.

Finally, I sat back down with a sigh.

Gosh. What a mess. But it could have been so much worse. The computer equipment belonged to the bookshop, and I had no desire to pay for replacements. Maria, the owner of Seaswept Books, would probably say it didn't matter, but I knew I would feel guilty and insist on paying. It wasn't her fault that I was so clumsy.

I returned to the stockroom and made myself a fresh cup of coffee. The simple activity steadied my nerves. Meanwhile, the bookshop remained empty.

This wasn't unusual, particularly for a Monday. Shellcliff was the sort of place best described as 'sleepy'. It had once been quite a vibrant seaside town, all arcades and donkey rides and picnics on the beach. Like many small seaside resorts, it had fallen victim to the rise in overseas holidays. Even as a child, I had only ever seen it slightly busy, and usually only at weekends. This suited me, because I've never liked crowds.

In many ways, the town was very dear to me.

Once I had recovered sufficiently from the coffee incident, I turned my attention to our monthly order. Maria assigned me a budget each month, which I could spend on whichever books I wanted. She always said that she trusted my judgement and my taste, an assessment which I found quite touching.

I flicked through the heavy buyer's notes catalogue, found the first title that caught my eye, and typed it into the wholesaler's search engine.

Or at least I tried to. It seemed that the 'A' on my keyboard was no longer working.

Maybe it was a fluke. I tried another title. This time, I found that the 'O' didn't work.

With a feeling of creeping dread, I opened a Word document and typed *A E I O U*. None of the letters appeared.

It seemed the coffee had consumed all the vowels. Swept them away.

If this was indeed the case, it was going to be a very long Monday. I wouldn't be able to do any buying, or search for anything on the internet, or take any customer orders. I had a mobile phone, but the stock control system was on the desktop.

It looked like I would have to replace the keyboard after all. For now, I would need to note everything down by hand. At least I could go through the catalogue and mark the titles I was interested in. Perhaps I could pop to Argos after work. I could replace the keyboard, and Maria would never have to know.

Ding-dong.

The sound of the doorbell made me look up. Maria entered the shop, followed by a woman I had never seen before. She looked about the same age as me, mid-forties, and she was wearing a long, flowery tunic dress and lots of bright, chunky jewellery.

'Hello, Greg,' said Maria, approaching the counter. 'How's business this morning?'

'A bit quiet,' I said. 'Mrs Johnson rang about the new Stephen King.'

'That's good,' said Maria. She turned to smile at the other woman. 'Sarah, this is Greg, the shop manager. He's been with us for twenty-five years, twenty in his current role. Greg, this is Sarah. She's going to be taking over the shop.'

I stared at Maria, then at Sarah. I blinked.

'Taking over the shop?'

'Yes.' Maria's smile faltered a little. 'I did tell you I was thinking of selling up.'

'I thought you meant a few years in the future.' This wasn't good at all. I liked Maria. I knew where I was with her. She wasn't exactly a hands-on shop owner, not anymore, and she tended to keep away, trusting me with day-to-day operations. We made a good team.

'I'm getting on a bit, Greg,' said Maria. 'It feels like the right time. And Sarah used to come here as a little girl. She has lots of brilliant ideas to develop the bookshop.'

This didn't reassure me. I turned to Sarah. 'Have you owned a bookshop before?'

Sarah narrowed her eyes.

'I'm a big reader,' she said. 'And this isn't my first business.'

Maria laughed. 'Greg's just interested, aren't you?'

I realised I'd made a slip, and nodded, even though I wasn't interested beyond knowing if my beloved shop was going to be in safe hands. 'Yes. Very.'

'He's an excellent manager,' said Maria. 'Very experienced.'

'I'm sure,' said Sarah. I didn't like the way she was looking at me. It felt like she was measuring me with her eyes, taking in every small detail. I dropped my gaze to the counter.

'If you'd like to stay for a bit, we can show you how the ordering system works,' said Maria.

I looked up. 'Um... I'm afraid that won't be possible.'

'Why not?'

'I can't look anything up. The keyboard's not working. There was an... incident with some coffee.'

'Oh dear,' said Maria. 'So you can't type anything?'

'I can type some things,' I said. 'It's the vowels, you see.'

Sarah looked confused. 'Vowels?'

'Yes. You know: A E I O U.'

'Yes, I know what vowels are,' said Sarah, a note of impatience creeping into her voice.

I looked at Maria. 'I'm sorry.'

Maria smiled, but the expression seemed a little forced. 'It's okay. We can soon buy a new keyboard.' She turned to Sarah. 'Maybe we should go and get a coffee somewhere? There are… things we need to talk about.'

Sarah looked at me again, her lips set in a thin line. 'Yes. I think there are.'

I watched them leave the shop. I was relieved to be alone again, but the entire exchange had given me a dreadful sense of foreboding. What if Sarah wanted to change everything about the shop? I had it exactly as I liked it, and I didn't relish the thought of 'development', or whatever it was that Maria had said.

Worse than that, there was the distinct feeling that I had shown myself up. What if Sarah decided to dismiss me?

The bookshop was my world. It was perhaps a small world, but it was mine. Leaving it didn't bear thinking about.

2

Charlotte

I hated matinees.

Picture, if you will, swathes of so-called 'theatregoers' who actually have no idea how to behave inside a theatre. Perhaps they're disappointed because they hoped the show would have a celebrity in it. Or maybe, if I'm being charitable, they're just a bit tired after their journey to London. Maybe they're a school party, forced to sit through the performance in the name of education. Whatever the reason, they're all set for two hours of scrolling through their phones, rustling sweet packets, chatting among themselves and – on one memorable occasion – chomping their way through a takeaway pizza.

Matinees – particularly Saturday matinees in early summer – are the antithesis of art.

They're bloody exhausting, quite frankly.

This particular Saturday started like any other. I arrived as late as I possibly could – thirty minutes before curtain-up – and looked up at the façade of the Oxford Theatre. As always, I allowed myself a slight smile at the sight of the huge billboard. Even after ten years, I still wasn't immune to the thrill of seeing the moody black and white photograph of myself and my co-star, Alex Paige, staring into each other's eyes, with both our names printed in swirling, elegant script. We looked like 1930s movie stars, which was the idea. Alex looked particularly handsome.

Above the photo was a neon sign which read: *The Next Thirty Years: A Musical*, followed by a couple more signs declaring that the show was 'Stupendous!' and 'A poignant evening filled with memorable tunes'.

I stepped through the stage door and exchanged a curt greeting with the doorman, who signed me in.

Then I walked down the gloomy, utilitarian backstage corridor to the star dressing room. I pushed open the door and looked at my dressing table.

Something was missing. It took me a moment to realise what it was, and my stomach dropped in dread.

There was one thing that made Saturday matinees tolerable, and that thing was nowhere to be seen.

I opened the door again and called into the corridor 'Fran?'

There was no reply.

'Fran, darling! Where are you?'

No answer. Fran was the assistant stage manager, but I also trusted her with some important non-tech related duties. Normally she came running. This simply would not do at all.

I left the dressing room and knocked on the door of the room opposite. Technically this was also a star dressing room, because Alex was my co-star, but I liked to think that my dressing room was the starriest. It had once been occupied by Sir Ian McKellen.

'Alex?'

There was some shuffling from inside, and then a mumbled: 'Just a minute.'

The door opened and Alex poked his head around the frame. He looked charmingly dishevelled, dark brown hair all messed up. Normally he would smile and invite me inside, but today he looked... worried.

'Charlotte,' he said. 'I... wasn't expecting you.'

'Have you seen my cupcakes?'

He scrunched his face up in puzzlement. 'What?'

'Cupcakes. Have you seen them? Fran always brings them on a Saturday.'

Alex ran a hand through his hair. 'Ah... no, sorry. No cupcakes here.'

'Oh.' This was not good news. 'Have you seen Fran?'

'I... er... well, she might be a bit preoccupied. What with the meeting.'

'What meeting?' I frowned. 'Is everything all right?'

'Ah... there was an announcement over the tannoy, probably before you arrived. Dominic is calling in between shows. He wants to talk to us. The musicians and crew, as well.'

Dominic was the producer of the show. He was extremely busy, and we only tended to see him in person when there was very good news (an award, a celebrity visit) or bad news (three years ago, we had been forced to close for a week while the theatre's roof was repaired).

'I hope it's nothing serious?' I said.

'I don't suppose so,' said Alex. He looked uncertain for a moment, then flashed me a smile. 'Wouldn't worry. See you onstage.'

The Next Thirty Years was a musical comedy with songs reminiscent of Cole Porter. The action begins in the 1930s, when we meet the two main characters, Constance and Gerald, on the night before their wedding. They are very much in love. But then, following a freak accident with a revolving door, Constance finds herself transported in time to various points during the following thirty years of her marriage to Gerald. There is much angst, laughter and tears. When Constance finally manages to return to the present day, she faces a difficult decision: should she still marry Gerald, with her knowledge of what their future will hold? Is love enough?

(Spoiler alert: of course it is, because this is a musical comedy, and if she didn't marry Gerald it would all feel a bit sad and pointless, really. At least in my humble opinion.)

Despite the usual matinee rustlings, we gave an excellent performance, as we always did. The size of the house was a little disappointing, but we were approaching the holiday season, and audience numbers sometimes dropped off a bit, before picking up again in the autumn.

I particularly loved the final scene, which was practically guaranteed to have the audience crying into their packets of Skittles.

Constance stands near the fireplace, her back to Gerald.
GERALD (Alex): Constance! Please, my darling. Neither of us know what the future might hold.
CONSTANCE (Me): You'd be surprised.
GERALD (*Taking her hand*): There's one thing of which I can be certain. I love you. I love you with all my heart. And I want you to go.

I blinked. It wasn't like Alex to fluff his lines.

CONSTANCE: You mean you want me to stay?

Alex froze for a moment. A subtle expression crossed his face, a look which said *oh bugger, sorry!* Imperceptible to the audience but clear to me.

GERALD: Of course I want you to stay, you silly thing! (*He sweeps Constance into his arms.*) I can't wait to see what the next thirty years have in store.
They kiss. The music swells. Cue a reprise of the show's big anthem 'What the Future Holds'.

We had a wonderful round of applause at the end, including a whole row of people in the stalls who stood up for us.

I returned to my dressing room in a surprisingly upbeat mood. I had almost forgotten about the missing cupcakes. I had been there for about five minutes when there was a knock on the door. I opened it to find Fran.

'Fran,' I said. 'What happened to my cupcakes, darling?'

Her hand flew to her mouth. 'Oh. I'm so sorry... I completely forgot. Er... Dominic's here. He wants us all onstage.'

The poor girl looked so worried that I didn't have the heart to press the matter. I pulled on the blue silk robe I used to cover my costume between performances, and followed her to the stage.

It had been reset for the evening's performance. The opening scene was a 1930s-style living room, so we all perched on the various pieces of furniture. I sat on the sofa next to Alex. I tried to smile at him, but he didn't quite meet my eyes.

When we were all assembled, Dominic rose from his chair. His face was grim.

'Thank you all for coming,' he said. 'I won't keep you for too long. But I'm afraid I have some very bad news.'

I held my breath. I didn't like the expression on Dominic's face at all. Something in the atmosphere told me this was rather more serious than a leaky roof.

'I'm very sorry to say that we're closing *The Next Thirty Years*,' he said. 'Our final performance will be next Saturday.'

Wait... *what?*

My mind whirled. This seemed like a physical impossibility. This show could not close. It had been running for ten years, and I had been in it for ten years. I'd only missed a handful of performances due to illness. It had been a massive, integral part of my life for a decade. That phrase 'the show must go on'? Well, this was most definitely a show that went on.

I looked around at the faces of the cast and crew. They all looked as shocked as me. The only person who didn't look shocked was Alex, which struck me as a little odd. Had he known about this? Surely not. Surely he would have told me...

'Are you okay?' Dominic was looking at me worriedly.

'Yes. I'm... just a little surprised. May I ask... why?'

Dominic raised his eyebrows. 'Why?'

'Why's the show closing?'

'Isn't it obvious?' said Alex, a slight edge to his voice. 'You must have seen the half-empty houses.'

'Yes, but... it's always like this in the spring,' I said. 'Things will pick up again in late summer. They always do.'

'That may be so,' said Dominic. He looked sympathetic. 'But I'm afraid we can't keep running on that basis.'

'I see.' It was taking all of my self-control not to burst into tears. I noticed that Fran was already crying. I had the sudden urge to go over and give her a hug. I pushed the thought away. Charlotte de la Mer was not a hugger.

'I'm really very sorry,' said Dominic. 'Obviously you'll be paid for the length of your current contracts.'

Our current contracts only ran for another month, so this wasn't exactly brilliant news.

'And I just know you'll all move on to bigger, better things,' said Dominic. He smiled at Alex, and something about that smile made me suspicious. Did Alex already have another job lined up? 'In the meantime, I would like to congratulate you all for your wonderful work.'

*

'Cheer up, Charley,' said Alex. 'It's not all bad.'

I sighed. 'I'm struggling to find any positives.'

Somehow, I had sleepwalked through the evening show. I knew I must have given a decent performance, because we had a good reception from the audience at the end, but I couldn't remember anything about the show itself. My mind had been very much elsewhere.

Now the performance was over, Alex and I had retreated to our favourite wine bar to decompress and analyse what had happened. Or rather, *I* wanted to analyse what had happened. Alex seemed weirdly upbeat.

'Well, for a start, we'll have the chance to do something else.' Alex sipped his wine. 'Come on, Charlotte. Weren't you getting the tiniest bit bored?'

'No. Not really.' The role of Constance fitted me like a glove. I knew where I was with Constance. I loved her. 'I like the show. I like my role. Don't you?'

'Of course. But things change, don't they? I think I'm ready for a new challenge.'

I narrowed my eyes at him.

He looked a little alarmed. 'What's wrong? Why are you glaring at me like that?'

'Did you know about this? About the show closing?'

He kept his eyes fixed on the wine in his glass, swirling it around. 'I'd heard a rumour, but I didn't want to worry anyone.'

'I see. Is that all?'

'What do you mean?'

'You're just being very... relaxed about this whole thing. Do you have another job lined up?'

Alex heaved a sigh and put his glass down on the table. 'All right. You've got me. I didn't want to say anything, because I wasn't sure what was going to happen, but I have been offered something, yes.'

'What?'

He glanced around the bar as if making sure he wouldn't be overheard. Then he leaned across the table. 'Does the name "Frederick Robertson" mean anything to you?'

I almost dropped my wine. 'Bloody hell, Alex!'

Frederick Robertson was an American director, famous in theatrical circles for his experimental approach to texts. His latest project was *Autumn Songs*, described in the advance publicity as 'a melancholy seasonal love story told in fragments, like falling leaves' (whatever that meant). It had that big film star in it, Selena Warrington, so it was highly anticipated, even among the most casual theatregoers.

'You see why I didn't want to say anything.'

'But that's… incredible.' A part of me was genuinely happy for him, but another equal part was quite jealous.

He laughed. 'It all feels a bit unreal.'

'So you would have had to leave anyway.' I also felt a little betrayed. Alex and I had been a team for ten years.

He gave a wistful smile. 'It was looking that way. I hadn't made up my mind. But it is the opportunity of a lifetime.'

'I wish you'd told me.'

'I was going to. I just hadn't found the right moment.'

'Hmm.'

Alex reached across the table for my hand and squeezed it gently. 'Look, I know this situation isn't ideal, but you'll find something else. Something better. I've always thought you were capable of far more.'

'I hope so.'

To be absolutely honest, I was no longer sure what I was capable of. It was over ten years since I'd last been to an audition. The thought of stepping back into that brutal world was enough to make me run screaming from the wine bar. It would be like stepping back into the dating pool after ten years.

Speaking of which…

'Are you coming back to mine?' I asked.

Alex hesitated for a moment, then shook his head. 'Better not. I've got an early start in the morning. A meeting about the new play. Maybe tomorrow night?'

'Oh. Okay.'

He collected his jacket from the back of his chair, and bent to kiss me on the cheek. 'Will you be all right?'

I forced a smile. 'You know me, Alex. I'll be fine. I'm always fine. And you're right. I should see this as a new challenge.'

He smiled back. 'That's what I like to hear.'

*

I'd told Alex I was fine, but I wasn't. *The Next Thirty Years* had given a structure to my days over the last decade.

After a sleepless night, the first thing I did the next day was phone Michael, my agent.

'I suppose you've heard,' I said.

'Yes. I'm so sorry. I was going to call you.'

'Any ideas?'

There was a short silence. 'Well... I can put you forward for a few things, but it is a bit quiet at the moment.'

'How about that new play, *Autumn Songs*? The one with that famous film actress?'

Perhaps Alex would put in a good word for me.

'Oh,' said Michael. 'You mean... right. Of course. The one that Alex is appearing in.'

'That's right.'

There was another pause. Then: 'Okay. Leave it with me. I'll look into it.'

'Thank you.'

'In the meantime, why don't you take a holiday? You haven't had one in... well, about ten years.'

'I don't do holidays. I like to work.'

A pause. 'Okay, if you're sure. I'll be in touch ASAP.'

This exchange didn't exactly fill me with confidence. Michael hadn't been required to do much work for me since I had landed the role of Constance. He had secured me a few voiceovers for adverts, but nothing in the theatre. Ah, well. He was a good agent. He would find something.

Ten minutes later, my mobile rang. I grabbed it, impressed by Michael's efficiency.

'Hi, Michael.'

'Charlotte! It's Sarah.'

My sister's voice took me by surprise. I didn't hear from her very often. We led such different lives, in very different parts of the country. She only ever called me when she had Big News.

'Hello, Sarah.'

'How are you? I have big news!'

My heart sank. Up until about five years ago, my sister had worked as a lawyer in London. She had been very good at it. Then, one day, seemingly out of the blue, she had declared that her career was 'no longer fulfilling' and that she was 'moving back home to try something new'. Apparently she missed the sea, and the small town community. So she returned to Shellcliff, where she became a serial entrepreneur. 'Big news' usually involved a new business opportunity. So far, these had ranged from a small 'glamping' site with luxury yurts, to her own brand of handmade cosmetics, to a marmalade stall at the local farmers' market, featuring 'alternative' flavours. She was nothing if not imaginative.

Some less charitable people would have called this a midlife crisis. Sarah referred to it as 'finding herself'. When she wasn't working, she spent a lot of time hiking and swimming and going on yoga retreats. It sounded exhausting.

'What are you up to now?' I asked.

'You know that old bookshop in Shellcliff town centre?'

I had a sudden, warm memory of being about eight and browsing through the children's shelves. I used to go there most Saturdays with Sarah and our mum.

'Yes?' I said.

'Well, the owner is retiring, so I've bought it. Isn't that wonderful?'

I was silent for a moment.

'Charlotte? Are you still there?'

'You've bought a bookshop? Just like that?'

'Yes! Well, not the building. The unit's rented. Just the business. And it wasn't "just like that", it was a carefully considered business decision. I've always wanted my own bookshop.'

'No you haven't, Sarah.'

'I have! We used to talk about it. Remember? We used to plan which famous authors we were going to invite.'

'You were ten.'

'So? What's wrong with reconnecting with childhood dreams? Anyway, I was wondering if you'd like to come and help me run it?'

Unbelievable.

'Sarah. I'm an *actress*. I have a career here in London.'

'Yes, but—'

'But *what*?'

Over the years I'd heard them all. From my parents, my teachers, and now, apparently, my sister.

But acting's not a real job.

But that's just a hobby.

And then, when I became successful: *But it's only temporary, right?*

'Nothing,' said Sarah, sounding sheepish. 'Sorry.'

I sighed. 'Look. I can't just... drop everything because you want to play shops.'

'Why not?' A brief pause. 'I heard about your show.'

I took a calming breath. 'How on earth do you know about that?'

'I saw it online last night.'

'Gosh, news really does travel fast, doesn't it?'

'Are you okay? It must have been a shock.'

I sat down on the sofa. 'I'm just waiting for my agent to get back to me. He says it might be a bit quiet over the summer, but I'm sure I'll find something.'

'Then come here for the summer! What have you got to lose? That's probably going to be the busiest time for us anyway, with the holidaymakers. There's one existing staff member, but I've got the other businesses to run. Yurts demand a lot of attention at this time of year, I can tell you.'

'I see.'

'We could really use some help. You can even bring that awful boyfriend with you, if you like.'

'You mean Alex? He's not awful. You just don't like him because you're prejudiced against actors.'

'Whatever. I'll tolerate him, is what I'm saying. What do you think?'

I hesitated for a moment, considering. On the one hand, it would be nice to see Sarah and spend some actual time with her. On the other hand, it would mean returning to Shellcliff, away from the bustle of the West End. Away from potential acting jobs.

'Let me think about it.'

'Thank you. That's all I ask.'

I ended the call, and went to the kitchen to make coffee.

I hadn't been home for any length of time since *The Next Thirty Years* opened. I visited my parents and sister at Christmas, and briefly over the summer, but that was about it. And Sarah liked London, so she would visit me more often than I visited her.

In some ways, Sarah was more sentimental than me. She enjoyed reconnecting with the things she had loved in her childhood and teenage years, like the bookshop. Which was lovely, if it made her happy. But I had fought for the life I now had. I had fought to become an actress. It could be exhausting and difficult, but I was damned if I was going to throw it away because of such a minor setback.

Going back meant giving up, and I wasn't ready to give up.

The next few days were awful. I went to work each night at the theatre, but Alex seemed preoccupied. For the first three nights, he didn't come back to my place after the show, saying he was too tired or that he had a meeting the next day.

On Thursday, two days before our official closing date, I found I needed a distraction. I took the tube to Trafalgar Square, and wandered around the National Gallery for a bit. Usually I loved looking at the paintings, but they didn't draw me in on this occasion. I kept thinking about Sarah's latest business venture.

Could it work?

I left the gallery and headed towards Charing Cross Road. I stood outside the largest bookshop, a place I hadn't visited for years. Slipping inside, I found it brightly lit and welcoming. I wandered between tables, picking up the odd book that caught my eye. This shop was beautiful. Clean, airy, with well-chosen, tidy stock. There was a café serving coffee and pastries, with free WiFi, and a wall of staff recommendations. Each book had a little review on a postcard, in neat handwriting. On the ground floor, I found an entire table display devoted to a particular author. I'd never heard of him, but a poster hailed him as *The star of postmodern literary fiction*. His latest book looked highly intellectual, and was written from the point of view of an ironing board over the course of several generations. His author photograph was in black and white, which somehow made him look extra intelligent.

There was also a large Children's section, which was charming and colourful. It had bright beanbags in one corner, and the tops of the bookcases were festooned with bunting.

I went upstairs to the café and bought a cappuccino and some sort of pastry with figs in it. I stared out of the window, thinking about my sister's bookshop. I was coming around to the idea. She clearly needed a creative consultant to help her. Someone with vision and ideas.

There was no reason why I couldn't be that someone, and there was no reason why her bookshop couldn't be like this one. A little slice of London, transferred to the Yorkshire coast. Good coffee, pastries, and visits from very important and critically acclaimed authors. Soirées with wine and poetry. A whole section devoted to radical modern art movements. A little haven from the hustle and bustle of the modern world. A place where people could go to read and think deep thoughts about... well, the books they were reading. And, in contrast, a colourful and fun kids' corner.

Perhaps I could go for the summer. Help out my sister, just for a little while. She was going to need it.

*

'I'm thinking about going back to Shellcliff.'

Friday night, one day before the curtain fell on *The Next Thirty Years*, and Alex had finally come back to my place. We were currently lying in bed, his arm draped across my chest. I felt him go tense when I spoke.

'What?' he said. 'You're joking.'

'No, I'm not.'

'But you always say what a dump the place is, and that you were glad to leave.'

'I may have been exaggerating a little. It's still my hometown.'

'What will you do there?' Alex gave a short laugh. 'Oh, no. Don't tell me: Michael has found you a role in some dreadful summer panto at a holiday park.'

'There's no holiday park,' I said. 'Actually, I'm thinking about helping my sister. She's just bought a bookshop.'

Alex was quiet for a moment. 'A bookshop?'

'Yes.'

'In Shellcliff?'

'Yes.' I bristled a little. 'What's wrong with that?'

'Nothing, nothing. It just feels like a bit of a risk, that's all.'

'She thinks it's worth a try. I'm inclined to agree with her.'

He wrinkled his forehead. 'You're serious, aren't you?'

'Yes.'

'But you can't give up acting! You're too good. You've worked so hard.'

'I wouldn't be giving up. I'd just be taking a break. Sarah needs some help over the summer. It would only be for a few weeks, while she gets up and running.' I paused, trying to gather my courage. 'Maybe you could come with me.'

He stared at me. 'Shellcliff? Me?'

'Yes, it would be a holiday. We could go walking. You always say you'd like to get outside more. The coast's lovely up there.'

He looked thoughtful, and for a moment I wondered if he was tempted. Then he frowned. 'I'm sorry. I can't. I've got rehearsals.'

'I thought you said they didn't start until July? You could come for a week, at least.'

'I... don't know, Charlotte. It's... tricky.'

'Tricky how?'

'Just... tricky.' He gave a short laugh, and reached out to stroke my hair. 'Can you really imagine me in Shellcliff?'

I thought about this. And the honest answer was no, I couldn't imagine Alex in Shellcliff. He was so very... London. If I was honest, I couldn't imagine him outside the boundary of the M25.

I sighed. 'No, not really.'

'Why don't you see how things turn out here before you do anything drastic? I think they're looking for an alternate for Selena in *Autumn Songs*. You'd be great for that.'

I was silent for a moment. 'Yes, that's probably a good idea.'

Alex was right. Acting was a big thing for me to give up. I had sacrificed a lot to get where I was, after all. More than he knew.

And yet, when I fell asleep, I dreamt of Shellcliff, and the bookshop.

3

Greg

It was a rainy Wednesday, and by 2pm, Seaswept Books had welcomed a grand total of four customers. Two of these had bought books, and the third had purchased a postcard. The fourth – a man in his fifties – was currently scanning the Crime section, pulling out each book in turn and reading the blurb on the back. He had been doing this for almost twenty minutes, and I was fairly sure he planned to tackle the entire bookcase.

I picked up my copy of *Middlemarch* and my second mug of coffee, reached beneath the counter for a chocolate biscuit, and settled in for a quiet afternoon.

Ding-dong.

The sound jarred me from my reading, and I looked up to see Sarah walking towards me. There was something in her expression that told me she meant business. Maybe the worst was about to happen. Maybe she intended to fire me and manage the shop herself.

I sat up straight in my chair, tried to ignore my pounding heart, and gave her a weak smile.

'Sarah. What can I do for you?'

Sarah smiled back, but the expression did not reach her eyes. 'I just thought I'd drop in and see what a typical afternoon was like.'

'Ah,' I said. 'Yes. Of course.'

She looked around the shop and frowned. 'Bit quiet today, is it?'

'Well, it is Wednesday, and the weather's bad, so…'

'Should you really be eating that?'

I had forgotten about the chocolate biscuit, which was in the process of gluing itself to my hand. A hot wave of embarrassment washed over me. 'Sorry... I was just having a coffee.'

'Don't you think it's a little unprofessional to eat at your desk?'

'Er, well... it's just me here, so I can't exactly shut up shop while I—'

'Excuse me.' The lone customer had abandoned the Crime section and was now looking at us both expectantly.

Grateful for the interruption, I stood to attention. 'How can I help?'

'I'm looking for a book for my wife.'

'What does she like to read?'

'Well, that's the thing,' said the man, rubbing the back of his neck. 'I don't really know.'

This opening gambit didn't exactly fill me with confidence.

'Well, have you noticed what she's read most recently?'

He looked thoughtful. 'I think she likes crime, but nothing too gory. Oh, and she likes cats, too.'

This was a bit more like it. I dared to glance at Sarah. Perhaps there was a chance I could impress her with my bookselling skills after all.

'We have just the thing,' I said, walking over to the relevant bookcase and pulling out a slim blue volume. 'Here you are. The first in the *Meow Crime Capers* series.'

The man took the book from my hand, read the blurb and frowned. 'So the detective's a cat?'

'Er... no. The detective's a person. But cats feature heavily, I believe.'

'Do you have anything where the cat solves the murder?'

'I don't think so.'

'Do you have any more cat books out the back?'

'No, sorry.'

'How about your warehouse?'

I scanned his face in an attempt to work out if he was joking, but I detected no trace of humour.

'We don't have our own warehouse. But I can have a look at our supplier's website and see if I can order something for you.'

'Could you get me something second-hand? It might be cheaper.'

I looked at Sarah. Her face was unreadable.

'No,' I said. 'I'm sorry. It's not our policy to do that.'

The man shrugged. 'Fair enough. I'll look online.'

He walked out of the shop.

'Honestly. Some people!' I turned to Sarah with a shrug and a smile, hoping we could bond over the sheer ridiculousness of that entire exchange. But her face was solemn. She pinched the bridge of her nose, then sighed.

'Okay, Greg, how do you think you could have handled that differently?'

'I'm sorry?'

'It's a question I used to ask trainees when we dealt with difficult clients,' she said, as if this would clarify things. 'You lost a sale there.'

'I don't think I did. I think he was always going to go online.'

'But you don't *know* that,' said Sarah. 'So what could you have done differently? How could you have given that customer a more positive book-buying experience?'

I thought about this. 'I suppose I could have offered him an alternative. A book about a detective with a dog, for example.'

'So why didn't you?'

'Because he was looking for something very specific. You develop an instinct for these things, after a while.'

Sarah looked about to protest, but then seemed to change her mind. 'Okay. What else could you have done?'

'I... could have offered him a biscuit.'

'A biscuit,' said Sarah, flatly.

'Yes.'

'I don't think so.'

'Why not?'

'Because the idea is to *sell* things, not to give things away.' She shook her head. 'Honestly, Greg. Have you never had any sales training? You should be selling something to everyone who comes into the shop.'

'Er... well, that's not always possible. Some people just want to have a look, get some ideas, then they might come back later.'

'You have to make more of an effort. This is a working environment.' She eyed the coffee mug with *Employee of the Year* printed on it. Then she looked me up and down in the same way she had when we met. Assessing. Measuring me against some standard that was unknown to me, although I could hazard a guess at what she was thinking. 'You know, I've asked my sister to come and work here for the summer. She's great with people, really charismatic. I think she'll make all the difference to this place.'

I stared at her, momentarily lost for words. 'You... want me to work with someone else?'

Sarah narrowed her eyes. 'Well, that remains to be seen, doesn't it?'

She walked away, letting the threat hang in the air. The sound of the doorbell jarred my nerves. Alone again, I reached for my coffee with hands that still shook.

I tried to imagine sharing my bookshop with someone else, but my imagination did not stretch that far. I was used to having my own space.

It was much better that way.

4

Charlotte

The curtain had fallen on the very last performance of *Thirty Years*. I could hardly believe it. All evening, I was thinking about last times. This is the last time I sing this song, the last time I drink from this glass, the last time I stand on this particular spot on the stage.

But maybe it didn't matter, because I had been presented with a serendipitous opportunity.

I had just arrived at the after-party, which was being held in a function room in a hotel across the road from the theatre. I had arrived slightly late, because as well as changing into my red party dress, I had also lingered for a while in my dressing room, and then backstage, not quite wanting to leave my theatre. But I had finally torn myself away.

The first person I noticed was Alex, standing in a corner and talking to a man I immediately recognised as Frederick Robertson, the director of his new play.

Fred was something of a visionary, and the recipient of several Tony and Olivier Awards. I had always wanted to work with him. This, I realised, was the ideal chance to introduce myself.

I swept over. 'Alex!'

His eyes went a little wide. He shot a quick glance at Frederick. 'Oh. Hello, Charlotte. I wondered where you'd gone.'

All three of us stood there awkwardly for a moment. Fred sipped his champagne. I gave him my biggest smile.

'I'm Charlotte de la Mer, Alex's co-star.' I extended a hand. 'It's good to meet you, Mr Robertson.'

'Oh,' said Fred, smiling weakly. 'Yes, of course. You were very good tonight.'

'Thank you,' I said. 'I'm sure Alex has told you all about me. About how keen I am to originate a new role.'

'He… might have mentioned you, yes.'

'Would you like a drink, Charlotte?' said Alex. 'Let's go and see what they have.'

'In a minute,' I said. 'Right now I'm talking to Mr Robertson.'

'I hear the cocktails are very good…'

I ignored him, and decided to go for it, on the basis that one should never be backward in coming forward.

I smiled again at Fred. 'Alex tells me you're looking for an alternate for the role of Catherine in *Autumn Songs*.'

Fred looked startled. 'Well… yes. Yes, I am.'

'Well! That's wonderful news, because I'm available and Alex and I work very well together. Would you perhaps consider auditioning me? I can put you in touch with my agent.'

Fred stared into his champagne glass. 'Thank you, Ms De la Mer, but that won't be necessary.'

'Oh? You mean you don't need to speak to my agent?'

He was very interested in his champagne. 'I mean, unfortunately, I don't think you're quite right for the part…'

'Oh.' I was taken aback. I glanced at Alex, but he didn't meet my eye. I realised he looked embarrassed. I turned back to Fred. 'May I ask why?'

Fred sighed, as if he really hadn't wanted to be pressed on the matter. 'It's just that we're looking for someone slightly, well… younger. That's all.'

I stared at him. I could feel the blood rushing to my cheeks. 'But Alex is—'

I was about to say 'the same age as me', but Fred cut me off.

'We need to cast an actress the same age as Selena,' he said. 'She's only twenty-five.'

Of course she is.

'Right,' I said. 'Yes. I see.'

'I'll of course keep you in mind for other roles,' said Fred, gallantly. 'There's Rochester's mother, for one thing.'

'His mother. Yes. Of course. Wonderful.'

An awful silence descended on us.

Fred cleared his throat. 'Excuse me. Er... I must just go and say hello to Dominic.'

I watched him scurry away. And as I did, I thought of all the things I should have said to his face, things about ageism in the arts, and sexism, and the patriarchy. Or maybe I should have bypassed all that, and simply poured a jug of Pimm's over his head. But his words had shocked me into silence, frozen me in stasis. I wanted to kick myself. I wasn't normally such a pushover.

Alex touched my shoulder. 'Are you okay?'

'Cheeky bastard,' I hissed. 'How old does he think I am, exactly?'

'Don't worry about it,' said Alex. 'Come on, let's go and get a drink.'

My anger boiled over. I flinched away from him. 'I don't want a drink! Why didn't you say something?'

Alex looked taken aback. 'What could I say? If he doesn't think you're right for the part—'

'I'm only forty-eight, Alex! You told me last night that you thought I'd be great.'

'That's what *I* think. I'm not him, am I?'

This was quite a reasonable argument, but I wasn't going to let it distract me. 'You're not seriously going to work with him, are you?'

Alex looked at me as if I had suddenly gone mad. 'What? Yes, I am. It's the chance of a lifetime. You know how tough this business is.'

'Not so tough for you, it seems.'

'That's not fair. Come on, people are staring—'

'So bloody what?'

'Come and get a drink—'

'No! I'm going home, Alex.'

I stalked off, pausing to grab my coat from the concierge. I was aware of some members of the cast looking at me as I bundled myself into it. Fred caught my eye and swiftly hid behind an ornamental palm tree.

Alex had not moved. I looked at him, willing him to follow me, for surely that would be the supportive thing to do. But he quickly averted his eyes.

I swept out into the night.

*

Stupid Alex.

Stupid Dominic.

Stupid Frederick Robertson.

I flounced around my flat, glaring at the framed theatre posters that adorned my walls. There was a big one for *Thirty Years* above the fireplace in the living room. I peered at it critically. Had I really changed so much in ten years?

No. I couldn't start thinking like that. I was *not* going to let this get to me. Little Charlotte Smith would have wilted like a flower, but Charlotte de la Mer was tough. She was resilient. She did not need the approval of others to be happy.

I sank onto the sofa. I suddenly felt desperately, crushingly tired, as if the last ten years of my working life had finally caught up with me. I was going to take a well-earned holiday, whether my treacherous boyfriend planned on joining me or not.

I took out my phone.

'...lo?'

'Sarah!'

There was a muffled groan. 'Charlotte, it's after midnight.'

'Never mind that. I've got good news. You've twisted my arm.'

'What?' She still sounded half asleep.

'You've convinced me! I want to help you with the bookshop.'

'Oh...' There was a long pause. 'Well, that's great news, Charlotte. Are you quite sure?'

'I've never been surer of anything in my life.'

'You just sounded a bit lukewarm about it the other day.'

'Yes, well, that's before I was truly *inspired*, darling. I've been to Charing Cross Road, and I had a vision for what you could do with the old place.'

'A vision?' My sister sounded wary.

'Yes. You know. A premonition of what the future could hold. Do you know what I mean?'

A longer pause. Then: 'Yes. I think I have a good idea. Er... when can you come up?'

'I was thinking tomorrow.'

'Tomorrow? That seems... quite soon. Where are you staying? Mum and Dad's?'

I frowned. 'No, thanks.'

'Why on earth not?'

'Because they'll spend the entire time asking if I'm going to quit acting and do something sensible. I know they mean well, but I don't think I can face that right now.'

'So what are you going to do?'

'Well, darling, I was hoping I could stay with you. You still have the spare room, don't you?'

'Er... Dave's turned it into a home gym.'

I bit my lip. *Of course* he had. Dave was Sarah's husband. He had made it clear, on more than one occasion, that he thought theatre was silly. So, by extension, he obviously thought I was silly, too.

I suppressed my annoyance. 'Not a problem. I'll stay in a B&B or something until I find somewhere more suitable. It's only for a few weeks, anyway.'

'Oh. Well, if you're sure?'

'Quite sure. I'll see you soon.'

I ended the call. Ten minutes later, I had looked up The Grand Hotel, the quite glamorous old place where Sarah had had her wedding reception. I booked a Double Deluxe Room with a sea view. It was easy to do, and the rates were surprisingly cheap. I booked for a week, which I thought would give me ample time to find somewhere else to stay.

I slept fitfully, filled with anticipation of my summer holiday. My first holiday in years. Because it *would* be a holiday. How hard could running a bookshop possibly be? It wasn't as though it was real work, not like acting. I would probably spend most of my time reading. Then, after a few weeks, I would return to London refreshed, reinvigorated and ready to take the West End by storm. I would find a new role, a much better role than some pretty film actress's alternate.

The next morning, I left my apartment with a single suitcase – I liked to travel light – and caught the early train. As it trundled out of King's Cross, I felt my spirits lift. Open spaces! Fields with sheep in them! The sea! Gosh, this was thrilling.

This was a wonderful idea.

*

This was an awful idea.

The taxi deposited me on the seafront, and I immediately regretted wearing a summer dress instead of a jumper and jeans.

All my favourite childhood memories were so sun-soaked that I always managed to forget how bloody *cold* this place usually was. Behind me, the sea was wild, and the sky was rain-grey. I shivered, hugging myself beneath my thin purple cardigan. This wasn't the gorgeous summer day I had pictured, but at least I was in Shellcliff.

I looked up at the façade of The Grand Hotel, and felt my heart sink into my shoes.

The place didn't look *terrible*, not by any means. I'd stayed in enough dubious digs in the early years of my career to know a dump when I saw it. But it had certainly gone downhill since I had last seen it. There was an air of sadness. Of slight creeping neglect. The 'R' and 'H' on the gold signage were both slightly wonky, and there were weeds growing through cracks on the steps leading to the entrance. The white paint was peeling from the walls.

I pushed open the heavy double doors and walked into the chilly foyer area. My heels clicked on the black and white parquet floor as I walked towards the reception desk.

It was presided over by a teenage girl with curly black hair, pale makeup, and black eyeshadow. She didn't look up when I entered. Instead, she kept her nose buried in a thick book, the sort of book I always said I'd read if I had time, but never did, and then felt guilty about it.

'Hello?' I said.

The girl looked up from her book. She blinked at me once. 'Hey.'

'Hello. I have a reservation.'

'Oh,' the girl said, finally closing her book. 'Right.'

'The name's De la Mer. It's for a week.'

The girl blinked at me again. 'A week? Really?'

'Yes. Why do you ask?'

She shrugged. 'People don't come here for a whole week very often.'

'Why ever not?'

The girl looked surprised, as if the reasons should be obvious. 'Well, there's not a lot to do around here.'

Honestly. Young people today had to be spoon-fed entertainment. It was sad, really.

'I'm sure that's not true,' I said, diplomatically.

She gave me a long-suffering look which seemed to say: *it absolutely is.* I chose to ignore it.

'So. Do you have a room for me? A Deluxe Double with a sea view?'

'Oh. Sure.' She reached for a key. 'Here you are. Room 4.'

'Thank you.'

'Don't mention it.' The girl smiled and went back to her book.

'May I make a dinner reservation?'

She looked up again. 'A what?'

'A reservation. For dinner.'

'Oh. Well, I'm afraid we're a bit short-staffed at the mo, so our restaurant's closed tonight, but I'm sure I could send out for a pizza or something...'

I sighed. 'All right. I suppose that'll do.'

'Okay.'

She was obviously not going to offer to help with my suitcase, so I picked it up and mounted the stairs.

In defiance of all logic, Room 4 was on the third floor. My heart sank as soon as I opened the door. This was not the luxurious accommodation I was expecting. The furnishings were dated and chintzy, and the pictures on the walls were faded. A net curtain obscured the view out of the window, and I had to crane my neck to glimpse a fragment of sea. It seemed I'd arrived at Fawlty Towers.

I sat down on the bed with an unexpected thud. The mattress was hard, and I grimaced.

At least there was a functioning kettle and a packet of shortbread, so I made myself a cup of tea and pondered my next move. My heart felt cold with homesickness. I suddenly longed for

London, for my friends, and for *Thirty Years*. I even longed for Alex. Maybe I'd been too harsh on him.

I took out my mobile and dialled his number. It rang and rang, and then went to voicemail. He had probably slept in after the party last night.

I didn't bother to leave a message. Instead I called my sister.

'Hi, Sarah. It's Charlotte. I'm here.'

*

I met Sarah at a little coffee shop in the town centre. I arrived early, but when I looked through the window I saw that she was already there, in a table in the corner, gazing down at her mobile phone.

I pushed open the door, and a bell rang to announce my presence. Sarah looked up and got to her feet, coming out from behind the table with a big smile on her face.

'Hello, Charlotte.'

'Sarah, darling, it's so good to see you!'

We hugged. Sarah was dressed casually in jeans and jumper, her long hair falling over her shoulders, and no makeup. She had never been one to care about such things. Maybe she thought they were a waste of time and money. I was still wearing my blue summer dress with the white polka dots, and I felt a little overdressed in comparison.

'You haven't changed a bit,' I said. 'It's been too long.'

'Nearly two years.' I was sure I heard a slight barb in her voice.

I felt a sting of guilt. 'I'm sorry, darling, I've just been so busy—'

She held up a hand. 'I know. It's fine. Shall we have a coffee?'

We took our seats at Sarah's table. It was covered with a pink and white checked cloth, with a vase of giant plastic sunflowers in the centre.

'Fake flowers are so pointless, aren't they?' I said.

'Shush!' Sarah glanced worriedly towards the counter, where a woman was arranging scones onto a plate.

'I'm just making an observation.'

'Yes, well. Please don't. I'm a regular.' She smiled. 'The brownies are to die for.'

I wasn't convinced, but when the woman came over, I ordered one anyway, along with a cappuccino. I was relieved to find that both coffee and cake were more than adequate, if not quite up to the standards of my favourite patisserie in London.

'So,' said Sarah, after a sip of coffee. 'You're finally out of that awful show.'

I almost dropped my own cup. 'The show was not awful. It has been hailed as a modern classic. And it's just a break. I'll find something else.'

My sister looked unconvinced, but she didn't ask me any further questions, much to my relief. She drained her coffee cup and put it down with an air of finality.

'Would you like to see my shop?'

*

I stared at the front window of Seaswept Books.

Much like the rest of Shellcliff, it didn't quite match up to the picture I had in my mind, which now seemed less like a memory and more like something I had plucked from my imagination. The shop I remembered had been colourful, all light blue and yellow paint to match the seaside, with a red and yellow striped awning reminiscent of the deckchairs you could hire on the beach.

This shop, however, appeared dark and antiquated. The paint-work was mostly dark green, and it was peeling in places. The windows were grimy around the edges, and there was no awning.

'It's not quite how I remember it,' I said.

Sarah nodded. 'Yes, it needs a bit of TLC. The last owner was spending more and more time away. I don't think she could quite keep up with it all.'

'That's a shame.'

Sarah shrugged. 'It happens, I guess.' She unlocked the door. 'Come on in.'

An old-fashioned doorbell jangled as we stepped inside. After the slightly sad façade, I wasn't surprised to find that the interior was a bit dingy. It could have been cosy, but the bookcases were all dark wood, and the only light came from a cast-iron chandelier in the centre of the ceiling.

'It's a bit dark,' I said.

Sarah nodded. 'My plan is to redecorate. Repaint the walls. Get some lighter-coloured furniture.'

The place was also stuffed with books. They were piled up in the corners, on the tops of the bookcases, and on a table in the centre of the room. By the window, there was a Children's section with racks of picture books, but this seemed to be the only part of the shop with its own unique identity. The rest was... well, chaos. A charming sort of chaos, but chaos nonetheless.

'There are a lot of books in here,' I said.

Sarah laughed. 'Yes. We need a bit of a sort out, possibly a sale.'

I began to peruse the bookcases. I was hoping for a shrine to intellectualism and the arts, and to be fair, the fiction selection did look interesting. But the non-fiction section appeared to be almost entirely stocked with books about the seaside. There was a whole bookcase devoted to memoirs written from the point of view of Clive, a seaside donkey who spent his working life on the local beach. He was a highly prolific donkey: his memoirs ran to sixteen volumes. Samuel Pepys had nothing on Clive. There was also a large cardboard cut-out of him, which stared at me balefully from beneath long, lustrous eyelashes.

'Do you have any plays?' I asked, hoping for some Chekhov or Ibsen at the very least.

'Oh, yes! We have the Complete Works of Shakespeare, the original *Blood Brothers*, and *The Importance of Being Earnest*.'

'So, apart from Shakespeare, you have two plays.'

'Yes. There isn't really much demand, you see.'

'Right.' I raised my eyes to the ceiling. There were cobwebs on the chandelier.

'So,' Sarah smiled at me. 'What do you think?'

'It's...' I paused. To be honest, the shop had rendered me somewhat speechless. I'd read somewhere that all independent bookshops were unique, reflecting the tastes and interests of their owners. This didn't appear to be a reflection of Sarah's mind, because Sarah liked things modern and clean and neat. Sarah's favourite shop was Ikea. Sarah had once told me she didn't like second-hand books, because 'they smelled funny'. This shop, on the other hand, had a whole bookcase full of second-hand books.

I was starting to feel suspicious. On the phone, Sarah had made it sound like she wanted me to help out behind the till, unpack the odd book, do a bit of light cleaning. But this looked like a project which was beyond anything I was expecting.

'Sarah,' I said, 'what is my job going to entail, exactly?'

'What do you mean?'

'It's just that... this shop doesn't really feel like *you*, darling.'

Sarah sighed. 'All right. I'll come clean. I took on the shop without realising just how much work there was to do.'

'I see.'

'But I thought that would be okay, because I could overhaul the place, start with a clean slate. But there's just one problem.'

'What?'

'Greg.'

'Who's Greg?'

'He's the manager. He's been here for twenty-five years.'

Ah, I thought, looking around the room. *That explains a lot.*

'Is he a bad manager?'

Sarah shook her head. 'It's... complicated. He's the only person who knows where everything is, which is helpful, obviously. And what he doesn't know about classic books isn't worth knowing. In many ways, he's great.'

'But?'

'But... he's just not quite right for the *vibe* I want to create here. You'll know what I mean when you meet him. He... he's not the sort of person you'd want as the public face of your company.'

I blinked. This was uncharacteristically cruel. Did the man have two heads?

'Why?'

'He's just... a bit stuffy. Old-fashioned. I mean, you should see his clothes.' She shuddered. 'I think he puts some people off... not intentionally, you understand. But he can come across as... abrupt.'

So I would be working with Bernard Black. Fantastic.

I was going to have to ask the obvious question. 'Can't you just get rid of him?'

Sarah shook her head. 'He's completely dedicated to the bookshop. He lives upstairs, in the flat.'

I glanced at the ceiling in alarm. 'Will he be able to hear us?'

'No. He always goes out on Sunday afternoons. And Wednesday evenings, regular as clockwork.' Sarah sighed. 'There's just something a bit *sad* about him, Charley. I can't put my finger on it. Even the previous owner made me promise to "look after her Greg". I don't think I have the heart to throw him out. But at the same time, I don't see how I can move things on with him here. He seems quite content just to sit around, ignoring customers. I had a chat with him yesterday, suggested some new ideas, like installing an electronic stock control system. He just looked completely confused and said, "But what good would that do?" I don't think I can face another conversation with him.'

'Right.' It did sound like my sister was facing some challenges. 'So, what can I do?'

'Well, I was thinking you could work with him. Impose some of your personality on this place. Bring some of your signature sparkle and glamour. I need someone with a winning personality, someone who's good with people.'

I felt myself straighten a little. It was nice that my sister viewed me in this way. 'I'm sure I can do that. But what about Greg?'

Sarah looked down at the floor. 'I'm hoping, once you've made a few changes, that he'll leave.'

My eyes widened. 'You want me to force him out?'

'Not force. Just… gently nudge him towards the door.'

'So, basically, you can't face firing him, so you've brought me here to play the bad cop?'

Sarah blushed. 'I wouldn't put it quite like that. Who knows? You might even make him up his game a bit. Then we won't have to get rid of him, will we?' She looked at the floor again. 'But I wouldn't count on it.'

None of this was especially reassuring, but I was committed now. I didn't like the idea of walking away from my sister in her hour of need.

'Right. Okay. When do I meet him?'

'Tomorrow morning. Come in at ten, and I'll introduce you and show you how everything works.'

'Okay. That sounds good.'

Sarah turned towards the door. 'I'm afraid I have to get going. The yurts are calling me. We'll have you over for dinner soon, okay? I'll invite Mum and Dad, too.'

This sounded optimistic. Despite being retired, my parents were possibly the only people I knew who were busier than Sarah.

Mum worked as a local councillor, and Dad ran three separate allotments. He regularly won prizes at flower shows for his roses, and country fairs for his carrots. They were difficult people to pin down. Compared to my parents and my sister, I had always felt rather unproductive and feckless. While I was the first to argue that acting fed one's creative soul, I sometimes feared I had never done anything quite so useful as grow a carrot from scratch.

I summoned a smile. 'Great.'

'See you tomorrow.'

'Yes. I can't wait to start.'

*

I asked the girl on reception to order me a takeaway pizza and retreated to my room, where I hunkered down for the evening.

Maybe, I thought, as I picked at my Spicy Pepperoni, maybe it wasn't too late to back out. I could apologise to Sarah, tell her that a new opportunity had come up in London. An audition, perhaps. Maybe Michael had found a suitable role for me.

My mobile rang. It was Alex. I hesitated only a moment before answering.

'Hi, Alex.'

'Charlotte. Where are you?'

'I'm in Shellcliff.'

'What are you doing there?'

'I've come to help my sister with her bookshop. The one I told you about.'

'You could've left me a message.'

'I tried phoning, but you were engaged.'

A pause.

'Listen, Charlotte. I wanted to apologise. I should have said something to that slimeball last night.'

I sighed, and felt myself soften. The conversation must have been just as awkward for Alex as it was for me.

'Thank you, Alex. I'm sorry too. I shouldn't have stormed off like that. I understand why you want to take the role. Just... don't make life too easy for him, will you?'

'I'll be sure to make some unreasonable demands. Oysters delivered to my dressing room, that sort of thing.'

I smiled. 'Good.'

'When are you coming home?'

'I'm not sure. I think I'll be here for a few weeks, at least. Maybe a month. There's lots to do in the shop.'

'A month? But what am I going to do?'

I bit my tongue. 'I thought you had meetings, Alex.'

'I do. I do. But... I'll miss you.'

'You could come and visit me.'

He sighed. 'All right. I'll see what I can do.'

'Great. Well, let me know when you've decided.'

'I will.'

'Alex?'

'Yes?'

'I do love you, you know.'

'Yes. Yes, me too.'

5

Greg

I had just settled down with my morning coffee when the shop doorbell rang. As usual, I ignored it. In my experience, customers liked to browse alone without my interference. If they asked for my help, I would give it to them. But they had to ask.

'Hello.'

I inclined my head slightly and gave my usual greeting, which sounded a little like 'Hmm.'

Footsteps. And then: 'Hi!'

The greeting was far too bright for a grim and rainy day on the Yorkshire coast. Half irritated, half curious, I looked up from my copy of *The Bookseller*.

A woman smiled back at me. I would have guessed she was in her late forties, and she wore a yellow summer dress with little blue flowers, and a wide-brimmed straw sunhat. The most bizarre thing was that she was the spitting image of Charlotte de la Mer, who had left Shellcliff about twenty-five years ago to become a West End actress. As far as I was aware, Charlotte hardly ever returned to Shellcliff, and I had certainly never seen her in the bookshop before. No, I must have been mistaken.

As generally occurred when confronted with a stylish member of the opposite sex (or anyone stylish, really), I looked down at her shoes, which were high-heeled red sandals. Her whole outfit was rather optimistic, as if she had dressed for a glorious day at the seaside. Which, of course, suggested that she was unprepared for the town's dramatic microclimate. This was further evidence that she was not, in fact, Charlotte de la Mer.

I forced myself to meet her gaze. 'Can I help you?'

'I'm Charlotte.' She stuck out her hand.

I stared at it, then snorted with laughter. 'No you're not.'

Her brow furrowed. 'I'm sorry?'

I immediately felt stupid. Honestly. How socially clumsy can you get?

'Sorry,' I said, offering my own hand. 'You took me by surprise, that's all. You're... Charlotte de la Mer?'

She smiled, a little sadly. 'I'm just plain Charlotte Smith here.'

Her voice didn't sound like it belonged to 'plain Charlotte Smith'. She had a posh London accent, the sort favoured by certain newsreaders and Shakespearean actors. Maybe she had dropped her Yorkshire accent at drama school. I was aware that some performers did that.

'Okay.' This was certainly a surreal turn of events. 'Er... are you looking for something in particular?'

I had visions of helping Charlotte de la Mer find her ideal book. She would then go away and tell her glamorous actor friends what good service she had received at Seaswept Books. This would attract a whole new set of customers who listened to the opinions of minor celebrities. We would end up on InstaThing.

Oh, God, no. That would be awful.

'I'm looking for Sarah.'

'Oh.' I felt relieved that whatever this was about, it was not my problem. 'She's not here.'

Charlotte looked startled. Then she frowned. 'Blooming typical. Are you Greg?'

'Yes. That's me.' Charlotte de la Mer knew my *name*. I wondered if she remembered me from school, or maybe the drama group. But she was a few years older, and we had had different friendship groups. 'Er... maybe I could give Sarah a message?'

She shook her head. 'No, that's all right. I'll wait. She wants to show me the ropes.'

'The ropes?'

'Yes. I'm working here for a few weeks. I'm Sarah's sister.'

This was a lot for me to process. Sarah had not mentioned that her sister was Charlotte de la Mer. That seemed like quite a big fact to omit. Not that we had engaged in much social chit-chat yet. Or any social chit-chat, really.

I wasn't sure I liked Sarah. She was very... businesslike. She always spoke to me in a very clipped tone which reminded me of my Year 10 English teacher ('Your handwriting is appalling, Gregory. And do you even *know* what a metaphor is?').

There was also the possibility that this was some sort of elaborate practical joke. Perhaps I should call Sarah and double check this person was who she said she was.

I was trying to mentally compose a response to 'Charlotte' when the doorbell rang again, and Sarah hurried into the shop.

'I'm so sorry,' she said to Charlotte. 'It was the yurts again.' She looked at me and gave that familiar forced smile. 'I see you've met.'

So this was real and not some strange hallucination. That was one good thing, at least.

'Yes,' I said, because I had the impression that a reply was expected of me.

'Charlotte's going to be helping out in the shop,' said Sarah. 'I know you'll make her very welcome.' Her tone implied that she wanted to add an 'or else', but was far too superficially polite to do so.

I forced a smile. 'Of course.'

Sarah turned to Charlotte. 'I'm afraid I can't stay. But Greg will show you what to do.'

'I will?' I said, weakly. 'I mean... yes. Certainly.'

Sarah smiled at Charlotte. 'You'll be fine. Thanks so much for doing this. You're a lifesaver.'

And then she was gone, and I was left alone with my new shop assistant (boss?), West End Superstar Charlotte de la Mer.

'Er...' I said.

'Well,' said Charlotte. 'Shall we get the kettle on?'

'Er, yes. Good idea.'

I went into our little kitchen-cum-stockroom. My hands were shaking. There was a lot I needed to do today. I needed to order next month's books, and dust the shop, and pay the local authors. Mainly, I wanted to drink coffee and read *The Bookseller*. But my mind was stuck on one track, and the track was saying *Charlotte de la Mer, Charlotte de la Mer is in my shop.*

How did she take her coffee? Did she even drink coffee? Would she prefer tea?

I stuck my head out of the stockroom. 'Charlotte?'

'Yes?'

'Would you like tea or coffee?'

'Oh... I'll have a latte, please.'

I looked at our refreshment making facilities. These comprised a plastic kettle (slightly tea-stained), a box of Yorkshire Tea bags and a jar of instant Nescafé. All of which was excellent, and suited me just fine. But Charlotte de la Mer was a West End star. Could I serve her instant tea and coffee? Was her constitution even suited to such a thing?

I guessed not.

I stuck my head out of the stockroom again.

'Charlotte?'

'Yes, darling?'

'I just need to pop out. Can you watch the counter while I'm gone? If anyone comes in, you can tell them I'll be back in five minutes.'

Her face lit up. 'Of course! You can rely on me.'

'Great. Thanks.'

I hurried down the street to Beans, my favourite coffee shop. Inevitably, Beans also happened to be the proprietor of the most expensive coffee in town.

Ten minutes later, having purchased two takeaway lattes and deciding I could not afford a holiday this year (not that I ever went away), I headed back to the bookshop.

Charlotte was sitting behind the counter. In my chair. Reading my copy of *The Bookseller*. This felt wrong on several different levels, but I decided to bite my tongue, because she was Charlotte de la Mer (Best Actress, *A Doll's House*, National Theatre, 2011).

She looked up from my magazine. 'That was quick.' She eyed the coffees in my hand. 'What's that?'

'Lattes.' I held one out to her.

She raised a perfectly manicured eyebrow. 'You went for takeaway coffees?'

'Yes.' I looked down at the floor, suddenly overcome with embarrassment. 'We don't have a coffee machine here.'

'You don't have a coffee machine? What if a customer wants a coffee?'

For a moment, my starstruck feeling vanished, and I wondered if she could possibly be for real. But when I looked up, she appeared genuinely surprised.

'They go to one of the cafés. We're not a café. We're a bookshop.'

She raised her other eyebrow. 'So... you don't serve coffee.'

'No.'

I had had this conversation many times in the past, but usually it was with customers. It was in my personal top three most annoying conversations, along with 'Is this a library?' and 'Are the books the price it says on the back?'

Charlotte shook her head in apparent wonder. 'No coffee.'

'But this coffee is very nice,' I said, gesturing towards the cardboard cup. 'Try it.'

She took a sip. Looked thoughtful, then smiled. 'Very good. But you really didn't have to go to all that trouble. You could have just told me you didn't have a coffee machine.'

I shrugged. 'Well, it's not every day I have a West End star in the bookshop.'

She cringed. 'We *are* just ordinary people, you know. And can we maybe not talk about that while I'm in here? I sort of want to take a break from it for a while.'

'Okay. Sorry. My lips are sealed.'

'Thank you.' She sipped her coffee, then clapped her hands together. 'So! What's on the agenda for today?'

'The agenda?'

'Yes. What would you like me to do?'

'Oh. Well...' I looked around the shop, seeking inspiration. Then I had a lightbulb moment. 'You could... er... reorganise the Sci-Fi, maybe? Check they're still all in alphabetical order. And sometimes people put the Iain Banks books back with Iain M. Banks. I know they're the same person, but these things are important.'

She looked at our Sci-Fi bookcase, and back at me. 'Is that all? Wouldn't it be a better use of my time to tidy the Children's section?'

I looked at the messier, more colourful quarter of the bookshop, and suppressed a shudder.

'I couldn't possibly ask you to do that,' I said.

'Why not? I'm no stranger to a bit of mess, darling.'

'I really think the Sci-Fi—'

'That'll take me about five minutes. Now where do you keep your cleaning stuff?'

*

Much to my astonishment, Charlotte made short work of the chaos in the Children's section. I tried not to watch as she swept up something that looked like crushed biscuits, reshelved the scattered books, and carefully relocated a large spider that was hiding under one of the novelty cushions.

An hour later, she announced that she was finished. And I have to say that she looked a bit smug.

I spent the afternoon showing her how to use the till and order books. She was a very quick learner, and asked plenty of questions. I had lots of questions I wanted to ask her, too, but I didn't quite dare. In the end, when I had exhausted the bookselling knowledge I had to pass on, we lapsed into silence.

She broke it about five minutes later. I had the impression that Charlotte and silence were not natural bedfellows.

'So... what do you do for fun around here?'

I looked up from my computer screen and blinked at her. 'Fun?'

'Yes. You know. Entertainment.'

I considered this. I wasn't sure my definition of fun would be quite the same as Charlotte's. 'Well, there are a couple of nice pubs that host live music. But not tonight. Usually just at weekends. And there are concerts at the bandstand, but again... just on Sundays.'

'Right.' She gave a tight smile. 'Any theatre?'

'Well, there's...'

'What?'

I hesitated. It perhaps wasn't such a good idea to tell Charlotte about the theatre group. It might be awkward to have her there. I wasn't sure I'd have the courage to stand on that stage knowing that a famous actress was watching my every move. She probably wouldn't be interested in amateur stuff anyway.

'...nothing on at the moment.'

'Oh.' She frowned. 'That's a shame. Is the Shellcliff Palace still open?'

For the time being. 'Only sporadically.'

She smiled. 'I basically spent my youth there.'

I wasn't surprised. We had been in several of the same productions. I could picture her now, all dressed up as Cinderella. Or was it Helena from *A Midsummer Night's Dream*? I considered saying something, but I didn't particularly enjoy talking about those times, and she probably didn't remember me anyway.

'Oh, yes?' I tried to keep my voice neutral.

'The summer shows were so much fun.'

I was starting to feel guilty. 'I can imagine.'

'So what do you do to pass the time? Have you been to any of these live music nights?'

'No. Well, I went once, but it was a bit loud for me...'

'Oh, dear. What was it? Heavy metal?'

God, this was exhausting. Why was she still talking to me? Couldn't she see that I was a terrible conversationalist?

'Er, no. It was a Madonna tribute night.'

She narrowed her eyes. 'The Madonna tribute night was too loud for you?'

'Well... yes.' I felt myself flush a little, and stared pointedly at the pile of books on the counter. 'To be honest, I prefer to stay in and read.'

6

Charlotte

By the end of my first week in Shellcliff, I had learned several things.

Greg was indeed stuffy and set in his ways. But Sarah had neglected to tell me that he was also something of a sweetheart, and terribly, terribly shy.

He would blush if I so much as looked at him. And he had actually gone out to buy coffee to go because he was, apparently, too nervous to admit that he only had instant. Yes, he came across as a little awkward. And he dressed like he was working in an office, in a pressed white shirt and dark grey jacket. He looked smart, if a bit formal. In short, he was hardly the ogre I had been picturing.

Sarah was right about the sadness, though. Sometimes I caught him staring into space, a haunted look in his blue eyes. When I asked if he was all right, he would look almost guilty.

There was also something vaguely familiar about him. Perhaps we had been in the same class at school. I knew I should ask, but I had a terrible memory for faces, and I didn't want to risk embarrassing myself, or him.

I spent the first few days following The Orders of Greg. In fairness, he ran the bookshop like a well-oiled, if slightly old-fashioned, machine. We opened up at 10am, and the UPS delivery man generally arrived at around 11am. We unpacked orders, shelved stock, phoned customers. In the afternoon, we did admin, and dusted. I was learning that bookshops produced a lot of dust.

Occasionally, an actual real-life customer would come into the shop, and sometimes they would buy a book.

Sarah came in a few times to check on things. There was a strange sort of tension between her and Greg. He would avoid her eye, and she would speak to him in a vaguely patronising way which I didn't especially like. But I didn't feel it was my place to comment on it. Not only was she my sister, but she was also technically my new boss, if only for a short time.

By the end of the week, I was starting to realise that it would be very difficult to either a) modernise the shop, or b) get Greg to leave.

I needed more information.

As an actress, I have always taken a psychological approach to my characters. Upon landing a new role, I list their strengths, weaknesses and motivations. I needed to know what motivated Greg, if anything.

'So, Greg,' I said, on my fifth afternoon in the bookshop. 'Have you always wanted to be a bookseller?'

It had been a particularly quiet day. We were standing behind the counter, drinking tea. I was halfway through making an inventory of the Classics section. I noticed that Greg had every book by Jane Austen, but nothing whatsoever by the Brontës. This struck me as something which needed to be rectified, post-haste. We were in Yorkshire, after all.

Greg looked a little startled by the question. He put down his mug. 'No. I just… sort of drifted into it.'

This was interesting. Maybe it could also be a potential motivation for Greg to leave the shop. Maybe, if he was to find his dream job, he would jump at the chance to do something new.

'It seems a very specialist thing to just drift into,' I said.

He shrugged. 'I love books. There was a job going. I took it.'

'Did you want to do anything else? When you were younger?'

Greg was quiet for a long moment. He didn't meet my eye. 'No...'

Ah-ha! I thought. *I don't believe you.*

'Go on,' I said. 'What would you be doing if you didn't work here?'

'I'd probably be working in another bookshop.'

'Fair enough. But if you could do something apart from working with books?'

'I've worked with books for over twenty years. I like working with books. I don't think I'd want to do anything else.'

Damn. So much for that, then.

'So you wouldn't consider changing jobs?'

'No.' His eyes narrowed. 'Why are you asking me all these questions?'

'Oh, no reason. Just curious.'

After that, Greg retreated to the stockroom. I had no idea what he was doing in there, but I suspected he was mainly avoiding me. I hoped he didn't realise what I was up to. I had no desire to be cruel, or to make him feel uncomfortable.

Fortunately, the next day he seemed back to his normal self. He even brought me one of those expensive takeaway coffees and a cinnamon bun. He was very sweet, really. He was probably too sheltered and bookish to suspect anything.

7

Greg

I knew what she was up to, and I wasn't going to fall for it.

I was quite sure that upon meeting me, most people thought I was a quiet person. Uninterested in others, and therefore oblivious. But I had spent decades working with the public, and I'd read a lot of books. I wasn't naïve: I knew when I was being played.

Charlotte and Sarah wanted me to leave. And the reason they wanted me to leave was that they didn't like the way I did things. Well, I'd been doing things my way for twenty years, and my way worked perfectly well, thank you very much.

These were the thoughts that went through my head as I stomped around my flat above the bookshop, watering my plants and putting bread in the toaster. Then I took my tea and toast into the living room, and looked out of the window at the grey, roiling sea.

I felt a touch of something close to vertigo. I have this, occasionally. It's the sense that the small, cosy life I've built for myself could slip through my fingers... and then what? I have no real skills, no training, no further education as such. And I can bluster in private all I like, but ultimately Sarah could fire me tomorrow if she wanted to. Then I would lose both my job and my home.

The only solution was to be what Sarah wanted me to be, but I wasn't sure I knew how to do that. I was like one of the old books in the antiquarian section: dry and dusty, and stuck in the past.

I couldn't be more different from Charlotte de la Mer.

I went into the kitchen and made myself another cup of tea. I wasn't too fond of Sunday mornings. They could feel a little empty. At one stage, many years ago, I had asked Maria if I could open the shop.

'You should really get a hobby, Greg,' she had said, not unkindly. 'Besides, it's too quiet on Sundays. Not worth the electricity bill.'

So that was that.

Still, I had followed Maria's advice. I had found a hobby. Or rather, I had reconnected with an old one. And while Sunday mornings were a drag, Sunday afternoons could be quite wonderful.

8

Charlotte

I managed to keep myself busy in the bookshop, but evenings were proving a challenge. The Grand Hotel's only form of entertainment was the television in my room, and while I did enjoy *Pointless,* there were only so many episodes I could watch. For some reason, reading didn't seem to hold much appeal.

The first Sunday was particularly tough. I found myself longing for my London Ladies, and the bustle of the theatre during the show. And I missed Alex. He hadn't yet told me when he was going to come and visit.

By lunchtime, I found I could take it no more. I decided to leave the hotel and go for a walk. Maybe refamiliarising myself with the neighbourhood was the best thing to do. Maybe I could check out one of those pubs Greg had mentioned. I was also feeling a little uninspired by the menu in the Grand's not-quite-restaurant, aka the pizza place down the road, so a decent meal was high on my list of priorities. Perhaps somewhere would be open for Sunday lunch.

Outside, the sea air was chilly. I walked several blocks along the promenade, passing a series of shuttered shops and empty units. There was an Italian restaurant, but it was closed.

A delicious smell drifted through the air and curled up my nostrils. Fish and chips. I hadn't had fish and chips for years. It wasn't what I'd hoped for, but it was certainly tempting.

I found the chippy a few doors down. There were a few customers waiting, and I stood in line, reading the posters tacked to the tiled walls. There were actually quite a few events and social groups in the town, most of which seemed to be at the library, or the Shellcliff Palace. I felt a small pang of nostalgia for the old theatre. I hadn't been to visit it yet.

A particular poster caught my eye. It was advertising auditions for a new play, *Theatre is Murder!*, which would be presented by the Shellcliff Amateur Theatre Society in late August. Funny. Greg told me there was no theatre happening in town. But some people could be snobbish about amateur dramatics, and I suspected Greg was a bit of a snob about all sorts of things. Dusty intellectuals generally were. Maybe that was why he didn't think to mention it.

I studied the poster. It seemed that the auditions were today, at 2pm. How interesting.

I paid for my small portion of fish and chips and wandered further along the seafront. At least it was nice and bright at this time of year. The beach was clean, and the sea had finally calmed. A few amusement arcades glittered with light, but there were very few people around. Just a couple of dog walkers on the beach.

I walked along, eating my chips – which were delicious – with the little wooden fork. I found a bench and sat for a while, looking out to sea as I finished eating. Then I stuffed the polystyrene carton in a nearby bin.

Ahead of me, the promenade swept around in a curve. The Shellcliff Palace was just on the other side of the bay. I hadn't planned to visit it today, but I was curious about the auditions. I found myself walking towards it, as if the theatre was drawing me in.

The first sight of it made my breath catch in my throat. I approached slowly, almost warily.

It had the same air of neglect as The Grand Hotel. Chipped paintwork, faded signage. There were cracks in the art deco panels on either side of the door, and the glass canopy over the entrance was streaked with grime and gull droppings. I did not consider myself a sentimental type, but I remembered how this place blazed with colour twenty-five years ago. What had happened?

When I looked closer, I saw that the theatre had not been entirely neglected. There were posters for upcoming concerts and comedy shows on the noticeboards, and as I peered through the glass door panels, I saw a light glowing in the foyer.

I could just pop in for the auditions. I wasn't seriously considering taking part, but it would be interesting to see what they were up to.

I grasped the big brass handle and pulled. The door swung open with a creak. I walked through the foyer and into the auditorium, where I was greeted by chaos. There were people everywhere. And they were making a lot of noise. Voices and laughter bounced off the walls. The acoustics had always been a tad echoey, as the theatre was effectively a giant shed with some plaster decorations stuck on it.

The Shellcliff Palace dated from the 1930s, but the interior had an art nouveau feel about it. The architect had evidently wanted the theatre to reflect its seaside setting. The walls and plasterwork were carved with swirls that resembled water, and painted in shades of blue and green. The proscenium arch was framed by two mermaids and various gold plaster fish. The walls were covered in murals depicting various colourful sea creatures, and the chandelier resembled a jellyfish, with strings of pink and white crystals hanging from a curved purple globe. It was startlingly beautiful, if a little tired.

There was a man standing at the front of the rickety old stage, his back to the auditorium. His plump figure was vaguely familiar, and dressed in a blue long-sleeved shirt and a pair of burgundy corduroy trousers. He clapped his hands in an attempt to quiet the cacophony. Everyone ignored him.

He tried again. 'Ladies and gentlemen! Can I have your attenTION *PLEEEEASE!*'

The theatre fell silent. I blinked. The last time I heard someone project like that, he was dressed as King Lear and going mad on a windswept moor. Respect to this director.

The man turned around. It was Greg.

My first thought was that meek, gentle Greg shouldn't possibly be able to project like that.

And my second thought was: well, well, well. The little liar!

In a much quieter, but still clear voice, he said: 'Thank you. Now, can we please take our places. I want to start the reading in two minutes.'

The actors fetched folding plastic chairs and began to organise themselves into a circle on the stage.

'Can I help you?'

I jumped. I had been so wrapped up in Greg's performance that I hadn't noticed a woman approaching me. She peered at me through thick-rimmed glasses.

And... I *recognised* her.

'Lydia?' I said. 'Lydia Harrison?'

'Sorry, I don't...' Her eyes widened. 'Charlotte?'

'Yes!' I gave a laugh.

Lydia was a couple of years older than me. At school, she had been super clever, always studying in the library at lunchtime. I had been friends with her younger sister, Vicky, who like me was very into acting. Vicky was always laughing about her swotty older sister.

There was a pang somewhere in my chest. Vicky. I still found myself thinking of her often.

I hadn't seen Lydia for years. She'd gone to Oxford to study Biology, or was it Psychology? And after... well, there was no reason for us to stay in touch.

If I were to list Lydia's character motivations, I would probably write *academic achievement* and *desire to be respected by others*.

'Lydia! Gosh... how have you been?'

'I've been... fine,' said Lydia, a little cautiously. 'You?'

'Oh, things are great, darling. I've been in London. My last part was in the West End.'

Lydia smiled. The expression looked forced. 'You mean that old time travel thing?'

I bristled a little. '*The Next Thirty Years* was a huge critical and commercial success. *The Times* called it "a blistering and insightful exploration of a marriage on the point of implosion, with tunes in the timeless style of Cole Porter".'

'Just closed, hasn't it?'

I had almost forgotten about Lydia's mean streak. It's amazing what time and distance can do. I was determined not to rise to the bait.

'Er... yes. Temporarily.' I paused. 'Are you performing in this play?'

'Not likely!' Lydia looked mildly horrified. 'No. I'm mainly here to help my brother. I do the admin and bookings and things. He's not the most practical of people.'

'Greg's your brother?' This was an unexpected development. I couldn't remember Vicky ever mentioning him.

Lydia nodded. 'Don't worry. He's a perfectly competent director.'

I glanced at Greg, who was handing out scripts. A sheaf of pages slipped from his hand and cascaded onto the stage. A few people went over to help. 'Er... yes. I'm sure he is.' My curiosity was piqued. Perhaps this was Greg's elusive dream career. I decided to dig a little deeper. 'Does he ever do any acting?'

Lydia looked briefly troubled, but chased it away with a smile. 'No. My daughter Sam's the performer in the family. She's going to try for a small part this time so it doesn't interfere with her exams. She's applying to Oxford this year.'

'Oh. Well. She must be very clever.'

'Yes. She is.' Lydia narrowed her eyes. 'What are you doing back in town?'

'I'm helping out at my sister's bookshop.'

She laughed. 'So you're working with Greg? You must have a lot to do. I don't think he's tidied up since about 2003.'

I had a sudden urge to defend Greg. 'It's not too bad.'

'You obviously haven't seen his cupboard.' She gave me a probing look. 'I'm guessing you won't have time to be in the play. I don't suppose you would be interested anyway, what with you being a *professional* actress.'

There was a barely suppressed sneer in her voice. And while I hadn't seriously considered auditioning for the play, I found that I now wanted to, just to show Lydia that I *could*. They say old habits die hard.

'Actually, I was thinking of giving it a go,' I said. 'It might be fun to work with *amateurs* for a change.'

Lydia blinked. 'Er... well, I'm not sure we're accepting new members at the moment...'

'Do I talk to Greg? Greg!'

Greg turned his attention from the scripts and looked in our direction. His eyes widened.

A moment later, he had come down from the stage. 'What are you doing here?'

'I'm here to audition,' I said. 'And I have a bone to pick with you.'

He looked alarmed. 'A bone?'

'You told me there was no theatre going on in town.'

Greg shuffled his feet. 'I... didn't think you'd be interested in amateur stuff.'

'Nonsense, darling! I *love* am-dram. It's where I started my career. In this very theatre, in fact. Ask me to do anything, play any role, and I'll give it one hundred and ten per cent!'

'I hardly think it's appropriate,' said Lydia, her nose slightly in the air. I seemed to recall that Lydia always had her nose in the air, even when we were teenagers.

'Why not?' I asked.

'Well, you're a professional, for a start,' said Lydia.

Greg ran a hand through his hair. 'She's right... we're an amateur theatre company. I'm just not sure it would be fair...'

I smiled. 'That's very considerate of you, Greg, but I'm not remotely snobbish. I don't mind working with amateurs.'

Greg stared at me for a moment. 'That's not what I meant.'

'Who knows? They might even learn something.'

'I just don't think it's a very good idea...'

'Listen,' I said. 'Let me audition like everyone else. What harm can it possibly do?'

Greg hesitated. Then he sighed. 'All right. We'll be reading some extracts from the script in a minute.'

Lydia stared at Greg. 'You're not serious?'

I smiled. 'That sounds perfect.'

Greg turned towards the stage and clapped his hands together again. 'All right, everyone. Can you take a seat onSTAGE PLEEEASE!'

Blimey. It was like a Jekyll and Hyde-esque transformation or something.

I made my way up the steps at the side of the stage, and found an empty chair. I sat down and smiled at my fellow thespians. Lydia sat down opposite me, a glare in her eyes.

Greg dropped a heavy printed script into my lap. 'There you go.'

'Thank you.'

He took a seat and looked around at the group. 'Okay, everyone. I'll assign some parts, and we can get on.'

I was taken aback. Oh, this was not good. Not good at all. There was a way of doing these things, and this was not it. I raised my hand.

'Yes, Charlotte?' said Greg.

'Aren't we going to do a few ice-breaker exercises first?'

'Ice-breaker exercises?'

'Yes, you know… drama games. Like throwing a ball around the circle to help us learn each other's names. Or making up a story by going around and each adding a sentence.'

He looked genuinely confused. 'Why would we do that?'

My God. Did this man know anything about acting?

'To get to know each other, and get our performance muscles warmed up. I mean, if we were a ballet company, we wouldn't launch straight into *Swan Lake*, would we? We'd at least do some stretches first.'

Greg massaged the bridge of his nose. 'Well, we're not a ballet company, are we? And I'm sure we'll soon learn each other's names… without throwing a ball. So let's make a start, shall we?'

So unimaginative.

'All right,' said Greg. 'Our play this August is *Theatre is Murder!*, by A. Hackson. It's set in a run-down theatre in the 1930s, and follows the fortunes of two actresses. They're friends, but also rivals. Maggie has been given the lead role in a play, while Opal is her understudy. Maggie believes the play will be her great comeback. But then the director is found murdered onstage, and Maggie becomes the prime suspect.'

A young woman raised a hand. 'Let me guess: Opal did it!'

There was some laughter from the circle of actors.

Greg smiled. 'Ah, you'll have to wait and see. Let's allocate the parts. Rose, will you please read Maggie?'

He went down the cast list on the front page of the script, moving around the circle and giving out parts. He reached the end of the list before he got to me.

'We'll read a few scenes, then reallocate to give everyone a chance,' said Greg.

Fair enough.

ACT ONE, SCENE ONE: The star dressing room, ten minutes before curtain-up. Maggie, the lead actress, is sitting at her dressing table, applying makeup and warming up her voice.

Greg read the stage directions. He had a lovely, clear voice. Perfect for reading aloud. I wondered if he ever gave readings in the bookshop. Something told me that he probably didn't, so I added it to my mental list of things to suggest.

One of the women cleared her throat loudly. She appeared to be in her fifties, and she was wearing what was possibly the world's most magnificent coat. It was printed with huge splashes of colour, as if a child had poured paint randomly all over it. My sister would be quite jealous if she saw her.

She peered at the script, her mouth set in an expression of utmost seriousness. Then she raised a hand, as if preparing to command all attention in the room. Everything about her demeanour screamed 'actress'.

MAGGIE (*Rose*): La la la la-la-la laaaaa!

OPAL: Are you all right, Maggie?

MAGGIE: I'm just warming up the old vocal cords.

OPAL: Oh, good. I thought for a moment you were ill.

MAGGIE: Any flowers?

OPAL: Yes. (*She places a bouquet of roses on the table.*) From His Lordship.

MAGGIE: Roses! How original.

I was completely fascinated. I had no idea how anyone could pack so much emotion into such inane dialogue. Rose was Acting with a capital A. Every line was enunciated at great volume, as if it were the most important, dramatic line in the play.

I decided that Rose's principal character motivation was *to be the centre of attention at all times.*

At one point, she caught my eye, and I dropped my gaze to my script.

We read on. It soon became apparent that, as a character, Maggie was an absolute pain in the proverbial behind. A complete diva. Which, of course, would make her tremendous fun to play. I won't lie: I coveted her.

Of course, if the play was on in August, there was a good chance I would be back in London by then. But if Greg cast me – and he would be mad not to – attending rehearsals would be a fun distraction. And I was sure he would find a replacement if I needed to leave before the play opened. In my experience, there was always a surfeit of wannabe lead actors in every group. I pushed any concerns from my mind.

After three scenes, Greg reassigned the parts.

'Charlotte, please could you read Opal?'

Well, that was a little disappointing. Still, I managed to give Greg a warm smile. 'Of course. It'll be my pleasure.'

'Thank you,' said Greg. 'Bex, could you read—' Rose peered at him over her dramatic spectacles. He seemed to deflate slightly. 'Actually, let's stick with Rose as Maggie for now.'

Well, this was going to be interesting.

The reading continued. Opal was quite an interesting character. Her primary motivation seemed to be jealousy, but it was interspersed with a sort of weary affection. The women were rivals, but they were very much defined by each other.

We reached the pivotal scene in which Maggie was arrested for the murder of the theatre director.

OPAL (*Charlotte*): You want to arrest her?
DI MORIARTY: Please let us through, Madam.

OPAL: But... she's innocent!

At this point, Rose stood up. She faced the unfortunate actor reading DI Moriarty, her features twisted in a pantomime of grief.

MAGGIE (*Rose*): Oh, no! Oh, noooo! I didn't do it! I'd never do that! It was Lord Moncrief! It was Lord Moncrief and his poisoned roses. Nooooo!

Rose wailed and sobbed, wringing her hands, clawing at her arms. Finally, she collapsed onto her plastic chair in a paroxysm of agony.

There was a short silence.

I knew one or two things about overacting. The best professional actors, myself included, delved deep into their own emotions to deliver performances based on psychological truths. Others, however, mistook wild gesticulation and talking very loudly for good acting.

Rose clearly fell into the latter camp.

Greg blinked and cleared his throat. I was intrigued to hear his reaction to Rose's 'performance'.

'Thank you. That was...' he glanced at Rose, who looked almost smug. 'That was... *interesting*. Er... would anyone else like to read the role of Maggie?'

For a moment, no one moved. Then the girl seated next to Lydia raised her hand. She must have been seventeen at the most. 'Please can I give it a go?'

Greg looked surprised. 'Sam?'

Lydia frowned at her. 'Are you sure? It's a big part, and there's your exams to think about.'

Ah. So this was Lydia's daughter. Which meant she was Greg's niece.

'I know that.' There was a defiant edge to Sam's voice. 'I would still like to give it a go.'

'It's really a role for an older lady,' said Greg, kindly. He received an odd look from Rose, an expression which hovered somewhere between grateful and offended. 'Why don't you read Eliza? She's the dresser. It's a good part.'

Sam looked slightly disappointed. She dropped her gaze to her script. 'Okay.'

'I'd love to read Maggie,' I said.

Rose looked at me sharply. 'I'm more than happy to carry on.'

'I'm sure you are,' I said. 'But Greg did ask.'

We both turned to Greg. An expression of mild panic flitted across his face.

'Well, if Charlotte wants to read—'

'Yes,' I said. 'I do.'

Rose folded her arms and glowered at me.

'Well!' said Greg. 'Now that's all settled, let's carry on, shall we?'

We continued with Act Two. I tried to give a subtle performance, to deliver an antidote to Rose's bombast. I was sure it was enough to make a good impression. After a while, I let myself relax and enjoy the reading. Sam was particularly good. Her delivery was understated and sensitive. She would go far.

'Thank you,' said Greg, when we reached the end of the play. 'That was great. I have a lot of thinking to do. I'll aim to get back to you all by the end of next week. Thanks again.'

The actors said their goodbyes and began to trickle out of the theatre. Rose shot me a glare as she strode out.

I was alone with Greg, who began to stack the plastic chairs.

'It's a great play,' I said. This was a slight exaggeration. The play was only quite good, but there was no harm in showing enthusiasm, especially to the director.

He grimaced. 'It's absolute rubbish, but it's fun. Would you mind giving me a hand?'

I helped Greg stack the chairs against the back wall of the stage area.

'So Lydia's your sister?'

'Yes.' Greg had a chair in each hand.

'I knew her a bit at school. I was friends with Vicky.'

Greg froze. He lowered both chairs to the floor.

'Oh,' he said lightly, without looking at me. 'Were you?'

'She was a great actress, and a lovely girl.' I swallowed hard. 'I was really sorry when I heard—'

Greg turned his back to me, and picked up the chairs again. 'Do you mind if we change the subject?'

I could have kicked myself. 'Of course. Sorry.' I stacked another chair. 'I really enjoyed the reading. I can't wait to get started.'

'Er, great. Thanks for coming, Charlotte. I'll let you know.'

I left him alone after that. The way he had suddenly frozen had startled me.

I decided not to mention Vicky again.

9

Greg

It was Charlotte's day off, and I was glad to have the shop to myself. This would not only give me a period of blissful silence in which to get some actual work done, but it also gave me the chance to grapple with the casting for *Theatre is Murder!*, which was proving a difficult task.

Sam was the obvious choice for Eliza. She was shy, but she was also a great young actor. The male parts were more or less sorted. Like most drama groups, we had limited men to choose from, especially younger ones, but fortunately the male actors we had were very good.

It was our leading ladies who were proving problematic.

At any other time, I would have had no hesitation casting Rose in the role of Maggie. She would be absolutely insufferable, and I would need to rein her in, but the character was also insufferable, so she would actually be a good fit. Rose had been a staple of the drama group long before I had rejoined. She had played many major roles, but she played all of them as if they were characters in a sensational Victorian novel. Sometimes this paid off. It was great for panto or, say, a production of *The Woman in White*, but less appropriate for Chekhov's *The Cherry Orchard*.

Theatre is Murder! would be a perfect vehicle for her.

But now there was also Charlotte. She had read Maggie beautifully, adding depth to a character who was rather two dimensional on paper. I had little doubt that she would be great in the role. She would be brilliant as Opal, too, come to that.

Except it didn't seem fair. She was a professional. Should I really give a main part to a professional actress? The whole idea of the group was to give opportunities to amateur performers. And Rose hadn't seemed happy when I had let Charlotte read. Neither had Lydia, for whatever reason. If I cast Charlotte and either of them left in a strop, I would be, not to put too fine a point on it, buggered.

I was just sipping a cup of tea and mulling over my dilemma when the doorbell jingled in its annoying merry way, and Charlotte stepped in.

'Greg, darling!'

I looked at her suspiciously. 'What are you doing here?'

Charlotte frowned. 'Nice to see you, too.'

I shook my head. 'No, I didn't mean that. I meant... what are you doing here on your day off?'

'To be honest, I was bored, so I thought I'd come in and see if you needed a hand with anything.'

'Well, er... I'm not sure.'

'Are you all right?'

I forced a smile. 'Yes, yes! Why wouldn't I be?'

'You sound a little... stressed.'

'I'm fine. Er... there's been a new delivery of postcards. You can get them out, if you like?'

She smiled. 'On it.'

I sipped my tea while Charlotte rummaged around in a cardboard box. The shop radio was playing Mozart, and I tried to focus on the music.

'Greg?' I jumped. Charlotte's voice was as jarring as a car alarm.

'Yes?'

'I was just wondering how you were getting on with casting the show?'

Damn.

'Oh. I'm getting there.'

'That's good. I'm really looking forward to it.'

Charlotte wasn't looking at me. She was holding a stack of postcards, examining each one as if they were the most interesting things in the world.

'Um... good. Er... Charlotte?'

She looked up. 'Yes, darling?'

'Are you absolutely sure you want to be in this play? Isn't it a bit of a comedown, after acting professionally?'

She shook her head. 'Certainly not. I'll enjoy it. It'll be nice to do some acting just for the fun of it.'

'Right. Yes. Of course.'

'But don't worry, I'll still take it extremely seriously.'

'Oh. Great.'

I spent the rest of the day in an agony of indecision while Charlotte hummed, and put out postcards, and dusted. We served precisely six customers, which wasn't at all bad for a Monday afternoon.

The shop closed at 5pm. I was starting to think about cashing up when, at precisely 4.58pm, the doorbell jingled. I looked up from the till, unreasonably annoyed by such a late customer, and froze.

It was him. He was here.

My first instinct was to hide. I ducked beneath the counter, but it was too late. He had already seen me.

'Hi, Greg,' said a soft voice from somewhere above my head.

There were two things that worried me about Nick. The first was that he was absolutely gorgeous. He had long hair, but it was beautifully combed and styled, and he gave off a slight rocker vibe... faded grey jeans and a jacket with lots of sewn-on patches. This was not a style I had ever much cared for myself, but Nick always carried it off with aplomb. He managed to look elegantly edgy, rather than scruffy.

'Oh,' I said, straightening up. 'Hello, Nick. Sorry, I thought I'd dropped my pen. Ah, there it is...'

Nick smiled. This was the second thing that worried me about him. Whenever he called into the bookshop, he always appeared to be amused by something, and I had the feeling that the thing he was amused by was me.

Sometimes, in quieter moments, I would imagine what would happen if Nick asked me out on a date. We would probably go somewhere on his motorbike – I honestly had no idea if he owned one, but he *looked* like he should. He would take me somewhere trendy, somewhere with loud music and... and this was the point when I remembered I was a plump, middle-aged bookseller who would always find the music just a *bit* too loud. And he probably never thought about me that way.

I could feel my face growing hot. Dammit.

'Are you okay?' he said, his own lovely face all furrowed with concern.

I cleared my throat. 'Yes, yes, fine. Why shouldn't I be?'

Nick looked about to reply, but at that moment Charlotte emerged from the stockroom.

'Hello,' she said to Nick.

'This is Charlotte,' I said, relieved by the interruption. 'She's working here for the summer.'

They shook hands.

'So you're the famous actress,' he said, with a smile.

Charlotte chuckled. 'Not that famous.'

'I'm Nick, from the library. I was wondering if you'd display a poster for us.' He placed an A4 printout on the counter. 'Beginners' IT class.'

'Of course,' said Charlotte. 'That's all right, isn't it, Greg?'

'I suppose so,' I said.

'There might be a few more,' said Nick. 'We've got lots of events coming up. Knit and Natter, coffee mornings, kids' story times. It would be nice to work together a bit more.'

'That sounds lovely,' said Charlotte.

'We'll think about it,' I said.

Charlotte looked at me. Her mouth narrowed into a frown. Then she turned back to Nick. 'So... have you always lived in Shellcliff?'

Oh, for goodness sake. Why wouldn't she just let him leave?

Nick shook his head. 'No. I moved here a couple of years ago. For my job. It's a nice place. Bit quiet, though.'

Charlotte nodded. 'Greg mentioned there were some music nights?'

'Oh. Yeah. One of the pubs runs them. They're mainly tribute acts.'

'Greg told me about the Madonna tribute.'

I cleared my throat again. Nick caught my eye. His face became serious. 'Yeah. That wasn't one of the better ones.'

Charlotte seemed oblivious to my residual embarrassment. 'Well, I'd better go and tidy the kids' section. Nice to meet you, Nick.' She raised her eyebrows at me, then walked away.

I was expecting Nick to leave, but he lingered by the counter. He straightened the pile of business cards next to the till. Then he reached over to the Book Tokens display, and started to straighten the gift cards. I resisted the urge to glower at him, and gave him a neutral, customer service smile instead. 'Is there something else I can help you with?'

'Well...' Nick looked down at the floor. 'I was thinking...'

'Yes?'

'How are you fixed for next Friday? There's a little gathering at the pub. For... local businesses, you know. But it's a social thing, as well.'

I frowned. 'I don't know... I might be busy.'

'Oh. That's a shame.' Nick became interested in the floor again. 'Well... maybe we could grab a coffee sometime instead?'

'A coffee,' I said, flatly.

'Yeah. You know. A marvellous drink made from beans?'

I heard Charlotte cough.

'Right,' I said.

Nick ran a hand through his greying dark hair. 'I was just thinking... we could talk about... books? If you like.'

'Like a work thing?'

'Er... yes.'

'I'll have to check my diary. Let you know.'

He nodded. 'Okay. Well... I'll be off, then.'

'Okay.'

'Okay.'

He turned around, gave Charlotte a quick wave goodbye, and left the shop.

Charlotte emerged from the Children's section and looked at me with an expression which was half amused, half pitying.

'Wow,' she said. 'That was truly spectacular. High romance indeed.'

I was taken aback. 'What on earth are you talking about?'

Charlotte stared at me for a moment. 'Well, darling, I may be wrong about this, but I think he was trying to ask you out.'

'What?' Heat rushed to my face. 'He was talking about a business meeting.'

'In my experience, people don't generally blush and play with their hair and look at the floor when they're inviting people to business meetings.'

'But...' I shook my head in wonder. 'He doesn't like me. Thinks I'm a joke.'

'Whatever gave you that idea?'

I was silent. I was not going to go there. I was *not* going to talk about the Madonna tribute night. The episode had been a disaster all round, one I had no desire to relive.

'Just trust me on this,' I said darkly.

'He likes you. He clearly likes you.' She smiled. 'And I think you like him.'

'I do not.' I was aware I sounded like an embarrassed teenager. Which, considering my limited experience in such matters, I might as well have been.

Charlotte shrugged. 'Well, I guess we'll have to agree to disagree about this.'

'Yes, I suppose we will.'

10

Charlotte

I had done it.

I had found Greg's weakness. His nemesis. His Achilles heel.

His name was Nick. He was a librarian.

It just made so much sense. They both loved books (at least, I assumed Nick loved books), and they both seemed to like each other, even if Greg was determined to pretend otherwise.

Greg seemed a bit lonely. Perhaps his primary character motivation was *to find love.*

A new boyfriend would be the perfect distraction. Something to bring Greg out of his shell, and, more importantly, coax him out of the bookshop.

There was something standing in the way, however. Was it simply a lack of confidence on Greg's part? Well, I was sure I could help with that. I was *all* about self-confidence. Ms Fake It Till You Make It, me.

I just needed to find the right opportunity to bring Greg and Nick together.

I spent the next few days watching and waiting for my chance. Inspiration came, quite unexpectedly, on Thursday afternoon.

Despite being a keen bookworm and taking great pride in the shop, Greg didn't seem to like customers very much. I couldn't help noticing the long-suffering look that crept into his eyes every time the doorbell jingled.

Today was a case in point.

The bell rang, and a slightly harassed-looking woman in her sixties hurried into the shop. I was busy tidying the books in the Children's section, so she made a beeline for Greg, who was presiding over the counter, master of all he surveyed.

'Hello! I think I need some help. I really need a book to take on holiday tomorrow.'

Greg put down his copy of *Bleak House* and gave the customer a look that suggested she was ill-prepared, and that clearly any thinking person would have purchased their holiday books months, nay, years in advance.

'Oh, yes?' he said, in a neutral voice.

'I was wondering what you could recommend?'

Greg's expression now vaguely resembled that of a rabbit caught in a pair of headlights. 'Well, what sort of thing do you enjoy?'

'I don't want any fantasy rubbish,' said the customer. 'No elves or ghosts or mermaids or nonsense like that. I don't like supernatural stuff.'

'Okay?'

'What I really fancy is a story about a young woman who is swept off her feet by a handsome aristocrat, but it turns out he's Not What He Seems.'

Greg perked up a little. 'All right. Well… what about a classic? *Rebecca* by Daphne du Maurier is very good and fits the bill.'

'Does it have any vampires?'

'No. Nothing like that.'

'Oh, that's a shame. I really fancy something with vampires.'

'But…' I could almost see the mental gymnastics taking place inside Greg's head. 'But you said you didn't like… supernatural stuff?'

The woman gave him a withering look. 'Vampires don't count.'

'Oh. Right then. It's just—'

'Do you have any books about vampires?'

'I really do think *Rebecca*...'

It was at this point that I decided to stop trying not to laugh, and swoop to Greg's rescue. The poor man was clearly out of his depth.

'We do indeed,' I said, smiling at the woman. 'Have you heard of the new *Regency Vampyre* series?'

'The what?' Greg had come out from behind the counter.

The customer's eyes lit up. 'No. What's that?'

'Regency vampire romance,' I said. 'It starts with *The Viscountess and the Vampyre*.' I lowered my voice. 'I'm told it's a little bit steamy, though.'

'Oh,' said the woman. 'Is it?'

I nodded solemnly. 'Let me show you our Romantasy section.'

I led the customer to the new subsection I had created in Science Fiction and Fantasy, where the hardback edition of *The Viscountess and the Vampyre* was displayed face-out in all its lurid Gothic glory.

'Good lord,' said Greg.

Five minutes later, the customer had left the shop with a smile on her face and the first two *Regency Vampyre* novels under her arm. I was definitely starting to get the hang of this bookselling business.

Greg paced around in front of the Fantasy shelves, occasionally leaning in to peer at a title.

'What on earth is Romantasy?'

'It's a popular new genre,' I said. 'Romance and Fantasy. I heard about it on TikTok. I thought it was worth a try.'

'You ordered all these new books without consulting me?' He sounded put out.

'I did consult Sarah,' I said. 'You know? Our boss.'

Greg pulled out a book and shook his head in wonder. '*The Day I Fell In Love With a Kraken*. Honestly. Do people really read this nonsense?'

'Who says it's nonsense? People enjoy it. Get with the times, Greg.'

Greg made a humphing noise and shuffled back behind the counter. 'You know what I don't understand?'

'What?'

'That lady clearly knew exactly what she wanted. Why not just tell me?'

I pondered this for a moment. 'Maybe she wanted to chat?'

'Chat?'

'To you.'

'Why?'

'Maybe she wanted to talk about books?' I smiled. The exchange had given me an idea. Oh, this was *perfect*. 'Have you ever thought of running a book group in here? I think people would come.'

'Why would I want to do that?'

'It would be a nice thing for our regular customers. We would meet new people... talk about books. I used to be in one in London. We'd share a bottle of wine. I mean... the wine was the main focus, really. But we read the odd book too.'

Greg looked unconvinced. 'I don't see the point in discussing books. I'd rather just read them.'

'What if I ran the book group? I'll advertise it and lead the discussion, and you can come if you want to. I'll bring the drinks.'

His expression turned to one of alarm. 'But... what if people spill wine on the books?'

'Greg, I'm talking about a book group. It's hardly going to be a wild night.' I prepared to deliver what I was sure would be the final, convincing argument. 'I'm sure Sarah would approve.'

Greg's mouth moved, as if he was trying to find words of protest. Then he sighed. 'Oh, all right.'

'Great. Maybe you could invite your nice friend from the library?'

A hopeful look crossed Greg's face, but it quickly turned dubious. 'I don't suppose he'd be interested.'

'There's no harm in asking, is there? I'm sure he'd put up a poster for us, at least.'

'Well... okay. If you like.'

The idea was actually quite exciting. I knew I would make an excellent book group host. I was very good at choosing biscuits. 'It'll be fun, you'll see.'

'Hmm.' He picked up his copy of *Bleak House*.

'Any news on the play?' It was almost a week since the reading. I thought that even Greg would have come to a decision by now.

'Oh. Yes.' He looked away. 'I was wondering how you felt about playing Opal?'

I felt a small stab of disappointment. 'Not Maggie?'

He shuffled a little in his chair. 'It's just... I think Rose is a little more... theatrical, shall we say. While your performance was more understated. I thought it would be a nice contrast.'

This was actually insightful. Maybe Greg was a competent director, after all. I was sorry not to get the starring role, but I knew I needed to stay humble. It wouldn't do for Greg, or anyone else, to think I was some sort of stuck-up prima donna. And Opal was almost as large a part as Maggie.

I forced a smile. 'I would love to. Thank you so much for entrusting me with this. I won't let you down. I might even be able to help Rose out a bit. Teach her a few lessons in subtlety.'

'Er... I don't think that will be necessary.'

'But—'

'You will be nice to Rose, won't you?' Greg's blue eyes were pleading. 'She is an amateur, after all.'

I wanted to say that being an amateur was no excuse for over-acting, but Greg looked so anxious that I relented. 'It'll be fine, darling. I'm sure we'll get along like a house on fire.'

*

The following Sunday, I met my sister for coffee.

'How are you getting on?' said Sarah.

I nodded. 'Fine, I think. Bookselling is a strange job.'

Sarah stirred her cappuccino. 'Any progress with Greg?'

'Well... I see what you mean about him being old-fashioned. But he seems keen enough to let me come up with ideas.'

'Oh,' said Sarah. She sounded a bit disappointed. 'Well... that's good. As long as things are working out between you.'

'I'm going to set up a book group. I've told Greg to invite his crush.'

'He has a crush?' Sarah looked surprised. I was starting to wonder what her problem with Greg was, exactly.

'Yes. It's sweet, really. He comes into the bookshop now and again. If they get together it might give Greg something else to think about.' I grinned. 'Then I can make more radical changes while he's distracted.'

'How sneaky of you.' She sipped her coffee and regarded me thoughtfully. 'I get the impression you're enjoying it. Working in the bookshop, I mean.'

'It's fine. I wouldn't want to do it forever, but it's a nice break. I wish I could move out of the hotel, though. It's starting to feel a bit claustrophobic.'

Sarah smiled. 'Actually, I have some news about that. A friend's flat is standing empty. Do you fancy moving into it for a while? She's travelling at the moment and would only charge a very small rent.'

'Really?' I frowned. 'That sounds a little too good to be true. What's the catch?'

'There's no catch.'

'Rubbish. There's always a catch. She doesn't have six semi-feral pet cats, does she?'

Sarah laughed. 'No. But... actually, she does have house plants. Prize-winning orchids. And cacti.'

My eyes widened. 'You can't be serious. I've never managed to keep a plant alive in my life.'

'You'll be fine. I'll help you. I've brought the keys with me, if you'd like to take a look.'

I considered this. My own space seemed infinitely preferable to yet another night in that cramped hotel room.

'All right. Why not?'

*

'So,' said Sarah. 'This is the living room.'

I stared at a space which resembled a scene from *The Day of the Triffids*.

'Your friend really likes her plants, doesn't she?'

'Yeah. She's a botanist. She sells me ingredients for my handmade soaps.'

'Of course she does.' I pushed my way through the jungle. The kitchen was much less green, apart from a Venus flytrap on the window ledge. It grinned at me with half a dozen long-toothed mouths, and I repressed a shudder.

'There's a balcony,' said Sarah. 'It's lovely.'

I followed her onto the balcony. It was small, but there was a little circular table and two metal chairs, and a view across the bay. I could even see the Shellcliff Palace in the distance, crouched on the seafront.

'Lovely,' I agreed. I would need to swot up on the care of house plants, but the balcony would be a lovely place to read if the weather was good. 'I'll take it.'

*

That evening, I arrived at the Shellcliff Palace in high spirits. Most of the actors were already seated in a circle onstage, chatting among themselves. I smiled around the circle at my new company. Rose did not return my smile. Instead, she looked straight down at her script.

'Welcome to our first rehearsal,' said Greg. 'Thank you all for arriving so promptly.'

I flicked through my script. I had spent the previous evening carefully highlighting Opal's lines with a bright yellow marker pen. To my displeasure, I had found that I had twenty fewer lines than Rose. But I had decided not to mention this, because it seemed petty.

'I'm sure you're all keen to get started,' said Greg, above the continuing hubbub. His tone was more pleading than enthusiastic.

I turned another page. Of course, it wasn't the number of lines, but the quality and impact of said lines. I had an excellent and very funny line about scones, for example.

'So,' said Greg, 'without any further ado—'

But Maggie had a fantastic monologue near the end of Act Two. I would have had tremendous fun with that monologue.

'Charlotte? CharLOTTE!'

I jumped and looked up from my script. 'Sorry, darling?'

Greg gave a prim little smile and reverted to his indoor voice. 'It's your line.'

'Oh. Right. Sorry.'

Rose smirked. I ignored her. Then I adapted the technique I always used before stepping onstage, which involved closing my eyes and taking a grounding breath. I thought: be Opal. And with that, I was there, inside the character.

MAGGIE (*Rose*): Look, Opal. Lord Henry has sent me roses.
OPAL (*Charlotte*): How exciting that His Lordship is coming to see our little show! I wonder if he's as handsome as the papers say?
MAGGIE: Oh, he's far more handsome than that. I've seen him in the flesh, you know. At Lady Redford's birthday party. Oh, I *do* hope everything goes to plan.

'Actually, Greg, do you mind if I stand up?' said Rose.

I stared at her.

'Pardon?' said Greg.

'It's just that I do some of my best acting standing up.' Rose sounded quite serious.

I rolled my eyes. 'Can we please get on?'

Greg shot me a warning look. Then he nodded at Rose. 'Fine, fine.'

OPAL (*Charlotte*): I'm sure everything will be fine. You'll be brilliant as always.

MAGGIE (*Rose*): I'm just so worried something might go wrong. That I'll trip over my dress or something. Or there'll be some sort of disaster in the theatre…

OPAL: What sort of disaster could possibly happen in a theatre?

MAGGIE: Fire. Flood. Critics. The usual.

And so it went on. I had to hand it to the playwright: he was capable of writing the most tremendous doggerel. Despite being nonsense, it was readable nonsense. And, more importantly, actable nonsense. I could just picture the blocking, and how Maggie would flaunt around the stage in a big flowing dressing gown. I was sure Rose would be very good at flaunting.

ELIZA (*Sam*): Excuse me, Miss Paige, but there's a letter for you.

MAGGIE: Thank you, Eliza. (*Reads message.*) Oh. Oh my. (*Sinks into a chair.*) Oh my God. Oh, noooo…

Rose's delivery jarred me out of character.

'Oh, come on,' I said.

Rose looked up from her script. 'Excuse me?'

'Aren't you over-egging it a bit?'

Rose scowled at me. 'She's just had terrible news. Her entire fortune has been lost at sea.'

'I just think you're overacting a bit.'

'Charlotte.' There was a quiet note of warning in Greg's voice. Rose turned to look at him. 'I'm not overacting, am I, Greg?'

Greg looked away. 'Er... maybe just a tad? If I'm being honest.'

Rose looked startled. Then she rolled her eyes. 'All right. I'll tone it down a *tad*.'

MAGGIE (*Rose*): Oh. Oh my. Oh, no...

'Better,' said Greg, with a nod.

OPAL: What's wrong?

MAGGIE: My entire fortune has been lost at sea!

OPAL: Oh dear.

MAGGIE: I can't possibly be expected to go on tonight. I'm too distressed.

OPAL: Maybe I could go on instead?

MAGGIE: No, it's fine. I'm not that desperate. I'm sure I'll rise to the challenge! The show must go on! I shall channel my emotions into my performance. It will be cathartic.

As I said, tremendous rubbish.

We reached the end of Act One. To be fair, Rose had reined her performance in slightly. There was still room for improvement, however.

'Right,' said Greg, clapping his hands together. He looked pleased. 'Let's have some tea, shall we?'

*

I soon learned that the tea breaks at Shellcliff Amateur Theatre Society were important social affairs. They lasted for almost half an hour, which was quite a chunk out of our two hour rehearsal time.

People collected their mugs from the kitchen and returned to the auditorium, where they stood around in small groups, chatting. I leaned against the stage, using it as a table for my mug.

Lydia arrived about ten minutes into the break. She was wearing a suit, as if she had come straight from the office. She paused by the tech booth at the rear of the auditorium, where she started talking to Bex. I had the distinct impression that Lydia and I had got off on the wrong foot, and I was just wondering if I should approach her when someone spoke to me.

'Hi.'

It was Lydia's daughter, Greg's niece. Sam. She seemed like a quiet sort of girl, but she was a good actor. I had been impressed with her reading of Eliza.

'Hello,' I said. 'Sam, isn't it?'

'Yes.' She was quiet for a moment, looking at the floor. There was something in her guarded manner that reminded me of Greg. She had the same large blue eyes, too. 'I was just wondering... is it true you were in a West End show for ten years?'

I smiled. 'Yes. And I was in other shows before that.' I was always careful to make this point. It was important not to be pigeonholed.

'How did you get into it?'

'The show? Or acting?'

'Acting professionally. Did you go to drama school?'

'I did indeed! One of the very best.'

She looked down at her feet again. 'I'd like to apply to drama school.'

Well, that was nice. The theatre bug obviously ran in the family.

'Really? Which one did you have in mind?'

Sam looked up at me. 'I haven't decided yet. I like the look of a couple of the London ones. And Liverpool and Manchester.'

'Some good choices there,' I said.

'I was wondering if you could help me?'

'In what way?'

'I need to prepare a monologue. For the auditions. I was wondering if you had any advice about what I should choose and... well... how I should do it?'

Well, this was lovely. How sweet of her to ask.

'I'm happy to help in any way I can,' I said. I glanced at Greg, who was seated onstage, writing in his script. 'Have you asked your uncle? He seems to know his stuff.'

Something strange happened to Sam's face. Her expression had been full of enthusiasm, but now it was as if some inner light had gone out. Her mouth twisted.

'I can't talk to Uncle Greg. He might tell Mum.'

'Oh?'

'Mum doesn't want me to go. She wants me to go to Oxford to study Maths.'

'Ah,' I said. This all sounded painfully familiar.

'I've tried to talk to her before, but she always says acting's not worth it. That it's too hard. But I know it's hard, and I still want to try.'

'Maybe you should talk to her again,' I said carefully. 'I'm sure she'd support you if she knew how much it meant to you.'

Sam shook her head. 'You don't know her. It's like it scares her or something.'

Oh. That was sad. Was this about Vicky?

I felt a twinge somewhere inside. It almost felt like guilt, which was ridiculous. This was a tough business, and what happened hadn't been my fault. And yet... sometimes it *felt* like my fault.

Maybe Lydia just needed to see that it could be done. Then she would have more confidence in her daughter. Maybe helping Sam would be a good way of building bridges.

I smiled. 'All right. I'll help in any way I can.'

Sam clasped her hands together and jigged up and down a bit. The internal light was well and truly back on.

'Brilliant! Thanks so much!'

'You're welcome,' I said. 'But I must warn you that I take acting very seriously. And so do the drama schools. I hope you're prepared to put in lots of hard work?'

'Yes! Definitely.'

'Then let me have a think about monologues. You have a think too, and we can talk at the next rehearsal.'

'I will! Thank you.'

Greg's voice broke through the buzz of conversation. 'Right, everyone. Shall we get back to it?'

I watched Sam hurry back to her chair with a big smile on her face. I found myself smiling, too. I had never really helped out any aspiring actors, because there had never been the opportunity. And for the past ten years, my career had been dominated by my West End role.

Lydia took a seat on the front row of the stalls. She caught my eye and frowned.

'Are you all right, Lydia?' I asked as I made my way up to the stage.

'Yes, thank you. Just wondering what treats are in store for the second act.'

I couldn't be sure if she was talking about me or the play, so I decided to change the subject.

'You know, it would be lovely to meet up for a coffee some time,' I said. 'We could have a proper catch-up.'

Lydia stared at me as if I had just suggested we swim naked in the North Sea.

'I just thought it might be nice,' I finished, trying my best to sound non-committal.

'I don't think so,' said Lydia, quietly.

'Oh. Well. I understand if you're busy...'

'I'm really *very* busy,' said Lydia.

I became aware of Greg watching us from the foot of the stage. I smiled, hoping to reassure him that everything was fine and my presence here was not a source of tension. He gave me a slightly uneasy smile back.

Then we carried on with the read-through.

*

'So,' said Greg, in the tone of someone who has been wanting to broach a subject for a while. 'Are you going to tell me why Lydia keeps glaring at you?'

It had been a quiet morning in the bookshop. So quiet, in fact, that I had resorted to watching YouTube videos in an attempt to teach myself how to refill the pricing gun. There were many, many videos, but I still wasn't getting anywhere fast.

I put the pricing gun down and scowled at it. 'I'd hoped you hadn't noticed.'

'It was a bit difficult to miss,' said Greg, not unkindly. 'Is there something wrong?'

'Yes, with this bloody thing,' I said, indicating the pricing gun. 'How do I change the roll again?'

'You don't,' said Greg, darkly. 'I've only known one bookseller capable of refilling a pricing gun. I think he's head of a major American book chain now. I believe he was headhunted because of his ability to refill pricing guns.'

I stared at him. 'Are you joking?'

'Maybe I am.' Greg sipped his tea and smiled enigmatically. 'Maybe I'm not.'

'But what do we do?'

He shrugged. 'We don't bother. Unless you have The Gift, you might as well spend the rest of your bookselling career writing out all the price labels. It'll be quicker that way.'

'Right.' I shoved the offending item into the cupboard under the counter. This was where Greg kept all the pieces of equipment which didn't work anymore – used Pritt Sticks, nice but redundant pens, chalkboard cleaner which didn't work on chalkboards. Oh, and lots of random pieces of wood which, in his words, 'might come in handy one day'. Maybe he thought the cupboard had a magical ability to make the items work again.

'So,' said Greg. 'You and Lydia. Is everything all right?'

I considered this. I was starting to formulate my own theory about why Lydia might have a problem with me. The theory revolved around Vicky. I knew I hadn't been the most supportive of friends. I didn't feel I could confide this fact to Greg, however; not after how he'd reacted the first time I'd mentioned his sister.

'I don't really know,' I said. 'She probably still thinks it's unfair that I'm performing with amateurs.'

Greg looked thoughtful. 'I do sometimes think she's threatened by big personalities. People who are... er... a bit domineering.'

'I'm not domineering.'

Greg held up a hand. 'I didn't say you were. But you are quite opinionated. You like to get your point across.'

'Yes, well, I've learned that you can't be a wallflower in this business.'

Greg was quiet for a moment. He placed his teacup down gently by the till. 'No. I suppose not.' He sounded a little sad. Then he gave a tiny smile. 'Lydia is... well, I suppose she's quite protective. Of me – not that I need it, of course. But mostly of Sam. Did you know she wants to go to drama school?'

'Er... she did mention it, yes. She seemed to think you didn't know.'

Greg sighed.

'What's wrong?'

'Nothing, nothing. It's just... sometimes I get the impression that my family think I'm sort of... clueless. But I'm not. I've known about Sam for ages. I don't think I've ever met anyone who loves performing as much as she does.' A shadow seemed to cross his face. 'Apart from... you know.'

I nodded in understanding. 'She said Lydia doesn't want her to go.'

'No,' said Greg. 'I don't suppose she does.'

'Do you agree?'

'I don't know. I mean... I bet she could do it. She's very good.'

'She's asked me if I'll help her prepare for her auditions.'

'Hmm,' said Greg. 'I would tread carefully there.'

I picked up my tea. 'I'd really like to help her, even if it just means finding her a good monologue. I know there's lots of stuff on the internet, but I think playscripts might be better. You don't have any, do you?'

Greg was quiet for a moment. He twisted his hands together.

'It's a very small thing,' I said. 'We'd just be finding her a few scripts. Lydia would never need to know.'

Something almost like a twinkle appeared in Greg's eye. 'You know, maybe I can help after all.'

*

At closing time, Greg led me outside and locked up the shop. Next to one of the bay windows, there was an unobtrusive green door with *Flat 1* on it. He opened it, and I found myself peering up at a shadowy staircase.

I followed him up. I wasn't nervous – there was nothing about Greg that made me feel ill at ease – but I did wonder what sort of flat a semi-reclusive bookseller would live in, especially one with a propensity to collect clutter. I had seen enough flats belonging to fellow drama students and ex-boyfriends, and I was bracing myself for a similar chaotic mess.

Greg opened the door at the top of the stairs, and my mouth fell open.

The place was beautiful. It had a huge front window overlooking the sea, polished wooden floors and a large, original fireplace with floral tiles. Greg's décor was lovely. He had a green velvet sofa, patterned rugs, and seascapes hanging on the walls. And there were, of course, books, but they were all lovingly arranged on bookcases at either side of the fireplace.

'Are you all right?' said Greg.

'Yes,' I said. 'This is lovely.'

He blushed a little. 'Thank you. I like it. I like the view of the sea.'

He opened another door, and clicked on a light.

I stared. The room was large, easily the size of my living room back in London, and lined from floor to ceiling with shelves. The shelves were full of files and plastic boxes. There was also a teetering pile of cardboard boxes in one corner.

'Wow,' I said. 'Er... what am I looking at, exactly?'

'These,' said Greg, with a note of pride in his voice, 'are the Shellcliff Palace Archives, 1932–2008 inclusive, with particular reference to the Shellcliff Amateur Theatre Society.'

'Wow,' I said again. 'And you have it in your flat because...'

'There isn't space for it in the theatre. The only suitable room was a bit damp.' He paused. 'And I like to have it here. I'm in the process of sorting it.'

I stared at the nearest shelf. There was a box file on it, bearing a sticky label which had *Summer Season, 1932* written in careful biro. I noticed the other files were labelled in the same way.

I had already concluded that Greg was a bit of a geek, but this took his obsessions to a whole new level.

'What's that in the corner?' I asked, indicating the tower of boxes.

Greg hesitated. His eyes seemed to mist over. 'Recent donations. I haven't had a chance to go through them yet.'

I had no idea why he sounded so sad, so I did my best to cheer him up. 'Greg, this is amazing.'

'Thank you.' He smiled, and reached for a file. 'Here, you'll like this.'

The file was labelled '1992–1998'. I opened it and gave a little gasp of surprise. There I was, dressed in a long, silver ballgown. 'That's me!'

Greg nodded. 'From *Cinderella*.'

'I loved that panto.'

'Yes,' said Greg, quietly. 'Me too.'

I looked up at him. 'Wait... you were involved?'

Greg smiled, flicked through several pages, and then pointed to a figure standing to one side of the ballroom scene, costumed as a pageboy.

I looked at the photo and smiled. 'I thought I recognised you!'

'I was in all the chorus scenes,' said Greg.

I turned another page. 'There I am again. How embarrassing.'

Actually, I wasn't remotely embarrassed. I loved reliving past triumphs.

The production was *A Midsummer Night's Dream*. I was Helena, wearing a white robe and flowers in my hair.

'Were you in *Midsummer*?'

He gave a little bow. 'Bottom the Weaver, at your service.'

'No!'

'Oh, yes.'

I shook my head. 'I'm so sorry, Greg. My memory must be hopeless.'

'It's okay. It's not as if we had many scenes together. Or any, really, except the last one.'

'Were you in any more shows after I left?'

'A few.'

'But you don't act now?'

He was quiet for a moment, staring at the *Midsummer* photo.

'I... haven't really had the inclination over the last few years.' He reached for the folder and placed it gently back on its shelf. Then he smiled. 'Right – plays!'

'Oh, yes.' I had completely forgotten why we were there.

Greg led me to a bookcase stuffed with playscripts. Some were actual books, while others were printed and stapled together.

'They're in alphabetical order by author's surname,' said Greg.

I nodded. 'I would expect nothing less. This is fabulous. We're bound to find something here.'

We spent half an hour looking through the scripts. Soon we had a shortlist of options: I selected *Romeo and Juliet* and *Lady Windermere's Fan,* while Greg pulled out Alan Bennett's *Talking Heads* and *Educating Rita* by Willy Russell. We also found a few books of more contemporary monologues aimed at young actors.

'These look perfect,' I said, flicking through the pages. 'We can show them to Sam. See what she thinks.'

Greg looked pensive. 'Are you sure we're doing the right thing? Encouraging Sam, I mean. It's incredibly tough, working as an actor.'

I smiled. 'You think I don't know that, darling? I've been doing this for twenty-five years. When it's hard, it's extremely hard. But when it all falls into place, it's wonderful.'

'I know. I... wanted to turn pro for a while. I even did some repertory theatre.'

'Oh, really?' At last: something to add to my Greg Character Profile. So much for only ever wanting to work with books.

Greg smiled briefly, his gaze going back to the archives. 'Sometimes I wonder...'

'What?'

He shook his head. 'Nothing.'

My instinct told me that this was far from being nothing. I looked at Greg and it was as if there was something hiding just beneath the surface.

'What happened?' I asked. 'Why did you give up acting?'

He looked startled, then waved a hand dismissively. 'It just didn't feel like the right fit anymore. I prefer to stay behind the scenes.'

His voice was rueful. I didn't believe him.

11

Greg

I had lied to Charlotte. It was true that I loved bookselling, but I also loved performing. It was in my blood.

When she had gone, I stayed in my spare room for a while, looking through the archives.

To someone who didn't know what they were looking at – e.g. almost everyone – the contents of the archives wouldn't appear particularly exciting. But they were deeply precious to me. I hadn't told Charlotte that the archives didn't just conserve our time in the theatre group, or the history of the Shellcliff Palace. They contained my entire family history. The story of the theatrical Harrison family, their theatre and their productions.

It had started with my great-grandfather. He was a music hall comedian. In fact, I had it on fairly good authority (*The North Yorkshire Times*, 1929) that he was one of the worst comedians in the history of comedy. But he didn't let that hold him back, because Charlie Harrison had a dream. His dream was to form his own troupe of theatricals, and bring a little bit of magic to Shellcliff seafront. He was a wonderful producer, and within three years, he had raised enough funds to construct his own purpose-built theatre (it helped that he also married an heiress, but that's by the by, and it led to all kinds of trouble later).

The Shellcliff Palace was his.

I looked again at the file from the mid-nineties, and I found myself staring at the *Cinderella* photos. I remembered Charlotte as a glamorous presence who didn't really pay much attention to the younger members of the cast, like me. She must have been seventeen or eighteen at the time, while I was only fourteen. I had thought she was fabulous. I wouldn't tell her that now, of course. She had a sufficiently high opinion of herself without my help.

I looked at my younger self, dressed in that ridiculous pageboy costume. As a teenager, those theatre productions had become the centre of my world for weeks on end. I enjoyed being someone else for a while. I enjoyed singing, and dancing (badly), and showing off.

Sometimes, I thought the boy in these photographs was a different person. That he had fled from the ball, much like Cinders, never to be seen again.

*

I had to hand it to Charlotte: once she had an idea, she never gave it less than one hundred per cent. Her latest fixation was the Shellcliff Book Group. She had printed posters and distributed them all around the town. So far, I had spotted them in two coffee shops, the Shellcliff Palace, the chippy and, most alarmingly, the window of the library.

Nick wouldn't turn up, of course. He would be far too busy. And he would probably have had his fill of books by closing time.

The day of the first meeting had finally arrived. Charlotte, who was chairing proceedings, picked up a packet of Hobnobs and brought it down on the table like a gavel.

'I declare the first meeting of the Shellcliff Book Group officially open!'

I looked around the room. Three people had turned up – the vampire fan, the man who owned Beans Coffee Emporium, and

Bex from the drama group. I thought this wasn't bad at all for a first attempt, but I had the impression that Charlotte was slightly disappointed, and trying to hide it.

I sat behind the counter, partly in case anyone wanted to buy something, but mainly so I could keep out of the way. I was half-obscured by the display of National Book Tokens, so hopefully I wouldn't be disturbed too often.

'So,' said Charlotte. She held up her copy of the unfortunate book that was due to be metaphorically torn apart. It was approximately the size of a large brick, and I had found it a tough read. I wasn't convinced it was the best choice for the first book group meeting. I suspected Charlotte had seen it on some prestigious prize list or other, and was trying to be clever. 'What did we think of *Undersea Rhapsody*?'

'It was okay,' said Vampire Fan.

'I loved it,' said Mr Beans.

'It was good,' said Bex. 'Bit long, though.'

There was a pause.

'Right,' said Charlotte. 'Would anyone like to expand on those... points?'

Silence. I heard the distant roar of the sea.

'Okay. Would anyone like a biscuit?'

'Oh, yes please!' said Vampire Fan.

I sighed and turned a page of my book. This wasn't going well. But then again, I hadn't expected it to. Talking about books always felt rather awkward to me.

The biscuits went around the circle twice.

The door opened.

I glanced up in time to see Nick step into the shop. He was wearing jeans, a faded blue T-shirt and a leather jacket. He looked rather grungy and casual compared to the rest of the group. He was also carrying a copy of the book under his arm.

He caught my eye and smiled. I hastily buried my face in my own book.

He approached the circle of a dozen chairs, and fewer people. 'Am I late?'

'Not at all!' said Charlotte. 'Welcome to the biscuit... I mean the book group!'

'Great,' he said, and flopped into a chair.

'We were just saying whether or not we enjoyed the book,' said Charlotte. 'What did you think of it?'

'Oh, I hated it,' said Nick.

I looked up at him with barely suppressed amazement. Nick was a librarian. He wasn't supposed to hate books. Any books. Not even objectively terrible ones.

The rest of the group seemed similarly scandalised. Mr Beans sat up straighter in his chair. 'What? How could you hate it?'

'I don't know,' said Nick. 'I just did. Please can I have a biscuit?'

'But... you can't have really hated it?' said Vampire Fan. 'Not really.'

'I'm afraid I did.'

'But *why*?' said Mr Beans.

Nick waved a hand. 'Does there have to be a reason?'

'I'm not sure you've quite grasped the point of a book group,' said Charlotte.

Nick eyed the biscuits, and then the bottle of white wine. Everyone was looking at him expectantly.

He sighed. It was a long-suffering sigh. A surprisingly intellectual sigh. 'All right. I disliked it because I thought it was derivative. I mean, the prose is excellent, and I liked the parts set under the sea – some nice touches of magical realism there. But the characters are paper-thin. That session musician was totally up himself. Real musicians don't behave like that, at least not if they want anyone to book them. And I couldn't get on board with the romance. People don't just meet and then fall in love instantly like that. It's nonsense. But I'm sure you all have different opinions. I think books are very personal.' He paused and looked around the group. '*Now* can I have a biscuit?'

I stared at him. He caught my eye again. Cheeks burning, I quickly averted my gaze.

There was a rustle of a biscuit packet.

'You know,' said Vampire Fan. 'I wasn't keen on it either. No vampires.'

'A fair observation,' said Nick. 'A few vampires would have livened things up.'

I wasn't at all sure if he was being serious or not.

'What did you think?'

I gave a start. Nick was looking at me again.

'Oh, I don't know,' I half-mumbled. 'It wasn't really my thing.'

'I was actually wondering about the ending,' said Mr Beans. 'I wasn't sure I quite understood it. What does everyone else think?'

The conversation flowed quite well after that. Biscuits were munched. I tried to concentrate on my book, but my attention kept being pulled towards the discussion.

After half an hour, Charlotte announced that it was time for a break, and opened the wine. The book talk descended into social chit-chat.

A shadow fell over the counter. 'Why are you hiding back here?'

I looked up to see Nick smiling at me. Again.

'I'm not hiding,' I said defensively. 'I'm just… concentrating. And someone has to watch the desk. In case of shoplifters. That sort of thing.'

Shoplifters? Get a grip, Gregory.

'Ah, yes,' said Nick. 'The great Shellcliff crime wave.'

'Hmm.'

'You can have a night off, can't you? Have a glass of wine?'

Charlotte caught my eye from the other side of the room, and gave me a thumbs up.

'Oh, I don't know...' I said.

Charlotte scowled.

I sighed. 'All right.'

I spent the rest of the meeting sitting next to Nick, sipping my wine. Occasionally I would contribute an opinion, usually in the form of a 'yes' or 'no'. Mainly, I enjoyed listening, and I learned one or two things about our customers. I learned that Vampire Fan was called Denise, and she had a collection of over five hundred vampire novels. When she wasn't reading about vampires, she liked to make jam for the WI. Mr Beans was called Brian. He had been in the army before opening his coffee shop, and he loved Scandinavian noir. I also learned that Charlotte was quite widely read, mainly in the fields of crime and romcoms.

'I like solving mysteries,' she said. 'Learning what makes people tick. It's useful for an actor.'

Nick seemed to have read absolutely everything (to the point that I almost felt intimidated). But he particularly loved Fantasy and Science Fiction, which I already knew.

It was actually quite pleasant, spending the evening talking to people about books. I even sold a few things, including a book about werewolves to Denise ('I really want to broaden my reading').

The meeting lasted for two hours. Nick was the last to leave.

'Thanks,' he said. 'I had a good time. Good to see you again, Greg.'

'You too,' I said.

He hesitated for a moment, then waved at us both, and walked out.

Charlotte turned to me with a big smile. 'What did I tell you?'

'I don't know. What did you tell me?'

'Didn't I say it would go well? What a lovely bunch of people.'

I sighed. 'All right. You win. It was a good idea.'

She clapped her hands together. 'Wasn't it just?'

'Shame there weren't a few more people.'

'I think word of mouth will spread, and we'll get more next time.' She handed me a sheet of paper. 'Here, I asked them to write down some suggestions. Would you like to contribute?'

I read the list. It said:

Twilight
Ulysses
The Lord of the Rings
Agatha Christie
Something by that Pointless *bloke*

'Certainly a diverse mix,' I said. I thought for a moment, then added *Jane Eyre* to the list.

12

Charlotte

The book group had been an absolute triumph.

I returned to my flat in high spirits, but it felt a little lonely after being around people for so long. It was interesting: my London friends rarely enjoyed discussing books.

At one point, I had set up a book group and roped in half a dozen actor friends, but the conversation would soon take a turn towards West End gossip. A memory arose unbidden: I saw myself seated in the coffee shop where we held our book group meetings. I could picture the scene quite clearly. I was flicking through our chosen novel – *Cat's Eye* by Margaret Atwood – when suddenly my friend Margot, who had spent most of the meeting scrolling through her phone, suddenly leapt to her feet and declared: 'Amelia's in *Vogue*!'

My friends instantly took up their own phones, and the discussion descended into a chorus of *what*s and *how*s and *you have got to be kidding me*s. My own phone was in my handbag, and I dutifully took it out and made a series of awe-struck exclamations about Amelia's latest fashion shoot. But, although I would never have admitted it, a part of me had felt a bit... well, bored. I mean, there was nothing wrong with fashion shoots and I liked *Vogue*. But I had wanted to get back to the book.

The thing I had enjoyed most about tonight's meeting was that the other people there also wanted to discuss the book. It had been fun to unpick it all.

Did this all mean I was officially a book lover?

Keen to talk to someone else, even at a distance, I decided to call Alex. He actually picked up for once.

'Hello, Charlotte.' He sounded tired.

'Hi. How's it going?'

'Oh, you know. The usual. How are things up there?'

'Good,' I said. 'I've just come back from a book group. Do you have a favourite book? I don't think you've ever mentioned one.'

'Not really. I don't get much time to read these days.'

'Did you have a favourite when you were a kid?'

'I don't really know, Charlotte.' Alex tried and failed to suppress a yawn. 'Sorry. Rehearsals are a bit intense.'

'You've started already? How exciting!'

'Yes. I suppose it is. Fred's a hard taskmaster. We didn't finish until nearly nine last night.'

'How terrible for you.'

'Yes. It's awful.' A note of humour crept into his voice. 'But one must suffer for one's art.'

'Poor baby.' I smiled. 'You should come and visit me at the weekend. Take your mind off things.'

There was a pause.

'Alex? Are you still there?'

'Yes. Sorry, I was just looking at my calendar. I'm not sure I can make this weekend. Fred wants us all to go to this big stately home somewhere. Research trip, apparently.'

'Oh. Okay. How about next weekend?'

'Maybe. Can I get back to you about that?'

I sighed. 'Listen, Alex, I know I haven't exactly spoken well of Shell-cliff over the years, but it's really quite nice here. The bookshop's lovely.'

Another pause. And then: 'Okay. Tell you what. I'll come the first weekend in July. I know I'm free then.'

This was still three weeks away, but at least he was coming. I pushed aside any disappointment.

'Lovely! I promise you won't regret it. We can go out to dinner. Maybe you could drop in on one of my rehearsals.'

'Rehearsals?'

'Oh, didn't I tell you? I've joined a drama group.'

'What? You mean like an am-dram society?'

'Yes. They're very good. Maybe, if you have time, you could come and see our show? It's on at the end of August, so before yours opens.'

There was a pause, and then something that sounded like Alex sucking in a breath.

'Are you sure you should be spending your time doing amateur stuff, Charley?'

'Well, I wasn't sure about it at first, but it's a lot of fun.'

'Fun?' Alex spoke the word as if it were an unfamiliar concept.

'Yes,' I said. 'Listen, don't worry about the play. I understand if you're not into it. I'll see you in a few weeks.'

'Okay.'

We said our goodbyes. I wasn't too downhearted about the play. One of the things I had always admired about Alex was his sheer commitment to his career. That was why he was such a popular actor, and why he had been cast in this new hit play. He was dedicated, as I was. We had always understood one another.

And he was finally visiting! I would be able to show him *my* Shellcliff. The beach, the theatre, the bookshop. We could have a coffee at Beans. It would be fun. Feeling my mood lift, I picked up my script for *Theatre is Murder!* and started to learn my lines.

13

Greg

I emerged from the stockroom with two mugs of coffee. I was just in time to see Charlotte having an animated conversation with a family of customers.

'Oh, yes. We love Clive here at the bookshop! He's our bestselling author.' She beamed as she handed over a full set of *Clive the Seaside Donkey* diaries, in an exclusive *Clive the Seaside Donkey* tote bag. The family left, smiling.

I placed the coffee on the counter. 'You're in a good mood this morning.'

'What makes you say that?'

'Well, you seem genuinely pleased about selling the oeuvre of Clive.'

'Alex is coming to visit soon.'

'Alex?'

'Oh. My boyfriend. He's an actor in London. He's very busy, but he's going to come down for a couple of days at the beginning of July. And I think I might be getting the hang of this bookselling thing. By the way, this arrived earlier.' She pointed to a box next to the counter. 'It's full of bunting. Posters, too.'

'Ah, yes. That'll be for Independent Bookshop Week.'

'What's that?'

'It's a sort of campaign. A celebration of bookshops. You can put the bunting in the window, if you really must.'

I settled in front of the computer and opened up the sales database. I planned to reorder the books sold the previous day. With a certain amount of annoyance, I noticed that the Romantasy titles were doing particularly well.

Charlotte opened the box and took out a letter. 'It says we should share our events on social media. Are we doing any events?'

'Usually some local authors ask to come in.'

'Hmm.'

I was clearly not going to get my ordering done today. 'What do you mean, "hmm"?'

'I was just thinking… maybe we could do something different?' Her eyes lit up. 'How about a children's story time?'

I shuddered. 'Oh, we tried that once. Chocolate everywhere.'

'Come on, it has to be worth a go. What's your bestselling kids' book?'

I thought about this. 'I… suppose that would be *The Witch on the Pitch*.'

'The what?'

I looked up from the computer screen. 'Are you telling me you've never heard of *The Witch on the Pitch*?'

'No, I can't say that I have.'

'I thought every bookseller knew it.'

'I haven't been doing this for very long, Greg.'

I softened. 'No. Sorry. Well, it's a sort of classic, really. It's a picture book about a witch who really wants to be a footballer.'

'I see.' Charlotte smiled. 'Up there with Dickens, clearly.'

'There's a whole pile of copies in the Children's section.'

Charlotte ventured into the most colourful corner of the shop. A few moments later, I heard laughter.

'You know, this is actually quite funny.'

'Is it? I've never read it.'

'I thought all booksellers knew *The Witch on the Pitch*.'

I raised both eyebrows at her. She smiled sweetly back at me.

'I've had an idea,' she said.

Oh God, I thought. *Not another one.*

'What?' I asked, warily.

'I could dress up as the witch while I read the story! All I would need is a pointy hat and a cape, and a football scarf. I could do all the voices and everything.'

I stared at her. 'I'm not sure that's such a good idea.'

'Why not? I could even cackle a bit, in a nice way, of course. I'm rather good at cackling. I used to do panto, you know.'

'I don't think Sarah would like that.'

This was a blatant lie. Sarah had already suggested that we should do an interactive story time, but I had been unable to face the mess, or the noise, or the general disruption to my peace.

'Sarah isn't here, is she? Besides, it's for the greater good. She did say she wants to get more people through the doors.' Charlotte gave a slightly evil smile which convinced me she would make a very good, if stereotypical, witch. 'How about this? I'll dress up as the witch, you can read the story, and I'll only cackle if it seems absolutely appropriate to do so.'

'What on earth does that mean?'

'Oh, sometimes, as an actor, you need to be able to read your audience, darling. Especially if improv is involved. So, what do you say? To witch, or not to witch?'

I threw up my hands. 'Okay! Fine! Whatever you like. Just... don't say I didn't warn you.'

She beamed. 'Brilliant. Now, do you know where I can find a pointy hat?'

14

Charlotte

One of the nicest things about being involved with amateur dramatics was that it felt comparatively unrushed.

The full rehearsal period for *Theatre is Murder!* would last around two and a half months, with meetings twice a week and an extra dress rehearsal two days before the show opened. In the professional theatre, it was common for us to have just three weeks to rehearse, although of course we would be rehearsing all day for five days a week.

I had expected to find this slow pace frustrating, but it actually left more time for my favourite part of the process: character analysis.

Oh, how I loved character analysis.

One warm, clear night a few days after the first book group meeting, I took my *Theatre is Murder!* script and a tall glass of lemonade onto my new, borrowed balcony. I sat on the little folding chair with the best view of the bay, took out a pen, and began to take methodical notes.

Opal: character motivations
Jealousy
Frustration
Feeling overlooked
Thwarted ambition

Revenge
Love???

I did this sort of analysis for every role I played. I learned it during a class at the London School of Performing Arts, where my tutor was a great follower of Stanislavski. Ideally, I would get a second person to hotseat Opal and ask my character questions, but I was alone in the flat. Maybe Greg could be persuaded to incorporate hotseating into rehearsals. I smiled as I imagined the perplexed look on his face.

It was funny, how things turned out. I had never expected to take acting so seriously. As a kid I had had no interest in it. Then, when I went to secondary school, I decided I wanted to befriend Vicky. She was beautiful, confident and cool. She was also popular, something I had never been. Something I longed to be. I was the sort of kid who looked forward to rainy breaktimes, because it meant I could sit in the school library with a book. I spent outdoor breaktimes wandering around the playground, unsure what to do with myself. I didn't understand sport, or the obsession with boys. But I did understand hierarchies. And as far as I could see, Vicky was at the top of the hierarchy. A friendship with her would raise my social status, and I wouldn't be lonely anymore.

Vicky loved performing. She was always the first to start dancing at the Christmas disco, the first to audition for the school play. I knew she was a member of the amateur drama group (then called The Shellcliff Players), so I joined too. And it was great. I offered to help Vicky learn her lines (she always played the lead). She adopted me into her friendship group, and soon we were inseparable, going to the cinema together and clothes shopping on Saturdays. There were visits to McDonald's and the roller skating rink. But much to my surprise, I enjoyed acting more than any of this.

I started small. I was cast in the chorus, then as one half of a pantomime cow, then as the Cheshire Cat in a production of *Alice in Wonderland*. And while I had no intention of outshining Vicky, it gradually became clear that I was her competition. The directors had a choice.

The year we performed *A Midsummer Night's Dream,* we had equal parts: Helena and Hermia, two former friends who now hated each other's guts. And that was the point when I started to get ideas.

I loved acting. I loved learning my lines, trying out new voices, being fitted for my costumes. I loved slipping into another person's skin, being someone else for a while. And when Vicky said she was planning to go to drama school, I knew I wanted to go, too.

'I want to be an actor.' I made the announcement at dinner one night, shortly before my seventeenth birthday.

'Don't be daft,' said Sarah.

I glared at her. 'I'm not being daft.'

'It's very difficult to be a professional actor,' said our mum, ever practical. 'Most of them are out of work most of the time.'

'I still want to do it,' I said.

'I thought you wanted to be a vet?' asked Dad.

'That was years ago,' I said. 'And I'm rubbish at science.'

'Well,' said Mum. 'It's up to you. I just don't think you should rush into it, that's all.'

Later that night, I overheard them talking.

'I'm a bit worried,' said Mum. 'I don't want her to throw everything away for a hobby.'

'I'm sure it's just a phase,' said Dad. 'She'll grow out of it.'

And, with typical teenage rebellion, I had thought: *a hobby, is it? Grow out of it, will I?*

Looking back, I know my parents were concerned because they cared about me. They knew nothing about acting or what it meant to work in the theatre, and they didn't know how to help. But at the time, I felt that my ambitions were being dismissed. Even when I got a place at drama school – the same school as Vicky – and left for London with their blessing, I still felt the need to prove something. Prove that this was not a hobby, and that I was a proper actress with genuine talent. Someone who had the right to be there.

And much later, after Vicky was gone, I felt I had even more to prove.

The sun was getting low across Shellcliff Bay. Having exhausted Opal's character analysis, I felt the need for some light relief (she was unexpectedly dark), so I turned my attention to *The Witch on the Pitch*.

I had borrowed a copy from the bookshop. It turned out to be a classic story of having a (rather modest) dream, overcoming various obstacles on the path to said dream, before finally achieving it. Basic dramatic stuff, really, but potentially quite meaty for a fine actor. There was a certain amount of angst involved, and the witch faced prejudice on account of... well, being a witch, before finally scoring a winning goal in a match, and becoming the heroine of the hour. I did think this was a little problematic, the fact that her peers only accepted her when she achieved something – if I were her, I would have turned them all into frogs. Still, I supposed it was uplifting in its way.

I turned to a fresh page in my notebook, and picked up my pen.

The Witch on the Pitch: character motivations
Ambitions
Dreams
Finding acceptance
Overcoming prejudice – historical persecution of witches
Revenge???

Never let it be said that Charlotte de la Mer does not take her vocation seriously.

15

Greg

I got to work to find a mountain of bunting on the counter. It was at least a dozen colours, sprawling over the till system like a many tentacled sea monster.

'Charlotte?' I said.

She stuck her head out of the stockroom. 'Yes, darling?'

'What's all this... stuff?'

'You said I could put bunting in the window.'

'Just the Indie Bookshop Week bunting. I didn't mean all this. Where did you get it, anyway?'

'The library. They had a Make Your Own Bunting workshop.'

I massaged the bridge of my nose. *Of course they did. The bastards.*

'You've been to the library?'

'Yes! It was very nice. A bit quaint. But the workshop was a lot of fun. Have you ever made your own bunting, Greg?'

This was it. I had finally reached the edge of my sanity. I supposed it was bound to happen, eventually. One can only be a bookseller for so long before falling off the proverbial deep end.

'No,' I said, in a carefully measured tone. 'I can't say I've ever had the pleasure.'

'It's an experience. Oh, and your friend Nick was there. He says hi, by the way.'

'Oh. Does he?'

'Yes. I said I wanted to decorate the shop, so lots of the ladies offered to donate their bunting. Nick even found some extra in storage. Isn't that nice?'

I stared at the bunting. This, I suspected, was Nick's idea of a joke. I was not going to rise to it.

'I thought we could hang it across the ceiling and around the tops of the bookcases,' said Charlotte.

I sighed. 'Fine. Just... don't overdo it, okay?'

Two hours later, the bookshop was festooned with bunting. Charlotte had started by hanging it from the central lighting fixture: a bronze four-armed chandelier. A string hung from each of the arms to a bookcase, creating something which looked a bit like a maypole.

Charlotte beamed at me, clearly proud of her handiwork. 'Really brightens the place up, doesn't it?'

Despite myself, I was impressed, but I didn't want to show her just how impressed I was. 'Hmm.'

'I'll hang some extra in the kids' section.'

Half an hour later, while Charlotte was still arranging the bunting and I was going through the monthly buyer's notes catalogue, the doorbell rang.

'Nick, darling!' Charlotte dismounted the stepladder. 'What do you think of the bunting?'

I did my best to hide behind the computer, but I couldn't resist a peek. Nick surveyed the bunting with raised eyebrows.

'It's... er... very nice,' he said. 'There's a lot of it, isn't there?'

'Yes,' said Charlotte happily. 'There is.'

Nick turned towards the counter. I quickly snapped my attention back to the computer screen. I hoped this would tell him, in no uncertain terms, that I was doing important work. But he didn't seem to be the sort to take a hint. He walked over.

'Hi, Greg. How are things?'

'Oh, you know,' I said. 'Busy.'

Nick glanced around the empty shop. 'Yes. I can see that.'

I resisted the urge to glower at him. 'How can we help you today?'

'Well, it's all quite exciting, really. I had an email from Crystal Moontide.'

'What's a Crystal Moontide?'

'You know? The bestselling fantasy author?'

'Oh!' I said. '*That* Crystal Moontide.'

I had no idea who he was talking about.

'She wants to visit Shellcliff for an event, as she's never been here before and she's going to be en route from a convention in Edinburgh. But the thing is, I really need someone to sell the books. Would you be up for it?'

'I—'

'That sounds marvellous!' said Charlotte. 'Just the sort of thing we'd love to do. Isn't it, Greg?'

'Er... I suppose so—'

Nick smiled. 'Ah, brilliant. I'll email her back. The event would be three weeks on Friday. Is that okay?'

'I'm sure that'll be perfect,' said Charlotte.

'Oh, fab. Thanks so much. I'll email her right away.' Nick gave us both a thumbs up, and hurried out of the shop, smiling.

I glared at Charlotte. 'What on earth are you doing?'

'Just building connections with the local community, darling. Like Sarah wants.'

'But we've never done an event at the library before. I don't even know who this Moontide person is.'

'Well, Nick's a librarian. He must have good taste. One must always trust librarians.'

'That...' I ran a hand through my hair. 'What you just said makes absolutely no sense.'

Charlotte smiled. 'Look. Why don't we just give it a try? Where's the harm?'

I considered this. The harm, as I saw it, was potentially three-fold: it would mean leaving the bookshop for an external event, investing money in books I had never heard of, and spending time with Nick, with all its potential for awkwardness.

'It might even be fun,' said Charlotte. She looked oddly hopeful. I wondered briefly why she cared so much. After all, she would be leaving us as soon as she found a new role in the West End.

I sighed. 'I'll think about it.'

16

Charlotte

It was the first Saturday of Independent Bookshop Week, which meant that I had a chance to flex my acting muscles in my role as resident Witch on the Pitch. I was looking forward to it.

I changed into my costume in the bookshop's stockroom. I tossed my red and white striped football scarf around my neck and uttered a loud cackle. I had watched *The Wizard of Oz* twice in the past week, thinking I should learn from the best. I threw back my head and cackled again. Yes. I was in good voice.

Gathering up my black cloak, I emerged from the stockroom. Greg was sitting behind the counter. His eyes widened.

'What do you think?' I asked.

'Er... very impressive,' said Greg.

Story time was due to start at eleven, so we prepared a little performance area by arranging the cushions on the floor in the Children's section. Five minutes before 'beginners', I concealed myself in the stockroom again, so I could make a dramatic entrance at the appropriate point in the story.

I was actually a bit nervous. It was a long time since I had publicly played a character besides Constance in *The Next Thirty Years*, a role that I could perform in my sleep. I told myself I was being silly. This wasn't even a play. It was just a little bit of fun for kids.

I heard the repeated jingle of the shop bell, accompanied by a gaggle of voices and some childish laughter. The kids sounded excited, and my nerves spiked. I took a deep breath. I should have spent longer doing my vocal warm-up.

The shop sounded very full. At last I heard Greg's voice cut through the din.

'Hello, everyone. Welcome to today's story time. Er... today's story is *The Witch on the Pitch...*'

He sounded a little formal and stilted. I hoped he wasn't going to put anyone off.

'Er... I'm pleased to say we have a very special guest: the witch herself!'

The children's voices rose in excitement again. Maybe this was going to work out well after all.

Greg cleared his throat and started reading. I waited for my cue. The witch entered on the third page, so I didn't have to wait for very long.

'*And then the witch leapt onto the pitch...*'

I swept open the curtain with a flourish. Then I beamed at the assembled children, threw back my head, and gave the loudest, most dramatic, witchiest cackle in my growing repertoire of cackles.

The kids stared at me wide-eyed. There was a moment of silence. Then one little girl burst into tears.

Greg looked up from the book in horror.

I tried to salvage the situation. It was many years since I'd done panto, and even then I'd played the goodies like *Cinderella* and *Snow White*. But I knew enough to be able to improvise.

'Don't worry, I won't turn you into a frog...' A dramatic pause. '...today.' And then I cackled again.

It was as if the crying was contagious. It spread from the girl to a neighbouring boy, and soon five children were crying. I looked at them in horror. Why were they so upset? The witch was supposed to be the heroine of the story, right?

I looked to Greg for help. He had gone pale, but like the intrepid bookseller he was, he attempted to carry on with the story. His delivery grew even more fragmented as it was drowned out by wails. I hung back, waving my football scarf half-heartedly, while several of the accompanying adults gave up and ushered their children out of the shop. A couple of them glared at me before leaving.

When the story was finished, and the last child (completely un-affected) had been given her Independent Bookshop Week goody bag, Greg snapped the book closed and strode up to me, hands on hips.

'What on earth were you thinking?' he asked.

I blinked in confusion. 'Sorry, what? I only did what we agreed.'

'Did you have to cackle quite so... evilly?'

'Oh, I didn't think it was evil. It was a standard witch cackle, really.'

'The Witch on the Pitch would never cackle like that, and she certainly wouldn't threaten to turn anyone into a frog.'

I was growing irritated. 'I thought you said you hadn't read the bloody thing.'

'Yes. Well. Everyone knows that!'

'Well, excuse me, Mister High-and-Mighty Literary Expert! I was only trying to make things more interesting.'

'You certainly did that.' Greg sighed and sank into a chair. 'Why do you always have to take things just a bit too far?'

'I was only trying to help.'

'No, you were trying to hog the limelight and make it all about you, as usual.'

This wounded me, but I was determined not to show it. I folded my arms. 'Tell you what. Next time, why don't I read the story, and you can dress up in a silly costume?'

Greg was silent. He looked down at the floor.

'Oh, I'm sorry,' I said. 'I forgot. You're frightened of acting, aren't you? Can't risk showing yourself up, can you? All because you never managed to turn pro.'

Greg winced. 'What? You think that's why... you think I'm *jealous* of you?'

'If the shoe fits.'

Greg gave a short laugh. It was an oddly startling sound, with none of his usual warmth. 'Trust me, Charlotte. I'm not remotely jealous of you.'

'And what's that supposed to mean?'

'What's going on here?' Sarah's voice cut through the shop. I turned to see her standing in the open doorway, an expression of barely repressed fury on her face.

'Oh,' I said. 'Hi, sis.'

Sarah strode towards me. 'Don't you "hi sis" me! I've just bumped into Mrs McLean. Literally bumped into her. Lily was in floods of tears. She said you'd terrified all the children at story time.'

I realised I was still wearing my witch's hat. I tore it from my head and hid it behind my back. 'Oh, for goodness sake! The kids of today really need to toughen up a bit.'

'Charlotte, Lily is three years old. You were terrified of witches when you were three.'

'I was not.'

'You were. Remember that panto at the Forum? We had to leave at the interval.'

I fiddled with my football scarf. 'That was different.'

'How? How was it different? You need to learn to read the room, Charlotte.' She turned to Greg. 'And where do you think you're going?'

Greg had risen from the chair and was surreptitiously edging towards the stockroom. Sarah's voice made him freeze.

'Er... I thought we could all do with some tea,' he said.

'Oh, no you don't,' said Sarah. 'You're staying right here. You're just as responsible as she is.'

Greg drew himself up to his full height. 'I really must protest—'

'Sit down!'

Greg blinked. He sat down.

Sarah raked a hand through her hair. 'You two really need to be more careful. This is my business. I have my reputation to consider.'

This was a bit rich. 'Sarah, with all due respect, you're hardly ever here.'

Sarah glared at me. 'That's why I hired you! I thought I could trust you to whip this place into shape. I know you're keen to rush back to the West End, and this is just a cosy little summer job for you, but you need to stop... *play-acting* and take it a bit more seriously.'

I flinched. I wasn't going to admit it, but I supposed Sarah had a point. I had viewed the bookshop as quirky and cosy, and I was working on the basis that I would be leaving soon.

'And as for you.' Sarah turned to Greg. 'You need to up your game, and stop hiding yourself away and treating this place like your personal library.'

Greg bristled. 'I don't—'

'Because if you don't, there won't be a bookshop for you to hide in. I reiterate: this is a *business*. Do I make myself absolutely clear?'

'Yes, Sarah.' Greg hung his head. 'Sorry, Sarah.'

Sarah raised an eyebrow at me.

'Sorry,' I said. 'You're right, of course.'

Sarah nodded. 'Thank you. I'm glad we all understand each other. I've drawn up a new business plan, and from now on this place is going to be run on much more efficient lines. We're going to start by trying to secure some big name authors.' She turned to Greg. 'I've been talking to Nick at the library. He was telling me he's been approached by that fantasy author. What's her name? Crystal Moontide, and you'd agreed to sell her books but no one has followed it up. Maybe you could drop in and chat to him, iron out the details.'

Greg looked even more alarmed. 'But the library—'

'I won't accept any buts, Greg.'

Greg wilted. 'All right.'

Sarah looked at me. 'And you can phone the council and sort out the recycling bin collections.'

My eyes widened. I knew I had messed up, but this felt like a cruel and unusual punishment.

'Can't we just email—'

'No. We can't. You need to phone them.'

I sighed. 'Okay.'

'I'm serious,' said Sarah. 'This place needs to start earning its keep. Otherwise, I'll have no choice but to cut my losses and sell up.'

We watched her leave. When she was gone, I turned to Greg. He was sitting in the armchair again. He looked pale, and he was shaking slightly.

My anger died.

'Greg?'

'I can't do it,' he said, his voice high-pitched. 'I can't lose my shop. My flat—'

'You won't have to.' I looked around the shop. Sarah's talk had given me new determination. 'We're going to turn this place around. Now, why don't we have some tea?'

Greg was silent. I was sure I could see tears in his eyes. At last he nodded. 'All right.'

17

Greg

That evening, when the bookshop was closed, I returned to my flat feeling shaken. The afternoon had passed in a bit of a blur. I had been operating on autopilot, serving customers and shelving stock, but Sarah's words kept going round and round in my mind.

If you don't, there won't be a bookshop for you to hide in.

I shuddered. I knew I needed to stop my thoughts spiralling, so I poured myself a glass of wine and went to my bookcase. For as long as I could remember, books had been a source of comfort for me. After what had happened to Vicky, books became a welcome escape. And for a while, after I got the job in the bookshop, my knowledge of fictional worlds was enough.

But it wasn't enough anymore. In order to save this place I held so dear, I would need to up my game. I would need to start 'networking' and – I shuddered – engaging with customers.

For the first time, I was truly grateful for Charlotte. She was better at this sort of thing than I was. Perhaps I could persuade her to do most of the public-facing work.

I would think about that tomorrow. Now, I needed to settle down with a good book.

I browsed my bookshelves, not sure exactly what took my fancy. Eventually, my hand fell on my copy of *Magic Flutes* by Eva Ibbotson. It was perfect – escapist, romantic, and about art and music.

I took my wine and book to my chair in the window, settled down, and began to read. But I kept getting distracted. My thoughts kept turning to the last time I had attempted to step out of my comfort zone and failed abysmally.

Outside of rehearsal hours, I had made it a habit not to socialise with the other members of the drama group. The long tea breaks were enough for me. I could have a chat, and then retire to my flat after the rehearsal, safe in the knowledge that I could spend the rest of the evening reading.

However, not all my drama group friends understood my need for quiet reading time.

'Come on, Greg,' said Bex, the most gregarious member of the group. It was early December, and we were rehearsing for the pantomime. 'It's Christmas! Come out with us. Just this once.'

'No, thanks.' I knew 'out' meant to the pub. I found pubs somewhat distressing in their disorganisation, and the pubs in Shellcliff were almost always crowded.

'Come for one drink,' said Bex. 'What harm can it do?'

I could feel the peer pressure weighing down on me. The group were all so kind and friendly, and I had no desire to appear mean.

'All right,' I said. 'Just one. Thank you.'

So I went with them to the pub. Of course, they chose The Crown. Its external signage proclaimed it to be *Shellcliff's Party Pub! The busiest place in town!* So I felt like a fish out of water before I even set foot through the door.

To make things yet more interesting, we were also greeted by a poster: *TONITE! MADONNA TRIBUTE!*

I relaxed a little. This actually sounded okay. I considered myself an occasional fan of Madonna. Who wasn't? And if there was a singer performing, at least there would be a focus of attention aside from making awkward small talk.

Bex and the others found a table just near the stage area. The pub wasn't too crowded yet, but it was only early. I decided to go to the bar and get a drink before it got too busy.

I was just buying wine for myself and Bex when I became aware of a presence to my left.

I turned to see an extremely handsome man. I could tell he was tall, even in his slouched position leaning on the bar. His long black hair was swept over one shoulder.

He smiled at me. The extremely handsome man was smiling at me. 'Hi. You work in the bookshop, don't you?'

For a moment, I couldn't reply.

'Hmm,' I said, eventually.

For goodness sake. Why was a simple 'yes' so difficult?

'I mean... yes. I do,' I said.

'I'm Nick. I work in the library.'

'Ah. Right. I'm Greg. I work in the bookshop.'

The man's smile widened. 'Yeah. I know.'

We lapsed into silence.

'So,' said Nick. 'Madonna tribute night.'

'Yes,' I said. I cringed. Was Madonna uncool now? Would Nick think I was uncool? Why did I suddenly care? 'Um. I didn't come here on purpose.'

'Oh. You mean you stumbled in by accident?'

'I mean I didn't realise it was on. I came with some friends. From my theatre group.'

'You're here with friends? Sorry, I hope I'm not keeping you.'

'No. They're not – I'm sure they won't mind. They're more like acquaintances really.'

'Right.'

I glanced over at the theatre group's table. Bex chose this moment to wave at me. 'Greg, love, we've got some of those crisps you like!'

I winced and looked back at Nick.

He raised his eyebrows. 'I think your acquaintances are trying to attract your attention.'

Wow. He probably thought I was a right miserable bugger. I felt a blush colour my cheeks. 'Yes... I just... maybe I should...'

Nick's mouth twitched. 'You obviously wanted an excuse to talk to me. It's fine. I know I'm irresistible.'

'What?' My blush deepened. 'No! Sorry, that's not... I didn't mean...'

Nick looked at me curiously for a moment. Then he sighed. 'All right. I get the picture.'

'I'm sorry.'

He waved a hand. 'It's fine.'

If I had been twenty years younger and a little more confident, I might have spoken up just then. Perhaps I would even have offered to buy Nick a drink. But he was already turning away, and I felt the chance slipping through my fingers.

Sighing, I went to rejoin the drama group. Bex presented me with a big bag of Worcester sauce flavoured crisps. 'You okay?'

'Yes,' I said.

She glanced towards the bar, and smiled. 'He's hot.'

I said nothing.

'Did you want to stay and talk?'

I was saved by a series of flashing lights and a burst of music. It seemed that the tribute act was beginning.

It's true that such performances don't require much concentration, but I couldn't even give the singer the minimum amount of attention. I kept thinking about Nick, fighting an urge to simultaneously look over my shoulder at him and kick myself.

Maybe it wouldn't be so difficult to break the habit of a lifetime, walk over to the bar, and give him my number. I could be bold for once. What did I have to lose?

After five songs, the MC announced a short break and invited us to replenish our drinks. I stood up and smoothed the creases from my jumper.

'Fancy another drink?' I asked Bex.

She nodded. 'Pinot, please.'

I headed over to the bar, and saw immediately that Nick had relocated to a table in the corner. He was still seated alone, however, which gave me hope.

I took a deep breath, and approached.

'Hi,' I said.

He looked up from his pint.

'Look,' I said. 'I'm sorry about earlier. I didn't mean to be unfriendly.'

'That's okay.' He smiled, and I was flooded with relief.

I swallowed. 'Um... I was wondering if you would like—'

The door burst open, bringing an icy cold blast of air and raucous laughter into the pub. I glanced over and froze.

Sean Henderson.

I hadn't seen him for more than fifteen years. He hadn't changed much. He was still handsome and well built, his blonde hair now greying around the temples.

As on the previous occasions I'd run into him as an adult, he made me feel about fourteen years old.

Two other men trailed behind him. Even at school, Sean Henderson had had a gang, at least two boys who were always just *there*. I glanced at their faces, trying to work out if these were the same two who had locked me in the toilets in Year 8. Then they strolled off towards the bar, and I realised they weren't with Sean Henderson after all.

Sean Henderson glanced around the pub, his gaze alighting on Nick. He smiled.

'Hey, Nick!'

Nick stood up to greet him. They shook hands. 'Hi, Sean.'

'You found us okay, then?' Sean was talking to Nick like a normal human being. The words of a functional mature adult were coming out of his mouth. I stood by the table, half horrified and half fascinated.

'Yeah, no worries.' Nick noticed I was still there. He frowned. 'Are you all right?'

I nodded, unable to speak.

Sean turned to look at me. His face broke into a big smile.

'Greg! Is that you? Wow, it's been years!'

I tried to coax my voice from my throat. I didn't want to look like a total drip in front of Nick.

'Yes,' I said. 'It has.'

'I can't believe it!' Sean reached out and thumped me on the arm. The gesture was affectionate and blokey. It made my skin crawl. 'Look at you!'

I didn't want to examine what that meant. I wanted to go and hide somewhere far, far away.

'How are you, mate?' said Sean.

'Oh,' I said, trying to twist my mouth into a smile. 'Fine, thanks.'

Sean turned to Nick. 'Greg was my mate at school. We go way back, don't we, Greg?'

'Yes,' I said.

The bullying had lasted for five years.

'I just wanted to welcome Nick to Shellcliff,' said Sean, his tone still perfectly amiable.

'Yes,' I said. This was apparently the only word left in my vocabulary.

Sean slid into the seat next to Nick. My legs suddenly felt wobbly.

'Maybe Greg could join us for a drink?' said Nick.

His voice was kind, and I felt a cold twinge in my chest. I had wanted so much to have a drink with him. But not now. Not with the figure from my nightmares sitting next to him.

'No, thanks,' I said. 'I should get going.'

'Come on, Greg,' said Sean. 'Join us.'

I hesitated. It was all in the past, this school stuff. I was probably overreacting, anyway. That's what the teachers had said at the time. Maybe they were right.

I sat stiffly on the chair opposite Nick.

The music started again, heralding the reappearance of the Madonna Tribute Act. I tried to focus on the singing.

'I'll get these,' said Sean, standing up.

I was left alone with Nick. He was still looking at me with furrowed brows. 'Are you sure you're okay?'

Beneath the table, I dug my fingers into the thick corduroy of my trousers. 'Yes.'

The Madonna Tribute Act moved on to 'Like a Virgin'.

Sean reappeared and put three pints of beer down on the table.

He turned to me with a big smile. 'Hey, Greg. They're playing your song!'

I felt the bottom fall out of my universe. I looked at him in horror.

'What's that?' said Nick.

'It was a joke we had in sixth form,' said Sean. 'We assigned everyone a song based on their... how do I put this? Social status. Prowess.' He laughed. I felt the heat rush to my face.

'Classy,' said Nick.

Sean's smile dropped. It was like a mask had slipped for a moment. 'It was just stupid kids' stuff. Banter. No hard feelings or anything. Isn't that right, Greg?'

I didn't say anything.

'It was funny, though,' said Sean. 'Wasn't it?'

I had had enough. I pushed my chair back and rose unsteadily to my feet.

'I'm sorry,' I said to Nick. 'I really have to go.'

I thought Nick looked a little disappointed. 'Oh. Okay.'

'I hope you're not leaving on my account,' said Sean.

I ignored him and began to walk away. Before I could collect my coat, I heard Sean speak again.

'Always was oversensitive, that one.'

Citing a headache, I said a hasty goodbye to Bex and the drama group, and headed outside. It had been snowing the day before, and it was still bitterly cold. I took a deep breath of the frigid air and leaned over, putting my hands on my knees. I had the most horrible feeling that I was about to throw up.

The door creaked open behind me and I heard the sound of footsteps in the sludge.

'Greg? You all right?' It was Nick's voice.

I looked up at him. 'Fine.'

'You looked really uncomfortable in there.'

'Did I?'

'Yeah.' Nick walked around so he could look me in the face. 'Is this about Sean? I hardly know him.'

'Consider yourself lucky,' I said.

'If you're embarrassed about what he said to you—'

I held up a hand. 'Please. Just leave it. It's nothing.'

'Greg—'

I pulled my coat tightly around myself. 'Don't let me keep you.'

Nick hesitated. He looked ready to argue, but then he seemed to change his mind. He turned back to the pub.

I put my head down, shoved my hands in my coat pockets, and trudged towards home.

18

Charlotte

As promised, I spent the morning on the phone to the council, trying to sort out the recycling bin collections. It seemed that the situation was positively Kafkaesque, with multiple missed collections, an email trail that went back months, confusion as to the address of the bookshop and the location of the bin, all compounded by a general sense that somehow it would all magically work out okay in the end (it hadn't).

I finally managed to secure a tentative pledge that they would collect the recycling 'sometime next week'. Then I turned my attention to the rest of the bookshop.

Since closing up last night, my mind had been swirling with ideas for how to keep the shop up and running. I was keen to share some of these with Greg.

He was currently shelving books in the Classics section. I walked over to him, holding my notebook.

'Greg?'

'Yes?'

'I've had a few new ideas for the bookshop.'

Greg slid another book onto the shelf. For a moment I thought he was going to ignore me, but then his shoulders sagged. 'All right. Let's hear them.'

'Well, I thought we could start by creating some social media accounts.'

Greg frowned. 'We're already on Facebook.'

'I know. But I was thinking more along the lines of Instagram and TikTok.'

'What's TikTok?'

I sighed. This was going to be harder than I'd anticipated. 'It's where people post short videos. If you're lucky, you can get a lot of hits.'

Greg's eyes widened. 'Videos? I don't want to appear on camera.'

'You wouldn't have to. I'd go on camera.' A new idea occurred to me. 'Maybe we could get some members of the drama group to make little videos? I'm sure they'd enjoy that. I could even ask Alex. He might be up for filming something.' Alex didn't give many endorsements, but it was worth a try. Maybe he could be persuaded.

'So I wouldn't have to appear on camera at all?' said Greg, twisting his hands together.

'Not if you don't want to. But it might be nice if you read something. You do have a lovely voice.'

He gave the slightest flicker of a smile, then went back to shelving. 'Maybe.'

This seemed as close to a 'yes' as I was going to get. I ticked *TikTok* off my list.

'Great! Right, next thing. I think we should install a coffee machine and use the furniture to make a "coffee corner".'

Greg froze, a copy of *Cold Comfort Farm* slipping from his hand. He turned around very slowly. 'Why? We already have a perfectly good coffee shop in town.'

'Because it'll make people stay longer. Then they might feel at home, and buy more books. Maybe we could come to an arrangement with Brian from Beans. He could supply the coffee and the pastries.'

He looked at me in confusion. 'Pastries?'

'You can't have coffee without pastries, darling. I think it would bring more people through the door.'

'But what if they spill the coffee on the books?'

I thought about this. 'I suppose there's always a chance of that. But they'll have two excellent baristas to supervise them.'

'But we can't afford to employ—' A look of realisation settled on Greg's face. 'Oh. No way.'

'Come on. How hard can it be to serve coffee? It might even be fun.'

Greg shook his head. 'What happened to the days when books were enough?'

'You have to diversify, darling. Just think about it, okay?'

He sighed. 'All right. I'll consider it.'

'Wonderful.' I ticked *coffee* off the list. 'We're doing well here. It's good to know we're on the same page.'

'Hmm.'

'I also wanted to talk to you about the shop front.'

'What about it?'

'Well, it's looking a little tired, darling. That horrible green paint! I don't know what they were thinking.'

Greg folded his arms. 'I chose that paint.'

'Did you?' I wrinkled my nose. 'I suppose you can't be good at everything. I was thinking it might be nice to freshen it up, maybe repaint it in brighter colours?'

'Brighter colours?'

'You know, something more eye-catching.'

'I suppose so. But it would be quite a big job.'

'I'm sure we could rope some people in to help.' I wondered if Nick was any good at painting. It would be a good way of getting him and Greg talking.

'Fine,' said Greg. 'Brighter colours it is.'

'Good.' I looked around the crowded shop. 'Last thing: I think we need fewer books.'

'What?' He looked thoroughly perplexed. 'But this is a bookshop.'

'My point exactly. It's a book*shop*. Which means we should be selling as much as we're buying.' I looked at the nearest teetering book pile and grimaced. 'I mean, do we really need another copy of *A Tale of Two Cities*? We already have one in stock.'

'But that's a nice new hardback edition. The other one's a paperback.'

'But we haven't sold the paperback.'

'But... we might sell it? One day.' Greg raked his hands through his hair. 'Oh, God. You're right.'

'What?'

'I'm a hoarder. A book hoarder.'

I smiled. 'Yes. You've got a serious problem.'

'Oh, please don't.'

I softened a little at the crestfallen look on his face. 'I'm joking. But I do think we need to cut back a little.'

We both stared at the book stacks, looming like paper megaliths around the edges of the room.

'I wouldn't even know where to start,' said Greg.

'Maybe we should organise them into boxes, and make a sale table. We could have a buy one get one free offer for the rest of the summer.'

Greg looked sadly at the nearest stack. 'All right. If we must.' He plucked *A Tale of Two Cities* from the top of the nearest tower. 'But I'm buying this one.'

'But I'm sure you've already got—' I gave up. 'Okay. Fine.' I went into the stockroom and found two empty boxes. 'Let's get started, shall we?'

19

Greg

Charlotte and I spent the next few days tidying up the bookshop. We organised the excess stock into cardboard boxes, and created a big *Buy One Get One Free* sign for the table, along with some posters for the window. Charlotte wanted to write BOGOF on everything with a big red pen, but I put my foot down at this, as it sounded unnecessarily vulgar to me.

We also had an argument about the armchair cushions.

'They're chintzy,' said Charlotte.

'They are *not*. They're William Morris. *The Strawberry Thief.* It's a classic design.'

'Whatever. They're faded and dusty.'

Charlotte wanted to throw out everything faded and dusty. I tried not to take her crusade personally.

'We need plain cushions,' said Charlotte. 'In bright colours. It'll make the place look cheerful and welcoming.' She brandished a black sack at me.

I picked up the nearest cushion and held it protectively to my chest. 'But these ones are cosy.'

'They're flat as pancakes.'

'They're not.'

'Give it here.'

'No!' I dived behind the counter, still clutching the cushion.

Charlotte rolled her eyes and stomped off in search of something else to bin.

Despite our occasional argument about the décor, I had to admit that we made a good team. Together, we managed to clear the floor, and Charlotte also had the idea of moving the heavy black bookcases out of the window and replacing them with plant stands. This made the shop much lighter.

Charlotte also posted about our two-for-one sale on Facebook, and word started to spread. Soon, a steady stream of local customers began to come through the door. Grudgingly, I was forced to admit that the sale had been a good idea.

It wasn't all pleasurable, however. On Wednesday afternoon, I finally made my dreaded journey to the library.

I approved of libraries in general – who doesn't? They provided a valuable public service. But I wasn't sure I approved of this library in particular. On my last visit, I found that half of it had been turned into what appeared to be an IT suite, another quarter had been given over to tourist information, and only one quarter seemed to be dedicated to books.

And then there was the little matter of selling books. Bookshops sell books, because that's how bookshops (sometimes) make money, but selling books in a library? There was something ugly, almost obscene, about it. Something that smacked of capitalism. I didn't like it one little bit.

Charlotte, of course, thought it was a wonderful idea.

'It'll be a nice community event,' she said. 'It'll help us reach more readers. That's the most important thing, surely?'

All of this sounded good, but I still felt uncomfortable. I was determined to make my visit as brief as possible.

I stepped through the automatic doors, and froze. Nick was sitting behind the reception desk. Of course he was.

Apparently he hadn't yet spotted me. I considered turning tail and heading straight back to the bookshop. But before I could coax my feet into action, he looked up from his computer screen, saw me, and gave me a big smile.

'Hey, Greg! Good to see you.'

He really was handsome. Annoyingly so. But he was also a librarian, and booksellers and librarians were natural adversaries. This exchange would be purely professional.

I squared my shoulders and walked smartly up to the desk. 'I'm here to talk about the event with Crystal Moontide.'

Nick looked a bit startled. 'Oh. Right. Straight to business. Nice.' He came out from behind the desk. 'Thanks so much for doing this. We're all very excited about her visit. This is a real coup for us, you know.'

'Yes,' I said, non-committally. I had looked up Crystal Moontide's books on the internet, and they didn't really sound like my cup of tea. She was the author of an epic fantasy series about fairies flying around on dragons, or dragons flying around on fairies, or something. It all sounded a bit tiresome. But she was immensely popular.

'I admit I'm a bit of a fan,' said Nick. 'She's probably my favourite author. She just has so much to say about the world and life in general, you know? Which is your favourite of her books?'

I blinked. 'Ah. I've never actually read her.'

'*What?*' Nick looked at me as if I had just confessed to armed robbery. 'You've never read her?'

'No. Er... sorry. I'm more of a classics man. Dickens. Austen. Virginia Woolf.'

'But you like fantasy, right?'

'Some. I like Tolkien. C. S. Lewis.'

Nick shook his head in apparent wonder. 'I thought everyone had read Crystal Moontide. And you work in a bookshop?'

This rankled. 'I don't have time to read every book in existence,' I said. 'I'm guessing you haven't read every book in this library.'

'I've read all the good ones.'

'Yes. Well. Good is a relative concept, isn't it?'

His smile became a thin line. I was aware that what I had just said made me sound like a book snob. And I wasn't a book snob.

I attempted to backtrack. 'Of course, if people enjoy her books, then that's good, isn't it?'

'Mm-hm,' said Nick. 'Got to cater to the masses.' There was something vaguely mocking about his tone.

'Yes,' I said. 'I suppose so.'

'Well, you'll be pleased to hear the event's sold out,' he said. 'We'll push a few of the bookcases back, make more space. We'll set you up with a table so you can sell the books.'

'That sounds fine.'

'We'll put you in the IT section, just over there.' He indicated the sea of computers.

I eyed the machines, my heart sinking. 'Wonderful.'

Nick smiled. 'See you on Friday. Looking forward to it!'

*

On Friday evening, I arrived at the library in good time for the event. I had asked Charlotte if she wanted to come with me, but she made some excuse about meeting up with Sarah for dinner ('And I would only get in the way, darling'). Nick had collected three boxes of books from the shop earlier in the day, and he had seemed upbeat. But now he was pacing around in front of the automatic doors, checking his watch, face set in a frown.

I approached warily. 'Is everything all right?'

'She's late.'

'What?'

'I was expecting her ten minutes ago.'

'Oh dear. Have you tried phoning her?'

He gave me a funny look. 'Of course I've tried phoning her.' He froze and stared past my shoulder, eyes wide. 'Oh, no.'

'What is it?'

Nick turned to me with eyes filled with darkness. 'They're *here*.'

I turned and saw a parade of people of all ages, dressed in various fairy and dragon costumes. Several of them were carrying flaming torches. It seemed that civilisation was about to collapse. Right here, on the Yorkshire coast.

'Good God!' I said. 'Who are they? Are they a mob? Are they coming to burn down the library?'

'They're the fandom,' said Nick. 'I'd heard they were dedicated, but I had no idea...'

The fandom advanced, torches held aloft.

'What are we going to do?' I said.

At this point, Nick did something very brave. He stepped forward, placing himself between me and the fandom. Then he held up a hand.

'Hello,' he said, amiable smile in place. 'I suppose you're here for the Crystal Moontide event?'

There was a cheer from the mob. Torches were brandished.

A very tall man stepped forward. He was wearing a dragon mask, its snout protruding over his face like a visor. 'We are here to pay homage to the most majestic Crystal Moontide.'

'Er... that's brilliant,' said Nick. 'It's just... well, I don't think I can let you bring those torches into the library.'

The man looked a bit disappointed. 'Oh. Why not?'

'It's just... well... books are quite famous for being flammable, I'm afraid.'

'Ah.' The dragon man nodded his scaly head. 'Of course. How silly of me.' He turned towards the group. 'No torches in the library, people. Sorry!'

There were a few grumbled complaints as the torches were extinguished.

'The costumes are great, though,' said Nick.

The dragon man would not be distracted from his purpose. 'Where is our Esteemed Author? Is she inside?'

'Er... there's been a tiny delay.'

Dragon man frowned. 'How tiny?'

'Oh, teeny-weeny tiny.' Nick stepped to one side. 'Please come in.'

The procession filed into the library. There were so many that a few of them had to perch on beanbags from the Children's section.

I sidled up to Nick. 'What are we going to do?'

'I guess we'll just have to sit tight and hope she's not too long.'

I retreated behind the book signing table, placing forty hardback books between myself and the fandom. They seemed a peaceful bunch, but I supposed I could build a makeshift book fort if things turned nasty.

Twenty minutes later, there was still no sign of Crystal Moontide. The fandom were dealing with the whole thing much better than I expected. One of the women had suggested a singsong. A man dressed as an elven prince had asked where the mugs were, and had proceeded to make tea for everyone.

'This is a bit odd,' I said.

'How so?' said Nick.

'Well, weren't you expecting them to be more... well, annoyed?'

Nick looked around at the fandom. One of them had taken out a Crystal Moontide board game and was setting up dozens of tiny playing pieces.

'You have a point,' said Nick. He approached the dragon man with a big smile. 'Listen... er, I didn't catch your name?'

'Bob,' said the dragon man.

'Well, Bob, I just wanted to apologise for the delay. I have no idea where she's got to.'

Bob laughed. 'Don't worry, mate. She's always like this.'

I blinked. 'She... is?'

'Yes. She's always late. It's all part of her mystique. That's why we bring board games and sleeping bags.'

'Sleeping bags? How late are you expecting her to be, exactly?' said Nick.

'Her personal record is two days.'

'Two days?'

'Yeah. Don't worry, it's no bother. It gives us a chance to have a catch-up. Like a mini convention.'

I leaned towards Nick. 'Please can I have a word?'

We retreated behind the signing table again.

'I don't think I can stay here for two days,' I said. 'I need to open my bookshop tomorrow.'

'Yes, well, I'm not exactly happy about it either,' said Nick. 'Why didn't you warn me she was like this?'

'I didn't know!' I said. *'You're* her biggest fan! Why didn't *you* warn *me?'*

'I said I like her books! I'm not on the same level as these guys!' He gestured towards two knights with foam swords, who appeared to be circling each other and preparing to engage in combat.

'Can't you have a word? Tell them to come back later?'

Nick stared at the board game players. 'They look kind of settled in, don't they? Seems a shame to spoil their fun.'

'This is a library event, not a sleepover!'

Nick frowned. He looked ready to reply, but we were saved from further argument by the appearance of an apparition at the sliding doors.

It was a woman, dressed from head to toe in silver, with a moon-shaped crown on her head, and she was brandishing an ornate silver fountain pen. I glanced at Nick. His mouth had fallen open.

'It's *her*,' he said, voice soft with awe.

Crystal Moontide swept into the library with a swish of silk. The fandom abandoned their games and stood up.

'All hail Crystal Moontide!' they chanted. 'All hail the Great Author!'

'Sorry, sorry, sorry!' said Crystal Moontide, who looked a bit flustered. 'The roads have been terrible. And it took me ages to find a parking space.'

Nick stepped forward. 'Would you like a cup of tea?'

Crystal beamed. 'Oh, yes please, love. I'm parched.'

Nick went over to the makeshift refreshment table. I stood behind the stack of books, poised and ready for sales.

Crystal walked over and smiled at me. 'I guess this is my chair? Thank you. Oh, look at all these lovely books!'

I decided I quite liked Crystal Moontide.

She looked over at her fandom. 'All right, everyone! The signing table's open.'

Twenty minutes later, Crystal Moontide had been furnished with a cup of tea, and I hadn't yet sold a single book.

It seemed that her books were so popular, and her fans so dedicated, that they already owned the entire series. Some of them even had multiple special editions. I watched as yet another dragon brought out a copy which looked like it had been dropped in a bath, dried on a radiator, and bound together with Sellotape.

'Ooh, this is a lovely well-loved one, isn't it?' said Crystal warmly, signing the book with a flourish of her fountain pen.

I caught Nick's eye. He was still standing by the refreshment table, looking slightly embarrassed. As well he might.

'I bought this one on Amazon,' said a knight. 'It has the original cover with the green butterflies!'

'How lovely,' said Crystal.

The evening continued. The fandom had their books signed and took photos with Crystal. Crystal read for ten minutes from her latest novel. I continued not to sell any books, and the fandom all left with big smiles on their faces.

'Well, that was lovely,' said Crystal Moontide. 'Thank you both so much!' She eyed the pile of unsold books, and her face fell slightly. 'Er... would you like me to sign these for you?'

'No thanks, that won't be necessary,' I said.

Nick plucked a copy off the top of the pile. 'Please can you sign this for me?'

'With pleasure.'

When Crystal Moontide had finally left, I turned to Nick. 'You didn't need to do that.'

'What? I wanted a signed copy.'

'Come on. I know you have the entire series. Like the rest of that lot.'

Nick looked sheepish. 'I'm sorry. I feel really bad. Still, it was a nice event, wasn't it? Good vibes.'

'Good *vibes*?' I stared at him in disbelief. 'I'm three hundred pounds out of pocket!'

'Can't you return the stock?'

I could. Of course I could. But I wasn't going to tell him that.

'That,' I said, drawing myself up to my full height, 'is not the point.'

There was a moment of silence. Nick looked crestfallen.

'No,' he said. 'I guess it isn't. Look, would you like me to drive you back to the shop? We could drop off the books.'

'I'll get them tomorrow,' I said.

'Maybe I could buy you a drink?'

'No, thank you.' I turned around and marched out of the library.

20

Charlotte

'How did the event go?'

Greg indicated the pile of unsold Crystal Moontide books on our central display table. 'Spectacularly well, as you can see.'

I winced. 'Sorry. Did you sell any at all?'

'Precisely one. To Nick.'

'Oh, well that's nice. Did you two get a chance to chat?'

'I have no desire to chat to him.' Greg took up the pricing gun.

I sighed. Obviously we were destined to fall out today.

The doorbell rang, and Nick stepped into the shop. He was carrying a shiny gold gift bag, the sort people use for bottles of wine.

I nudged Greg. 'You might not have any choice.'

Greg looked over his shoulder and rolled his eyes.

Nick approached the counter, his shoulders slightly hunched. Greg pretended to be focused on sorting customer orders.

'Hey,' said Nick.

Greg glanced up, his mouth set in a disapproving line. Standing behind piles of books, he looked like a small, fierce literature professor. I felt sorry for Nick, who was clearly floundering.

'Hello, Nick,' I said. 'Nice to see you.'

'Hi, Charlotte.' He flashed me a brief smile, then placed the gift bag on the counter in front of Greg. 'Look, I've brought you this. By way of apology for last night. You wouldn't let me buy you a drink, so...' He shrugged. 'It's wine. I don't know if you like it, but, yes. That's what it is.'

Greg looked up. His gaze went from the gift bag, to Nick, and his face softened. 'Thank you. That's very thoughtful.'

'So we're okay?'

Greg gave a small smile. 'We're okay.'

'Oh, good.' Nick lingered by the counter for a moment, as if he wanted to say something else. But then he seemed to change his mind, and walked over to the Science Fiction section. He often did this. He rarely bought anything, but he would stare with feigned concentration at the shelves, occasionally stealing a glance at Greg when he thought he wasn't looking. Meanwhile, Greg would focus on his work and do everything to avoid meeting his eye.

I wanted to knock their heads together. I was just trying to find a way to resume the conversation when the doorbell rang again.

A boy of about fifteen entered the shop. He walked over to the General Fiction section and stood there, looking lost.

'Can I help you?' I said.

The boy jumped. Then he made a sniffing noise, and wiped his eyes with the cuff of his coat. His cheeks were red.

'Are you all right?' said a soft voice from behind the counter.

I looked at Greg in surprise. He rarely took the initiative with customers, instead waiting for them to approach him for help.

The boy sniffed again and nodded. He took a few tentative steps towards the counter.

Then, in a small voice, he said: 'Do you have any graphic novels?'

This was the sort of thing that normally provoked an eyeroll from Greg. I knew he was not a fan of graphic novels because they had, in his words, 'too many pictures and not enough writing'. I braced myself.

'We do,' said Greg gently. 'May I ask which ones you've enjoyed recently?'

I blinked. This was not the reaction I had expected.

The boy looked thoughtful. 'I liked the *Heartstopper* books and *The Sad Ghost Club*. Do you have anything like that?'

'Er... I'm not quite sure,' said Greg. He looked at me. 'Do we?'

'A nice one came in the other day,' I said, turning towards the Young Adult section and pulling out a book with a colourful cover. 'It's about a group of friends putting on a play at school.'

I offered it to the boy. He took it, and flicked through the pages.

'I'm in the school play,' he said after a moment. 'The other boys say I look stupid. And gay.'

I wasn't sure what to say. There was a cough from Nick in the Sci-Fi section. I turned to look at Greg, who was still standing behind the counter. He was perfectly still, apart from his hands, which he was twisting together in obvious discomfort.

'I'm... sorry they said that,' he said.

The boy shrugged. 'It doesn't matter. I mean, I *am* gay. But I don't want to look stupid.'

Some of the tension seemed to leave the room. Greg stopped wringing his hands. Determination crept into his features.

'Plays are great,' he said. 'You should be in them if it makes you happy.'

I was rather taken aback by the hypocrisy of this statement. It was a pity Greg couldn't follow his own advice.

'Yeah, I guess acting does make me happy. I should probably just ignore the others,' said the boy. He gave Greg a small smile.

'I'm glad to hear that,' said Greg, with utmost solemnity.

There was a soft chuckle from the Science Fiction section. I turned to see Nick, who was watching the scene as if it were a particularly fascinating soap opera.

'I'd like to buy this book.' The boy approached the counter. 'I only have three quid, though. Would you keep it for me?'

'That's all right,' said Greg. 'You can have it for three pounds.'

His face lit up. 'Thanks!'

'Now go and enjoy that play. Don't listen to those other kids.'

'I will.'

The boy left the shop. I turned back to Greg. 'Wow, look at you, inspiring the kids.'

'Oh, do shut up.' Greg refused to meet my eye. He opened the till, threw in a fiver from his own wallet (presumably to make up for the boy's seventy per cent discount), then shut the drawer with a small *crash*. 'And what are *you* smiling about?'

Nick had emerged from the Sci-Fi section, and was looking at Greg with a big grin on his face. 'That was very sweet.'

'It was nothing.'

'Do I get a discount, too? Mates' rates?'

'No!'

'Why not?' Nick placed a thick hardback tome on the counter. Greg looked down at the book. 'Because you're not being bullied at school.'

He was silent for a moment. He looked sad, I realised, his features closed-off and pale.

Nick looked at me questioningly. I shrugged.

'Well, I'd like to buy this book anyway,' he said.

Greg took his payment, put the book in a paper bag and held it out to Nick, all without saying anything.

'You know,' said Nick. 'If you'd like to grab that coffee... just to talk?' He took the bag, and as he did his fingers brushed against Greg's hand. 'Well. You know where I am.'

'I'm fine.' Greg hastily withdrew his hand. 'But thank you.'

Nick gave him a soft smile. Then he waved to us both and left.

'He's lovely,' I said, after a moment had passed.

'Hmm.' Greg's gaze was focused on the computer screen, but a bit of colour had crept into his cheeks.

'You should definitely go for coffee with him.'

'Maybe.'

'What are you so afraid of?'

Greg's head snapped up from the screen. 'I beg your pardon?'

'It's just... you're obviously nervous, that's all. Why?'

'I'm not nervous.' He turned back to the computer. 'Why do you care so much, anyway?'

If Greg had asked me this question just a few weeks earlier, the answer would have been that I was trying to distract him and coax him out of the bookshop. But I wasn't sure this was true anymore, so there was no need to lie.

'Because you're my friend,' I said.

He looked at me again, his eyes soft. For a moment, I thought he was going to confide in me. But then his face fell back into its usual, neutral mask. The one he wore in front of the majority of customers.

'Thank you,' he said. 'But I'm not scared.'

21

Greg

I was scared. Of course I was.

I was scared because I had been on my own for so long, and although I wasn't entirely happy with this situation, I had made it work. And now I was afraid of letting someone else in, of disrupting my peace. It had happened before.

His name was Andy. I was in my mid-thirties, and he was my first serious boyfriend. We met through the bookshop. He was a regular customer, coming in to order business books from me. He had a high-powered job, something in banking or finance. One day, out of the blue, he asked me on a date. I was surprised, but I leapt at the chance.

At first, everything was lovely.

Andy was the very model of an attentive boyfriend. He bought me gifts, even if they weren't the sort of things I would have chosen. We went on holiday together to Greece, where we spent a lot of time lounging around on the beach, or sitting by the pool. I didn't see the point in going all that way just to lie on a beach when there were interesting cities and classical ruins to explore. A beach was just a beach, after all.

I tried to tell him this.

'We could do this at home,' I said.

He raised his head from the sun lounger and smiled at me. 'I suppose we could, if you wanted to catch pneumonia.'

I was forced to concede that this was a fair point. The sun *was* lovely. But I wasn't ready to give up on the wonders of classical antiquity just yet.

'We've been here for three days,' I said, referring to the beach resort. 'Don't you fancy going into the city? There's this walking tour—'

He held up a hand. 'Look, you go if you like. You need the exercise. I've come here to relax. You know what work's like right now.'

'I—' I stopped, as my mind went back over the last few sentences and honed in on one in particular. 'What do you mean, I need the exercise?'

'Nothing. Just… you know.' He waved a hand, the gesture taking in most of the length of my body.

'No,' I said. 'I don't know. Please enlighten me.'

He laughed. 'It was just a throwaway remark. You're so uptight! Relax, why don't you? We're supposed to be on holiday.'

I lay back on the sun lounger. I brought my hand to my belly, and pressed it self-consciously. He was right, of course. Andy was always right. Still, I had no desire to go on the walking tour now. This was partly down to sheer awkwardness – an old stubbornness that I could not quite shake, even with Andy, the boyfriend who I loved and who had my best interests at heart.

I picked up my book and tried to read.

'That's right,' Andy's voice purred near my left ear. 'Who wants to go on a boring old tour anyway?'

After that, everything was objectively wonderful. It was a little like being stuck inside a film, a cute gay romcom entitled *Andy's Perfect Holiday*. We posed for pictures. We went for romantic walks along the beach at sunset. We ate excellent food. We went swimming in the sea.

I was bored stiff. But this was a dream holiday, so I was sure this was my problem. Andy was great. Did it really matter that we had nothing in common?

*

Back home in Shellcliff, everything seemed to be going well. Andy and I spent a lot of time together. Even my parents liked him.

'We're so glad you've finally found someone,' said my mum, at one Sunday lunch.

'It took him long enough,' said Andy, who was seated next to me. 'I hope I was worth the wait.'

There were fond chuckles from both my parents. I felt myself blush. Andy smiled at me and found my hand beneath the table. It was nice to feel included in this way, in the whole family thing. My sister Lydia was married with two kids, and ever since the wedding our family events increasingly revolved around her. It was hard not to feel like the odd one out, sometimes. But now I had Andy. Charming, sociable Andy. Things seemed to be back on track.

Dad rose from his chair. 'Anyone for sticky toffee pudding?'

'Yes pl—' Under the table, I felt Andy squeeze my hand. Quite hard. 'No, thanks. I'm full.'

Andy let go of my hand.

*

'Maybe we should move to London.' We were eating dinner in my flat, and the statement seemed to come out of nowhere. I dropped my fork into my bowl of Greek salad.

'What?' I said.

'I've been offered a promotion,' said Andy. 'It's a great opportunity, but it's based at head office. What do you think? Would you come with me?'

'London,' I said, flatly.

'Yes!' Andy beamed at me. 'Didn't you want to move there when you were younger?'

I stared sadly at the rather limp salad. 'Yes, but... that was *before*.'

Andy was quiet for a moment. Then he picked up both our bowls and stomped into the kitchen.

I followed him. 'What's wrong?'

'Nothing, I just thought you might be a bit more excited, that's all. A bit happy for me.'

I stared at him in bewilderment. 'I am happy for you. Of course I am. It's brilliant you've been offered a promotion. It's just... I have a life here.'

He turned to look at me. Then he gave a short laugh. 'A life? What life? You're *stuck*, Greg. You spend every day in that dusty old bookshop.'

'It's my job, Andy.'

'That's not a job. I have a job. A proper job that earns real money.'

I flinched at that, because of course Andy's job was better paid than mine. One didn't go into bookselling to become a millionaire.

'I thought you wanted to do something with your life,' said Andy.

A tiny spark of annoyance flared into life among the layers of insecurity. 'I *am*. I enjoy working in the bookshop. And there's the drama group. I might audition for a part next time.'

He smiled and looked me up and down. 'You're not serious?'

I folded my arms. 'I'm quite serious, Andy.'

'Well, you'd need to start making more of an effort, if you want theatre types to notice you. Dress better. Maybe lose a bit more weight.'

My bottom lip quivered. I bit down on it. 'I don't need to lose weight.'

He stared at me for a moment. Then he laughed.

'What's so funny?' I said, hurt and anger coiling in my chest.

'You know your problem?' he said. 'You're so bloody boring and set in your ways. I've tried to help you see sense, to get up off your backside and do something constructive. But you won't listen.'

I thought about the last six months, about our holiday abroad that had been entirely planned by Andy, our dates that had been orchestrated by him. A horrible realisation was starting to creep up on me: he had slowly taken over every aspect of our lives together, always choosing where we went, even the food we both ate.

How had I let this happen? Had I really been so desperate to love him?

'If I'm such a bore,' I said, slowly, 'why are you still here?'

A strange mix of expressions crossed Andy's face. He looked at me as if I was some strange mathematical equation which had surprised him during an exam. Then his confusion twisted into a sneer.

'You know what?' he said. 'I don't fucking know anymore.'

'Then perhaps...' There were tears rising in my throat. I swallowed them. 'Perhaps you should leave.'

He shook his head in apparent wonder. 'You do realise you got lucky, don't you? Do you really think anyone else is going to want a dull old loser like you?'

'I think that's a risk I'm going to have to take,' I said softly.

For a moment I thought he was going to say something else, that the confrontation was going to descend into a shouting match. But then he turned his back on me and stomped down the stairs. I heard the door slam. It was suddenly much easier to breathe in the flat above the bookshop.

Later, one of my customers mentioned in passing that Andy had moved to London. I never saw or heard from him again.

Sometimes, though, in my lonelier moments, I would hear his words in my head. They would go round and round like a faulty vinyl record. *Lose more weight. You got lucky. Dull old loser.*

And in my loneliest moments, I believed him.

22

Charlotte

It was three days before Alex was due to visit, and Greg had popped out for our habitual takeaway coffee. I was alone in the bookshop, sorting through customer orders, when Lydia arrived.

She looked at me in vague disapproval. 'Is Greg about?'

'He's just gone for coffee,' I said.

'Do you mind if I wait?'

'Of course not.'

Lydia and I had reached an uneasy truce during the rehearsals for *Theatre is Murder!*. She generally stayed away from me, only speaking to me when there was an administrative matter to attend to, such as my drama group membership fee. At first I had been disappointed that she didn't want to talk, but I had now accepted it. It seemed immature, but it was her choice, after all.

'I see you've settled in all right,' she volunteered unexpectedly.

'Yes,' I said. 'Thank you.'

'I hope my brother isn't proving too much of a pain.'

I frowned. 'On the contrary. He's a sweetheart, mostly.'

At that moment, Greg hurried in, carrying two takeaway coffees. 'I'm so sorry. There was a queue.' He saw Lydia. 'Oh, hello. I'm sorry, I didn't know you were coming. Coffee?'

Lydia waved the cup away. 'No, thank you. I'm just here to give you this.' She handed him a white envelope. 'And to wish you a happy birthday.'

'Er... thank you, Lydia.'

'Oh!' I said. 'Is it your birthday?'

'Yes,' said Greg, in a resigned tone. 'It is.'

'I also came to remind you about dinner,' said Lydia. 'You are coming, aren't you?'

'Yes. Of course. I wouldn't forget.'

'Mum and Dad are looking forward to it. They say, if you want to bring a plus one—'

Greg held up a hand. 'No, thank you. It'll just be me.'

'Okay, well... that's fine. That's what I thought.' She turned towards the door, but then paused. 'Seven o'clock, remember?'

'Yes, Lydia. I'll be there.'

Lydia left the shop before I had a chance to wish her goodbye. Greg opened the card, glanced at it, and then placed it on the shelf behind the counter. It had a picture of a cake and balloons on the front. I stared at it for a moment.

'I can't believe you didn't tell me it's your birthday.'

He looked down at the counter. 'It's not important.'

'Of course it is!' I smiled and clapped my hands together. 'Maybe we could go out after the rehearsal on Sunday? I could invite Alex along.'

'No, thank you.'

'But you must celebrate your birthday.'

'I'd really rather not,' said Greg. 'It's not a big deal.'

I couldn't understand this at all. I always made a big deal of my own birthday. Usually, Alex would buy me a ridiculously blingy piece of jewellery, something which should look tacky but which actually looked fabulous when I wore it. And I always met up with my London Ladies, either for a meal or drinks or karaoke, sometimes all three.

'But... it's your birthday!' I said. 'You're one year older.'

'Thanks for the reminder,' said Greg. 'Now are we going to finish processing these orders?'

*

It was the night before Alex's visit, and we still hadn't made any firm arrangements. I decided to call him.

'Hi, Alex. I was just wondering what time you were getting here tomorrow?'

'Ah, right...' Alex sounded distracted. 'I've been meaning to call you about that. I'm going to have to reschedule. Sorry.'

'Oh.' The wave of disappointment was unexpectedly strong. I actually felt my eyes prick. It was pathetic, really. 'Why?'

'Fred wants the whole cast to attend this gala thing. There'll be lots of photo ops, apparently. Good publicity for the play.' I heard him sigh. 'To be honest, I need it like a hole in the head. I'm absolutely knackered.'

'Can't you just make an excuse? Give it a miss?'

'Ah. No. I've already promised I'd go.'

'You made a promise to me, Alex. You promised to come and visit.'

'Please don't be like that, Charley. You know what it's like.' He sounded tired. 'Look. I'll come and see you as soon as I can get away. I promise. It'll be great. Okay?'

I was quiet for a moment.

'Charley? Are you still there?'

'Yes, I'm still here. Okay, fine, Alex. I lo—'

'Sorry, I've got to go.'

'—ove you.'

Too late. He was gone.

I sat for a moment, staring at the phone in the hope that he had been cut off, that he would ring me back and apologise and maybe say that he loved me too. But the phone was silent.

I shoved it into my handbag so I didn't need to look at it anymore.

The weekend stretched ahead of me, looking lonely and empty. I couldn't even go to the bookshop. Expecting to entertain Alex, I had taken the Friday and Saturday off work. So much for that.

I pushed the self-pitying thoughts away. I would not allow myself to wallow. Alex was busy, and I could be equally busy. I did not require him to organise my social life.

Perhaps it was time to begin Operation Greg in earnest. He might not care about his birthday, but I did, and I was pretty sure that Nick would, too.

I opened the Facebook app on my phone, and went to the Shellcliff Amateur Theatre Society members' page. I started a private message thread and added everyone except Greg. Then I went in search of Nick's profile.

23

Greg

It was 4.45pm. It hadn't been a bad day; there had been a steady flow of summer visitors. I had sold plenty of Clive the Donkey books, and even a few cut-price Crystal Moontides. Things could have been significantly worse. It had cheered me up a little after the awkward dinner with my parents and sister. The evening had felt a little like an episode of *Mastermind*, complete with all the tension of the 'Approaching Menace' theme music, with myself in the big black chair. My specialist subject? Greg's love life.

Are you seeing anyone at the moment?

Have you tried online dating?

Did you know there was a dating app aimed at gay men?

Have you heard from Andy?

Among other questions. I had several passes, and gave quite a few wrong answers (or at least they felt that way to me).

I loved my parents and Lydia dearly. I also knew they just wanted me to be happy. But sometimes I felt like a disappointment.

It was good to be back in the familiar surroundings of my bookshop. It would be Christmas before I would be quizzed again.

I was starting to consider shutting the shop ten minutes early when the door flew open and Charlotte strode in. She was dressed in a long, polka dot vintage swing gown and red high heels. She looked impossibly glamorous. She was probably off to meet that boyfriend of hers.

'Hello, Charlotte,' I said. 'I wasn't expecting to see you today.'

'I thought I'd surprise you,' she said. 'We're going out.'

'Who is?'

'Us. Me and you.'

'Why?'

'Because it's your birthday, of course.'

I lingered behind the counter as if it were a protective barrier. Charlotte had caught me completely off-guard, and I searched desperately for an excuse.

'Er... I don't think I'm really dressed for going out.'

Charlotte rolled her eyes. 'I'm not taking you anywhere posh, Greg. Come on. Everyone's waiting.'

'I just...' I realised what she had said. 'What do you mean, everyone?'

'Oh. I invited some of the drama group.'

I stared at her in horror. 'You told the drama group it was my birthday?'

'Of course I did. They were all very keen to come along. I mean, you're not... how old are you again?'

'Forty-five.'

'You're not forty-five every day, are you?'

I looked at the stack of unopened boxes from the wholesaler. 'I need to unpack this delivery.'

Charlotte narrowed her eyes. 'Greg, you and I both know that you never work after five. The delivery can wait.'

I twisted my hands together. I was rapidly running out of excuses.

'Come on. You have to celebrate your birthday. What else have you got to do with your time?'

This stung a little. 'I do have interests, Charlotte.'

Charlotte looked awkward. 'Sorry. I didn't mean it like that.'

I sighed. 'No, no. You're absolutely right.' I tried to smile. This was kind of her, even if it wasn't what I would have chosen to do. 'All right. Why not?'

She clapped her hands together. 'Great! Come on. We'll be late.'

Ten minutes later, I was somewhat relieved to find myself standing outside Olive's, the little Italian restaurant on the seafront. I had been convinced that Charlotte was going to take me to the pub. Some of the tension left my body. Perhaps the evening would prove enjoyable, after all.

Charlotte pushed open the door, and I was greeted by an inviting smell of cooked bread and garlic. I hadn't been to Olive's in years. There had been no one to go with, and I had never enjoyed dining alone in restaurants. I often wished I could revel in my freedom and independence (this was what the guides in our Self Help section all seemed to advise, not that I spent much time looking at them, of course). Unfortunately, I was starting to think I would never be that sort of person.

A small cheer went up from a table in the corner. I looked over and saw a small gang from the drama group: Bex, Harry, Iris, Rose and Matt. And, seated right against the wall, Nick.

'What's he doing here?' I whispered.

Charlotte smiled. 'He's joined the drama group, darling. He's interested in operating the lights, so I thought tonight might be a good opportunity for you to chat about ideas.'

'Chat about ideas? I thought this was supposed to be my birthday party.'

'Yes, well, I know how much you enjoy this nerdy stuff.'

'Nerdy stuff? It's not—' I shook my head. 'Never mind.'

We walked over to the table, where I received a small chorus of 'Happy Birthdays'. While I was thanking everyone, Charlotte slid into the seat opposite Bex, which left only one chair empty.

Nick waved at me. 'Hey, Greg.'

'Hello,' I said. I glanced briefly around the table, in a forlorn hope that I would psychically communicate that I wished to change seats. It didn't work, so I sat down opposite my library nemesis.

Nick smiled at me. 'Happy birthday.'

'Thank you.' I picked up the menu. After a brief perusal, I was relieved to discover that it had not changed since 2004.

'What are you having?' said Nick.

'Oh. The lasagne's good. I think I'll have that.'

'Do you come here a lot?'

'No.'

'I think I'll have this Bolognese pizza,' said Nick. 'Two classic Italian dishes in one.'

'Sounds good.'

'Do you think if I asked, they'd include the actual pasta, too? Like, a bowl of spaghetti Bolognese but on a pizza?'

I stared at him. 'I honestly have no idea.'

Nick laughed. 'There's no need to look so horrified. I wouldn't dare ask such a thing. I might try it at home, though. I like a bit of culinary experimentation.'

I looked to my right. Rose was deep in conversation with Harry, and could not be distracted. Charlotte caught my eye, smiled, and resumed her chat with Bex. I vowed to get my revenge in due course. I would empty *both* the pricing guns so she would be forced to refill them. Yes. That would be a good start.

'I'm just joking, you know,' said Nick.

'What?'

'About the spaghetti pizza.'

'Are you?'

'Well... sort of.' He gave a short laugh, then drank a large mouthful of wine. 'I'm babbling, aren't I? I'm sorry. I'm a little nervous.'

This took me by surprise. Nick struck me as naturally outgoing. 'Why?'

Nick's face took on a serious expression. He glanced around the table as if to make sure we weren't being observed, then leaned forward slightly.

'I'm not sure what I'm doing here, to be honest. I sort of feel like I'm gatecrashing.'

A part of me was tempted to agree, but Nick looked quite worried. He began to play with a napkin. I softened a little.

'Don't be silly. Charlotte invited you. You asked to join the drama group, didn't you?'

'Ah.' Nick ran a hand through his hair. 'Not exactly. She messaged me on Facebook. Said something like "Hey, Nick. We desperately need someone to help us with the lights for our show. Are you free tonight?" And I said okay, and then she told me to meet her at the Italian restaurant, and then she said, "oh, by the way, it's Greg's birthday." Don't you think that's a bit odd?'

'Yes.' I lowered my voice to a whisper. 'Well, she *is* a bit odd.'

Nick laughed lightly. 'If I didn't know better, I would think she was trying to play Cupid.'

'Pardon?'

'You know. Set us up.'

'Oh.' I felt heat rush to my face. 'Well, that would be ridiculous.'

Nick's smile faded. 'Yes. I suppose so.'

There was a short silence, during which I kept my gaze fixed to the menu.

'By the way. I brought you something.' Nick reached under the table, and produced a brown paper bag. 'Sorry it isn't wrapped. It was all a bit short notice, you see. But happy birthday, anyway.'

'Oh,' I said, slightly taken aback. 'Thank you.'

'It's a first edition Crystal Moontide novel,' said Nick.

I hesitated, looking at the bag in mild horror.

Nick smiled. 'Only joking.'

I reached inside the bag. My hand closed around something large and book-shaped. I pulled it out. The book was worn, evidently well-loved, and the title was *Jonathan Strange and Mr Norrell* by Susanna Clarke.

'I know you said you didn't read much fantasy,' said Nick. 'But I thought you might like that. It's brilliant. It has footnotes and everything.'

A part of me wondered why Nick thought footnotes would be such a selling point for me, but a larger part was actually quite touched.

Once you become a bookseller, people rarely buy you books as gifts. I suppose they just assume you have all the books you could possibly want. Nick, however, had not only gifted me a book, but had spent time thinking about what sort of book I would like.

'Thank you,' I said, smiling. 'That's very kind of you.'

He waved a hand. 'I know it's a bit boring, giving you a book when you have a whole shop full of them.'

'They're not actually my books,' I said. 'People rarely give me books.'

Nick nodded. 'I don't think anyone's given me a book since I started working in libraries.'

I slipped the book back into the bag. 'Thank you, Nick. I'll look forward to reading it.'

I met his eyes. He smiled. Nick, I realised, had a nice smile. Warm.

'And if you don't like it, I figured you could always stick it in your second-hand section.'

*

The evening was quite enjoyable after that. I began to relax, and talked to the other members of the drama group. I'd always known they were a nice bunch, and I wondered why I had ever been so reluctant to spend more time with them.

It turned out that Nick had some very good ideas about the lighting for *Theatre is Murder!*.

'I used to do lighting for bands,' he said. 'Some really big names, too. Have you heard of a band called Shattered Chandelier?'

I confessed that I hadn't.

'I was on tour with them for a full year. The frontman scared the hell out of me. Had all these mad creative ideas. Full theatrical production stuff. I think lighting a play would be quite easy, in comparison.'

'That sounds dreadful.'

'No. I loved it. I just got a bit tired of touring. I worked in admin for a while before I did the lighting stuff. I wasn't expecting to get the job in the library, after doing other things for so long. I feel really lucky.' He sawed away at his pizza. 'Not as much working with books as I would like, though.'

'I never expected to work in a bookshop,' I said, without thinking.

'What did you want to do?'

I glanced at Charlotte, but she was still busy talking to Bex. They were sharing a bottle of wine, and their laughter was getting increasingly loud.

'I wanted to be an actor,' I said quietly.

'Oh, right. So that's why you're so active in the theatre group.'

'I suppose so.'

'I guess you could still be an actor. You could ask Charlotte for advice.'

I shook my head and stared down at my empty plate. 'I don't think so. I'm too old now.'

'Hey, don't be ridiculous.' Nick smiled. 'I'd like to see you act.'

'I think I'm probably a bit rusty.' I drained my wine glass. My eyes were pricking a bit.

Nick frowned. 'You okay?'

'Oh. Yes. Fine. Look, can we change the subject?'

'Sure.'

When the meal was over and the rather complex bill had been split, Charlotte looked around the group, her gaze settling on me. 'So! Where next?'

I was feeling pretty stuffed, and my head was a little light from the wine (I rarely drank more than two glasses). I was looking forward to crawling into bed with a book. 'I should really be going.'

'Don't be silly. It's your birthday! You need to celebrate!'

I indicated the empty plates and glasses. 'I *have* celebrated.'

'The night's still young.' Charlotte giggled. Her cheeks were a little flushed. 'How about we go to the pub for a bit? Just one more drink.'

Nick looked at me. 'I'd be up for another drink, if you are?'

I was now torn between my need to return to the bookshop and a desire to spend more time with Nick. 'All right. Just one.'

We walked down Shellcliff high street. Charlotte marched on ahead with the air of a woman on a mission. The street was quiet – it was the main thoroughfare through the town, and it had once been vibrant, but now several of the shops were boarded up. There were a few pubs and takeaways, however, and I felt myself growing tense, because each pub we passed increased the chance we would end up in The Crown. I had no desire to relive my first embarrassing meeting with Nick.

He fell into step beside me.

'Do you think she's all right?' he asked.

'Who?'

'Charlotte. She seems a bit... I don't know. Determined to have a good time? Like she needs a distraction or something.'

I had no reply to this. I didn't feel that I knew Charlotte well enough to hypothesise about her personal life.

There was light and music spilling out of the door of The King's Head, one of the town's cosier pubs. Charlotte stopped outside, and turned to beam at me. 'You're going to love this.'

She practically pushed me across the threshold, right into a crush of people standing at the bar. I found myself staring at a blackboard, which informed me there was *KARAOKE TONIGHT!*

'Surprise!' said Charlotte.

'Sur...prise?'

'You can sing any genre you like. I checked.'

'Er... I don't know.'

'Oh, don't be boring, darling! I bet Nick's up for some karaoke. Aren't you, Nick?'

Nick shoved his hands into his pockets. 'It's not really my scene, to be honest.'

Charlotte rolled her eyes theatrically. 'Whatever. I'll get us some drinks.'

She walked off towards the bar.

Bex caught my eye. 'I'd better go with her.'

'Thank you.'

A few minutes later, we were all squashed around a tiny table, alarmingly close to the makeshift karaoke stage. I couldn't concentrate on what anyone was saying above the hubbub, so I did what I vaguely remembered doing when I had gone out with friends when I was in my late teens, namely: sit there with a fixed smile in place, nod occasionally, and hope my responses were appropriate.

I really, really wanted my book.

'Isn't this nice?' said Charlotte. Her eyes were slightly red-rimmed.

A woman wearing a sparkly gold top stepped up to the microphone and waved her arms around a bit, trying to quell the noise.

'Hello, everyone. Welcome to our weekly karaoke night!'

There were a few whoops from around the bar.

The woman smiled. 'I'm Gemma, and I'll be your MC for the evening. Can I have my first victim... I mean, volunteer. Ah, it's Baz! Come on up, Baz. I can tell this is going to be something special.'

It seemed that Baz was a regular around the local karaoke scene. What followed was a spectacularly awful yet enthusiastic rendition of 'Bat Out of Hell' by Meat Loaf. Baz's sheer energy made the performance oddly compelling. He was rewarded with a round of happy applause.

'That'll take some beating,' said Gemma. 'Who's next? Clarissa? What have you got for us tonight?'

At least the karaoke freed me from any obligation to make small talk. Around me, the company laughed and clapped and sang along with the choruses, and I joined in in a low voice. We listened to 'Jolene' and 'Bad Romance' and 'Bohemian Rhapsody'. At one point, Charlotte asked me if I would like another wine, and I said yes. Then, while I was drinking it, we listened to 'Born to Run', 'Gimme Gimme Gimme' and 'Life on Mars?'.

'Okay,' said Gemma. 'Who's next? How about someone from this table over here?' Her gaze fell on our party.

Harry slapped me on the back. 'Go on, Greg!'

I shook my head. 'Oh, no...'

'Yes!' said Charlotte. 'Go on, darling!'

I really, really wanted to.

'Yeah, go on,' said Bex.

'Maybe Charlotte should go first...'

'Greg! Greg! Greg!'

'Oh, all right,' I stood up. 'Er... what should I sing?'

'Anything you like,' said Charlotte.

I went up to the stage area. Gemma gave me the remote, and I flicked through the song categories. Perhaps I should sing something in the same vein as what had come before. Something poppy or rocky. I wasn't particularly au fait with recent music, so I wasn't sure I wanted to risk something from the last ten years.

A title caught my eye. An old favourite from the eighties. 'This one.'

Gemma smiled.

I launched into a rendition of 'Total Eclipse of the Heart' by Bonnie Tyler. After three glasses of wine, which was one more than I usually drank, it sounded a little shaky. Slightly off-key, perhaps. I closed my eyes in the hope this would help me focus. I was already wondering how I was going to deal with the big key change at the end, but there were at least two more verses to go before then.

The drama group cheered. At this point, I made the mistake of opening my eyes again.

Sean Henderson was sitting at the bar, nursing a pint of beer. He was smiling. Another man leaned over and whispered something in his ear. Sean laughed, and I knew, with absolute certainty, that he was laughing at me.

And just like that, I was back there, at that party, and Vicky was telling me that I was embarrassing and spoiled everything, and Lydia, on a separate occasion, was asking why couldn't I be like everyone else?

A whine of feedback brought me back to reality. I blinked, and realised that it wasn't Sean Henderson at the bar after all. Just a man with a similar haircut, in poor lighting.

But I kept hearing those words: *Why can't you be like everyone else?*

I looked at the microphone, and at the drama group, and I wondered what on earth I was doing up there, singing in front of all those people. Because I didn't do things like this. Not anymore.

My gaze rested on Nick. He was sitting straight in his chair, giving me his full attention. And he was smiling. He inclined his head in a slight, encouraging nod.

I took a breath, closed my eyes, and went for it. I drowned out the other voices, if only for now. And then the song was at an end.

The pub gave me a round of applause.

'Well,' said Gemma, 'wasn't that something?'

I went back to the table, shaking slightly.

'That was great,' said Charlotte, grinning. 'Go you!'

'Thanks…' I picked up my jacket from the back of my chair. 'I'd better be going.'

Charlotte's expression fell into a pout. 'But the evening's just getting started.'

'I need to get home. Thank you, everyone, I had a good time.'

I smiled at the company, hoping my face was making the correct sort of grateful shape.

Charlotte frowned. 'What's wrong?'

'Nothing. I've had a great time. I just need to get home now.'

'Come on. Stay. Don't be so boring.'

The pub was starting to feel overwhelming. Loud, smelly and crowded. I gripped the back of my chair. 'I can't.'

My voice was embarrassingly small. Charlotte was right, of course. I was being boring.

A gentle hand fell on my arm.

'I think he wants to go, Charlotte,' said Nick.

Charlotte's smile vanished. She blinked, as if awakening from some sort of daze. 'Of course. So sorry.' She got to her feet, swaying slightly, and addressed the MC. 'I'll sing next!'

We watched Charlotte take her place onstage. She took quite a long time to make a selection, then looked around the pub with an intensity that was almost alarming.

Nick's hand brushed against my arm. 'Would you like to get out of here?'

I nodded. 'Yes, please.'

'Okay.'

Charlotte raised the microphone. The first bars of 'I Will Survive' thrummed through the room.

'She really isn't okay, is she?' said Nick.

'It's all right,' said Bex. 'We'll stay with her.'

Nick nodded. I followed him out of the pub on shaky legs.

'You feeling all right?' he said, once we were outside.

'Yes. I just had a bit too much to drink, that's all. Sorry to be boring.'

'Don't be daft. Come on. I'll walk back to the bookshop with you.'

'There's really no need...'

Nick sighed. 'Greg, I *want* to walk back to the bookshop with you.'

'Oh. Right.'

We fell into step beside each other again. It was only a five-minute walk, and we spent it in silence. I really wanted to turn back time, to prove to Nick I was capable of enjoying myself, but it seemed a little late for that. It was a shame, really. For the first time in years, it had felt possible to grow close to someone.

We reached the bookshop. I lingered at the door to my flat, searching clumsily in my pocket for the key.

'Goodnight, Nick,' I said. 'Thanks for... well, you know.'

He smiled. 'It's okay.'

I finally found the key. I was about to turn away when Nick reached out and placed a hand on my shoulder.

'Hey,' he said. 'You're not boring, okay? I enjoyed tonight.'

'Oh.' I blinked. 'Me too.'

'Maybe we could do it again? Without the drama group and the karaoke, I mean.'

'Yes. Yes, I would like that.'

'And I guess I'll see you at rehearsal?'

'Yes. See you there.'

Nick's hand went to my cheek. He brushed a lock of hair behind my ear.

''Night,' he said.

I watched him leave. I was slightly disappointed he hadn't leaned in for a kiss, but this hardly mattered. He wanted to see me again. The evening hadn't been a disaster, after all.

I went upstairs feeling considerably lighter, but I still felt a little bad about leaving the pub in such a hurry. Charlotte had made a real effort to celebrate my birthday. I should probably have taken more time to thank her.

I wondered if I should text her, but I wasn't sure what to say besides a simple 'thank you.' So I went back downstairs, turned on a light in the bookshop, and spent fifteen minutes browsing the shelves. Charlotte had mentioned she wasn't one for the classics, but perhaps I could give her something else. Something more 'her'. As a thank you.

One of the spines caught my eye. I started to smile.

Perfect.

24

Charlotte

Charlotte de la Mer had always known how to party.

I had finished 'I Will Survive' to rapturous applause, and immediately asked the MC if I could have another go. She barely protested, so I moved onto 'Flowers' by Miley Cyrus. I had decided that I absolutely did not care about Alex and his stupid gala night. I was not sad, I was not jealous, and I was going to sing all the empowering songs to prove it.

The first photos had come through while we were having dinner. I had been eating the most marvellous plate of meatballs and rigatoni, when my phone had pinged.

It was Margot, one of my London Ladies, currently appearing in *The Glass Menagerie* by Tennessee Williams.

Her message said: *Have you seen this???*

She linked to an article from an entertainment news website. The headline read: *Selena Warrington Attends Star-studded Gala on the Arm of Co-Star Alex Paige.*

Alex, looking sharp and handsome in an evening suit, had his arm around Selena, who was wearing a gown of peacock blue. They both looked very happy. Big smiles all round.

I had put my phone down and carried on eating. I supposed it was nice that Alex was having a good time at the gala without me. After all, we had both always been independent, and quite capable of attending events on our own.

Another ping. It was Margot again. Apparently the internet was going wild.

I did not care. I would not look online.

I sipped my wine.

I went online.

OMG! Who's that?

Bit old for her, isn't he?

They make a cute couple!

They're in the same show together!!! Awww! (Heart-eyes smiley face emoji.)

I slammed my phone down and skewered a meatball with my fork. I did not care.

Now, an hour later, I was proving how much I didn't care. I've found that it's always best to channel one's emotions into delivering a perfect performance.

I finished singing 'Flowers'. I bathed in the applause, looking around the pub. It was so nice to have an appreciative audience.

'Thank you, everyone. For my next number, I will sing "Sisters Are Doin' It...", er... "Doin' It For... "' My mind went blank. I momentarily couldn't remember who the sisters were doing it for. I realised the MC – was it Gemma? – was starting to look a little alarmed.

A hand fell on my arm. It was Bex.

'Maybe you should let someone else have a go, Charlotte.'

This seemed like a highly unreasonable suggestion. 'Nonono, it'll come to me in a minute—'

'Come on,' said Bex. 'Come and have another drink. Lemonade this time, maybe.'

Her voice was kind. So kind that I burst into tears.

'He's a bastard,' I said.

Bex nodded sagely, although she probably didn't have the faintest idea who I was talking about. 'I know.'

She led me back to the table.

The rest of the evening was a bit of a blur.

*

I awoke to the sound of crying seagulls. This confused me: at first, I was convinced that I was in London, because I had vague memories of attending a karaoke night and this was something I did with my London Ladies.

I cracked open an eye, and saw an annoyed-looking gull staring at me through the window. And I remembered I was in Shellcliff.

I sat up in bed and groaned, fighting an urge to lie straight back down again. I'd reached the age when I didn't have to drink excessively in order to acquire a hangover. I needed coffee, and I didn't think the instant stuff in the kitchen was going to cut it.

As I showered and dressed, more memories of the previous night started to come back to me. I had an uncomfortable feeling that I had embarrassed myself. Had I cried after singing karaoke? Had I told them all about Alex?

I also remembered that I had said something mean to Greg. Had I called him boring? Oh, dear. That wasn't good. And on his birthday, too.

Well, that settled it. I would call into Beans on my way to the bookshop, and pick up coffee and pastries for both of us.

Twenty minutes later, I was standing outside Seaswept Books. The lights were off, and when I tried the door I found it locked.

I checked my watch. 10.15am. Greg was a full fifteen minutes late opening up, which was absolutely unprecedented. I hoped he was okay. Fortunately, Sarah had given me a key. I unlocked the shop, flipped the sign to *OPEN*, and switched everything on.

Another ten minutes later, the door opened and Greg hurried in, looking a little worse for wear.

'I'm so sorry,' he said. 'I'm so, so sorry.' He stopped, pressed a hand to his head, and abruptly sat down in an armchair. 'Ugh. I only had a few glasses of wine. How embarrassing.'

'Dirty stop-out.' I grinned, and picked up the coffee. 'Here, I got you a cappuccino.'

'Ah, thank you so much.' He took it from me and drank a long swig. 'Oh, God. I needed that.'

'Listen, Greg,' I said. 'I wanted to apologise if I said anything… harsh last night. I didn't mean it. I'd had a bit too much to drink. And… well, I was missing Alex.'

Greg's eyes widened. 'What? Don't be silly. I had a really nice night. Thank you for organising it. If anything, I should be apologising to you.'

'Whatever for?'

'For rushing off like that.' He fiddled with his cuff. 'I… find the pub a little overwhelming sometimes.'

'That's quite all right.' I was flooded with relief. I smiled. 'Did you have a good chat with Nick?'

'Oh. Yes.' Greg's cheeks coloured slightly. He turned his face away. 'And?'

'And what?'

'What did you think?'

Greg sighed. 'Okay. You were right. He's very nice.'

I laughed. 'Told you. And he's going to help out with the lights?'

'Yes. I believe he is.'

'So you'll be seeing a lot more of him.'

'I suppose I will.' He stood up and went behind the counter. He started rummaging around in the cupboard, and I wondered if he was trying to avoid further conversation. But then he emerged again, and held out a book wrapped in brown paper. 'This is for you. To say thank you for the party.'

'You didn't have to do that,' I said, taking the package.

'Don't get too excited. I think I was still feeling the effects of the drink when I chose it, so apologies if it's something inappropriate.'

I hesitated. 'It's not *Fifty Shades of Grey*, is it?'

'I… don't think so.'

Intrigued, I opened the bag and pulled out the book. I had heard of the author, but the title was unfamiliar. I turned it over and read the blurb.

I smiled. 'That sounds lovely.'

'I hope you enjoy it. Ibbotson's one of my favourite writers. She writes a lot about the theatre. And musicians.'

'Sounds right up my street.'

Fortunately for our sore heads, it was a quiet morning in the bookshop. The weather was foul, with rain lashing against the front door. At one point, Greg even stuffed a towel into the letterbox to stop water coming in.

We had three customers. The first wanted to know if we sold umbrellas, and the second had read Google Maps wrong and thought we were a shoe shop. The third, however, bought a copy of *I Capture the Castle*, which made Greg very happy.

'Such a lovely book,' he said, when the customer had gone, a rather soppy smile plastered across his face.

'I've never read it.'

'Oh, you'd love it,' he said. 'It's about this family in the 1930s, and they live in this wreck of a castle. The aristocratic owners turn up and the older sister decides she wants to marry one of them. But then the younger sister falls in love with him. It's all very romantic.'

'I'm not sure that's quite my thing. Sounds a bit mushy.'

He looked mildly offended. 'It's not. It's very sharp and witty.'

'If you say so.'

He pulled another copy from the shelf and held it out to me. 'Try it.'

'Maybe another time. You've already given me one book today.'

'Just read the first chapter. See what you think.'

I took the book from him. 'All right. But only if you promise to read a crime novel. Even if it's a classic, like Sherlock Holmes or an Agatha Christie.'

He sighed. 'Okay. Fine. I'll read one of your silly mysteries.' He turned away and began to tidy the nearest bookcase. 'Though why anyone wants to read about death and murder all the time is... well, a mystery to me.'

I was about to reply when the doorbell rang, and Sam hurried into the shop. Her eyes looked a little red, as if she had been crying.

'Whatever's the matter?' I asked.

'I've got an audition at the London School of Performing Arts.'

Greg and I exchanged glances.

'But that's wonderful,' I said. 'Why are you upset?'

'I'm trying to learn my audition speeches.' Sam slammed a thin book down on the counter. 'I hate this stupid play. I can't do it. It's too hard.'

I looked down at the script. It was *Romeo and Juliet*.

'What seems to be the problem?' said Greg.

'It's just... I can't get my head around how I'm supposed to say the bloody words. There are so many of them.'

A smile flickered across Greg's face. 'Ah, yes. A bit wordy, old Shakespeare.'

'I've been watching some YouTube videos of *Romeo and Juliet*. It sounds like poetry.'

'That's because it is poetry,' I said.

'I can't do it,' said Sam. 'I sound silly when I talk in poetry.'

'I'm sure you don't,' said Greg.

'I do!' Sam wrung her hands in frustration. Then she scowled at the floor. 'All those actors sound lovely. They're all so *posh*. I just sound stupid.'

Ah. This was familiar. I remembered my first few weeks at drama school in London. I had soon come to the realisation that very few of the other students sounded like me. I learned to disguise my accent, to adopt what my voice tutor called 'received pronunciation'. This had become a habit, the way I spoke in everyday life as well as on the stage. Since returning to Shellcliff, I had noticed my real accent coming back. I was surprised how natural it felt.

Greg frowned. 'You must never say that.'

'But it's true,' said Sam.

'No, it's not.' He actually sounded angry, which surprised me. Greg rarely showed anger. 'You have a lovely voice, Sam. You're a great actor.'

Sam looked sadly down at the script. 'I just don't think this is me.'

'You don't have to do Shakespeare,' I said. 'You could choose something else.'

'I need a modern monologue and a classic monologue,' said Sam. 'I don't know what else to choose.'

Greg looked thoughtful. 'Do you want to play Juliet? In a production, I mean, if given the chance?'

'Not really. I think she's kind of annoying.'

'Blasphemy!' I gasped, pressing my hand to my throat in mock horror.

Greg ignored me. 'Maybe you just need to pick a different Shakespeare.' He turned to the shelf of scripts in the Classics section, which were still mostly by good old William. 'What sort of character would you like to play?'

'I think I'd like to be a villain,' said Sam. She gave a slightly worrying smile. 'More fun.'

'Lady Macbeth?' I suggested. 'I've always wanted to play Lady Macbeth.'

'A possibility,' said Greg. He paused, and pulled a script from the shelf. 'Ah. Now this could be right up your street.'

He offered Sam the script.

I eyed it dubiously. '*Richard the Third*? Really?'

'It's quite action-packed,' said Greg. 'And he's a great villain. Psychologically complex. Here... read his opening monologue.'

'Now is the winter of our discontent...' read Sam. She looked up at Greg. 'Isn't this a speech for a man?'

'Does it matter?' said Greg. 'You just need to show the audition panel what you can do.'

Sam squinted at the text. 'I'm not sure I quite get it.' She held the script out to me. 'Could you read it out? Show me how it should be done?'

'I think you have to decide that, Sam,' I said.

'Please? I won't copy you. It'll just give me some idea.'

I reached out for the script, and then changed my mind. An idea had occurred to me. Here, at last, was the opportunity I had been waiting for.

'Maybe your uncle should read it,' I said.

Greg shot me a panicked look. 'No. I couldn't possibly.'

'He's obviously more familiar with the play than I am,' I said. Then I smiled.

'I'd really rather not—'

'Please,' said Sam. She looked at him with a similar pair of wide blue eyes.

Greg seemed to deflate. 'Oh, all right, then. But I might be a bit rusty.'

We waited as he cleared his throat. Twisted his hands together. Peered at the script. Paced up and down a bit. Just when I was starting to think this was a bad idea, his whole posture and manner suddenly changed. His soft figure seemed to grow tense, stiff, as if he was coiled ready to spring. Then he began to speak, and the voice that emerged was not Greg's voice at all. It was low, and deep, and tortured. The dissimilarity to his usual voice was rather unnerving.

'I am determined to prove a villain/And hate the idle pleasures of these days.'

Sam and I both stared at him. A cold shiver ran down the back of my neck.

'Dive, thoughts, down to my soul: here/Clarence comes.'

There was a short silence. Then Greg relaxed, melting back into himself. He gave a small, shy smile. 'What do you think?'

Sam was looking at her uncle as if he had suddenly started levitating. 'Wow. Okay, you're amazing and I can't believe I didn't know you could do that.'

He waved a dismissive hand. 'Don't be silly. You'll do a much better job.' He handed her the script.

'I like this speech,' said Sam. She smiled. 'I'm going to give it a try.'

Five minutes later, when Sam had left, looking much happier, I turned to face Greg.

'What in the name of Laurence Olivier was *that*?'

Greg looked startled. 'Well, you did ask me to read it.'

'When did you get so... *good*? I mean, I knew you could act. But I didn't know you could do *that*.'

'I don't know what you're talking about,' said Greg. But as I stared at him there was something there that belied his words. Some slight sparkle in his eyes. A little upturn at the corner of his mouth.

'Oh, come on! You know how good you are. I can tell.'

Greg sighed. 'You're not going to let this go, are you?'

'No, I'm not.'

'All right. Just a minute.' Greg went to the bookshop's door, locked it, and hung up the *Back in Five Minutes* notice.

'You're actually closing the bookshop?' I said, rather scandalised.

'If we're going to talk about this, I'd rather not be overheard.'

'Okay. Fair enough.'

We settled in the armchairs near the Fantasy section.

'So,' I said. 'What else can you do? We already know you can sing. Can you dance? Perform acts of ventriloquism?'

He laughed a little. 'I wouldn't exactly call what I did last night "singing". It was always acting, for me.'

'What happened?'

He stared at his hands, which were clasped on his lap. 'I think the phrase is "life happened".'

'Greg. Don't give me that. They're not your words.'

He shrugged. 'Well, I am an actor.' He looked sad for a moment. 'Was. Was an actor.'

'Once an actor, always an actor.' I spoke as gently as I could. 'Tell me what happened.'

He was silent, and I started to think he wasn't going to reply. Then, suddenly, he started to speak. 'I wanted to go to drama school. I even went for an audition.'

'Did you get in?'

'Yes.'

'But you didn't take up the place?'

He shook his head. 'I lied to my family. Told them I didn't get in. It felt like—' He paused, and closed his eyes briefly. 'After Vicky... it didn't feel right. I wanted to stay here. It felt like the right thing to do.'

'I see,' I said, although I didn't, not quite. I realised I had had the opposite reaction. I had needed to get away from Shellcliff at the first opportunity, and keep away. This felt like a misplaced sense of duty from Greg. 'What about now?'

'Now?'

'Well, it's been a long time...'

He looked up sharply. 'It doesn't really fade, Charlotte.'

'No! No, of course not. I'm sorry, I don't mean that. I just mean... there's nothing to stop you acting now, is there?'

'I'm busy with work. Busy directing the play.'

'Those sound like excuses, Greg.'

He lifted his hands and let them drop. 'Okay. Fine. You want my last shred of dignity? I'm middle-aged. Chubby. Shy. No one wants to see me act.'

I stared at him for a long moment.

'That,' I said, 'is absolute *tosh*, and I think you know it.'

He raised an eyebrow. 'Tosh?'

'Yes. Tosh. Or, to put it in modern parlance, utter bollocks. Have you even *seen* your drama group? There are people of all ages, shapes and abilities.'

Greg frowned. 'I can't believe you just used the word "bollocks" in my bookshop.'

'Stop trying to distract me. Just listen. There are people who barely know one side of the stage from the other. And then there's *you*. If only you could have seen yourself read that speech. You were like some... shape-shifter or something.'

A blush crept to his cheeks. He looked away. 'You're very kind.'

'No. I'm not kind. I'm honest. Come on, Greg. When have I ever pulled any punches about this sort of thing?'

He looked uncertain. 'Never?'

'Damn right. So why not listen to me? Listen to your friend, the award-winning actress, and just give it a go, why don't you? I notice you still haven't cast the servant in *Theatre is Murder!*. He only has a few lines. It would be a start.'

He shook his head. 'Oh, no. I'm the director. It wouldn't be appropriate.'

'Why not?'

'I can't cast myself. It would feel like I was taking advantage.'

I scoffed. 'Darling, I know a director in London who cast himself as both Vladimir and Estragon in his own production of *Waiting for Godot*. Do you know what part I played?'

Greg shook his head.

'I played the *tree*. I didn't even have any lines. I just stood there, for nearly two hours, while he had a conversation with himself.'

He looked thoughtful. 'I suppose there'd be no harm in giving it a go.'

I smiled. 'No harm at all.'

An unexpected spark of fire crept into his blue eyes. He smiled. 'Right. Fine. I'll do it.'

I clasped my hands together. Victory was mine. 'Wonderful!'

*

There was still a little under a month to go until *Theatre is Murder!* opened, and things were starting to come together in rehearsal. Some props and pieces of costume had already been acquired, mainly after searching the local charity shops.

It was time for our first full run-through, and Nick arrived to help out with the lighting. There were many stops and starts as Greg shouted very low-tech directions at the lighting booth.

'Can you make the big light in the middle brighter? No, that's too bright. Better. Okay, can that other light be more... er... glittery?'

Nick emerged from the booth and walked up the aisle, brushing dust from his jeans. 'You're going to have to be more specific than "other light" and "glittery".'

'The light upstage left. It's supposed to represent a chandelier. So more... I don't know? *Glinty.* And we need moonlight in the next scene. That particular quality of romantic moonlight, you know? Gentle.'

'So, a gentle moon like in romantic comedies, as opposed to an aggressive moon like in werewolf movies.'

'That's it! You've got it.' Greg smiled, but the expression was quickly replaced by a frown. 'You're joking, aren't you?'

Nick sighed. 'I think we need a lighting plan.'

I sidled up to him. 'I bet you're wondering what you've let yourself in for.'

'A bit, yeah.'

'Just ignore his instructions, and you'll be fine.'

Greg glared at me and turned back towards the stage. 'All right, places for Scene Three, everyone.'

Fortunately, when we were actually performing, we ran through the scenes in good time. This was helped by the fact that several of the actors were now off script and word perfect, including – to my surprise – Rose.

I liked to think we had turned our rivalry into something positive. When Greg gave us his notes at the end of the first act, he said he could 'feel the animosity in the air', which I was starting to think was the best I could hope for. I still thought her approach to acting was completely over the top, but I had decided, if this was to work, I would need to ham it up a little, too. And it was actually proving quite good fun.

'Rose, maybe you don't need to swoon quite so dramatically onto the chaise longue,' said Greg, pacing around downstage. 'And Charlotte, I think you should look a little more disturbed when the police come to arrest Maggie. She's your rival, but she's also your friend.'

I saluted him. 'On it!'

'And Nick?' Greg paused centre stage and squinted at the tech booth. 'Nick? *Nick!*'

Nick stuck his head out of the booth. 'What, what, *what?*'

'Can you find a way to represent a snowstorm for the next scene? There should be some slidey whatsits, somewhere.'

'Slidey whatsits?'

'Yes. You know. Gobbles.'

Nick took a moment to compute this. 'You mean gobos.'

'Yes. That's the one.' Greg clapped his hands together. 'Positions for Act Two, please, everyone!'

Nick shook his head and disappeared back into the booth.

'I think love is in the air,' said a voice at my shoulder. I turned to see Harry, the actor playing Lord Moncrief. He smiled.

'You think so?' I said.

Harry lowered his voice. 'That man is about fifty per cent more intense than usual. And he was pretty tightly wound in the first place. He seems happy, though.'

I couldn't help smiling. 'Yes. I suppose he does.'

'You don't remember me, do you?'

I cringed internally. Not again. I really had the most dreadful memory.

I shook my head. 'No, sorry.'

'We were in *A Midsummer Night's Dream* together. I was Lysander.'

I stared at him for a moment. He was tall, and he had a beard, but there was something familiar about his eyes...

My hand flew to my mouth. 'You're *that* Harry! I'm so sorry. I'm utterly hopeless.'

He laughed. 'It's okay. I'm considerably hairier these days. You look exactly the same.'

'Oh, rubbish.'

'You do. I recognised you straight away.' He paused, gaze flicking to the stage floor. 'Maybe we could have a catch-up? A drink after rehearsal one night?'

'Ah.' There was, of course, every chance Harry was just being friendly. But it still didn't feel right. I had been hurt when Alex had gone to the gala with Selena, and I had no desire to become a hypocrite. 'I'm not sure.'

'Just as friends?' His voice was hopeful.

'Maybe. Let me get back to you.'

He looked a little disappointed, but smiled and nodded.

Greg bustled up to us. 'Why are you all still talking? Positions, please! Honestly. They expect me to work in these conditions.' He hurried away again.

I raised my eyebrows. 'Perhaps we'd better do as he says.'

25

Greg

Wednesdays tended to be quiet in the bookshop, so I would use them to catch up on admin, or tidy the shelves. I glanced out of the window. It had started to rain again, and the street was deserted. Of course this wasn't great for business, but we'd had a good Saturday, so I allowed myself a little smile of satisfaction.

Charlotte was tidying the stockroom, so I decided to flick a duster around. This gave me ample opportunity to practise my lines.

'Your tea, Madam,' I said, dusting the top of a boxed Jeeves and Wooster collection.

'I'm afraid I didn't hear anything, Chief Inspector.' I dusted the Crime shelves, smiling at the Vera Stanhopes.

'Did you call, Madam?' I ran the duster over the standee of Clive the Donkey, paying particular attention to his ears.

Ding-dong.

I jumped and glanced up. A man had entered the bookshop. He appeared to be in his late forties, with a handsome face which looked vaguely familiar. He was wearing a smart blue jacket, possibly silk, and definitely unsuited to the wet weather. He ineffectually tried to brush the water away, scowling the whole time. Then he approached the counter.

'I'm looking for Charlotte,' he said, in a velvety smooth voice. A voice that made me think of melted chocolate. And vampires, for some reason. 'Is she here?'

'Er... may I ask who you are?'

The man looked affronted. 'I'm Alex. Her boyfriend.'

'Oh,' I said, caught off-guard. Sometimes, when I was working in the shop, I got a feeling about certain people. This man was very attractive, and he didn't seem threatening, but he gave off... I suppose Nick would describe it as a certain 'vibe'. There was just something about him that I didn't trust. Something that felt wrong. But if someone were to ask me exactly *why* it felt wrong, I wouldn't be able to tell them.

'Well?' said Alex, an impatient edge to his voice. 'Is she here?'

'I'll... just go and check.'

I went to the stockroom door and knocked softly, half hoping Charlotte wouldn't answer.

'Yes?'

'Charlotte, Alex is here to see you.'

A long pause. And then: 'Just a minute.'

The door opened and Charlotte came out. After everything she had said about Alex, I was expecting an appropriately theatrical reunion: Charlotte rushing into his arms and kissing him. But instead she hung back, looking unsure.

'Alex,' she said. 'What are you doing here?'

He stepped closer. 'Do I need a reason to visit my gorgeous girlfriend?'

His voice was all smooth sweetness.

'I just... I didn't think you were coming. What with rehearsals and everything.'

Alex pushed a hand through his hair. 'Yes, well... we have a few days off, and I thought I needed a holiday. To be honest, they're all doing my head in.'

'Oh,' said Charlotte. 'I guess that's as good a reason as any to visit me.'

Alex frowned. 'Aren't you glad to see me?'

Charlotte laughed. It was slightly too high and tinkly, different from her usual deep, warm laugh. It sounded similar to the laugh I had used when I was dating Andy. 'Of course I am! I'm just a little surprised, that's all.'

'Ah, good. I was aiming for surprised.'

Alex bent down for a kiss. I glanced away, because obviously I had an excess of squirming English reserve. Sometimes I wondered how people kissed so effortlessly, particularly in front of strangers.

I coughed.

Alex looked in my direction. 'You haven't introduced me to your friend.'

'That's just Greg,' said Charlotte. 'He's the manager. Greg, this is Alex.'

'Yes,' I said, trying to keep an unexpected wobble out of my voice. *Just Greg. The manager.* 'I was here when he arrived.'

'Oh,' said Charlotte. 'Yes! How silly of me.' Again, that tinkly laugh.

Alex smiled at me. It was a wide smile, but it didn't reach his eyes. 'Nice bookshop, Greg. Bit old-fashioned. Does anyone actually read books these days?'

I tensed. So he was one of *those*. My instincts had been right.

Charlotte tapped him playfully on the arm. 'Stop it. Of course they do.'

Alex laughed. 'Fancy coming for lunch? My treat.'

'Oh,' Charlotte glanced at the clock. 'I'm sorry, Alex. I don't think I have the time. I have to work until five.'

Alex looked around the empty shop and sneered. 'There's no one here. Can't you just bunk off?'

I now knew, in no uncertain terms, that this chap Alex was a complete arse. There was honestly no other word for it. He exuded arrogance and entitlement from every pore. And Charlotte liked him. Possibly loved him. It was honestly baffling.

Charlotte frowned. 'I can't just bunk off. This is my job.'

That sounded more like the Charlotte I knew. Perhaps there was hope after all.

Alex smiled. 'Not for much longer.'

'What does that mean?'

'Come for lunch, and I'll tell you.' Alex turned his gaze towards me. 'Maybe Greg can cover for you?'

For a moment, I allowed myself to hope that Charlotte would refuse. She would stay in the bookshop, and I would make tea, and it would be a normal afternoon. But instead, she looked at me hopefully.

'Would you, Greg?'

I nodded, because of course I did. 'Certainly.'

'Good man!' said Alex. He kissed Charlotte on the cheek. 'Come on. I'm going to spoil you rotten.'

I watched them go, Alex's arm draped possessively around Charlotte's shoulders.

The doorbell went *ding*.

I was left alone in the bookshop. I knew, in no uncertain terms, what was going to happen. Charlotte was a tolerable work colleague, and the first real friend I had made in years, and now Alex was going to whisk her back to London.

'Bugger,' I said, aloud.

26

Charlotte

Alex stood on the high street, grimacing.

'Is this it?'

'Is what it?'

'I thought you said this place had come up in the world.'

'It has! There's the new Italian restaurant, for one thing. Well, it's not exactly new. It opened about twenty years ago. But you know what I mean.'

'Wow. How cosmopolitan.'

I laughed. 'Don't be a snob. You like Italian. We'd probably go to an Italian if we were in London.'

Alex sighed. 'I know. It's just… it's so long since I've seen you. I was hoping for something a bit more upmarket. Something special.'

I squeezed his hand. 'I'm quite happy with pizza. Honestly.'

'Oh, all right.'

We went inside. The waiter showed me to my usual table, the one in the corner where I liked to sit alone with a book. Most recently, I had been here for Greg's birthday. That had been a lovely evening, before I had allowed myself to spoil things. I pushed the memory of the gala photographs to the back of my mind. I would ask Alex about them, but not yet.

Alex raised an eyebrow. 'Are you all right?'

'Yes.' I forced a smile. I was not going to wallow in self-pity. Not when Alex was finally here. I was determined to have a nice evening. 'Are you going to tell me this exciting news, or what?'

Alex smiled. 'All in good time. Let's order first. And I think we should get some champagne.'

He clicked his fingers at Luca, the young waiter, who was standing behind the dessert counter. Luca gave me a funny look, and I found myself smiling apologetically. Although a treacherous voice in my head wondered why I needed to apologise for Alex's bad manners.

Five minutes later, we each had a glass of sparkling champagne in front of us.

'All right,' I said. 'We have our drinks. Now please will you tell me what's going on?'

Alex's face broke into a wide grin. 'You're going to love this.'

'Love what?'

'Guess!'

'What?'

'Come on, humour me. Guess.'

'You're the new James Bond?'

Alex laughed. 'I wish!'

'You're the new Doctor Who?'

'No. Way off!'

I glanced out of the window. If I craned my neck at the right angle, I could just about see the front of the bookshop. I wondered how Greg was getting on and if he was busy.

'Then I've no idea,' I said.

'Well, it turns out that Selena can't manage the performance schedule.' Alex grimaced a bit. 'Eight shows a week isn't at all what she's used to.'

Why did this not surprise me?

'So there's an opening for an alternate Catherine in *Autumn Songs*.'

'I see,' I said.

'They asked me if I had any ideas.' Alex twirled his champagne glass between his fingers. 'And of course I told them I wanted to play opposite you. I said I wouldn't countenance working with anyone else.'

'Oh,' I said. 'Well, that's... very considerate, Alex.'

He put down his glass. 'What's up?'

'Nothing's up.'

'I thought you'd be happy.' He sounded nonplussed.

I stared at the red and white checked tablecloth. In truth, I was confused, too. On the face of it, this was very good news. It meant I could go back to work. I would be able to act again. I could even play opposite Alex. That was what I wanted... wasn't it?

'I'm just a little surprised, that's all,' I said. 'When I spoke to the director, he made it abundantly clear that he thought I was too old for the role.'

Alex nodded. 'Yes, I've spoken to him about that. He was very apologetic. Said he didn't mean to cause any offence.'

'Really. Well, he'll have to speak to my agent.'

Alex sighed. 'Come on, Charlotte, don't be like this.'

'Like what? Did you think I would just say yes without giving it any thought?'

His bewildered expression told me that, yes, this was exactly what he had been thinking. He looked genuinely confused and hurt, and I felt myself soften a little.

'I appreciate the offer, Alex. I really do. And I will think about it. It's just... I'm quite enjoying working here. At the bookshop. I've told my sister I'll stay for a couple more months. And I'm involved in that lovely am-dram group I was telling you about.' I felt myself smile.

Alex gave a disapproving sigh and steepled his fingers together. 'You really need to prioritise, Charley. Start taking things seriously.'

I felt a little stab of annoyance. 'It is serious, though. The company are great. Greg's such a good director. A good actor, too.'

'They're amateurs, Charlotte.'

'Not this again. So what?'

'I just think you need to consider your future. That's all I'm saying.'

I folded my arms. 'What's that supposed to mean?'

He reached across the table and took my hand. 'This is a tough business. You're beautiful, and I know how good you are, but... well, you're not getting any younger, are you?'

I snatched my hand away. 'For God's sake, Alex! Neither are you.'

He looked momentarily wounded. Then he waved a hand dismissively. 'Yeah, yeah. I know—'

'I don't think you do know. Not really. You've barely spoken to me the last few weeks.'

'You're the one who moved away, Charley. I thought you'd be pleased to see me. I thought you'd be over the moon about the part. But instead you're going on and on about how happy you are in this dump.' His eyes were sad. He reached for my hand again. 'This means you can go home. We can both act together, just like before.'

I felt myself relent a little. 'I know that. But...'

'Please. At least consider it. I miss you.'

I sighed. 'I'm sorry. It's just... before I got here, I didn't realise how much I needed a break.'

He narrowed his eyes. 'A break?'

'Not from us! I don't mean that. I just... Don't you get tired of the grind of it all, Alex? The same show, day after day, week after week. And then as soon as that show closes, we're expected to jump straight into another one.'

'Yes, well, that's generally how theatre works.'

'I think I just needed a rest. In the proper sense of the word. Not the unemployed actor sense. But I will think about it. I promise.'

Alex was quiet for a moment. Then he rose from his chair and picked up his jacket. 'Maybe I should go back to the hotel.'

'There's really no need... Come on, Alex, you've come all this way. Let's just enjoy our meal, shall we? We can talk about this when I've had time to think about it.'

Alex gave a frown which was almost a pout. In the past, I had found this expression sexy. But today I found it irritating.

'Oh, sit down, won't you? Stop being such a grump.'

'Fine.' Alex slid gracelessly back into his seat.

The rest of the meal was awkward. I asked Alex about rehearsals for his new play, and he gave quite terse and lukewarm answers. I realised he was sulking, but I was determined not to rise to it. I would enjoy my pizza, come what may.

Things warmed up a bit when I told him more about the am-dram production, which he seemed to find hilariously funny. Almost a bit too funny, really, but I was glad to see him in a better mood.

'And you say that Greg bloke is a good actor?'

'Apparently. From the bits I've heard him read. He may look a bit... well, *dusty*. But he's a dark horse.'

His eyes sparkled. 'Maybe I could come and watch you. Drop in on a rehearsal.'

'Don't you dare!'

Alex laughed.

When we had finished, we walked back to my flat together. Things felt much more relaxed. I slipped my hand into his as we strolled along the seafront. It was late afternoon by that point, and the rain had cleared. A few people were walking their dogs on the beach, and a couple of families were seated outside the ice cream parlour. A burst of bright music came from one of the amusement arcades, accompanied by the cry of a seagull. A salty tang blew in from the sea, mixing with the smell of frying fish.

'You know,' said Alex, 'this place is actually quite charming, in a faded sort of way.'

'I'm glad you like it.'

'Ha! I wouldn't go quite that far. Nice place for a cheap holiday, maybe.'

'Snob.' I nudged him with my shoulder, then smiled. 'It is good to see you, you know.'

'Yeah, I know.'

'And I do appreciate the news about the show. I really will think about it.'

'I know you will. Just... don't leave it too long, okay? Fred says there are other actresses queuing up to play the role.'

Alex slipped his hand into mine, and we walked the rest of the way in silence. An old, comfortable, companionable silence. I hadn't realised just how much I had missed him. Deep down, I knew Alex was right. Shellcliff was a good place for a holiday, but one couldn't stay on holiday forever. Eventually, I would have to go home, and my home was with Alex, in the West End. I knew this was true.

So why did the idea of going back there feel so hollow?

27

Greg

Charlotte was late.

I didn't want to think about why she was late. She had not come back from her lunch with Alex, and she had sent her apologies for missing the evening's play rehearsal, but she had made no mention of taking the next morning off, too. I tried to distract myself with a cup of tea, but it was no good. I felt uneasy.

I didn't like this Alex character at all.

The doorbell rang at quarter to eleven, forty-five minutes after I had opened. I looked up, expecting to see Charlotte, but instead I saw Alex.

He walked up to the counter with his big movie-star smile in place.

'Morning, Greg,' he said. 'Charlotte's just coming. She went to get coffee.'

'I see,' I said, making a show of tidying the National Book Tokens on the countertop display. 'That's fine.'

Alex's smile widened. 'May I have a quick word with you, man to man?'

'Of course.' I tried to keep my voice as neutral as possible. 'How can I help?'

'Well, it's a bit awkward, really. Charlotte has the chance to originate a wonderful West End role, starting in September.'

'Oh,' I said, feeling a flicker of disappointment, because this meant that Charlotte would definitely be leaving soon. She would be required for rehearsals. I would need to recast *Theatre is Murder!*. 'That's... great news.'

'But she's in two minds. She seems to think she has an... obligation... to you and your bookshop. And the drama group.'

I felt myself perk up a little. How nice. But I didn't like Alex's tone. There was something vaguely unpleasant in it.

'I'm sure that's Charlotte's decision,' I said.

'Will you tell her she's under no obligation to stay?' Alex went on. 'You wouldn't want to hold her back, would you? You don't strike me as the selfish type, Greg.'

Now I did look at him.

'Of course not,' I said. 'But as I say, it's up to her—'

He smiled. Looked me up and down. Gave a little chuckle.

'What's so funny?' I asked, irritated now.

'Charlotte told me what a good actor you are,' said Alex. 'Despite being a bit dull and dusty, she said.'

I looked down at my shirt, cheeks burning. 'She said that?'

'Yes.' He patted me on the shoulder. I flinched. 'Don't worry, she was being nice. She's like that, Charley. Kind to... lost causes.' He grinned. 'Hey, it's great that you've found an outlet. It must be hard for someone like you, even in amateur circles.'

I stared at him.

'I came across lots of people like you at drama school,' Alex continued in a reasonable tone. 'Good actors, but nothing much to look at. No real star quality. Instantly forgettable.'

At this point, if I had been a more assertive or intimidating person, I could have done one of several things.

I could have asked him who the hell he thought he was.

I could have told him to leave the bookshop and never darken my door again.

I could, quite possibly, have punched him. Not that I would ever condone such behaviour.

But I didn't do any of these things, because I was shy, weak Greg. Greg the dull and dusty. I couldn't even be there for my sister when she needed me.

'Here she comes now,' said Alex, and strode towards the door.

I watched through the windows as Charlotte passed Alex a coffee. Then they shared a one-armed hug, and a kiss. The kiss made my skin crawl, and I looked away.

When I turned around again, Alex had mercifully disappeared, and Charlotte had stepped inside the bookshop. She was wearing a blue dress with big sunflowers printed on it, a real splash of colour against the dusty shelves.

The dull and dusty shelves.

She approached the counter, smiling as if nothing had happened.

'Hey, Greg.'

'Hello,' I said, somewhat icily.

'I've brought you a coffee.' She offered me a takeaway cup.

'Thank you.'

I made no move to take it, so she put it on the counter.

She frowned. 'Are you okay? You look a bit... down.'

'I'm fine.' I began to tidy the bookmarks next to the till. 'Just been busy.'

'Sorry I was a bit late.'

'That's all right. I managed just fine.'

'Er... good.' There was a pause. I hoped Charlotte would go and find something to do. Maybe hang even more bunting up in the Children's section. But she did not move from her position in front of the counter. 'There's something I've been meaning to talk to you about.'

'What's that?'

Another pause. Charlotte looked a little uncomfortable. Maybe she was going to tell me she was leaving. I braced myself.

'It's just... well...'

'Yes?' I said.

'I've... been thinking about Christmas.'

I blinked. 'What about Christmas?'

'Well, it's the most important time of year for trading, isn't it? I was thinking we ought to start planning. Maybe I could design the Christmas window.'

I kept my eyes fixed on the bookmark display. 'Yes, if you like.'

'And... I was thinking. Maybe we could put on a special evening for our customers. Late night shopping. Drinks. Performances. Maybe Sam could perform a monologue. You could read something Christmassy. You have such a lovely voice. Maybe you could read from *A Christmas Carol*. You would make a fantastic Scrooge.'

I had always loved *A Christmas Carol*, so under normal circumstances this would not have upset me. But now her words struck a nerve.

'Do you really think so?' I said quietly.

'Yes. I mean, you act all grumpy and guarded but we all know you're a softie really.'

'Is that really how you see me?'

'Well... yes...'

'Grumpy. Dull. Guarded?'

'I didn't say anything about dull...'

I sighed and ran a hand through my hair. 'Look. I don't want to be a part of any ridiculous bookshop performance, okay? I'm not an actor. I'm a bookseller.'

Charlotte's mouth turned down at the corners. 'But you're so, so good—'

Charley is kind to lost causes...

'Look,' I said, attempting a smile. 'I know you mean well, Charlotte, and I appreciate the encouragement. But the servant in *Theatre is Murder!* is enough for me, for now. So can we please change the subject?'

Charlotte looked a little put out, but she nodded. 'All right.'

I turned away and started to tidy the greetings cards. Unfortunately, having suggested a subject change, I could not think of a way to revive the conversation. We continued our work in silence.

28

Charlotte

Greg was quiet over the next few days. His quick change in attitude confused me. Less than a week earlier, he had seemed excited about performing again, frequently going over his lines in the bookshop (with full theatrical blocking and gestures). But now it was as if some barrier had been raised between us. He seemed upset, and not his usual self at all.

I supposed it was something I'd said. I thought back over our conversation about the Christmas celebration. What I had meant to do was ask Greg if he wanted me to stay. I still hadn't made up my mind about the role in Alex's play, and I had really wanted to ask Greg for his views on the matter. Unfortunately, the discussion had not progressed that far.

Fortunately, we were kept busy in the bookshop. The weather had finally cleared, and we were enjoying a warm spell, with families flocking to the beach. A steady stream of customers came through our doors, which put an end to any awkward silences.

One evening, I was making dinner and mulling over my career options when my phone rang. I checked the display. It was my sister.

'Hi, Sarah.'

'Hi, Charlotte. Er... are you free to meet up?'

'I was just about to have dinner. Are you okay?'

'Yes.' There was a brief pause. And then: 'Can I come over? It's urgent.' There was an odd wobble in her voice. Sarah rarely sounded upset. There was clearly something wrong.

'Yes, of course.'

I poured extra fusilli and pasta sauce into the respective pans, and tried to keep myself occupied while I waited for my sister. I grated cheese and made a salad. Then, as an afterthought, I went to the cupboard and took out a bottle of red wine and two glasses. I rarely drank during the week, but something told me that Sarah might appreciate one.

She arrived half an hour after our phone call, looking tired and flustered. Her eyes were red-rimmed, as if she had actually been crying.

'Oh, come here,' I said, folding her into a hug. We rarely embraced, but this time she hugged me back tightly. 'Sit down.'

She took a seat at the kitchen table while I plated up the pasta.

'Thanks,' Sarah sniffed.

'What's wrong?'

She looked at me with watery eyes. 'I think I'll have to close the shop.'

I almost dropped the parmesan. 'I'm sorry?'

'Everything's going up. The rent, the electricity... I've been looking at the sales figures for the last few months, and I don't think I can make it work.'

'Oh, no.' There was a leaden feeling in my stomach. 'But I thought we were doing well?'

'I thought so, too. But what can we do if prices are increasing everywhere?'

'Isn't there anything we can do?'

'I've thought about diversifying. More cards, toys, souvenirs, that sort of thing. But even with those things, I just don't think we're going to get enough people through the doors, if the first half of the summer is anything to go by. I think I can keep going until the end of September, and then I'm going to have to close the shop.'

'But that would be so sad,' I said. 'It's been here forever.'

Sarah wiped her eyes. 'I should have known I wouldn't be able to make it work. You were right, Charley.'

'No,' I shook my head. 'No, I was wrong. People really love the place. We just need to look at other ways to get the word out. You're saying September. That still gives us almost a month, yes?'

Sarah nodded. 'I should tell Greg. Just in case.'

I thought of the state Greg was in after our last meeting with Sarah, his distress at the thought of losing his shop and home.

He would be devastated.

'No,' I said.

Sarah looked startled. 'But he needs to know.'

'Yes, of course. But not yet. Leave it with me. I'll see if I can work something out. Then I'll talk to him. I promise.'

Sarah looked unconvinced. But then she nodded. 'All right.'

Neither of us had much of an appetite, so we picked at our pasta, and then drank a large glass of wine each. We didn't talk much: there didn't seem to be much left to say.

We hugged again on the doorstep, and Sarah walked away, still looking sad, but with a slightly more confident posture than before. She seemed to really trust me. I was determined to make things right. I just needed time to think.

I was pacing around the living room when an idea struck me: Alex. He knew lots of famous people, far more than I did. And he had a huge following on social media. He had always embraced that sort of thing, while I had been cautious and stayed off the platforms. Now, I could see how advantageous it could be.

Alex was in the ideal position to highlight the plight of a small bookshop.

I rang him.

'Hi, Alex.'

'Oh. Hi, Charlotte. I didn't expect to hear from you so soon.'

'Not busy, are you?'

'No. Of course not.'

'Good. I really need your help. I've been talking to my sister, and she says she might have to close the bookshop.'

'Oh, dear. Well, that's hardly surprising, is it? It was always a long shot.'

I suppressed my annoyance. 'I'm sure we can make it work. We just need more attention, a few more customers. I was wondering if you could get word out to your followers? Endorse the shop.'

'You want me to help save an indie bookshop?'

'Yes.'

'Are you sure I'm the best person for this? I'm not much of a reader, Charley.'

'I know. But that doesn't matter, does it? You would be helping out a small business.'

'I see. So you're saying it would make me look good?'

'Well... yes. But that's not really the point. You'd be doing my sister and me a big favour.'

'Right. And it would be good PR.'

I rolled my eyes. 'Sure, Alex.'

'All right, then. I'll do it.'

I was actually a little surprised. 'Oh. Right. Thank you!'

'When should I come up again? I could take a few selfies in the bookshop, show that I really do endorse it.'

'Whenever you like, really. But Alex, could you please keep this to yourself for the time being? There are... staff... who haven't been told yet.'

There was a brief silence.

'Oh,' said Alex. 'I see. Staff. Don't worry, my lips are sealed. Height of discretion, me.'

'That's wonderful, Alex. Thank you.'

We said our goodbyes, and I went to bed feeling slightly more optimistic about the situation.

Now, I just needed to work out how to break the news to Greg.

*

The next day was Sunday, so I didn't have the chance to speak with Greg. I reluctantly made my way to a *Theatre is Murder!* rehearsal. I was tempted to stay in my flat, but I knew from experience that this never made me feel better. Keeping busy made me feel better. And the rehearsal would keep me busy, even if it meant I had to face Greg while knowing I was keeping quite a big secret from him.

I had prevaricated a little too long, which meant I was five minutes late. This was annoying, but I knew it wouldn't matter, because there was always ten minutes of chit-chat before the rehearsal actually started.

I pushed open the auditorium door, and immediately knew there was something odd going on. Most of the company was clustered around a figure at the front of the stalls. Greg stood a little way apart, hands thrust into his trouser pockets.

'Hello?' I said, walking down the centre aisle.

The group parted to reveal Alex. He gave me a big smile.

'Surprise!' He stepped forward, arms open.

I stepped back a little. 'Alex. I wasn't expecting you back so soon.'

'I figured there was no time like the present,' said Alex. 'And I thought I'd make good on my threat to come and watch you rehearse this thing.'

I glanced towards the stage, and saw Greg immediately look away. Had he found out? Had Alex let something slip? No. Surely he wouldn't do that. 'I see.'

Alex's face fell a little. 'Aren't you pleased? Don't I get a hug?'

I stepped forward and allowed myself to be embraced. It felt a little awkward, with the company watching us.

'You haven't said anything about the shop, have you?' I whispered.

He raised an eyebrow. 'Of course not. I just wanted to be here. As you seem to have fallen in love with this place, I thought: if I can't beat her, join her!'

'Right. Well, it's... great you could make it.'

'I was just chatting with the group. They seem like a lovely lot.'

'Yes. They are.'

'They're very taken with you.'

'Are they?'

'Absolutely.' Alex smiled, and gestured towards the middle of the front row. 'Shall I sit...?'

'Anywhere's fine.'

He flopped into a seat, gracefully draping one long leg over the other. I caught a few of the chorus members staring at him. They quickly averted their eyes when they saw me looking.

We embarked on a full run-through. My route to the back-stage area meant that I was obliged to walk past Greg. He looked at me accusingly.

'What's he doing here?'

'He's here to give me a bit of moral support,' I said. 'And I'd thank you to be nice to him.'

'Oh, don't worry, I'm always nice,' said Greg.

I sighed. 'Greg, if this is about what I said in the bookshop—'

'What did you say? I've forgotten.'

'I really didn't mean anything by it.'

'It's fine. Now can we please get on?'

I gave my most dramatic sigh and strode past him. Honestly. If he knew the lengths I was going to to spare his feelings.

'Beginners onstage, please!'

*

I really wasn't in the mood.

It happens to all actors, and you plough on through anyway. It's like any public-facing job. Actor, waiter, bookseller. You paint on a smile, and you carry on.

That's what I did. I gave the role everything I could. I stomped and swooned and screamed in all the dramatic places, and I think the bits in between were quite good, too. But all the time, a part of me was aware of Alex, a polite smile on his face. He probably thought the play was awful, and he would probably tell me so later.

One person who was incapable of hiding his feelings was Greg. He looked miserable. I wondered why he was so unhappy. One thing I did notice: he was keeping as far away from Alex as possible.

'All right,' he said, when the curtain had fallen on Act One. 'Tea.'

The word 'tea' lacked his usual enthusiasm. I watched as he slunk towards the kitchen. He resembled a walking, talking raincloud.

I was about to follow him, but before I could, a hand fell on my shoulder. I turned to see Alex.

'Hi,' I said. 'Did you enjoy?'

'I wasn't going to say anything,' he said, glancing over his shoulder to make sure the others were out of earshot. 'But seriously... what the fuck?'

'I'm sorry?'

He laughed. 'This play is terrible.'

'Shush! Yes, I know.'

'If you know, why are you doing it?'

'Because it's fun. And the acting is good.'

'*Some* of the acting is good. Mainly yours. Why are you wasting your time on this? Not to mention your talent.'

'Not this again.' I took a deep breath. 'I'm going to get some tea. Would you like some?'

'I may need something stronger, if I'm going to sit through Act Two.'

'Oh, stop being so unpleasant, Alex.' I swept past him towards the kitchen.

'Chill out. I was only joking.'

I turned to look at him. The thing was, I knew he wasn't joking. Not really. Once I would have laughed along with him, but now I was starting to recognise Alex's jokes for what they were: arrogant little nuggets of meanness. I was almost tempted to tell him this, but I didn't want to spoil my own evening.

'Would you like some tea or not?' I said.

He shrugged. 'Okay, whatever.'

Alex followed me into the kitchen, where Greg was fulfilling his secondary role as Guardian of the Kettle and Dispenser of the Tea.

'Two teas, please,' I said.

Greg gave me a curt nod.

'I don't suppose you have a coffee machine, do you?' asked Alex.

Greg gave him a look which seemed to say: *Oh, God, not another one.* 'No, sorry,' he said. He presented each of us with a mug of tea. 'Sugar's over there.'

Alex inspected his mug and scowled. It had a picture of Noddy and Big Ears on it, from the Enid Blyton books. It was the oldest mug in our motley collection of mugs, and one we generally avoided due to excessive tea staining.

I looked at Greg, wondering if this was his version of being passive aggressive. But he was the picture of innocence, as usual.

Alex took a sip, and grimaced.

'Is it okay?' I asked.

He coughed. 'Yeah. Great.'

'Excuse me,' said Bex, sidling up to us. 'Please can I get a picture with you, Alex?'

Alex's face lit up. 'Sure!' He passed me his mug, and I took it automatically.

It always took Alex a long time to orchestrate the perfect selfie – I had seen him in action many times at the stage door after *The Next Thirty Years*. It was mildly annoying, but at least it gave me a chance to speak to Greg.

'Are you okay?' I asked, softly.

'Never better,' he said.

'Are you still up for... you know?'

Greg hesitated, throwing a nervous glance at Alex. But then his face hardened. 'Of course. Why shouldn't I be?'

'Well, that's... good.'

I turned around. The photoshoot seemed to be coming to a close. Alex handed Bex her phone and gave her his most charming smile. 'There you go.'

'Thanks,' said Bex. 'My mum loves you! She's seen all your shows in the West End.'

Alex's face fell slightly. I suppressed a smile.

He sauntered back over to me. 'Right. Are we starting again, or what?'

'Beginners onstage in five minutes,' said Greg. Then he drained his tea, his hand shaking slightly, and left the kitchen.

29

Greg

I paced up and down the narrow backstage area.

During Act One, I had spoken my lines from the front of the stalls. I had made the excuse that I needed to see the blocking again, but really I hadn't been in the mood to go onstage, not with Alex watching. He had soured the atmosphere, somewhat. But when Charlotte asked me if I was still up for performing, I found that I couldn't say no. So here I was.

It would be fine.

True, this was my first acting role in... what? Twenty years? More? But it would be fine. I had been practising in front of the mirror at home. My performance was as polished as I could make it.

I paused in my pacing and took a breath. Then I projected as loudly as I could. 'Act Two beginners, please!'

I heard footsteps onstage, followed by Charlotte and Rose's raised voices. I stood in the wings, awaiting my cue.

MAGGIE (*Rose*): How dare you!

OPAL (*Charlotte*): I'm sorry. I had to ask.

MAGGIE: I'm not capable of murder!

OPAL: You may not be, but His Lordship is more than capable of acting on your behalf.

MAGGIE: But... he's my patron!
OPAL: Exactly.
MAGGIE: He's a respected member of the aristocracy.
OPAL: And your point is...?
There is a knock on the door.

This was it. I straightened my waistcoat.

MAGGIE: Enter!
A SERVANT enters.

I stepped onto the stage.

SERVANT *(Greg)*: Did you call, Madam?
MAGGIE: Yes. Please give this message to Lord Moncrief.
She hands him a letter. The servant exits.

I hurried off.

*

'Well done, Greg,' said Charlotte, when Act Two was finished and I had gathered the company together for notes.

'Yes,' said Rose. 'Well done.'

'Thank you.' I didn't wish to be patronised, and I was still a bit annoyed with Charlotte, but I felt quite pleased with myself. It wasn't much, but it was a start. 'It went quite well, didn't it?'

'Very well,' said Nick. 'You were great.'

Sam whipped her hands out from behind her back and produced a small plastic Oscar, which she offered to me. 'Congratulations!'

I gave a peal of laughter. 'Well, I would have preferred an Olivier, but I suppose it will have to do.'

'Acceptance speech!' said Nick.

I chuckled and held the 'Oscar' aloft. 'I would like to thank all of you for browbeating me into submission.'

Sam and Nick applauded.

'I don't understand,' said Alex. I turned and saw that he had risen from his seat on the front row of the stalls. He was looking at me with an indulgent smile on his face, as if I had just performed an interesting trick. 'What's the big deal?'

'This is Greg's first stage appearance in over twenty years,' said Charlotte.

Alex looked perplexed. Then he gave a bark of laughter. 'That? You're making a big fuss about *that*? It was honestly pathetic.' He stood ramrod straight and parroted my words in a monotone: 'Did you call, Madam?'

I stared at him. 'It... I did my best...'

'If you think that's such a big deal, maybe you're not cut out for life onstage,' said Alex. 'Stick to bookselling. I would.'

Charlotte glared at him. 'Alex!'

I looked at Alex, all swagger and arrogance. And I decided I had finally had enough.

'Just who do you think you are?' I said softly.

Alex blinked. 'I beg your pardon?'

'You barge in here, interrupting our rehearsal, and then you humiliate me in front of my company. Why are you even here?'

Alex grinned and took a step closer to me. 'You want to know why I'm here?'

'Alex...' Charlotte reached for his arm, but he brushed her off.

'I'm here,' said Alex, 'because Charlotte begged me to come. She wants me to help save your precious bookshop.'

I froze. Something clenched in my stomach. 'My bookshop?'

Alex slapped his forehead. 'Oh, silly me! Did Charlotte not tell you? The bookshop's closing. Some rich git will probably turn it into yet another coffee place. Well, bring it on, I say. This place could do with some decent coffee.'

'No... that can't be right.' I looked at Charlotte. 'Tell me he's lying?'

Charlotte shook her head. 'I'm sorry, Greg. I was going to tell you—'

'You didn't even think I deserved to know? I've been running it for twenty years.'

'Yes, I know, I'm sorry.'

I felt tears rush to my eyes. I turned away from them and hurried up the aisle.

'Greg, wait...'

I ignored Charlotte. I needed to get away from them all.

I needed to save my bookshop.

30

Charlotte

I rounded on Alex. 'Was that really necessary?'

Alex held up his hands. 'He was going to find out sooner or later.'

'You promised you wouldn't tell him.'

His smile faded. 'Did you hear how he spoke to me? I won't let a pathetic little creep like him show me up.'

My anger finally spilled over. I put my hands on my hips. 'No, Alex. You're showing yourself up! How dare you come here and insult my friends?'

Alex laughed. 'Friends? I thought you said Rose hated you.'

'Excuse me?' said Rose.

I sighed. 'Sorry, Rose. I didn't mean it.'

'That's what you told me at lunch. You said she was a nightmare to work with.' Alex was warming to his theme. 'Oh, and Sam is needy, and Lydia just gives you the cold shoulder all the time.'

'I think you should go, Alex,' I said.

'Why, so you can run after your precious Greg? The Greg you said was dull and stuffy and irritating? He's probably the worst actor I've ever seen.'

Nick, who had been standing half in shadow in the wings, suddenly sprang forward, fists clenched at his sides. 'Why don't you just shut the *fuck* up?'

Alex blinked at him. 'Excuse me?'

'Nicholas, please,' said Rose. 'This is a *theatre*.'

Nick ignored her. He was completely focused on Alex, his sharp brown eyes boring into his skull. 'You walk in here, all: "Look at me, I'm a West End star, blah blah blah, aren't I great?" Then you treat the kindest, nicest man in town like he's dirt.'

'How dare you!' seethed Alex. 'Don't you know who I am?'

'No,' said Nick. 'I don't. But for what it's worth, I think you're a fucking wanker.'

'Nick!' Rose clutched at her pearl necklace.

Nick looked at her for a moment. Then he sighed and glared down at the floor, deflated.

'You know what?' he said. 'I'm done.'

'But... what about the lights?' I said.

'Find someone else.' Nick thrust his hands into the pockets of his jeans and slunk down the aisle. The auditorium door slammed shut behind him.

Alex looked at me in wonder. 'Really, Charlotte. How do you tolerate these... *people*?'

'I beg your pardon?' said Rose.

'Not you, Rose, obviously,' said Alex. 'You seem to have a bit of class. But, Charlotte, between the ridiculous bookseller and that... whoever *that* was? You'll be glad to get back to London.'

I stared at him. I couldn't believe that, after everything he'd said, he was still assuming I would go along with his plan.

I straightened my shoulders. 'I'm not going back to London, Alex.'

His eyes widened. 'Sorry?'

'You heard me.'

'But... you can't stay here.'

'Just *watch* me.'

'But... what about your career?'

'Theatre isn't limited to London, Alex.'

'What about me? I miss you, Charlotte.'

'I'm quite sure you'll survive. You've got your little friend Selena, for a start.'

He looked stunned. Under any other circumstances, his expression might have been comic. 'What are you talking about?'

'I saw the gala photo. I'm not stupid.'

'We went as a cast. She's my co-star. I would much rather have gone with you.' He reached for my hand. I pulled away. 'Come on, Charley. Come home with me.'

'I can't.'

'But... there's the play. Our friends. We had plans.'

'They were your plans, Alex,' I said. 'And they were your friends. We never talked about what I wanted. There never seemed to be time. I just got swept up in it all.'

'But... it was *our* show. Ten years, Charlotte.'

I softened a little. 'That's as may be,' I said. 'But sometimes it's good to move on.'

Alex shook his head. 'I don't believe you. You'll get bored. Once the novelty wears off, you'll be on the first train out of here.'

'We'll see,' I said.

Alex hesitated for a moment. Then he turned on his heel and stalked out of the theatre.

I felt a hand brush my shoulder. I turned and was startled to see it was Rose.

'Are you all right?' she asked, softly.

'Yes.' I felt tears rush to my eyes. 'Yes, I'm fine.'

Rose frowned, apparently unconvinced.

I sniffed, swallowing the tears. 'We should probably find Greg and Nick.'

31

Greg

I stood in my spare room, surrounded by ninety years of theatre memorabilia. I was currently staring at the three large boxes in the corner, still taped closed. Twenty years they had stood there, and I had not been able to bring myself to open them.

Perhaps now was as good a time as any. I needed a reminder of why I hadn't stepped on a stage in so many years. Something to ground me in reality.

I took a deep breath, and tucked my fingernail under the edge of the brown tape on the top box. The glue had deteriorated, and the tape soon came loose. Best get it over with: I tore the whole strip away, and opened the box.

The first item was a theatre programme. No surprises there. I had so many. But this wasn't from the Shellcliff Palace. This was all the way from London.

Anything Goes.

My breath caught in my throat. We had all gone down to watch her professional debut. My mum and dad and me. I had watched in wonder as she twirled and high-kicked in a line of dancers, part of a chorus, but still completely herself, and completely recognisable.

Vicky. My sister.

I was seventeen at the time. My sister had been in London for a little over three years, studying Musical Theatre at the London School of Performing Arts, with a particular focus on dance. She had attended on a full scholarship. I wanted to be a performer, like her.

I knew I couldn't be a dancer. I was completely uncoordinated. Rubbish at anything remotely physical. Besides, it wasn't something that boys tended to do, not where I came from. But I could act. I had been told this in my English class, when we had to read out extracts from Shakespeare's plays. I had always been the first to volunteer.

There was no drama programme at my school, so the theatre group had filled a real void. It opened up a new social life for me. I was popular, and I was happy. Two things I had never been at school.

Whenever Vicky came home, it was like sharing the space with a person from another world. Her voice had changed, grown softer and, at the same time, more precise. She told me about London, about the famous actors who gave masterclasses on her course, of her visits to the theatre. It all sounded impossibly glamorous to me. I wanted to go, too. And I told her that.

She looked at me in surprise, her forehead crinkling. 'But what would you do?'

'I'll be an actor,' I said.

She laughed at that, not unkindly.

There was no money for me to audition, let alone train. I realised later that it was expensive enough paying for Vicky's dance lessons, even before she got her scholarship. This was why my parents hadn't supported me. They couldn't. But as a teenager, I thought they wouldn't, and I was jealous of my sister, who seemed to have everything.

'You can still act as a hobby,' said my mum. 'You love the drama group.'

This was true. I did love the drama group. But I wanted more.

'Maybe I can introduce you to some people,' said Vicky, when I spoke to her about it. 'Put in a good word for you.'

By some miracle, she managed to get a director friend to give me a chance. At the age of eighteen, I found my first professional acting job at a theatre in nearby Hull.

It was the best year of my life. I had a ridiculously small part in an Agatha Christie play, and spent the rest of the time working as a stagehand (or assistant stage manager, to be more precise). But I loved every minute. And I soon learned that not everyone in the company had gone to drama school. There were other routes. I started to think I would be able to work my way up, to build a career through experience alone.

Things were going well.

Then Vicky had an accident. It was a fall onstage. A broken ankle. For anyone but a dancer or an athlete, it wouldn't have mattered so much. But my sister was off work for weeks. And when she finally started dancing again, it was clear something had been lost. Some flexibility. But more than that, some spark.

She took extra singing lessons in the hope of securing leading musical theatre roles. There followed a period of failed auditions, of *not what we're looking for*s. Of doors shut in her face.

Finally, my sister came home.

I had just turned nineteen, and was 'resting' at the time. I had appeared in a couple more plays at Hull, but I hadn't been needed for the latest production. I saw a job advertised in the window of Seaswept Books, handwritten in biro: Bookseller Wanted. I applied for the job, thinking working with books would still leave me with the time and energy I needed to attend auditions and keep up with my amateur dramatics. Although it was harder work than I'd expected, it helped up to a point. I saved some money and began to give serious consideration to attending drama school. Perhaps I could make it work.

Vicky was not so optimistic. She tried to put on a brave face. She helped coach the children at a local dance school. She talked about retraining as a teacher, or maybe teaching dance classes full time. She returned to London briefly to attend an audition for a new production of *The Wizard of Oz*, but was rejected in favour of one of her theatrical friends.

After that day, it was as if a light had gone out. She spent more and more time at home, shut in her old bedroom, away from us. I assumed all she needed was time, that after a while she would emerge from this shell and be her usual bubbly self again.

Her family and friends wanted to help, to find a way to cheer her up. The Grand Hotel had started to hold summer party nights. I thought my sister, with her love of dancing, might appreciate a night out, with drinks and a disco. I invited some of her old school friends.

Vicky seemed less than enthusiastic about the idea.

'I'll only come if I can invite my boyfriend.'

I hadn't known she had a boyfriend, but of course I agreed.

I invited Thomas. I had known him since school, and we had grown close while attending the drama group together. I had developed quite a crush on him. While I might have been a little naïve, I had decided that this could be the evening I finally told him how I felt. I planned on asking him to dance.

I spent a lot of time getting ready. I wore my one and only suit, complete with a William Morris-patterned tie I had found in a local charity shop.

Despite being a bit of a throwback, the hotel had done everything possible to create a party atmosphere, with disco lights, balloons and streamers.

I arrived early and found a table near the main entrance. I checked my watch. Thomas was late.

Lydia had been chatting to a group of Vicky's school friends. She saw that I was on my own and came over, carrying two glasses of wine. She handed one to me.

'Thanks,' I said.

Lydia frowned. 'Are you all right?'

'Yes. I'm fine.'

Lydia wandered off again. I waited for fifteen minutes. The door opened, and I looked up hopefully. But it wasn't Thomas. It was Sean Henderson.

I went very still in my seat. I had tried to forget about Sean, but now it all came rushing back. The chanted insults, the punch to the stomach, the locked toilet door.

Sean sauntered over to my sister, who was chatting to another girl near the bar. He placed a hand on her waist, then leaned down for a kiss. Then they continued to make their way around the room, Sean smiling at Vicky's mates, and generally playing the role of the attentive boyfriend.

Finally, they reached my table.

'Hello, Greg,' said Vicky. She gestured at Sean. 'This is—'

'Yes,' I said stiffly. 'I know who this is.'

Sean stuck out a hand. 'Hi, mate.'

I ignored the offered hand, and addressed Vicky. 'What's he doing here?'

Vicky narrowed her eyes. 'Sean's my boyfriend.'

'He used to beat me up,' I said.

'Ah, come on, we were just kids,' said Sean.

'It went on for years,' I said. My voice was almost a whine. 'You knew about it, Vic.'

'Oh, grow the fuck up, Greg,' snapped Vicky. 'The world doesn't revolve around you.'

'I never said it did.'

Lydia appeared at Vicky's shoulder. 'What's going on?'

'Nothing,' said Vicky. 'Just our little brother being a brat, as usual.'

'I'm not being a brat,' I said.

Sean held up a hand. 'Look... I get the feeling I'm not welcome here.'

'No,' I said. 'You're not.'

'I'll go and get us a drink, shall I?' said Sean. 'Let you talk to your brother.' He pressed a kiss to Vicky's cheek, then sloped off towards the bar.

Vicky glared at me. 'What's wrong with you?'

'Nothing. I just wondered why you've brought my school bully to the evening I organised for you.'

'You don't get to decide who I spend time with.' My sister's voice rose in anger. 'You think I want all this? Balloons and a stupid disco? I'm not a kid! Sean makes me happy.' She glanced around the room, and then, in a lower voice: 'We're getting married.'

I stared at her for a moment. Lydia's eyes had also gone very wide.

'You can't marry him,' I said.

'I think you'll find I can.'

'But... he's a loser. He's bad news, Vicky.'

'I can do whatever I like,' she said, and now her own voice sounded petulant. 'It's none of your business.'

'But what about your career?' said Lydia. 'Your life onstage?'

She gave a harsh laugh. 'What career? I don't have a career, not anymore. Look at this dump, Lyd. Do you really think there are any opportunities for someone like me here?'

The fact that she'd just referred to our hometown as a dump made me sad. I tried to ignore the feeling. 'You could move back to London.'

'They don't want me.' Her voice shook. 'No one cares about me. No one except Sean.'

'That's not true,' I said. 'Please don't give up your dreams, Vic. Not for a man you don't even love.'

She flinched backward as if I'd hurt her. Then her eyes narrowed. She straightened her shoulders.

'How do you know I don't love him? What do you even know about love? You live your life like it's some sort of fairytale, dreaming of success. And you dare to call Sean a loser?' She looked around with a sneer. 'Where's your date, anyway? Stand you up, did he?'

I was still young enough for her words to hurt. She was only parroting the things I had told myself in my more insecure moments, but it was as if hearing them spoken aloud, by a person who I had always loved and looked up to, suddenly gave them real power. My eyes stung.

Lydia put a hand on Vicky's arm. 'Come on. There's no need for that.'

Vicky flinched away. 'You both think you can run my life for me. You know nothing about me or what I want. Well, fuck this. Fuck both of you.'

Lydia held out a hand. 'Vicky. Please...'

Vicky turned away from us. She walked towards the bar, took Sean's hand, and together they strode through the disco lights, past the balloons and streamers, and towards the door. Lydia and I both called her name, but she didn't answer. She didn't even look back.

The party went on without her.

*

He dumped her.

I wasn't entirely surprised. In some ways, this is what I had been hoping for (though I would have preferred her to walk away from him). But I couldn't take any comfort from it, because my sister was just so sad.

I didn't have time to help. I finally had an audition at the London School of Performing Arts. Night after night I rehearsed my monologue, trying to make sure it was perfect. One day, while my parents were both at work, I caught the train to York, and then to London. I was excited. Perhaps this would be it. A brand new chapter in my life.

The audition went well, and I left the college in high spirits.

I got back to King's Cross to find that multiple successive trains were cancelled. I was stuck at the station for hours, and didn't arrive home until after 1am.

I knew something was wrong before I even stepped through the garden gate, because the lights were still on downstairs. Neither of my parents stayed up so late, and Lydia and Vicky were always home by midnight.

Inside, I found my mother crying on the sofa, and my father pacing the floor. Lydia was standing by the phone, wringing her hands.

They looked at me with frightened eyes.

Where have you been, Greg?

Where's your sister?

Do you know where she is?

I shook my head. Managed to reply that I didn't. That I had been in London all day.

An hour later, there was a knock on the door. The police had arrived. There had been an accident, they said. I felt as if I was standing outside my own body. I could hear the police officer talking, but the words seemed distorted, far away, as if they had nothing to do with me. Vicky was in her car. There had been a sharp corner, taken at speed. A wall. Alcohol may have been involved.

Afterwards, my mother looked straight at me.

'You should have been here,' she said.

I was numb. The world felt unreal. I didn't know what to say.

'I'm sorry,' I said. 'I was at my drama school audition. The train was cancelled.'

'He's not even upset.' Lydia looked at me with swollen eyes. 'Why can't you just be like everyone else?'

*

Nothing was quite the same after that.

The day after my sister's funeral, I took all the theatre posters down from my walls. I packed my theatre programmes into a box, and put them on the top of my wardrobe. Later, I moved them into the bookshop.

A couple of weeks later, an acceptance letter arrived from the London School of Performing Arts. I tore it up.

Performing had lost its appeal. Apart from anything else, it would mean I couldn't always be here. And I needed to be here.

When I wasn't here, bad things happened.

Back in the present, my phone rang. I peered at the illuminated display. It was Nick.

I let the call go to voicemail. Then I made an effort to pull myself together, wiping my eyes on my sleeve.

For many years, I had dwelt on the if onlys. If only I had been kinder, if only I hadn't spoken that way to Vicky, if only I hadn't gone to the audition and had stopped my sister driving away from Shellcliff that night. If only, if only, if only... But I had been too much of a coward to stand my ground, to help my sister in any meaningful way. We had lost her, because I had been a coward.

Well, I wasn't going to be a coward anymore. This time, I was going to fight.

32

Charlotte

After Greg left the rehearsal, I went round to the bookshop and knocked on his door. I also tried his mobile, but there was no answer. When I looked up at the windows of his flat, I saw they were dark. I left him a message, saying I hoped he was okay and asking him to call me.

The next morning, I was surprised to find Greg in the bookshop, unpacking a box of books and shelving them in the General Fiction section.

'Morning,' I said, as gently as I could.

He turned and smiled at me. 'Morning, Charlotte. Here, put this in Fantasy, would you?' He thrust a copy of *A Wizard of Earthsea* into my hands.

Greg had apparently started early; there were already three empty boxes on the floor. I took the book to the Fantasy section and shelved it under Le Guin.

'Are you all right, Greg?'

'Never better!' His tone was one of forced cheer.

I tried again. 'We were a bit worried about you last night.'

'Oh, there's no need to worry about me.' He picked up a stack of books and walked over to Crime, where he began to shelve with a manic fervour. I had never seen Greg move so fast, or work so hard. It was discombobulating.

'I'm really sorry about last night. I didn't want you to find out like that.'

Greg froze for a second, then shelved another novel. 'It's fine. It's given me a lot to think about... In fact, I think it's helped me achieve some clarity.'

This didn't sound good at all. 'What do you mean?'

'Well, I've realised this theatre malarkey really isn't for me at all. I've decided to focus on the bookshop. Rose will take rehearsals from now on.'

'I'm sorry?'

He turned to look at me, that forced little smile still in place. 'Don't be sorry! I'm not. It feels... liberating. I'm going to get so much more work done. This place needs my full attention now.'

The sound of a Mozart ringtone filled the shop. Greg paused, took out his phone, frowned, and shoved it back in his pocket again. Then he carried on shelving books.

'Greg... you do know if Sarah closes the shop, there's nothing we can really do about that, right?'

He gave a nervous laugh. 'Nonsense! If we just work hard enough, we can turn this place around.'

'But it's completely out of our hands...'

'I'm not giving up my bookshop,' said Greg. 'They'll have to drag me out of here by my ankles.' He paused. 'You know, I was thinking of increasing our opening hours. Seven am to ten pm, maybe, to catch the evening crowd. I wonder if we could finally install that coffee machine?'

I was silent for a moment. Then I made a decision.

'Excuse me, Greg. I just need to pop out for ten minutes.'

*

I went straight to the library. Nick was on the front desk, exactly where I had hoped to find him. I waited until he had finished assisting a customer, then approached. He looked at me in surprise.

'I need your help,' I said.

'What can I do for you?' He smiled. 'I'm assuming you don't want to borrow any books.'

'I'm worried about Greg. Have you spoken to him?'

His mouth twisted. 'I've tried. He's not answering my calls.'

'He's pretending everything's okay, but he's really upset about the shop. He's threatening to work twelve hour days.'

Nick looked thoughtful for a moment. Then he shrugged. 'Well, he does enjoy his job.'

'He wants to install a coffee machine. And he's quit the theatre group.'

'Bollocks,' said Nick.

A woman shot him a disapproving look from Romance and Sagas. Nick ignored her.

'Would you come and talk some sense into him?' I said. 'He likes you. I think he'll listen to you.'

Nick sighed. 'Okay. I'll do my best.' He waved to his colleague. 'Anna? Please could you watch the desk? I'll be back soon.'

We got to the bookshop to find Greg pricing postcards, individually, even though there was a big sign on the card rack which said: *Postcards £1.*

Nick and I exchanged glances.

'Greg,' I said. 'There's someone here to see you.'

Greg looked over. His brow furrowed when he saw Nick. 'Oh. It's you.'

Nick was apparently undeterred by this slightly cold reception.

'Hey, Greg. What's going on?' His voice was soft, warm, gentle.

Greg blinked at him, then began to price the postcards again. 'Nothing. I'm just getting a few jobs done around the place. Really, I've been lax.'

'Come and have a cup of tea with me.'

'I've got too much to do.'

Click, went the pricing gun.

'I'm sure that can wait,' said Nick.

'No, it can't.'

Click.

'Charlotte tells me you've left the theatre group. That doesn't sound like you.'

'It's fine. I wasn't good enough.'

Click.

'I disagree,' said Nick. 'I don't know much about these things, but I thought you were great.'

'We need you,' I said.

Greg was still for a second. Then his shoulders hitched. He threw down the pricing gun, and spun to face us.

'Didn't you hear me? I'm not good enough! I've never been good enough, but I used to think I was and I was so... bloody... selfish.' His eyes filled with tears. 'My sister died because I was selfish. Did you know that? I should have been with her, and I wasn't!'

Greg started to shake.

'No one needs me...' he said. Then he sobbed.

The display had me frozen, helpless, to the spot. But Nick didn't hesitate. He swooped forward and gathered Greg into his arms. Greg clutched at him, crying into his shoulder.

'Hey.' Nick rubbed Greg's back. 'Hey, love. It's okay. You've done nothing wrong, okay?'

'It was all my fault.'

'No, no, it wasn't.' He held Greg tighter.

Greg made a sniffing noise. 'I'm hopeless. I can't even make this place work.'

I stepped forward. 'That's just not true. We know how much you care about the bookshop.'

Nick patted Greg's back. 'I think we all need that tea now, yes? And maybe some cake?' He began to disentangle himself.

'No,' I said. 'I'll get it.'

I left them to it. By the time I returned with the tea tray, they were sitting huddled together on the old sofa, Nick's arm still around Greg, and Greg leaning on his shoulder. He looked washed out, his eyes red and swollen, but he had stopped crying.

I put the tea things on the counter and handed a mug to Greg. He smiled weakly. 'I... maybe I should take some time off.'

'That sounds like a good idea,' I said.

Nick smiled. 'Maybe we could finally go for that coffee.'

Greg nodded. 'Yes. Yes, I think I'd like that.'

We sat in silence for a while, sipping our drinks.

'I just wish there was something I could do,' said Greg.

Nick looked thoughtful. 'We could try and get some more publicity for the place. Drum up some support.' He started to smile. 'I think I know someone.'

'Who?'

He pointed to the stack of Crystal Moontide books on the display table.

'Oh, no,' said Greg. 'You're not serious?'

'I'm dead serious. I think she'd help us. She once arranged a sit-in at a big bookstore in New York that was marked for closure. Stayed there for about a week with a load of her fans. It made world news.'

'And did it work?'

'Well... no. The shop still closed. But it *could* have worked.'

Greg sighed. 'All right. Call her. It's got to be worth a try.'

*

I offered to look after the bookshop while Greg took a few days off. It felt strange being there alone, but I took the opportunity to do some serious sorting out. I tidied the Children's section, changed the window display, and threw away all the out of date publishers' catalogues.

By lunchtime on the third day, I was feeling very pleased with myself. I decided that I had earned a jacket potato, topped with beans and quite possibly cheese as well. I'd been eating a lot of jacket potatoes recently. I wondered briefly what Alex would think of my new culinary favourite, and then realised I didn't care.

It was so liberating, not caring what he thought.

Shortly after lunch, the door flew open and a tall woman strode into the shop. She looked positively ethereal in her long silver dress, like the Snow Queen from a pantomime version of Anderssen's story. But when she smiled, the expression was as warm as the sun.

I stared, utterly enchanted. I had seen the author photos, and I knew there was only one person this could possibly be.

'Crystal Moontide?' I asked.

'You must be Charlotte,' said Crystal Moontide. She looked around the bookshop. 'What a lovely shop! It smells of chips in here.'

'Sorry. That's my jacket potato.'

'It's making me hungry, whatever it is,' she said. 'Your nice librarian friend said the bookshop's in a spot of trouble?'

I nodded. 'Sadly, yes.'

'I've been thinking of how I can help,' said Crystal Moontide. 'And I've had an idea.'

'Oh. Great.'

'I have a first edition copy of my very first novel,' said Crystal. 'I thought I could auction it and donate all proceeds to the bookshop. I'll even sign it.'

'Oh.' I felt slightly disappointed. I'd hoped for something bigger. I wasn't convinced that a signed book would help as much as Crystal seemed to think it would. 'That sounds wonderful. Thank you.'

'I'll sign every page,' said Crystal. 'So the lucky fan will have my signature four-hundred-and-fifty-seven-times.'

'Right,' I said. 'Good.'

'And I'll include a handwritten micro-story on the inside back cover. The last edition with a micro-story sold for quite a lot of money!'

I was no longer entirely sure what Crystal was talking about. 'Thank you. We really appreciate it.'

'Just leave it with me, love. There's hope for your lovely shop yet.'

With that, Crystal Moontide swept out of the shop in a swish of glitter and silk. Well, at least it was a start.

Intrigued in spite of myself, I went on the internet and did a search for 'Signed First Edition Crystal Moontide with Micro-Story.' When I saw the amount raised at Crystal's last auction, I almost dropped my coffee. This couldn't be right. But the more I read, it seemed that it was. Apparently, there were some very wealthy Crystal Moontide fans out there.

I immediately called Sarah to tell her.

33

Greg

After three months of rehearsals, it was finally opening night. *Theatre is Murder!* was about to be unleashed on an unsuspecting public.

I wasn't ready. I had always felt a bit nervous on the first night of each production I had directed, but that was more of a second-hand feeling, born of hoping the cast would do well. By that point, my job was more or less done, so it was easy to hide backstage. But tonight I would step into the spotlight for the first time in years. And my nervousness was on a completely different scale.

'What are you doing?' said Lydia as I rearranged the display of raffle prizes for the fourth time that evening. We always held a raffle to raise extra funds for the drama group. It suddenly felt very important that the donated items, which included two bottles of wine, a box of Quality Street and a pack of assorted soaps, were perfectly spaced out on the table, in order of height.

'Just, you know, making things look nice,' I said.

Lydia frowned. 'I really don't need your help.'

'It's fine.' I fussed with the tablecloth, smoothing out invisible wrinkles.

'Shouldn't you be getting changed?'

'In a bit.'

My sister rolled her eyes. 'Greg. You're trying to distract yourself. Go backstage and put your costume on.'

'But don't you need some help selling—'

'No.' I flinched a little, and her expression softened. 'You'll be fine. Now get lost, why don't you? And for heaven's sake, enjoy yourself.'

I went backstage. I was the first to arrive in the dressing room, which suited me fine. I didn't want the other men in the company to see how anxious I was. They didn't need a nervous director making them nervous, too.

When I had donned my costume, I inspected my reflection in the full-length mirror. At least, in my waistcoat and tie, I looked the part of an impeccably dressed servant. I adopted an expression of judgemental snootiness.

I reminded myself that this was supposed to be fun, that I had been looking forward to it. It was just a play, after all. Nothing bad was going to happen. I mean, I could miss my cue, or forget my lines, or trip over the furniture, but other than that...

I felt like I was going to throw up.

Look at you, said an intrusive voice inside my mind. *Getting all worked up over nothing. It's pathetic.*

I shook my head.

You should really be over this by now. Everyone else just gets on with it. Why can't you?

I wondered if it was too late to back out. Maybe I could persuade Lydia to go on as the servant instead.

You're so bloody boring and set in your ways. Did you really think you could do this? You're no good at it, anyway.

Then, another remembered voice: *I don't know much about these things, but I thought you were great.*

Nick.

Despite the circumstances, it had felt nice when he had comforted me in the bookshop. When Charlotte had gone to make the tea, we sat down together on the sofa, and he draped his arm around my shoulders, pulling me close.

'You're all right, you know,' he said, giving me a gentle squeeze. 'There's nothing wrong with you.'

I sniffed. 'I'm sorry to make such a scene.'

'Don't be daft.' I could see him smiling out of the corner of my eye. 'If you get nervous in the play, just imagine the audience is naked.'

I grimaced. 'I'd really rather not.'

'Imagine them in silly hats, then.'

We had stayed like that for quite a while, even after Charlotte brought the tea.

Now, in the dressing room, I straightened my shoulders. Nick wanted me to go on. And more importantly, *I* wanted to go on.

If anything went wrong, I would follow Nick's suggestion, and imagine the audience wearing silly hats.

Taking a deep breath, I left the dressing room and made my way to the wings.

34

Charlotte

As instructed, I arrived forty-five minutes before curtain-up. I was relieved to see Nick back in the tech booth. At least as far as the lighting was concerned, we were in safe hands.

I stuck my head around the door. 'Is Greg here?'

Nick smiled. 'Yes.'

'Is he okay?'

'He's a bit nervous, but I think he's looking forward to it, actually.'

A wave of relief washed over me. 'Good.'

I went to the slightly gloomy backstage area where the dressing rooms were located. It was more than ten years since I'd last shared a dressing room, so the arrangements at the Shellcliff Palace had come as a bit of a shock.

It was the very same dressing room I'd used as a teenager, but I'd forgotten just how chaotic it was. I find you notice these things less when you're young and hyped up on adrenaline, caffeinated pop and dreams of fame and glory.

When I'd arrived for our dress rehearsal a few nights before, I'd just stood in the doorway for a while and stared. It was certainly much smaller than I remembered. The dressing table was already covered in makeup, makeup brushes, hair accessories, packets of sweets, hats, gloves, and cans of hairspray. The costumes were squashed onto two small clothes rails. There were only two mirrors in the room – one above the dressing table, and a full-length one leaning against the wall next to the adjoining shower room.

Unfortunately, on opening night I was the last to arrive, and there were already six women in the room. They were getting ready, constantly reaching around and over each other to grab items of clothing, to take turns in front of the mirror, and to help adjust each other's costumes. The dressing room resembled a scene from a modern ballet, or possibly an interpretive dance.

Sam was the first to notice me. 'Charlotte! Hi! We saved you a place.'

She pointed to the corner of the dressing table, where there was a clear space the approximate size of a paperback book.

'Er… thanks,' I said, putting my handbag on top of it, lest it should be claimed by someone else.

At least there was a plastic chair, so I was able to sit in front of the mirror to do my makeup.

Ten minutes later, I was all dressed and ready to go. I looked in the full-length mirror, and Opal stared back at me. I felt a little shiver of excitement. With the exception of the Witch on the Pitch (who didn't really count), this was the first time I'd been in costume as a new character for more than a decade. Opal was so different to Constance – so much more assertive and stroppy – that this felt genuinely refreshing. I couldn't wait to stand on that stage and share her with the audience.

A bell rang, alerting us that it was five minutes until curtain-up. The play opened with Maggie and Opal already onstage, so I left the dressing room and went to get into position, reclining on the chaise longue.

I took a letter from the pocket of my dress and began to 'read' it. Meanwhile, Rose had seated herself at the dressing table, and was 'applying' Maggie's makeup. This was the first image the audience would see.

There was a snatch of 1930s jazz music, and a whirring noise as the faded red curtains slid open. Beyond the edge of that small, contained world onstage, there was a vast, dark cavern, filled with amorphous shapes. A darkness that could quite easily swallow you, if you set one foot wrong.

I realised my palms were sweating. I hadn't experienced stage fright for years, so the sudden rush of nerves was startling. I thought of Greg. Maybe it was contagious. I tried to forget about the audience, and focus on the fictional dressing room, and on Maggie and Opal.

MAGGIE (*Rose*): La la la la-la-la laaaaa!
OPAL (*Charlotte*): Are you all right, Maggie?
MAGGIE: I'm just warming up the old vocal cords.

And, just like that, we were off.

It all felt a little stilted at first. The response from the audience was muted, as if they didn't quite know what to make of the play. Perhaps they were expecting a serious crime drama, something more like Agatha Christie. But then, around ten minutes in, something changed in the atmosphere.

The audience started to laugh.

I particularly enjoyed my scene with Lord Moncrief, which was rubbish of the highest order, but still marvellous fun to perform.

LORD MONCRIEF (*Harry*): You misunderstand, my darling. I want only to make you a star!
OPAL: But what about Maggie?
LORD MONCRIEF: Ah! I thought I loved her, but ever since I learned that her fortune had been lost at sea, I have felt my passion cool. Entirely coincidentally, of course.
OPAL: Of course.

In the context of the play, Lord Moncrief is described as a 'villain' and a 'blackguard'. Harry took these instructions to heart; if Lord Moncrief had had a moustache, he would have twirled it. He also had excellent comic timing, and was very handsome to boot.

I found I was rather looking forward to the kiss we would share in Act Two.

It was soon time for Greg's first scene. Opal was offstage at that point, so I stood in the wings to watch him.

He entered with the tea tray, and I saw immediately that he was shaking. The teapot was almost rattling as he made his way across the stage.

SERVANT (*Greg*): Your tea, Madam.
MAGGIE (*Rose*): Thank you.

Greg plonked the tray down on the dressing table. But he must have performed this action with unexpected force, because it destabilised the teapot. It toppled over, rolled as if in slow motion towards the edge of the tray, and then fell with a *clunk* to the stage floor. Fortunately, it did not shatter. The spell of the performance, however, was temporarily broken.

There was a loud guffaw from somewhere in the auditorium. Greg looked out at the audience, cheeks flushed, his face a mask of frozen horror. My heart ached for him. After working so hard to overcome his nerves, it felt like such terrible luck.

Then, quite suddenly, he snapped back into character. He bent over, retrieved the fallen teapot, and placed it back on the tray. Then he addressed Maggie.

SERVANT (*Greg*): I'm awfully sorry, Madam. I shall brew a fresh pot.

There were chuckles from the audience. Greg turned around, looking surprised. And pleased. He hurried off, clutching the teapot.

At the interval, we all reconvened on the stage, with real tea this time.

'I can't believe it,' said Greg, shaking his head. 'I've spent ten years making tea for you lot, with barely a spillage, and *this* is the night I drop the bloody teapot.'

'Sod's law,' said Nick, who was taking a break from the tech booth. 'You were great, by the way. Very funny.'

'Yes, well. I'm glad you enjoyed it.' Greg sounded irritated, but I had the impression that this was an act. He was still smiling.

After that, there was no stopping him. During the second act, he made full use of his range of comedic facial expressions – quite a useful skill when you don't have many lines. His look of shock and outrage when Lord Moncrief declined a scone would stay with me for a very long time, as would his ad-libbed line in the final revelation scene ('The man doesn't like scones. I knew he was a wrong 'un').

The evening went by in a blur of low level panic, laughter, lost and found shoes, lost and found makeup, people shushing each other, forgotten lines, remembered lines, ad-libbed lines, a temperamental sound system, and the overpowering scent of hairspray. And a kiss from Lord Moncrief AKA Harry, which I think we both quite enjoyed.

I hadn't had so much fun onstage for years. It was just so good to act for the sheer pleasure of it. I thought of Constance, the part I had played opposite Alex. I had loved that role, but perhaps I had been going through the motions a little by the end of the ten-year run. It had felt like a job – albeit one with a touch of glamour – while tonight felt like a joy.

After we'd taken our bows, and the curtain fell, we all looked at each other and smiled. Then Sam let out a cheer, and I joined in, and suddenly the company was exchanging hugs and claps on the back. I looked at these people – my company and friends – with real warmth.

I realised I had been Charlotte de la Mer for a very long time. Charlotte de la Mer had been a survivor, and a professional. She had been intimidating, glamorous and aloof, but, if I was honest with myself, not entirely real. Of course, I still missed Alex. We had been together for ten years. But I was starting to think that he liked my professional persona more than he liked me.

Charlotte de la Mer was at home in the West End. But perhaps Charlotte Smith belonged right here, in this little theatre by the sea.

35

Greg

The first night was over. The audience had left, and our volunteer ushers – led by Lydia – had already finished tidying the auditorium, collecting any abandoned wine glasses or sweet packets. I was alone onstage, resetting the scene for the opening of Act One. I heard the occasional peal of laughter from the dressing rooms, where some of the cast were still getting changed.

I was just pushing the chaise longue back into place when I heard a floorboard creak behind me. I looked around to see Nick.

He smiled at me. 'Need a hand with that?'

'Yes please. Thanks.'

He placed his weight against the other end, and together we manoeuvred the bulky piece of furniture back into position.

'I thought that went well,' said Nick. 'Didn't you?'

'Yes.' I gave him a broad smile. 'Couldn't have been better, really. Apart from me dropping the teapot.'

Nick waved a hand. 'It doesn't matter. All part of the magic of live theatre.'

'I suppose so.' The memory of my mistake cast a sudden shadow over the evening. 'You don't think it was too much, do you? Ad-libbing like that?'

'Not at all.' He took a step closer to me and took my hand in his. 'I meant it when I said I thought you were great.'

I looked down at the floor. 'It's silly, I know. But I have such a fear of looking ridiculous.'

'You're not ridiculous.' He reached out with his free hand and brushed my cheek. 'You're brave and clever, and I think you're...' He tailed off and turned his face away, mumbling something under his breath.

'I'm sorry?' I said. 'What did you say?'

'I said I think you're lovely.' He blushed, still not meeting my eyes.

I stared at him for several long, silent moments.

Nick, handsome, kind, wonderful Nick thought I was *lovely*.

'Oh,' I said. 'I see. Right. Gosh. Thank you.'

I instantly wanted to melt with shame. All the classic romances I'd read, and *that* was the best I could come up with? I waited for Nick to let go of my hand, to turn away. It was no more than I deserved. But he didn't move.

I forced myself to meet Nick's eyes. He stared back at me. The corner of his mouth twitched. Then he burst out laughing.

Which was so much worse.

Heat rushed to my face. 'Oh no. I'm so sorry, I didn't mean it to sound like that. I like you too... please don't laugh.'

'I'm sorry.' He shook his head. 'I'm not laughing at you. Well, I am, but probably not for the reasons you think.'

I continued to stare at him, completely flummoxed.

He leaned in closer. 'You're very sweet. And I would really like to kiss you. If you don't mind?'

'I... think I would like that.'

A warm expression crossed Nick's face. Every feature seemed to grow soft. He tilted his head and touched his lips to mine.

My last kiss had been with Andy. Our kisses had always been somewhat... perfunctory, as if he was going through the motions. I had played along in the hope that something would spark between us, that he would finally notice just how much I cared for him.

Cared being the operative word; recently, I had begun to doubt that I had really loved him. It had all felt like a performance, by the end.

Nick's kiss was not strained or dismissive. It was deep and warm. And I knew within about half a second that I would not have to pretend with him. His arms came around to rest on the small of my back, pulling me into a closer embrace. Any remaining feelings of self-consciousness flew out of the metaphorical window. I kissed him back and held him tight.

We stood like that, wrapped around each other on the empty stage, for quite some time.

There were raised voices from the direction of the ladies' dressing room, growing louder. I heard a door bang, and the sound jolted me out of my romantic haze. I broke the kiss.

'We should go,' I said. 'I have to lock up.'

Two gentle hands slid around my waist again. 'Are you okay?'

'Yes.' I gave a wide smile. 'Never better. You?'

'Yeah. I'm great.' He narrowed his eyes. 'You know, we don't have to leave.'

'They'll want to go for a first night drink.'

Nick gave a playful smile. 'That chaise longue looks very comfortable. We could just stay here all night.'

I adopted an expression of mock outrage. 'How dare you! This is a refined cultural institution, you know.'

'Just joking.' His smile turned wicked. 'Maybe after the last performance?'

I laughed. 'Stop it!'

Nick planted a kiss on my cheek. 'Pub?'

'All right.'

I offered him my hand, and we left the stage together. I turned off the house lights and locked up the theatre, and we went to catch up with the company. For once, I was in the mood to celebrate.

*

The rest of the week was a delight. The performances were successful, with enthusiastic, responsive audiences who laughed in all the right places. I didn't drop the teapot again, although I did indulge in a spot of ad-libbing.

Nick and I started to spend more time together. We went out for coffee twice, and lunch once. We kissed onstage after each performance, and once in the tech booth. I was positively giddy; even the uncertainty about the future of Seaswept Books didn't sour my mood.

Speaking of which, Charlotte and I made good progress in the shop. Maybe it was my high spirits, but I found myself agreeing to most of her interior design ideas. I agreed to get rid of the dusty brass lighting fixtures, and we installed new cream lampshades so that the shop was now bathed in soft, natural-looking light. I even let her swap the cushions on the armchairs.

After learning that Nick was prepared to wield a paintbrush, I asked him to come over, and the three of us spent a pleasant day repainting the shop's exterior. We chose a deep blue for the door, and a pinkish red for the shop sign. Nick went up the ladder to paint the sign, and I avoided the stray drops while keeping everyone supplied with coffee. We made a good team.

Inside, Charlotte and I tidied most of the clutter and rearranged the stock so more books were face-out and on prominent display. The shop was already looking brighter and, much to my surprise, I found that I liked it. It was still cosy, just a little more welcoming and easier to navigate.

I did, however, draw the line at Charlotte's new 'up-cycling' idea.

'But I saw it on Instagram, darling! Apparently it's quite trendy.'

'Charlotte, I am *not* cutting up books to make Christmas decorations.'

'Why not? They're only proofs. It's not as though we can sell them.'

I folded my arms. 'You can't cut up books.'

'Why not?'

'Because they're books! It just feels wrong.'

Charlotte sighed. 'Well, you're going to have to store them in your flat, because they're not staying down here.'

'Fine, fine.'

I packed the old proofs into three boxes and took them upstairs, where they would be safe from Charlotte and her scissors. When I got back to the bookshop, I found her behind the counter, systematically going through my cupboard of useful nick-nacks, a bin liner clutched ominously in one hand.

I didn't even feel like protesting. Maybe I truly was a changed man.

36

Charlotte

Lydia raised her glass of wine. 'An absolute triumph!'

Theatre is Murder! had just played its final performance. It had been quite a week; invigorating, exhausting and fun in equal measure. Now, we were gathered at the front of the auditorium, by the table which we had used as our makeshift bar during shows. The audience had left, and now we were free to celebrate... and pick apart the entire evening.

'Act Two could have been a little faster,' said Greg. 'The pace, I mean.'

'Really?' Nick smiled. 'I noticed you milked your entrance for all it was worth. It shouldn't take that long for a man to serve tea. You were ad-libbing again and everything.'

'Yes, well, there are no small parts, only small actors,' said Greg.

'I'll drink to that.' I clinked my glass against his. 'You were wonderful, darling.'

He blushed a little. 'Thank you.'

'I'm knackered,' said Sam, reaching for a can of Pepsi. 'I need sugar.'

I laughed. 'If you think you're tired now, just wait until you start your course.'

The theatre went quiet. Sam's eyes went wide with panic. Then she glared at me, and I realised what I had just said.

'What course?' asked Lydia.

'Nothing,' said Sam.

'What course?' Lydia was insistent. Her tone was sharp.

Sam sighed. 'I've been applying to drama schools.'

'What?' said Lydia. 'We've talked about this. I thought you were going to university. I thought we'd agreed.'

I exchanged an uncomfortable glance with Greg. The atmosphere suddenly felt very tense.

'I don't want to go to uni, Mum,' said Sam. 'I want to be an actor. I've got an audition in a couple of weeks. One of the top London drama schools.'

Lydia looked at me. 'And you knew all about this?'

'Sam told me,' I said quietly. 'She wanted some advice about her auditions.'

'Just who do you think you are? Putting these silly thoughts into my daughter's head—'

'*Mum!*' cried Sam.

I felt anger bubble up to the surface. 'Sam came to me! She *asked* me if I would help her. And do you know why? It's because she was scared to talk to you.'

Lydia flinched. A look of pain flashed across her face, but she quickly recovered. 'How dare you?'

'She said you wouldn't understand, that you didn't want her to go to drama school. I tried to persuade her to tell you, Lydia, I really did. But she wouldn't have it! What was I supposed to do?'

'Oh, I don't know, maybe stay out of things that are none of your business?'

I took a deep breath. 'Look. I'm very sorry if I overstepped the mark—'

'*If?*'

'I didn't mean to hurt anyone's feelings. I'm sure, if you talk to Sam, you'll be able to work things out. She only wants to follow her dream, that's all.'

'Follow her dream?' Lydia narrowed her eyes. 'How can you say that? After what happened to Vicky. After what *you* did to Vicky?'

I felt as if Lydia had just struck me. I took a step back, and glanced at Greg. He had gone pale.

'What are you talking about?' asked Greg.

'That last audition, the one that pushed Vicky away from performing? That was *her!*' Something had snapped inside Lydia. She was almost spitting with rage. 'She was supposed to be Vicky's friend, and she snatched that opportunity from her. Stole it from under her nose.'

Greg looked at me with wide eyes. 'Is this true?'

I shook my head. 'It wasn't my fault.'

'It never is, is it?' seethed Lydia. 'But you were quite happy to go along with it, as I recall. After everything she did for you. All the support and encouragement. Then, you just happily dumped her and went swanning off to your new life in London.'

'It wasn't like that at all!' I said. 'I was really upset by the whole thing.'

'Oh, yes, *really* upset,' said Lydia. 'Upset enough to not come to the funeral, to avoid us for twenty years. And now what? You come back up here and think you can interfere in our lives? In my daughter's life?'

I trembled. I had the horrible feeling I was going to burst into tears. I hadn't wanted to admit it to myself, but everything Lydia had said was true.

'I was trying to make things right,' I said, staring at the floor. 'I know what I did all those years ago was wrong. I was just trying to help.'

'By pushing my daughter down the same road?' said Lydia.

'I'm right here,' said Sam. 'And you're the one pushing me!'

Lydia was quiet for a moment. Then she shook her head, and looked at me again. 'You know, I actually thought you'd changed. When I saw you at the drama group, and helping Greg, I actually thought you'd become a better person. More fool me. You're still the selfish little bitch you always were.'

Tears rushed to my eyes. 'Lydia...'

'You're not welcome here,' she spat. 'You're not welcome in Shellcliff, and you're certainly not welcome in the drama group. Why don't you sod off back to London and give us all some peace. You and that horrible boyfriend of yours are perfect for each other.'

I looked to Greg for help. Confusion and disappointment were written across his features. He opened his mouth as if he was going to say something, but then he seemed to change his mind, and turned away, towards Nick.

'Greg?' I said quietly.

'I think, perhaps, it might be best if you went home,' he said.

I blinked. 'Right. Yes. You're right, of course.'

I spun on my heel and hurried up the aisle. I had thought that I finally belonged somewhere, that the past was behind me. But I had been wrong. Well, I would not interfere again.

It was only when I was outside the theatre, in the cool sea air, that I allowed myself to weep.

*

The audition had been for a production of *The Wizard of Oz*.

I had wanted the part of Dorothy. I had wanted the part more than any other part before it, but I knew it would go to Vicky. Vicky was beautiful and glamorous and a wonderful all-round performer. She would be perfect for the role.

We had kept in touch since leaving drama school, even when she got cast in show after show, and I was seemingly unable to catch a break. I had returned to Shellcliff after six months of failed auditions, and I was considering giving up acting and choosing a more 'sensible' career (in my sister's words). Then, one day, Vicky returned home too. A broken ankle had meant some time away from the stage, and now she was also struggling to find her next role.

It felt good to have my friend back, to have a partner in adversity. For a while, we cheered each other on, even auditioning for some of the same roles.

Finally, Vicky got a callback for the role of Dorothy. I offered to accompany her to the final audition in London, because that's what friends were for. Lydia had wanted to go too, but she hadn't been able to get the day off work. So I had gone instead.

Vicky was excited about the callback. And surprised. I wasn't remotely surprised, but I was a little bit jealous, and disappointed not to have made the shortlist myself.

She chattered for the entire train journey. I knew it was because she was nervous, but by the time we reached Doncaster, it was starting to give me a headache. I didn't have the heart to tell her to be quiet. After all, it was the first sign of success she had had in months.

When we finally got to the theatre, we were shown to a dressing room, where she unceremoniously threw her coat at me. 'Hang this up for me, will you?'

I obligingly found a hanger for the coat.

'Could you get me a drink of water? I'm parched.'

The words *get it yourself* were on the tip of my tongue. But I didn't say them. Instead, I went in search of a glass of water.

I returned to the dressing room in time to hear horrible vomiting noises coming from the toilet cubicle.

I knocked tentatively. 'Are you all right?'

'Yes.' The door opened, and Vicky poked her head around the frame. She looked pale. 'Will you go and tell them I'll only be a few minutes?'

I went to the auditorium.

A woman approached me with a clipboard. 'What name is it?'

'Vicky Harrison,' I said. 'But she's—'

'Great,' she said, cutting me off. 'Take a seat.'

'But I'm...'

It was too late. She was already walking away.

I took a seat at the end of the front row. I watched the parade of Dorothys, all of whom were very good. I kept glancing at the auditorium door, but there was no sign of Vicky.

After six auditionees, I was starting to tire of 'Over the Rainbow'. I was also starting to get worried. I checked my watch. Where *was* she?

Clipboard Woman's voice rang out around the theatre: 'Vicky Harrison!'

I stood up. I would have to go and retrieve my friend from the dressing room.

The woman looked straight at me. 'Vicky Harrison?'

'No,' I said. 'That's my... listen, I just need to fetch my friend...'

The audition panel was seated at a table at the front of the auditorium, near the orchestra pit. A man rose to his feet and turned to face me. He had an air of... creative officialdom about him, stylish hair and smart shirt coupled with sharp, discerning eyes. I was reminded of Boris Lermontov in *The Red Shoes*, which wasn't exactly comforting.

'Do you want to audition, or not?' he asked.

I shook my head. 'You don't understand. I'm not—'

'It's a simple enough question,' he said, not unkindly. 'Do you want to audition, or not?'

Time seemed to slow down. He was right, of course. It was a simple question, with a simple answer. I glanced towards the door. Still no sign of Vicky.

Did I dare? It wasn't as if I hadn't worked for it. I had attended the first round of auditions, after all. I knew I hadn't been at my best, and now here I was, being offered a second chance.

'Well?' said the man.

I took a deep breath, and briefly closed my eyes. I decided to give him an honest answer.

'Yes,' I said. 'I do.'

He waved a hand towards the stage. I mounted the steps with shaking legs, stood centre stage, and waited for the accompanist to play the introduction on the piano.

Where was the harm? As soon as I'd performed, I would come clean, explain there had been a misunderstanding. Then they would ask Vicky to audition. This was just a way of showing them what I could do. There was no way I would get the part of Dorothy, but they might bear me in mind for future roles.

The accompanist began to play.

And I went for it.

I had almost reached the final chorus when the door banged open and Vicky walked in. She still looked pale, but now she was staring at me with wide eyes. She stood rigidly, her entire demeanour emanating a sense of betrayal.

I couldn't look at her anymore, but neither could I stop. So I fixed my gaze on the auditorium's chandelier, and sang the final high notes.

*

Vicky didn't speak to me for almost two weeks. In direct contrast to our journey to London, she was silent on the way home. I tried calling her several times over the following days, but she either hung up on me, or I was informed by her mother that she was 'out'.

She finally spoke to me the day before I was due to leave for London.

'What do you want, Charlotte?' Her voice sounded tired, even over the phone line.

'I just… don't want us to part on bad terms.'

'It's a bit late for that,' she said. 'It was my part. You didn't even get through the first round of auditions.'

I felt a stab of irritation. 'I did explain everything. You still got to sing.'

'Yes, after you… you…'

'After I what? Blew their socks off?'

'You're not even sorry, are you?'

'Why should I be sorry, Vicky? I won that part fair and square.'

'You stole it from me!'

I sighed. 'Listen. If you really can't be happy for me, then maybe it's better we don't talk anymore.'

'That suits me just fine.'

'Great. Bye, then.'

The line went dead.

*

Later, when I was alone in London, sharing the grottiest digs imaginable with a bunch of people I didn't know, I found that I missed Vicky.

And as I attended rehearsals, pretending that I could dance, that I had in fact taken dance lessons, I started to think that she was right. This should have been Vicky's part. She was the true musical theatre performer, far more accomplished and professional than me. Vicky wouldn't return from each performance exhausted and unable to socialise. Vicky wouldn't cry in her dressing room because the director had told her that she had 'all the grace of a bull'. Vicky wouldn't strain her voice to the point that she had to visit the doctor, be advised not to sing for three weeks… then sing through it anyway. Vicky was real. She wasn't a fake like me.

But as the run entered its second month, I gradually stopped thinking like this. I grew used to the tiring schedule. My voice got better. I was able to ignore the jibes from the director. I made friends. I suppose I faked it until I made it.

Then my sister called and told me about the accident.

When she called, I was in my dressing room before the show, in Dorothy's gingham dress, waiting to go on. I managed to keep it together until the interval, when I came offstage and burst into tears. For the first time, my understudy went on for the second act, and I took three nights off work.

I wanted to go back to Shellcliff for the funeral. I got as far as King's Cross station. But in the end, a combination of guilt and fear made me turn back. Guilt, because I felt I was somehow responsible for this, that I was performing Vicky's role, living Vicky's life. And fear, at the thought that my Shellcliff friends – who were really Vicky's Shellcliff friends – would blame me too.

So I went back to work. Every night, for a full year, my Dorothy found her way home. After all, there was no place like it. I only wished I had the courage to do the same.

*

Now, back in my borrowed flat, I stuffed my clothes into my suitcase without bothering to fold them properly. Then I tore the poster for *Theatre is Murder!* from the living room wall, scrunched it up, and threw it in the waste paper bin.

I would leave for London first thing in the morning. I knew I couldn't stay here. Not after everything Lydia had said. Not after what I'd done.

It was time to go back to my real home.

*

I arranged to meet Sarah in the coffee shop. She was already there when I arrived, and she stood up to offer me a hug. I kept my distance, too nervous and wrapped up in what I needed to say.

Sarah's smile vanished, her arms falling to her sides. 'Are you okay? What's happened?'

I took a deep breath. It was probably best that I just got on with it.

'I'm sorry,' I said. 'But I have to go back to London.'

'What?' Sarah's eyes widened. 'Why?'

'I've tried my best,' I said. 'I really have. But I just don't feel particularly welcome here. I've messed things up with Lydia. You know? From the drama group.'

Sarah sat down. 'What's Lydia got to do with anything? I'm sure there's no need to leave.'

'She's Greg's sister,' I said. 'Remember what happened to Vicky? His older sister? I think they blame me.'

Sarah shook her head. 'But that was an accident. It had nothing to do with you.'

'I tried to help Sam. Lydia's daughter. She wants to go to drama school. It seems stupid now, but I think I was trying to make amends. Lydia hit the roof when she found out, and Greg said it was probably best if I went home.'

Sarah's hands curled into fists. Her face was suddenly thunderous. 'Oh, did he now?'

'Yes...' I was slightly alarmed by the look on Sarah's face. 'He was just a bit upset, I think.'

'I knew it,' said Sarah. 'I knew he was bad for the bookshop. You're not going anywhere. I'd rather fire him and keep you.'

I held up a hand. 'No... please don't do that. Look, it's time for me to move on anyway. The summer's almost over, and I might stand a chance of getting an acting job. Alex says there's a role for a standby in his new play.'

Sarah narrowed her eyes. 'Is that really what you want?'

I looked down at the floor. 'Yes. I'm so sorry to leave you in the lurch like this.'

'I'm not sure I believe you,' she said. 'But if you really must go, then I'm sure I can sort something out.'

I forced myself to meet her eye. 'Thank you. Yes. It's what I want.'

37

Greg

It was almost 11am, and I was worried about Charlotte. She still hadn't turned up for work, which was most unlike her. I hoped she hadn't taken what Lydia had said to heart. I felt awful about it in retrospect. She was my friend. I should have stood up for her. After all, I had been helping Sam as well.

I knew Charlotte had never meant to hurt Vicky. Auditions were tough. I understood that. When she did arrive at the bookshop, I would be sure to explain everything, and to make amends if she would let me.

I tried to keep myself busy by sorting stock. Someone had filed our vampire books under Natural History again, and I was just moving them when the doorbell jingled. I looked up, hoping it was Charlotte.

It was Sarah. And she looked angry.

'Hello, Sarah,' I said, smiling nervously.

She marched up to the counter. 'How dare you speak to my sister like that.'

'I'm sorry?'

'You told her she should go home. Apparently you made it clear she was no longer welcome.'

'What? No! That is... I didn't mean... Lydia was upset...'

'I'm not interested in Lydia. I'm interested in you, Greg. You're supposed to be the manager of this bookshop, and you've driven our star employee away.'

'What do you mean?'

Sarah rolled her eyes. 'She's gone, Greg. Gone back to London. She didn't think she could work here anymore.'

'But I didn't say anything—'

Sarah held up her hand. 'You know what? I don't care. I'm tired of making allowances for you. I'm tired of your bumbling excuses, and your incompetence, and your awkwardness. Your sheer unwillingness to change.'

'But I—'

'I'm sorry, Greg,' said Sarah. 'I'm afraid I have to ask you to leave.'

'Leave?' For a moment, I didn't process what she had said to me. I knew the meaning of the individual words, but together they made no sense. 'What about the bookshop?'

'I'll find someone else. Or I'll run it myself. How hard can it possibly be? The point is, I can't keep you on.' Sarah couldn't quite look me in the eye anymore. 'I hoped it would all work out, but it hasn't. I need to look ahead now. And I don't think you're the right person to take this shop into the future.'

'You're firing me,' I said.

'I'm letting you go,' said Sarah.

'Go where?' For the first time, I felt a spark of anger. After everything I had given to the bookshop, all that time and devotion for more than twenty years, I was being tossed aside because I didn't align with Sarah's 'vision'.

'You can continue to rent the flat, of course,' said Sarah. 'And I'll write you a good reference. Not that you deserve it.'

'Oh, well that's all right, then,' I said.

'Please don't use that tone with me,' said Sarah. 'I gave you a chance. I gave you plenty of chances, really, and you just carried on doing exactly as you liked.'

'That's not fair,' I said, quietly.

'Welcome to the real world,' said Sarah. 'I'd like you to leave now, please.'

I had expected to weep, but I just felt numb, as though the bookshop was no longer real. As if I was inside a dream.

'All right,' I said to Sarah. 'I'll be off, then.'

I walked unsteadily out of the shop. The front door slammed behind me. Somehow, I drifted upstairs to my flat, where I stood in the middle of the living room, staring out of the window.

This couldn't be happening. Any moment now, I would wake up from this nightmare.

Minutes ticked by, and I realised this was all real. The numbness drained out of me, to be replaced by panic.

What was I going to do?

38

Charlotte

I caught the train to York, then to London. When I finally disembarked at King's Cross, I felt a rush of relief. This was home, and it had been for twenty-five years. There was no point in kidding myself that there was anything left for me in Shellcliff. I had tried to reproduce my happy teenage years, and it hadn't worked. I was living proof that you really couldn't go back.

I went to a coffee shop just across from the station, bought a latte and an eye-wateringly expensive sandwich, and called Alex.

It was like Lydia had said. We were perfect for each other. Alex had a competitive spirit. He knew this was a tough industry. If I told him the full story, he would probably tell me I had nothing to feel guilty about. I really needed his careless company right now. And perhaps the role in his new play was still available.

The phone rang almost a dozen times before he picked up. 'Yeah, hi?'

'Alex! It's me.'

'Huh?' He sounded as if I had just roused him from sleep. Maybe he'd been at a party last night.

'It's Charlotte. Guess what? I'm back in town.'

There was a pause. 'Oh. That's nice, Charlotte.'

'I was just thinking it would be nice to see you if you're free?'

'I'm... this is a little unexpected, Charley. After everything.'

I winced. 'I know. I'm sorry. I hate to think we parted on bad terms. Are you free for a coffee? Or maybe I could come over—'

'NO!' The urgency of the word almost made me drop the phone. 'I mean, no, sorry. I'm a little busy. Performance tonight.'

'Oh. Of course. Maybe tomorrow, then?'

'Yes. Maybe. Look, I'll call you, okay?'

'Okay, Alex. Break a leg.'

He ended the call. I sipped my coffee, feeling a little bereft. I supposed it was natural that he didn't really want to see me. I hadn't exactly welcomed him with open arms when he had visited Shellcliff. And of course he was busy with his play.

The play! Maybe there was a way I could build bridges, make things up to him. I tapped *Autumn Songs* into my phone. It was currently in previews, and I was delighted to see there were still a few single seats left. They were shockingly expensive (the price of my sandwich times about one hundred) but it would be worth it. I booked one.

*

Four hours later, wearing my favourite burgundy evening gown and a very blingy diamanté necklace Alex had given me for my last birthday, I ascended the stairs to the entrance of the Shakespeare Theatre. I had to briefly surrender the large box of chocolates beneath my arm to a member of the front of house team for a security inspection, before being waved across the threshold.

The foyer was packed. This was going to be a very popular play. There had been a lot of buzz for months. I bought a programme from an usher, and raised my eyebrows at the cover. The photograph was very similar to the publicity photo of Alex and myself that had long been used for *The Next Thirty Years*. Except this time, he had Selena in his arms. It was a little disconcerting. I straightened up, reminded myself it was just a posed photo, and went to find my seat.

*

A part of me was annoyed to discover that *Autumn Songs* was glorious. Funny, poignant, well directed, beautifully performed. Selena was stunning. There was really no other word for her. She was beautiful, but more importantly she was an amazing actress. I felt a little guilty that I had ever judged her to be a lightweight, simply because she was young.

Alex was wonderful, as I had known he would be. He received a standing ovation at the end. He looked delighted, and bent to kiss Selena's hand. I felt a little bit jealous, but the kiss was a common enough thing. Lead actors did it all the time.

The ovation continued. I smiled to myself. Alex was going to be insufferable after this.

When the audience finally started to leave, I went around to the stage door, and spoke to the woman looking after the entrance.

'I'm here to see Alex,' I said. 'My name's Charlotte de la Mer.'

My stage name sounded awkward on my tongue. I realised it was a while since I had used it.

The woman smiled. 'Is he expecting you?'

'Well… no. It's a surprise. I'm his girlfriend.'

Her brows knitted together in a frown. 'I'm afraid we need to know about visitors in advance. But he should be down soon, if you'd like to wait outside?'

'Oh,' I said, a little taken aback. Perhaps Alex hadn't mentioned me. 'All right. I understand, of course.'

I went outside. There was a slight chill in the air, and I huddled into my wrap. I wished I'd brought a proper jacket.

I waited while several of the supporting actors came out. A couple of them smiled at me and looked expectantly at my programme, but I explained that I was waiting for someone.

After about fifteen minutes, the door opened, and Alex appeared. He had his arm around Selena. They were both laughing.

I was about to say his name, but then Alex swung around and kissed Selena, quickly, on the mouth. A cold shard of jealousy knifed through me.

'Alex,' I said.

He gave a start and looked up. His eyes widened. 'Charlotte! What are you doing here?'

'I... came to see your play,' I said. My voice sounded hoarse. I swallowed tears.

'Oh,' he said. 'That's very nice of you. Sorry, I wasn't expecting—'

'Yes,' I said. 'I can see that.'

'Alex?' Selena was eyeing me curiously. 'Aren't you going to introduce me?'

Panic flitted across Alex's face. He was so suave that only someone who knew his expressions very well would have noticed it. He recovered almost instantly, and gave a charming smile. 'Sorry! Where are my manners? Selena, this is Charlotte de la Mer. She was my co-star for ten years.'

I stared at him.

Co-star.

Co-star?

Selena's face lit up. It was like watching an incredibly glamorous sun. She swooped forward and grasped my hand. 'Of course! Alex has told me so much about you!'

'Has he really?' I looked at Alex and saw a brief, pleading look in his eyes.

'Yes! He said you're wonderful. A legend! In fact, I think I even saw you in panto. I was just a kid at the time.'

Oh, this was just getting better and better.

'You're like theatrical royalty, or something,' gushed Selena.

'Thank you,' I said, still looking at Alex.

'Er... darling?' Alex put a hand on Selena's upper arm. 'Could you do me a favour and go to the restaurant? I don't want us to lose the booking, and I need a quick word with Charlotte. Work stuff.'

Selena looked momentarily puzzled, but nodded. 'Okay.' She smiled at me again. 'It was so lovely to meet you, Charlotte.'

'You too,' I said.

We watched Selena hurry off down the street.

'She's very nice,' I said. 'Sweet. And she saw me in panto. How lovely. You two been together long?'

Alex stepped towards me, a desperate look on his face. 'Charlotte, please—'

I glared at him. '*Co-star*? Really?'

'I'm sorry. I didn't mean... Look, she doesn't know about us, okay?'

'I'm sure she doesn't. Tell me. Were you seeing her before or after you decided to visit me in Shellcliff?'

He rubbed the back of his neck and glanced away. 'We'd... *met* a few times. But I had no idea if it was going anywhere. And you'd gone, Charlotte. You'd built this whole new life, without me. And Selena... well, she was there.'

'I was *there*, Alex!' I met his eyes. 'I was there, for ten years! And looking back, I think you barely noticed.'

He looked down at the pavement. 'I'm sorry. I thought it was what you wanted. Casual, like.'

'Did I not drop enough hints? All those times I said how nice it would be to get our own place? You seriously didn't think I meant it?' He didn't reply, and I shook my head in wonder. 'God, I've been such a fool.'

'Charlotte, please don't do this. Come and have dinner with Selena and me. She'd love to meet you properly.'

'Are you kidding me? I'm not staying just to spare your feelings, Alex. And I'm certainly not having dinner with your new girlfriend.'

'She's not my girlfriend.'

'Well, she seems to think she is.'

'I told you. It's not serious.' He took a step towards me and put his hand beneath my chin. 'Darling, you know I care about you.'

He leaned forward and touched his lips to mine. I drew back and stared at him in disbelief. 'How could you?'

'Charlotte...'

I started to turn away, paused, then spun around again. 'Actually, you know what? I accept your invitation to dinner.'

Alex blinked. 'What?'

'Come on, let's go, we don't want to lose the booking.'

'Charlotte, please...'

I set off at a trot down Haymarket. It only took me a few minutes to reach the restaurant, because of course I knew it would be our favourite restaurant. Alex's and mine.

Selena was seated at a table in a corner. I was about to approach when I was intercepted by the maître d'.

'Can I help you, madam?'

It was at this point that Alex caught up with me. His hand fell on my shoulder. 'Come on, Charlotte, let's not make a scene.'

I ignored him and focused my attention on the young maître d'. 'Yes, I rather think you can. That's my friend over there. Coo-eee! Selena!'

Selena looked up from her menu. She saw Alex and me, looked briefly confused, but then smiled and waved at us.

The young man stepped to one side. I strode towards the table. 'Hello, Selena. Alex invited me to join you for dinner.'

'Oh.' Selena narrowed her eyes at Alex. 'That's... nice.'

'Don't worry, I'm not staying,' I said cheerfully. 'I just thought you should know that Alex and I were together for ten years. Or rather, I thought we were. Alex seems to have had other ideas. It seems that, at one stage, he was seeing us both at the same time. There was a certain degree of overlap. Oh, and he tried to kiss me just now. But not to worry, I'm sure you'll sort it all out, talk it all through. Alex is very good at spinning a yarn, making things sound reasonable. But, quite frankly, you seem like a very nice girl and I think you deserve better.' I realised I was still holding the chocolates. I plonked them down on the table. 'You might as well have these. Enjoy.'

I turned around and, ignoring Alex's pleas for me to come back and explain myself, walked out of the restaurant with my head held high.

*

My feeling of pride and euphoria lasted until I got back to my flat. As soon as I turned on the lights and looked around the empty living room, I felt the adrenaline start to drain away.

What on earth had I been thinking? Why had I even come back here?

What the hell was I going to do now?

I had not allowed myself to think beyond reuniting with Alex and getting a part in the new play. I supposed I still could, potentially, get a part in the play. But that would mean working with Alex, something that now seemed about as appealing as bathing in the Thames.

I took off my velvet wrap and the ridiculous diamanté necklace, and poured myself a large glass of wine. I had always been an optimist. Maybe things would look better in the morning.

39

Greg

Over the next few days, I found myself retreating from the world. I didn't attend readings for the theatre company's panto. I even declined Nick's repeated invitations to meet him for coffee. I just sort of... froze.

Every now and then, I would go on the internet and look at jobs. I managed to find some bookselling jobs, but they were all too far away, or part time, or in London, or casual, or they wanted you to be able to speak a second language. Soon, I had fallen into my own huge skills gap, and was mentally listing all the things I was unable to do, that I had never learned to do. Maybe Sarah was right. Maybe I was completely behind the times.

I tried to dig myself out of this dark place by rereading my favourite novels, but I couldn't concentrate. The words danced around on the pages as if trying to run away from me. I was reminded of the day all the vowels stopped working on my keyboard, the day of my disastrous first meeting with Sarah.

So I closed my books, and moved on to my favourite films. I watched several back to back. Occasionally my mobile would ring, warm bright Mozart blazing into the room. I ignored it, my gaze glued to the television.

Eventually, some time around day four, there was a heavy knock on the door. I ignored that, too, burrowing myself deeper into the sofa and pulling a blanket up to my chin. But the visitor was insistent. They kept on knocking, louder now.

I threw the blanket aside with a sigh and padded downstairs. I flung the door open, fully prepared to tell my unwelcome visitor to bugger off.

It was Nick.

'Hey,' he said, with a smile which quickly faded. 'God. You look awful.'

His blunt honesty disarmed me. 'I'm not well. I have the flu.'

Nick raised an eyebrow. 'Are you sure? Shouldn't you be in bed?'

'I was in bed. Sort of. But you got me up by thumping on the door.' I realised I sounded irritated. I didn't care. 'What are you doing here?'

'I came to see if you were all right,' said Nick. 'You haven't been answering my calls.'

'I told you. I'm—'

'Ill. Yeah. You said. Can I come in?'

'What?'

'Can I come in?' He raised a hand. He was holding a plastic carrier bag. A strange smell was emanating from it. 'I've brought lunch.'

I wrinkled my nose. 'What is it?'

'My homemade veg curry.'

'Ah. That's kind. But I don't think I can manage—'

'Let me guess. You've been up there for three days, living off cheese on toast and cup-a-soup, right?'

I stared at him. 'How on earth do you know that?'

Nick rolled his eyes. 'Because I've been there, you daft sod. I've been fired, too.'

I looked down at the doorstep. 'So you heard.'

'Everybody's heard, Greg. The entire theatre company, the Shellcliff Business Association… they're all up in arms. Lydia's on the warpath. She's threatened to form a Committee to Reinstate Greg. Have you even looked at Facebook recently?'

'No. I only really use it to post drama group news.'

'Oh, for goodness...' Nick pushed past me and thumped up the stairs. 'Come on. I'll show you.'

Faced with no choice, I wearily followed him upstairs.

'Wow,' said Nick, looking around. 'Nice place you've got here.'

'Thank you.'

'Where's the kitchen?'

'Just through there. But—'

He went into the kitchen and dumped the carrier bag on the worktop. Something inside it appeared to be leaking yellow liquid.

Nick surveyed the kitchen, which I realised was in the most terrible mess. Three days' worth of washing-up was piled in the sink. There were also scattered empty cup-a-soup sachets and a small pyramid of empty baked beans cans.

Nick wrinkled his nose. 'Remind me not to sit too close to you. And to open a window.'

I almost laughed at that, but I quickly swallowed the sound. 'Don't be disgusting.'

'Right,' he said. 'Lunchtime.' He reached into the carrier bag, took out a transparent plastic container that appeared to be full of lumpy yellow gunge, and put it in the microwave.

'I'm really not hungry,' I said. 'You don't need to go to all this trouble.'

'It's hardly trouble. You just bung it in. It only takes five minutes.' He began to search my cupboards for empty plates. Finding none, he settled on cereal bowls instead. I wanted to tell him that I did not want his curry in my breakfast bowls, but I suddenly found that I did not have the energy.

We stood in the kitchen, the only sound the whir of the microwave.

'Listen,' I said. 'I'm really sorry I didn't ring you back. I just... needed some time alone, that's all.'

Nick frowned. Fortunately, the *ding* from the microwave saved me from any further bumbling attempts at an apology.

Nick took out the container, steaming now, and deposited it on top of the oven. 'You don't need to justify yourself to me. It's shit being fired.'

'Well... I wouldn't have put it exactly like that. But yes, you're right. It is.'

I watched him spoon the congealed yellow gunk into the bowls. I was starting to feel a bit queasy.

'Here,' he said, handing a bowl to me.

'I'm sorry, Nick, but I'm really not hungry.'

'Just try it. It might make you feel better.'

I picked up one of my few remaining clean spoons and scooped up a tiny amount of curry.

At first all I could taste was heat, but this soon resolved itself into an elaborate symphony of flavours, including cinnamon, one of my favourites. My eyes widened.

'Wow,' I said. 'That's... actually extremely nice.'

'Told you.' Nick picked up his own bowl and gestured towards the living room. 'Can we go and sit down?'

I nodded. I sat on the sofa, and Nick sat opposite me in the armchair.

'Right,' he said, after we had enjoyed our food in silence for a few minutes. 'Facebook.'

He reached into his pocket and took out his phone. He scrolled around a bit, then held it out to me. I put my bowl on the coffee table, took the phone, and stared at it.

I was looking at a page called Shellcliff Community Focus, where someone had posted a message entitled: *Help Bookseller Greg.*

I read on: *It seems that Greg has been unceremoniously fired from his job at Seaswept Books, with no reason given. I am appalled by his treatment at the hands of the new owner, and I hope you all are, too. BRING BACK GREG!*

Well, this was embarrassing.

'Look at the comments,' said Nick.

I scrolled down. The comments were certainly varied.

That's a shame. Greg's a legend.

Whos Geg?

I always thought he was a bit grumpy myself.

This is why I shop on Amazon. Boycott Seaswept Books!

No one even buys books anymore.

I looked at Nick. 'But this is awful! I don't want them to boycott the bookshop.'

'Ignore all that. It's just trolls.'

'Trolls?'

'Yeah.' Nick waved a hand. 'Scroll down a bit further.'

I did as instructed and saw a longer comment from someone called Lynne.

Greg really cheered me up when I was having a bad day and he recommended I Capture the Castle to me. It's now my favourite book. He made the bookshop feel so welcoming and cosy. I hope he finds a better job. He's always so helpful.

I looked up again. My eyes were pricking. 'But this can't be about me. She must have me confused with someone else.'

'What makes you say that?'

'Sarah. She said I was stuffy and grumpy and irritating.'

Nick smiled gently. 'It would seem Sarah's in the minority.'

I scrolled a bit further. A lot of people agreed with Lynne's comment. They said they were very sorry I had lost my job, and wished me all the best for the future.

I handed the phone back to Nick. 'Thank you for showing me this.'

'You're welcome.'

We picked up our bowls of curry again.

'Well?' said Nick.

'Well what?'

'What are you going to do?'

'I don't know.' I let my spoon fall into the bowl. 'I mean...
those comments are lovely, but they don't really change anything,
do they? I've tried looking for another bookselling job, but there's
nothing around here.'

'Would you consider doing something else?'

'I don't think I have much choice. I'm just not sure what.' I
stirred the curry absently. 'I never thought I'd leave the bookshop.'

'Do you think if you talk to Sarah... apologise...'

I shook my head. 'I think I've burned those bridges, to be honest.'

'Maybe this could be a good opportunity to do something
different? You wanted to be an actor, right?'

My mind drifted to my short time at the repertory theatre in
Hull. It seemed so long ago, a completely different life. I knew it
wasn't possible to go back to that old life, even if I wanted to. A
sudden, intense longing closed around my heart. Did I want to?

I pushed the feelings away. 'I don't think that's going to be practical.'

Nick laid his empty bowl aside. 'At least say you'll come back
to the drama group?'

'Maybe.'

'Please. Rose is doing my head in. She wants an underwater
ballet sequence in the panto, and she's sent me this list of all the
special effects she needs. She wants a chorus of deep-sea angler-
fish... you know, with the little lights dangling at the front. And
moving jellyfish projections. I think I preferred working with you.
You don't know anything about lights.'

I gave a tiny smile. 'Thank you. I think.'

'Please,' he said, meeting my eyes. 'Everyone misses you. I
miss you.'

I wasn't sure how to respond to that. I was tempted to say
something self-deprecating like 'I'm sure that's not the case'. But
Nick sounded completely sincere, and I didn't know what to do
with such unexpected warmth.

'I'll think about it.' I swallowed hard. 'In the meantime... maybe we could go out again? Properly, I mean. For dinner. It would be nice to return the favour.' I waved towards the empty bowls.

Nick raised an eyebrow. 'Is that your way of asking me on a date?'

I shrugged helplessly. 'Yes?'

He smiled. 'I would like that.'

40

Charlotte

Things did not, in fact, look better in the morning.

I awoke with a wine-thick head and a feeling of crushing existential despair. Alex was gone. The show was gone. The bookshop was gone. My career was over.

I sat up and winced. I would have to do something proactive, maybe call Michael, my agent. But first, I desperately needed to clear my head. So I showered and dressed, and headed out, towards Charing Cross Road.

I found myself standing outside my favourite bookshop. Well, my *second* favourite bookshop, I thought with a brief pang of regret. The windows glowed in welcome, and I stepped inside.

I wandered between the tables, much as I had done the day after my sister had called and told me about Seaswept Books. I noticed that Ironing Board Novelist had been replaced by a display of Crystal Moontide's latest fantasy epic, about fairies fighting with water nymphs. This seemed like quite the literary pivot. I wondered if she had done anything to help promote the bookshop.

I hoped Greg was okay.

A few minutes later, I was inspecting the Children's department. There was a lone copy of *Clive the Seaside Donkey Volume One* in the Middle Grade section. I looked around to check that no booksellers were watching, and then surreptitiously turned it to face outwards.

'No, darling, that book's for babies.'

Behind me, a small girl of about four had found a book which made a noise like a duck. *Quack. Quack. Quack.*

'Let's look at the big girl books, shall we?' The mum looked a bit harried and tugged her daughter's hand. The girl continued to *quack* the book.

I watched out of the corner of my eye as the woman scanned the racks of picture books. 'Do you like the look of any of these?'

Quack, said the book.

'Excuse me,' I said, automatically. 'Would you like some help?'

The woman smiled at me. 'Yes please! I've no idea where to start.'

I looked over the shelves, hoping that they had it. And... yes, they did!

'I can recommend this,' I said, pulling out the picture book. '*The Witch on the Pitch*. It's about a witch who really wants to be a footballer.'

'Football?' The woman's face fell. 'Are you sure that's not a book for boys?'

I suppressed a sigh. 'No. I mean... it's for anyone, really. The witch is a girl, and it's about friendship and overcoming adversity.'

The woman turned a page and laughed. 'Oh, that looks great, actually. Thank you so much! Look at this, Rosie.'

There was another *quack*. But Rosie was looking at *The Witch on the Pitch*, and she was grinning.

'You must really enjoy working here,' said the woman.

'Oh, I don't work...' I began, but Rosie had become distracted by a giant plush Gruffalo, and was tugging her mum towards it.

I went to the coffee shop upstairs, bought a latte and a pastry, and stared out of the window. Then I took my phone out, and stared at that instead. I found myself looking at Crystal Moontide's website. Bids for the signed book had closed the previous day, raising over four thousand pounds. My eyes widened. This wouldn't necessarily help Seaswept Books in the long term, but it was certainly an excellent start.

I wondered if Greg had seen it. I scrolled through my contacts and brought up his number.

Maybe it wasn't too late to call him. Maybe he would take me back.

My finger hovered over the call button, but my courage failed me. What was I going to say? That my triumphant return to London had been a disaster? He had looked so disappointed when he'd heard about my past with Vicky. He probably wouldn't forgive me.

I flipped the phone case closed and pushed it away.

41

Greg

It was strange, being unemployed after so long in the same job. It was made even stranger by the fact that my former place of employment was currently beneath my feet, and yet completely inaccessible to me. Seaswept Books had been closed for almost a fortnight. There was a notice in the window advertising for a new manager. Apparently Sarah had no real desire to run the bookshop herself.

After Nick's visit I tried to keep to a routine. I still made a mid-morning cup of tea, still listened to Classic FM while I did my job search. I had a few interviews lined up, mainly in administration and retail roles, but my hopes weren't particularly high. I was relieved that I had lived fairly frugally over the last few years – my savings bought me a little time to think.

What I was mainly thinking was that I really, really didn't want to work in admin.

There was one new change to my routine. Nick and I had gone on our date to the Italian restaurant, and for the last few days, I had met him for lunch. We had taken to sitting on a bench on the seafront, just near the chippy. I always brought sandwiches. I did quite enjoy eating outside.

That day, I wasn't eating. I was staring out to sea.

A hand brushed my arm.

'Hey, Eeyore? What are you thinking about?'

I glanced at Nick. He smiled at me.

'Nothing much,' I said.

Nick gestured towards the closed bookshop, where the bunting still hung in the window, looking ironically cheerful.

'Any sign of the place opening up again?'

'Not yet.'

'Maybe you could apply for the manager role. You could use a pseudonym.'

I rolled my eyes. 'No thank you.'

He nudged me. 'Bet you miss your glamorous assistant, too.'

Damn. How on earth did he know that? I had been trying not to think about Charlotte. I still felt bad about the way we'd parted.

I sighed. 'A little. Silly really. I managed quite well for years by myself.'

Nick followed my gaze towards the sea. 'Hmm.'

'What do you mean, "hmm"?'

'I guess that's what happens when you start to let people in.'

'Sentimental rubbish. I'll be fine. I mean, I should be fine, shouldn't I?'

We were silent for a moment. Then Nick said: 'You know, you could just give her a ring. If she comes back and talks to Sarah, maybe you could patch things up. Get your old job back.'

'She hasn't even called me. She's probably going to get a new part in a play, or something.'

Nick was quiet for a moment. Then he said: 'Are you angry with her? About Vicky, I mean.'

Was I? That was a good question. 'No. At least, I don't think so.'

'Do you think she did anything wrong?'

'I think she was dishonest.'

'But do you think... do you really think that's why Vicky gave up acting?'

I looked down at the pavement. 'I don't know. I don't know what Vicky was thinking. I'm starting to think I never will. Maybe it was nobody's fault?'

Nick nodded. 'Maybe it wasn't.'

'Do you think Charlotte would come back if I asked her?' I said.

'I guess there's only one way to find out,' said Nick. 'Will you call her? The worst she can say is no.'

'I sort of feel like I owe her an apology for what I said after the show.'

'You were upset. I'm sure she'll understand.' His gaze slid to my sandwiches. 'They look grim. What's in them?'

'Cheese.'

'Just cheese?'

'Yes. They're nice.' I picked one up and bit off a corner. It was like eating damp polystyrene. I put on a brave face. 'Mmm!'

Nick grimaced. 'Fancy the chippy?'

'God, yes.'

*

The next morning, I awoke in much higher spirits. Nick really did have a way of cheering me up, of making me see the brighter side of things. Maybe he was right, and it wasn't too late to mend my friendship with Charlotte. Perhaps I'd give her a call later.

It was just after 10am, and I'd turned on my computer to begin my daily job search when I heard someone knocking on the door. The knocks soon graduated to a quite desperate thumping.

I hurried downstairs to answer.

Lydia was on the doorstep. She looked pale, and her eyes were red-rimmed.

'Lydia,' I said. We hadn't spoken since the disastrous showdown at the *Theatre is Murder!* after-party. I had a horrible feeling that she also blamed me for conspiring with Charlotte to help Sam. 'Are you all right?'

Lydia didn't bother with pleasantries. 'Is she here?'

'Who?'

'Sam.'

I felt a pang of alarm. 'No. Why? Should she be?'

'She's gone. Took off early this morning. I texted her and she says she's okay, but she's not answering her phone and she won't tell me where she is. And I know she's seventeen now, but... well, it's just so out of character.' Lydia twisted her hands together. I had always been slightly in awe of her unflappability, her way of just getting on with things. It was disconcerting to see her so distressed. She looked at me with wide, frightened eyes. 'What if something's happened to her?'

The mild alarm turned into a strong stab of fear. Memories flashed through my mind: my childhood home with the downstairs lights on at 1am, the knock on the door. I swayed slightly, putting one hand on the doorframe to steady myself.

This seemed to pull Lydia out of her own spiral. 'Greg! Come on. Focus.'

'Sorry.' I shook my head and straightened up.

'Do you have any idea where she might have gone?'

'I don't...' I paused. Surely not. 'Wait... It was supposed to be her drama school audition this week. In London.'

Lydia stared at me. 'You don't think she's gone there, do you? All alone?'

'She... seemed pretty determined to get in.' On the one hand, I thought this was incredibly brave of her, particularly in the light of everything that had happened. But on the other hand, she was young, and upset. And she had told me she'd never been to London before.

'Which drama school was it?' said Lydia.

'I think... it was the London School of Performing Arts.'

'But that's where Vicky... where *you*—'

I winced. 'I know.'

'Right.' Lydia straightened her back. She looked determined: this was the Lydia who sat on four local committees and was forever metaphorically knocking people's heads together. 'Okay. We'd better go after her.'

'What?'

'Do you really think I'm going to stay here and let my daughter throw her future away like this? I'm going after her.'

I had my own thoughts about this, and most of them revolved around the idea that maybe Sam should be allowed to attend the audition. But I kept these thoughts to myself.

'But... it'll take hours to get there,' I said.

Lydia looked ready to protest. Then she sighed. 'You're right. But what else can we do?'

I hesitated. 'We could call Charlotte.'

'What?'

'She's back in London. And she trained at that school, so she knows it. We could ask her to go and meet Sam.'

Lydia's mouth twisted. 'Out of the question. It's her fault we're in this mess in the first place.'

This seemed a little unfair, but I wasn't about to argue under the circumstances. 'I know it's not ideal, but at least she wouldn't be on her own.'

Lydia sighed. 'All right. *Fine.* But I'm still going to get her.'

42

Charlotte

In theory, I was having a late breakfast in my flat. In actuality, I was staring disconsolately at a plate of scrambled eggs on toast, and wondering what on earth I was going to do with the rest of my life. I had spent the last fortnight wandering around my old West End stomping grounds, haunting my old life. I had been back to Charing Cross Road several times, passing in and out of the bookshops. And yesterday, I had stopped in front of the Oxford Theatre, where the billboard for *The Next Thirty Years* had been replaced by a sign advertising the tenth London revival of cult musical *Feathers.*

I was approaching an existential crisis. If an actor wasn't acting, was she really an actor? And if I wasn't an actor, who was I?

My phone rang. I reached for it with a mixture of relief and dread. It was probably Michael, my agent, calling to say there were no parts available, or that I had been offered an audition. I couldn't quite decide which was worse.

But no. To my vast surprise, it was Greg.

'Hello, Greg,' I said.

'Charlotte. Are you busy?'

I stared at my breakfast. 'Oh, you know. Lots of glamorous parties and first nights, that sort of thing...'

'Oh. Sorry to disturb.'

I sighed. 'I'm not busy, Greg. Are you okay?'

'Not really.' He sounded a bit breathless. 'I was wondering if you could do me a favour?'

'What?'

'Sam's gone missing. We think she's taken herself off to the drama school audition.'

I couldn't help smiling at that. *Good girl, Sam.* 'I see. What would you like me to do about it?'

'Lydia's really worried,' said Greg. 'We were wondering if you could go to the school and... intercept her.'

'Intercept?'

'Meet her. Check that she's okay. Stay with her until Lydia gets there.'

I had no idea what to say. It was as if our confrontation after the play had never happened.

'Are you sure about that?'

'Listen,' said Greg, 'I know we didn't exactly say goodbye on the best of terms. And I'm very sorry I overreacted.'

'You didn't overreact,' I said. 'Lydia was just telling the truth. I should have been a better friend to Vicky.'

'I'm... not sure there's anything you could have done.'

This was too difficult a conversation to have over the phone. I decided to change the subject.

'So you want me to accompany Sam to the audition?'

There was a pause. 'I don't think Lydia wants her to audition.'

'I'm... well, I'm not sure I can stop her, Greg. If she's made up her mind—'

'Please,' said Greg. 'Please would you just meet her? It would set my... Lydia's mind at rest.'

'Fine,' I said. 'I'll intercept your wayward niece.'

There was a sigh on the other end of the line. 'Thank you. Lydia will meet you there.'

43

Greg

I ended the call. 'She says she'll do it.'

'Good,' said Lydia. She turned towards the door of my flat. 'We'd better go.'

'We?'

'Aren't you coming with me?'

'I'm not sure how much that'll help.'

For the first time in years, Lydia looked at me with a genuine plea in her eyes. 'Please, Greg. I'd appreciate the moral support. She listens to you.'

I gave a short laugh. 'No, she doesn't.'

'She does. I don't think you realise how much she respects you.'

This surprised me. I'd always thought Sam regarded me as her dull, sad uncle who had never moved away from home or even gone to university. The idea that she might actually respect me was quite uplifting.

'All right,' I said.

'Thank you.' She held up her mobile. 'We'd better look at trains.'

'There might not be any need.' I smiled. 'I have a better idea.'

*

Nick looked at me with his head cocked slightly to one side. 'Come again?'

'I'd like you to drive me and Lydia to London so we can stop Sam auditioning for drama school.'

His brow furrowed. 'Why do you want to stop her auditioning for drama school?'

'*I* don't. Lydia does. *I* think she should audition.'

'So... why are you trying to stop her?'

'Because Lydia...' I threw up my hands. 'Look. Please could you drive us to London? I might be able to persuade Lydia on the way.'

'Well, it would be a jaunt, I suppose. We could see some of the sights.'

'This is a mission, Nick, not a day trip.'

Nick wilted a bit. 'All right. I'll fetch the Bookmobile.'

'The what?'

He smiled. 'You'll see. I'll meet you at your place in fifteen minutes.'

A short time later, Lydia and I stood waiting outside my flat when something that might once have been a mobile library rounded the corner.

Lydia's eyes widened. 'What on earth is that?'

'I'm guessing it's the Bookmobile,' I said.

'It looks like it's about to fall apart.'

The Bookmobile sputtered to a halt in a cloud of exhaust fumes. We both stared at it. It had obviously seen better days. The small windows had tired net curtains hanging in them. Blazoned along the side was the slogan: *Bookmobile: Gets you from A to B, and all the way to Z*, but the blue letters were slightly faded.

Nick poked his head out of the window. 'Are you getting in, or what?'

'Is it safe?' I said.

'Of course it's safe,' said Nick. 'It came from another library. I'm planning to do it up, but it's completely sound.'

'I thought you were bringing a car,' I said.

'I can go and get the motorbike, if you'd prefer?' said Nick.

'So you do have a motorbike.' I gave a soft sigh of admiration, even though I had never considered myself an admirer of motorbikes.

'What?' said Nick.

I shook my head. 'Nothing.'

Lydia rolled her eyes. 'I'm not riding a motorbike. Come on.'

We climbed into the cab, which fortunately had three seats. Something cracked beneath my heel. I glanced down at the footwell, and found myself staring at a mess of CD cases, discarded crisp packets, and half-empty bottles of mineral water. Lydia followed my gaze, and grimaced.

'Yeah, I've been meaning to clean that out,' said Nick, without a hint of apology.

Lydia clicked her tongue. 'You two are obviously made for each other.'

I blushed, and avoided Nick's eye.

'Right,' said Nick. 'London, here we come.'

44

Charlotte

It took me almost an hour to get to the drama school by taxi. I hadn't visited the place since graduating in my early twenties, and I was surprised to find a collection of modern glass-fronted buildings clustered around its grand Gothic façade.

I paused, took a breath, and went inside.

'Where are the auditions, please?' I asked the young man on the front desk.

He smiled at me amicably. 'May I take your name?'

'My name's Charlotte de la Mer – I mean, Charlotte Smith, but that's not—'

'What course are you auditioning for?'

I was taken aback. 'You think *I'm* auditioning?'

He looked confused. 'Why? Aren't you?'

Gosh. He thought I was auditioning. I almost laughed at the absurdity. Whatever next?

'No, darling,' I said. 'I'm an alumna. It's my friend's daughter. Her name's Sam. Samantha Harrison. BA Acting, I think.'

'Right. And where's Sam now?'

'I'd rather hoped you'd be able to tell me that. Her mother asked me if I'd come and see her.'

The man frowned. 'I'm really sorry. I can't just let you in.'

'I have ID if that would help?' I reached into my handbag, opened my purse, and took out my Equity Card.

The man peered at it. 'I'm sorry, that's not—'

'Please,' I said. 'Maybe you recognise me? From *The Next Thirty Years*? Don't you know who I am?' He stared at me blankly. I felt something inside me wilt. 'No. No. Of course you don't. How silly of me...'

I turned away. I could feel tears welling up in my eyes. It was absurd, that this was going to be the thing that finally pushed me over the edge. The fact that I couldn't even use my tenuous fame to do one small thing for Lydia, after everything she'd been through...

'Wait.' I paused and turned around. The man was looking at me sympathetically. 'I can't let you in, and I can't give you any information about the auditions, but you can always wait here in reception? See if Sam shows up?'

This was better than nothing. 'Okay. Thank you.'

I sat on a red vinyl chair near the door, and waited. Greg had texted me Sam's number, and I tried calling her again, but she wasn't picking up.

Ten minutes ticked by. Fifteen. Thirty. Maybe Sam had already been and gone. Maybe I was too late...

I waited for almost three hours. Lydia called me several times, and each time I had to apologise, to say there was no sign of her daughter.

Finally, just before 3pm, the door opened and a familiar figure entered the reception area and approached the desk.

'Sam!' I was on my feet in an instant.

Sam turned around. Her eyes widened, then narrowed. 'What are you doing here?'

'Lydia told me you'd gone missing. We knew it was your audition today—'

'Yeah,' said Sam. 'It is. So, if you don't mind...' She turned back towards the desk.

'Your mum's worried sick. She asked if I would come and check on you.'

Sam glared at me. 'Really? So you're in league with her now? I suppose you've come to tell me that I'm crap and shouldn't bother. That's what you all think, isn't it? I know it's what Mum thinks.'

I cleared my throat. 'That's not what she said.'

'She said auditions were a waste of time for someone like me.'

'I'm sure she didn't mean that,' I said carefully. 'She was probably talking about what happened to your Aunt Vicky. Her experience rather... changed your mum's view of the acting profession.'

Sam made no reply, so I continued. 'For what it's worth, I don't think you're wasting your time, and I don't think your mum does, either. Not really. Does it have to be like this? Can't you just phone her and tell her you're okay?'

'She doesn't care. She's not interested in what I want to do.' Sam sounded very close to tears.

My mobile started to ring. 'That'll be her now. Won't you just talk to her?'

'You talk to her, if you're so bothered,' said Sam. 'I'm going to be late.'

I watched helplessly as she gave her name to the nice young man on the front desk.

'Ah, here you are,' he said, with a smile. 'Auditorium Two.' His smile faded. 'Are you all right?'

Sam had blanched. 'Where are the loos?'

'Just through there.'

Sam hurried past me, her face ashen. She pushed open the door to the visitor toilets. Ignoring the disapproving look of the man on the desk, I dived in after her, only to be confronted with a cubicle door slamming shut in my face.

I knocked gently. 'Sam?'

'Go away!'

'Are you okay in there?'

'I'm fine.' There was a pause, followed by the sound of retching. I winced.

'You know, I used to get terribly sick before auditions.'

Sam groaned. 'Please just leave me alone.'

I sighed. 'Okay. But you know where I am if you need me, right?'

There was no reply, so I went back to the reception area and sank into a chair. My phone rang again, and I fished it out of my pocket.

'Hello, Lydia.'

'Well? Do you have her?'

'Not exactly.'

'What does that mean?'

'She's here. But she doesn't want to talk to me.'

'What's she doing now?'

'She's... in the toilets. Nerves, I think. But she still seems pretty determined to go through with it.'

There was a pause. 'Shit. Poor girl. We won't be long. Can you wait for her?'

'Of course.'

She hung up.

45

Greg

Lydia glared at her phone.

It had taken us over five hours to drive to London, and it had been an awkward, tense journey. Lydia had spent most of the time checking her phone and hiding the fact that she was on the verge of tears. She had called Charlotte several times, only to learn that there was no sign of Sam. I tried to think of something to say, to comfort her, but nothing helpful came to mind. Nick, meanwhile, had attempted to cheer everyone up by putting on his 'trucking music': a CD of power ballads by Bonnie Tyler, Tina Turner, Journey, et al. But this had just made Lydia sigh dramatically, so he had turned it off again.

'Is everything all right?' I asked.

'She's there,' said Lydia. 'At the audition. Charlotte spoke to her, but she's determined to go through with it.' She stared out of the window. 'I suppose I shouldn't be surprised.'

'What?'

'All the sneaking about. Pretending she was revising. I even found a script in her room, but she insisted she was studying it in English.' She paused and sniffed. 'I only want what's best for her. I don't want her to get hurt.'

'She's a very determined young lady,' I said, choosing my words carefully.

Lydia gave a short laugh. 'Yes. She certainly is.'

'She's also very good.'

'Yes. She is. I know she is.'

'She's a smart girl. She'll be okay.'

'I hope so.'

We drove on in silence.

*

After another forty minutes negotiating our way through London traffic, and many choice words spoken by Lydia, we finally reached the drama school. Lydia tried Sam's mobile several times during our convoluted journey, but it went through to voicemail every time. I could feel her frustration rising, and was concerned that the next part of the day was not going to be pleasant.

We left the Bookmobile in the staff car park and hurried to reception. Charlotte was sitting just inside the door. She stood up to greet us.

'Lydia, I'm so sorry, I've tried talking to her—'

'Where is she now?'

'Still locked in the toilets. Refusing to come out.'

Lydia closed her eyes briefly. 'Of *course* she is.' She looked at me. 'Will you wait here? This might take a while.'

'Of course.'

'I'll... just...' Nick waved his arms awkwardly towards the car park, where the Bookmobile was taking up two spaces.

'Would you wait with me?' I said, aware how needy I sounded. This place was putting me on edge. It had been nearly twenty-five years, and apparently I still wasn't over the disappointment. Or the shock.

Nick sighed. 'Oh, all right.' He sank into a chair.

Lydia grasped Charlotte's arm. 'Okay. Show me where she is.'

46

Charlotte

The toilet cubicle was still locked.

Lydia knocked gently on the door. 'Sam?'

No reply.

'Sam? Are you in there?'

'Go away.' Sam's voice was hoarse, and there was a catch in it, as if she was struggling to hold back tears.

'Charlotte told me you were having a wobble. Would you... would you like to talk about it?'

There was a pause, followed by the click of a lock. The door opened to reveal Sam, her eyes red with tears and her makeup all smudged.

She glared at Lydia. 'Why do you care? You've never wanted me to do this.'

Standing in the corner, I braced myself for a showdown. But all trace of anger had left Lydia's face. Now she just looked hurt. 'That's not true.'

'Yes, it is. You said you didn't want me to be an actor, that it was no life—'

'You could have talked to me about it.'

'What difference would that have made? You'd have told me not to come.'

Lydia was quiet for a moment. Then she nodded. 'Yes. That's probably true. It's just because I know how hard it is, love.'

'Yeah, well. You'll be glad to know I've changed my mind.'

'What?!' I said. I couldn't help myself. 'But you were so keen.'

'I know, but after everything... I'm not sure this is for me. It just feels wrong. After what happened to Aunt Vicky...'

Lydia flinched.

'I just... don't think I can do it,' said Sam quietly. She wiped her eyes.

Lydia and I both stared at her. I was half expecting Lydia to declare victory, and sweep her out of the toilets. But instead she reached forward and put both hands on Sam's shoulders.

'Listen,' she said. 'You're right. I didn't want you to go down this route. That's because I was afraid. But I don't want my own fears to rub off on you. I've never wanted that.'

Sam sniffed. 'But you said—'

'I know what I said. I was wrong. Whatever you decide to do, I'll support you one hundred per cent. And for what it's worth, I know you can do it. And Charlotte thinks so, too. Isn't that right?'

Lydia looked at me.

'Of course,' I said, feeling oddly touched that Lydia should ask.

'If you really want to leave, we can go right now,' said Lydia. 'But please don't leave because you think you're not good enough, because that's just not true.'

Sam gave a little sob. Lydia folded her into a hug. They stood like that for a few moments, Sam shaking and Lydia rubbing her back.

'So,' said Lydia. 'What do you think?'

Sam wiped her eyes again. 'I... think I'd like to try.' She glanced in the mirror, and laughed. 'But I'll need to get cleaned up first.'

'Is there anything I can do to help?'

'No. Everything's here,' Sam nodded towards her rucksack.

Lydia and I left the toilets. A few minutes later, Sam emerged, head held high. I had to admire her determination. As a young actress, a similar bout of nerves would have flattened me (and it had done, on more than one occasion).

'Let's go,' she said, and strode off towards the auditorium.

I exchanged a glance with Lydia, who smiled.

47

Greg

'Are you okay?' said Nick.

I was pacing around the reception area, trying to avoid eye contact with any auditionees who came out of the main building. I didn't want to see the disappointment or triumph written on their faces.

'Of course I'm okay,' I said, turning around and pacing back towards the door. 'Why shouldn't I be? Everything's fine.'

Nick frowned. 'Why don't we get a coffee? I think I saw a place just over the road.'

'No, thanks.' I didn't want a coffee. What I wanted was something much stronger. Possibly of the hard liquor variety.

'Oh, for goodness sake, would you please stop pacing?' Nick leapt up and walked over to me. 'She'll be absolutely fine. There are other schools, if it doesn't work out.'

'I know that.' I finally allowed myself to take a seat, where I replaced pacing with wringing my hands.

Nick pulled his chair closer to mine. 'Why are you so nervous?'

I brought my hands up to my forehead. 'I don't know! I'm sorry, I think it's just the memories... This place...'

'Did you study here?'

'No. No, that's sort of the point... I really wanted to. I even passed the audition. But then my sister... This was where I was when...'

'Ah,' said Nick. 'I'm sorry, love.'

There was a pause.

'You know,' said Nick. 'It's never too late.'

I looked up at him. 'No, please let's not go there. I don't want to go through all that "chase your dreams" carpe diem nonsense.'

Nick looked hurt. He shrugged. 'I was just saying, is all.'

'Sorry to be so grumpy. I know you mean well.' I took his hand and gave it a quick squeeze. 'I'm absolutely fine. Honestly.'

He attempted a smile. 'I know.'

'There's nothing wrong with being a bookseller.'

'Of course there isn't.'

'I really liked running the bookshop.'

'I know you did.' He paused again. 'It's just, sometimes—'

I was saved from this uncomfortable conversation by the door swinging open. Lydia, Charlotte and Sam appeared. Sam looked a little flushed, her expression serious.

I was on my feet in an instant. 'Well? Did you get in?'

Sam frowned. 'I don't know yet. They'll let me know by the end of the week.'

I deflated slightly. I had been waiting for a dramatic revelation, either tears or a joyful cry of 'I got in'. Obviously I was still a thespian at heart.

'Are you happy with how you did?' I asked.

'Yeah. I think so.'

I smiled. 'That's good.'

'I don't know about anyone else, but I'm starving,' said Lydia. 'Pizza?'

48

Charlotte

We found a restaurant just down the road from the drama school. It was proving to be a strange meal: Greg was quiet, picking at a plate of spaghetti. Nick kept trying to coax him out of his shell, but he was getting nowhere fast.

'Are you all right?' I asked.

Greg smiled weakly. 'Absolutely fine.'

Then he retreated into his own world again. I caught Nick's eye. He just shrugged.

'How are things at the bookshop?' I said.

Nick gave a warning shake of his head, but Greg looked up in surprise. 'Oh. I thought Sarah would have told you.'

'Told me what?'

'I don't work there anymore.' Greg avoided my eye, and curled pasta around his fork. 'She sacked me.'

'What?' It took all my self-control not to jump out of my chair. 'Why?'

Greg shrugged. 'The usual stuff. She thought I was grumpy, stuffy, old-fashioned. But mainly she thought I was responsible for driving you away.'

I glanced at Lydia. She gave an awkward cough.

'That's not true,' I said. 'I was upset, but it was hardly your fault.'

'Still, I'm sorry,' said Greg. 'I shouldn't have told you to leave like that.'

I shook my head. 'I can't believe she fired you. After all that time.'

'She never liked me much. I think we both know that.'

'Maybe, if I talk to her—'

'That's kind of you, but I'd rather you didn't.'

I exchanged a glance with Nick, who shrugged again. The atmosphere had become considerably cool. I felt the need to change the subject.

'So,' I said. 'What have you chosen for the Shellcliff panto this year?'

'*The Little Mermaid*,' said Sam, brightening up.

'Bleugh,' said Nick. 'It's so soppy.'

Lydia glared at him. 'No it's *not*. I think you'll find the script we've found is subversively feminist.'

I smiled at Sam. 'Will you be auditioning for Ariel?'

Sam stared contemplatively at her pizza. 'I think I'd rather play the prince. Or maybe one of the Sea Witch's henchmen. They look fun.'

'You know, I've always wanted to play a villain in panto.'

'You'd be a great Sea Witch,' said Sam. 'You'd have to fight it out with Rose, though.'

I gave her a glower of mock offence. Sam laughed.

'You know,' said Lydia, skewering a piece of pasta with her fork and not quite meeting my eye. 'You could always come back.'

I stared at her. 'Are you sure that's such a good idea? After everything that was said?'

'I... realise I probably overreacted,' said Lydia.

I blinked. 'Is that an apology?'

'Yes... I suppose it is.'

'Then I'm sorry too.' I smiled, a little sadly. 'I would love to come back, but I'm not sure it's going to be practical. I should probably call my agent again, start looking for acting jobs.' I realised, as I spoke, that I sounded less than enthusiastic.

'You could run the bookshop,' said Sam.

I looked at Greg, who didn't meet my eye. 'I'm not sure that would be fair on your uncle.'

'You could rehire him,' said Sam. 'I mean, it's not as if it's even been open.'

I dropped my fork. 'Are you telling me the bookshop has been closed since I left?'

'Sarah's looking for a new manager,' said Lydia.

I looked at Greg again. 'And all that time, you've been stuck upstairs in the flat. I'm so sorry, Greg. My sister is... I don't quite know *what* she is.'

'It's fine,' said Greg. 'It's given me some time to think.'

'Please talk to Sarah,' said Nick. 'I want Greg to stop moping.'

Greg glared at him. 'I am not moping.'

'I caught him buying bunting the other day,' said Nick. He grinned. 'I think it reminds him of the bookshop. And you.'

'I did no such thing!' Greg flushed.

'He absolutely did,' said Nick. 'It's a problem. An addiction. Bunting and tote bags.'

'Leave it with me,' I said. 'I'll talk to Sarah.'

*

It was too late for Nick's Bookmobile to drive back to Shellcliff, so my friends found rooms in a nearby Premier Inn, with the intention of travelling home the next morning. Nick gave me an open invitation to join them; Lydia said she would catch the train with Sam, so there was a space for me if I wanted it.

I returned to my London flat. I made myself a cup of tea, picked up my new copy of *I Capture the Castle*, and settled down on the sofa. But I couldn't concentrate. I kept thinking about the bookshop.

I missed it. I missed the daily routine, the unexpected creativity, the sense of community. I missed being able to go home at the end of the day and relax with a book on my balcony. I missed the drama group rehearsals, which gave me all the joy of acting without the worry about if and when I would find another job. I missed Shellcliff. I missed Greg.

It was time to be honest with myself. I didn't want to live in London anymore. I wanted to be a bookseller. And I wanted to go home.

It wouldn't even mean I had to abandon my acting career. There were theatres nearby. Perhaps I could look for some less demanding acting jobs, small speaking parts, maybe. It wasn't as if I was leaving professional theatre behind forever. But for now, I would give myself space to think, and time to try some new things.

I called Sarah. She answered immediately, which was unusual for her. Previously, I always had the impression that she had more important things to do than talk on the phone, unless she was the person making the call.

'Hi, Charlotte. How are things?'

'Fine,' I said. 'How's the bookshop?'

'Oh, you know. It's okay. Still touch and go. But at least Christmas is coming. The busy season.'

'I've just been talking to Greg.'

'Oh,' said my sister again. She went silent.

'He told me what happened. Said you'd been closed for two weeks. For God's sake, Sarah. What were you thinking?'

'I don't know,' said Sarah. Her voice sounded shaky. 'I don't know. I panicked. You said you were leaving, and I was angry with Greg, and I didn't think I could manage on my own—'

'You could have told me.'

'Yes, well. You'd buggered off back to London, hadn't you?' There was a pause. 'Please don't say "I told you so". I know I've messed up utterly.'

'I wasn't going to say "I told you so",' I said. I paused and took a breath. 'I'm sorry for running away like that. Leaving you in the lurch. Coming back here was a mistake.'

'What?'

'I wish I hadn't left Shellcliff. I didn't really want to leave. I loved working in the bookshop.' I hesitated again. 'Would you consider letting me come back?'

There was a moment of silence.

'Sarah? Are you still there?'

'Oh, thank God,' said Sarah. 'I thought you'd never ask. When can you start?'

'Thank you.' I smiled, feeling a huge weight lift from my shoulders. 'I can start almost immediately. But I do have one condition.'

'Anything.'

'I'd like you to give Greg his job back.'

'But Charlotte—'

'He's an excellent bookseller. We're a team. If you don't offer Greg the job, I'm not coming back either.'

There was a pause.

'Could you ask him to dress like someone from the twenty-first century?'

'No. He can dress however he likes.'

Sarah sighed. 'Okay. But will you run the social media accounts? I can't see Greg on TikTok.'

'Sarah, I can promise you that Greg doesn't want to go anywhere near TikTok, even though it would be absolutely charming.'

'Oh, fine. It's a deal.'

I said goodbye to my sister. Then I pulled my suitcase down from the top of the wardrobe. This time, I was going to pack more knitwear.

Epilogue – Christmas

Greg

Seaswept Books had never looked better. Charlotte had put hours of work into creating our Christmas window displays. The large bay window had a Christmas tree bedecked with baubles and tiny books. With the help of the craft group at the library, she had used the pages of old proofs to create hanging snowflakes and special, book-themed bunting. Despite my misgivings about cutting up books, I couldn't deny that the final effect was quite lovely. The windows twinkled with tiny white fairy lights.

It was, I had to admit, the very epitome of good taste. There wasn't a piece of pink tinsel in sight.

It was a week before Christmas, and members of the drama group had gathered in the bookshop to read from *A Christmas Carol*. I was playing Scrooge. And, I realised, I was happy about it, not least because it meant I could wear an excellent top hat (I had to wear a night cap for the night-time scenes, but one couldn't have everything).

Our regular customers sipped glasses of mulled wine as the readings commenced. Charlotte was the narrator, and Sam and Rose played the Ghosts of Christmas Past and Present respectively. Nick had constructed an excellent puppet to represent the Ghost of Christmas Yet to Come, using a couple of wire coat hangers, two bright fairy lights for eyes and a piece of black fabric from wardrobe. The puppet was quite terrifying, and probably received the biggest round of applause of the evening.

Harry played all the other male roles, employing a variety of voices to great comedic effect. He and Charlotte had been spending a lot of time together over the last few months, but Charlotte refused to talk about it, or even admit they were an item ('We're just seeing how things go, darling!'). This seemed a bit rich after all the times she had quizzed me about Nick. I was determined to get more juicy details out of her at the first opportunity.

When the performance was over and we had all taken a bow, Lydia stepped forward and raised a glass.

'Thank you so much, everyone. As we're among friends, I would like to take this opportunity to make an exciting announcement.'

A hush fell over the small crowd. Lydia smiled. 'As you all know, Sam has been offered a place at the London School of Performing Arts. Yesterday, we found out that she's been offered a scholarship to support her studies. These are for *exceptionally* talented students.'

There was another round of clapping. A few members of the drama group whooped their approval.

Sam rolled her eyes. 'Mum! It's not a big deal or anything.'

'It is! Come on, you knew I was going to do this. It's just because I'm proud.'

Sam smiled. 'Whatever, Mum.'

Fortunately, Sam's embarrassment only lasted for a moment. She was instantly surrounded by the drama group.

Charlotte gave her a hug. 'Congratulations, darling. Well deserved!'

At a loose end, I retreated to the refreshment table, where I opened a new packet of posh crisps and poured them into a bowl.

A shadow fell over the table. 'Hey, love.'

I looked up to see Nick. 'Oh. Hello.'

'Are you okay? You seem a bit quiet.'

I smiled. 'I'm fine.'

'Come on. I know that face. Something's bothering you.'

I didn't want to tell him that Sam's news had made me feel a bit melancholy. I would miss her, of course, but it was more than that. A slight twinge of something that felt almost like regret. Or even jealousy.

Nick brushed my hand with his. 'Could we pop outside for a minute? There's something I'd like to show you.'

I glanced at the party. Charlotte was hosting with aplomb. I decided it would be fine to leave for a few minutes. We slipped outside.

The bookshop had been doing well in the run-up to Christmas. Crystal Moontide's signed book auction had raised enough money for us to cover our bills for two months, which was nothing short of amazing, and the additional publicity had brought new customers through our doors. The future was still uncertain, but I felt more confident than I had in months, not least because Charlotte and I made such a good team. She came up with the mad creative ideas, then I complained about them for a while, before helping to put them into practice. Everyone was happy.

And yet, there was still a shadow at the back of my mind. A sense that, during my temporary unemployment, I had glimpsed other possibilities, and promptly dismissed them.

I followed Nick across the road and into the small Italian pleasure garden on the seafront. He stopped next to the town's Christmas tree, lit up with coloured bulbs.

'This is all very mysterious,' I said.

'I wanted the right setting,' he said, gesturing towards the tree. Then he reached into his jacket pocket and took out an envelope.

'What's that?'

'It's your Christmas gift.' I opened my mouth to protest, but he held up a hand. 'And yes, I know you've got me something, and I know it's back at the bookshop, probably hidden in that stupid cupboard of yours. Please don't worry about it.' He handed me the envelope.

'What is it?'

'Just open it. Please.'

I opened the envelope, and drew out a thin brochure for a theatre in Scarborough, a venue where I had seen several excellent productions. Nick had marked one of the pages with a Post-it note.

'Oh, lovely!' I said. 'Theatre tickets?'

Nick smiled. 'Even better.'

I turned to the relevant page. There was an advert for an acting course for adults, with the chance to appear in a professional production.

'What's this?' I said.

'I've paid for the first three sessions.' Nick rubbed the back of his neck. 'When we were at the drama school, I know you said you didn't want to look back. But you're just so good and you couldn't go when you were Sam's age, and I just thought, well, this would be a way of trying it out again. Look, I'm sorry if it was a silly idea...'

My eyes filled with tears. I stared down at the brochure, and then looked up into Nick's anxious face.

'No,' I said. 'No. This is... I don't know what to say. This is the nicest thing anyone's ever done for me.'

'Gah, don't!' Nick rubbed his eyes. 'You'll start me off.'

I put my arm around his neck and drew his head down to mine. We kissed, softly, in front of the Christmas tree.

'You will go?' said Nick. 'On the acting course?'

'Yes. I'll go.' I smiled and squeezed his hand. 'Come on. Let's get back to the bookshop.'

Holding hands, we walked back across the road, where the windows of Seaswept Books glowed in welcome.

Acknowledgements

This novel is partly a love letter to booksellers and independent bookshops. It feels fitting that I should start by thanking the wonderful indies who were so supportive of my debut novel *The Moon and Stars*. Special thanks to the Grove Bookshop, Imagined Things, the Guisborough Bookshop, DRAKE the Bookshop, Pickering Book Tree and the Little Ripon Bookshop.

Thanks to my customers at Book Corner. You are wonderfully supportive, even when I'm a bit like Greg.

Thank you to Teesside University for being such brilliant champions of my writing and inviting me to your lovely library.

Thanks to Crossing the Tees Book Festival for having me back for a second time.

Thank you to my wonderful writer friends, especially Carmen, Em, Helen, Sarah and Sussi, who have given me so much encouragement over the years.

Thanks to all at Fairlight Books for believing in my work. I'm delighted my second novel has found a home with you. Special thanks to Louise Boland, my brilliant editor Laura Shanahan, and Beccy Fish for the gorgeous cover design.

Thanks to my friends Catherine, Isabel and Kate for your support and encouragement.

Special thanks to Mam and Dad for all your love and support.

About the Author

Jenna Warren was born in Middlesbrough and grew up in Saltburn-by-the-Sea. She studied Theatre at the University of Hull, and completed an MA in Creative Writing at Teesside University. Her first novel, *The Moon and Stars*, was published by Fairlight Books in 2022. Her short stories have featured in the anthologies *Whitby Abbey: Pure Inspiration* and *Through the Cracks: The Teesside Literary Society's Inaugural Anthology*. After she worked for several years as an assistant in an art gallery, her passion for books led her to open Book Corner, an independent bookshop in Saltburn. *The Hometown Bookshop* is her second novel.

TEMPORARY PALACES

TEMPORARY PALACES

The Great House in European Prehistory

Richard Bradley

OXBOW | books
Oxford & Philadelphia

Published in the United Kingdom in 2021 by

OXBOW BOOKS
The Old Music Hall, 106–108 Cowley Road, Oxford OX4 1JE

and in the United States by

OXBOW BOOKS
1950 Lawrence Road, Havertown, PA 19083

Paperback Edition: ISBN 978-1-78925-661-1
Digital Edition: ISBN 978-1-78925-662-8 (epub)

A CIP record for this book is available from the British Library

Library of Congress Control Number: 2021935097

Printed in the United Kingdom by Short Run Press

Typeset by Lapiz Digital Services

For a complete list of Oxbow titles, please contact:

United Kingdom	United States of America
Oxbow Books	Oxbow Books
Telephone (01865) 241249	Telephone (610) 853-9131
Fax (01865) 794449	Fax (610) 853-9146
Email: oxbow@oxbowbooks.com	Email: queries@casemateacademic.com
www.oxbowbooks.com	www.casemateacademic.com/oxbow

Oxbow Books is part of the Casemate group

Front cover: Edin's Hall: a lowland broch inside a hillfort in the Scottish borders. Photograph: Richard Bradley.
Back cover: A modern wood carving at the entrance to the early medieval site of Yeavering. Photograph: Richard Bradley.

Contents

Preface and acknowledgements   vii

List of figures   ix

Part One. A problem shared   1

  1. 'Nobody on earth knew of another building like it'   3

  2. From Anatolia to Zealand: an A to Z of Great Houses   28

Part Two. Dream houses   57

  3. From the foundations   59

  4. Castles in the air   81

Part Three. Setting the house in order   105

  5. On a larger scale   107

  6. Social distances   141

  7. Halls of residence and Halls of Fame   173

  8. Building societies: a summary and some conclusions   205

Bibliography   221

Preface and acknowledgements

I have written this book to explore a topic which has fascinated me for more than a decade. I began to organise my thoughts for a lecture to the Prehistoric Society in 2012, but I wrote this version in unusual circumstances. I was starting to sketch my ideas when the 2020 pandemic broke out. It felt as if I was under house arrest, and I could not visit any libraries. Digital access to a small selection of journals was a poor substitute, yet it did make me concentrate on a project that might have developed much more slowly. I gave little thought to publication until a draft was complete. It was necessarily restricted to sources that remained accessible and, where possible, to sites which I had visited, but, freed from the normal restraints of academic research, I was able to consider material that is usually out of bounds to a British prehistorian. Like my earlier book, *A Geography of Offerings*, it extends from the last hunter gatherers to the Viking Age. The problems raised by modern fieldwork do not arrange themselves according to period divisions.

Although it was written in isolation, the text has benefitted greatly from the comments of three friends and colleagues: John Blair, Helena Hamerow and Tanja Romankiewicz. Their advice has been invaluable in framing the arguments more clearly. They helped me to correct some errors, but any mistakes that remain are entirely my own. Two conferences provided a stimulus. One was held in Reading and organised by Gabor Thomas. The second was convened by Julie Lund in Oslo. I must thank Fraser Hunter who sent me his forthcoming article on the first Roman contacts with Scotland, and Marianne Hem Eriksen for letting me to read her recent book before publication. As so often, Courtney Nimura mediated between an impatient author and a temperamental laptop. Aaron Watson produced all the figure drawings to his usual high standard. I cannot thank them enough. Throughout the writing Katherine sustained an increasingly restless hermit.

I was allowed to go for walks during the lockdown (which is still not over). I often met Anwen Cooper and Duncan Garrow for coffee in a nearby park. That helped me to retain some sense of perspective when my manuscript ran aground. It was eventually refloated, and here is the result. Now that I have finished the book, they are the dedicatees.

List of figures

(all the drawings are by Aaron Watson)

Frontispiece   The site of the palace at Yeavering.

Fig. 1   The main regions studied in the book.

Fig. 2   The halls at Doon Hill, Yeavering and Balbridie.

Fig. 3   Earthworks and excavated structures at Durrington Walls and Knockaulin.

Fig. 4   Timber structures at Woodhenge and Knockaulin.

Fig. 5   Excavated buildings at Göbekli Tepe.

Fig. 6   The Trypillia mega-site at Nebelivka.

Fig. 7   The Bronze Age longhouse at Skrydstrup.

Fig. 8   A monumental timber building on Mont Lassois.

Fig. 9   Two Late Iron Age halls at Silchester.

Fig. 10   Timber buildings and associated structures at Lejre.

Fig. 11   The Iron Age roundhouse at Pimperne and the Neolithic longhouse at Elsloo.

Fig. 12   Plans of the large timber buildings at Navan Fort and Borg.

Fig. 13   The Neolithic house at Rastorf in relation to later burial monuments.

Fig. 14   Two Viking longhouses associated with round barrows.

Fig. 15   Contrasting plans of two Irish ringforts.

Fig. 16   A timber hall and ship setting at Lejre.

Fig. 17   The locations and plans of the halls at Crathes and Balbridie.

Fig. 18   Timber buildings inside the the enclosure at Mairy.

Fig. 19   Monumental Neolithic buildings at sites in northern and western France.

Fig. 20   Four timber buildings associated with Grooved Ware.

Fig. 21 Three stone settings comprising a square within a circle.

Fig. 22 Outline plans of Maeshowe and Stonehenge.

Fig. 23 Figure-of-eight structures sealed by the mound at Navan Fort.

Fig. 24 Paired Iron Age structures at Knockaulin and Thetford.

Fig. 25 Plan of the principal prehistoric monuments at Tara.

Fig. 26 Distributions of four regional groups of brochs in relation to the Roman frontier.

Fig. 27 Outline plan of the royal complex at Jelling.

Fig. 28 Outline plans of Gamla Uppsala and Uppåkra.

Fig. 29 The principal alignment of structures in an early phase at Yeavering.

Fig. 30 The early medieval monuments at Tara.

Part One

A problem shared

A modern wood carving at the entrance to the early medieval site of Yeavering. Photograph: Richard Bradley.

CHAPTER 1

'Nobody on earth knew of another building like it'

Introduction

The title of this book comes from a 'light poem' by the Scottish artist Robert Montgomery which has been displayed in a variety of settings across Europe (www. robertmontgomery.org/recycledlightpoems). It featured in the 2011 Venice Biennale and at a disused swimming pool in former East Berlin. It was also shown in Stavanger, at a dock for unloading fish in Lyon, at the Palais de Tokyo in Paris, and on the side of a multi-storey carpark in Cardiff. The inscription was powered by solar energy and read 'All palaces are temporary palaces'.

Like Montgomery's other work, this installation raises questions about ownership and power, but the idea that palaces might be temporary constructions has a particular resonance for archaeology where enormous but short-lived buildings are a recurrent and puzzling phenomenon. They have often been studied individually but are rarely considered as a group, and that is the aim of this book. It extends from the west of Asia as far as the Atlantic coastline, and from the time of the last hunter gatherers to the Viking Age (Fig. 1). It considers timber buildings more often than stone constructions and investigates their relationship with domestic architecture. Like the text from which it takes its name, its main concern is with social and political questions.

The starting point is another of Montgomery's installations: 'There are wooden houses on land in far-away places ….' One such place was close to the North Sea in Scotland. That is where this account begins.

Fig. 1 The main regions studied in this book, with the locations of additional examples used in Chapters Two and Four.

Cases of mistaken identity

Britain: the influence of Yeavering

In the 1960s an important excavation took place outside Dunbar (Fig. 2). Its results have featured in many studies of early medieval Scotland, but their authors confronted the problem that the results of such influential work were never published (Ralston 2019). The original project was undertaken by the Cambridge archaeologist Brian Hope-Taylor who was undoubtedly one of the most accomplished fieldworkers of his time, but very few of his projects were brought

Doon Hill

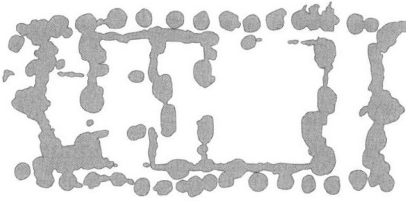

Yeavering

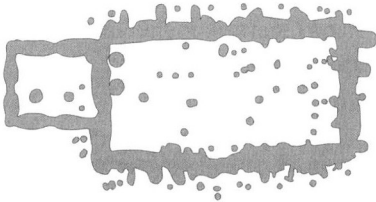

10 m

Balbridie

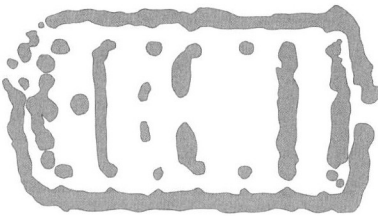

Fig. 2 Outline plans of two superimposed halls on Doon Hill, compared with timber buildings of similar size at Yeavering and Balbridie. Information from Ralston (2019), Hope-Taylor (1977) and Fairweather and Ralston (1993).

to completion. The one important exception was at the remarkable complex of Yeavering in northeast England where he investigated a royal centre documented by the historian Bede. His monograph recorded the traces of a series of timber buildings whose plans had been identified from the air (Hope-Taylor 1977).

The same process led to the new discoveries at Doon Hill, Dunbar, and Hope-Taylor followed his work at Yeavering with a project on that site. Again he recovered the ground plans of large wooden buildings.

There were two of them and in this case they were enclosed by a palisade. The first structure may have been repaired during the course of its history and was eventually destroyed by fire. It was replaced in the same position by a smaller rectangular construction. It was the later building that the excavator compared with those at Yeavering. Emboldened by this comparison, he dated the second structure to the Anglian settlement of the region in the seventh century AD and suggested that its predecessor was a hundred years older and must have been the work of the indigenous population. Until recently, many authorities were content to follow all, or part, of that interpretation. When the site was displayed to the public the outlines of the successive structures were marked on the ground by cement of two different colours.

Problems began when a third site found by air photography was excavated. This was at Balbridie in the northeast of Scotland. Here fieldwork identified a considerable rectangular building whose dimensions and method of construction were virtually the same as those of the first structure on Doon Hill, but in this case it was associated with Neolithic pottery and returned dates in the early fourth millennium BC. Although it seemed possible that it had been built of ancient bog oak, analysis of the burnt grain from the site confirmed its prehistoric origin (Fairweather & Ralston 1993). How could the problem be explained?

A compromise solution was considered but was never plausible. Maybe the earlier and larger building was indeed of Neolithic origin. It would explain its resemblance to that at Balbridie. The later structure at Dunbar would have been built more than four thousand years afterwards, as there seemed no other way of explaining why it looked like buildings at Yeavering whose chronology was not in any doubt. For a time this influenced the form in which Doon Hill was presented to visitors. It seemed possible that the people who erected the second structure at Dunbar recognised the Neolithic foundation trenches and followed them in their work. The idea was highly improbable, for it would have required skills that archaeologists developed more than a thousand years later.

New research has disposed of many of these problems because samples of charcoal associated with both buildings on Doon Hill have returned dates in the early fourth millennium BC. They are consistent with those from Balbridie and from more recently excavated structures of the same kind at Claish, Crathes and Carnoustie in other parts of Scotland (Brophy 2007; Sheridan 2013). Analysis of the surviving records even suggests that the resemblance between the later 'hall' at Dunbar and timber structures at Yeavering may have been exaggerated (Ralston 2019). This is understandable as both projects were undertaken by the same person. Hope-Taylor pursued a similar historical narrative in both cases and may have been led astray by his own expectations.

Now a different problem arises. There is no reason to contest the Neolithic date of the structures at Balbridie and Doon Hill, nor is there any case for a radical reappraisal of Yeavering. Not only was that site described in an important historical source, similar buildings have been excavated elsewhere in England and have a secure chronology. The problem is not to choose between a Neolithic context and a medieval one, but to consider why these extraordinary buildings were erected at such different times. Analogous structures dating from the intervening period have never been found.

An added complication is another discovery in Scotland. In 2011 Magnus Kirby published the results of his work at Lockerbie Academy. The site is a located in an area with a rich and varied archaeology and was on a route leading inland from the coast. It produced evidence of Early Bronze Age burials which focused on a low knoll, but what could not have been anticipated were the presence of another unusually large Neolithic building and the discovery of two superimposed structures of similar proportions dating from the first millennium AD. In this case there was no ambiguity as the prehistoric and medieval halls were in different parts of the site. The prehistoric example was associated with diagnostic pottery and a series of radiocarbon dates between 3950 and 3630 BC. The medieval structures provided dates between AD 540 and 670. The excavator emphasised the strategic locations of all these buildings, and this is reflected by the establishment of an Early Bronze Age cemetery at the highest point where its position seems to have been marked by a cairn. That monument could still have been visible in the early medieval period, but no trace of the Neolithic construction would have remained during either phase.

The report on the medieval halls at Lockerbie was published before Hope-Taylor's dating of Doon Hill was challenged, and for that reason Kirby proposed a similar interpretation for the successive medieval buildings. The earlier was described as 'British', and its more substantial successor was 'Anglian'. Its form was influenced by contacts with the kingdom of Northumbria. Again these unusual structures were related to the politics of the first millennium AD.

In fact there are similarities and differences between structures of these two periods, but they have been overlooked. The buildings on Doon Hill and the comparable structure at Balbridie are all of similar proportions and their lengths are approximately twice their widths. Hope-Taylor's Hall A (the older of the pair) was 23 m long, compared with lengths of 24 m at Claish (Barclay *et al.* 2002), 22 m at Balbridie (Fairweather & Ralston 1993), and 22.5 m at Crathes (Murray *et al.* 2009). All three were very similar to one another. The Neolithic example at Lockerbie was even bigger and measured about 27 m by 8 m. The equivalent figures for the larger of two structures recently excavated at Carnoustie were 35 m by 9 m (www.guard-archaeology.co.uk/carnoustiehoard); the smaller building on that site had similar dimensions to the second construction on Doon Hill. Few Neolithic houses have been identified in Britain (Darvill 1996), but many more are recorded in Ireland where their chronology is comparable to that of the Scottish structures. Jessica Smyth's (2014) research suggests that almost all of them were square or rectangular. One group was between 6 m and 8 m long and between 4 m and 7 m wide. The dimensions of the larger buildings were less consistent and extended between 9 m and 13 m in length and from 6 m to 8 m in width. It means that a hall like the first building on Doon Hill was truly exceptional and enclosed about 70% more floor space than any of these houses. The enclosed area was five times greater than it was in the smaller Irish dwellings.

Similar considerations apply to the medieval structures. The successive halls at Lockerbie Academy were 15 m and 20 m long, and their widths were 6.5 m and 7 m respectively. Most domestic buildings of the same date were considerably smaller, and on average they enclosed between a third and half as much space. Helena Hamerow (2012) defines early medieval 'Great Halls' as structures over 18 m long, and on Hope-Taylor's site at Yeavering the largest building attained a length of 24 m; their equivalents on extensively excavated sites at Lyminge and Cowdery's Down in southern England were 21 m and 22 m long respectively (G. Thomas 2018; Millett & James 1983). There is no question about their ages, yet they were the same size as Neolithic halls in northern Britain. At Sutton Courtenay in the upper Thames valley an early medieval structure of the same kind was 30 m in length and 10 m wide (Brennan & Hamerow 2015): almost the dimensions of the Neolithic monument at Carnoustie.

Despite such a remarkable coincidence, there were important differences between the prehistoric and early medieval buildings. Although their dimensions overlap, there were practical limits to their scale. Where any evidence survives the principal timbers were of oak. The widths of these structures must have posed a special problem as experimental reconstructions show that it would have been difficult to manoeuvre rafters of more than 10 m. That may be why longhouses of any date in Northwest Europe were usually about the same width (Bradley 2013a). On the other hand, a rectilinear structure could extend to almost any length provided it could stand up to strong winds.

The halls of both periods made considerable demands. In his report on the excavation at Yeavering Hope-Taylor argues that the wood used in their construction had been acquired from a 'significantly large' area and in a striking phrase he refers to the 'oaken extravagance' of individual structures at the site (Hope-Taylor 1977, 333–34). That would apply even more directly to the Neolithic building at Balbridie which had an unusual width of 11 m: a higher figure than most of the medieval examples. Its neighbour at Crathes might have posed still greater problems, as pollen analysis shows it was situated in an area of open land, suggesting that the wood was brought from a distance. The raising of all these structures involved the conspicuous consumption of raw material. Assuming, as most reconstructions do, a roof pitch of about 45 degrees, unusually wide buildings of this sort must have been higher than the others and might have appeared more monumental. Oliver Rackham (1976, 73–74) observes that few structures surviving from the Middle Ages used oak timbers much over 6 m long and that those with lengths of 9 m or more were altogether exceptional. They were usually public buildings like cathedrals. Constructing prehistoric halls must have presented a significant challenge. Oak is very heavy. Whatever the dimensions of the individual timbers, their erection required a significant workforce.

If some of the posts were 10 m long and dispersed within an area of forest, this must have made their construction even more demanding. It may be no accident that the dimensions of the Neo-lithic halls were so similar to one another. Because of the constraints imposed by sourcing and transporting the raw material they *might have approached the limit* of what could be built at the time. Similar constraints may have influenced the scale of their early medieval counterparts, although they were undoubtedly more sophisticated structures, and by that time woodland was carefully managed. Even so there was an obvious emphasis on display. It is unfortunate that little can be said about the external appearance of both groups of buildings. Their walls could have been lavishly decorated and the posts might well have been carved. That much is suggested by pictorial evidence and surviving church buildings in Scandinavia.

The external dimensions of prehistoric and medieval halls may have been strikingly similar, but their interiors were organised in distinctive ways. The earlier architectural tradition was characterised by structures with massive gables and a number of internal partitions which divided them into separate compartments. They would have impeded movement within the structure and their existence has never been explained (Debert 2016). The Great Halls of the first millennium AD had a very different character. The internal space remained largely open, although small rooms might be provided towards the ends of these buildings. External annexes could be added in order to lengthen the structure. In contrast to some of their counterparts in Northern Europe, they did not include a byre.

There were other contrasts between them. Most of the Neolithic examples were isolated, although there were two halls of different sizes at Carnoustie and the successive buildings on Doon Hill appear to have been enclosed by a polygonal palisade. There were very few features around them. By contrast, early medieval Great Halls were usually part of a larger complex in which the structures shared common alignments and were organised in relation to one another. That is evident at the most extensively excavated sites – Yeavering, Cowdery's Down and Lyminge – and a similar configuration can be recognised on air photographs (McBride 2020). Of the sites considered here only the successive halls at Lockerbie did not conform to this pattern.

There are still further differences between the histories of individual sites. The Neolithic structures show signs of piecemeal repair but only at Doon Hill was one of them demolished and replaced in the same position. Despite their enormous sizes, these buildings may have been used for short periods and one result of fieldwork has been to show that at least some examples were destroyed by fire. The evidence from Crathes is a little ambiguous as the wood may have been ignited after the hall was taken down, but this seems unlikely as so many other monuments were set alight during the same period. It was equally common with the houses in Ireland. There is little to indicate a similar practice in early medieval Britain, although burnt structures were identified during two of the main phases at Yeavering and were also found at Cowdery's Down. On the other hand, it was usual for halls to be replaced. Either the new construction was in exactly the same position as its predecessor, or it was erected nearby and conformed to the same alignment. This was clearly documented by excavations at Yeavering and Lyminge. Despite their monumental aspect, the structures may not have been intended for a long period of use, and in this respect they share an important feature with their Neolithic counterparts.

A characteristic of some of these buildings is the paucity of artefacts. The Neolithic structures are found with fine pottery and deposits of burnt grain, but the stone tools that would usually be associated with settlements are extremely rare. In the same way, not all the Great Halls of the early medieval period have produced many finds, despite the number and quality of artefacts buried in graves during the same period. In this case there is regional patterning, so that elaborate objects are comparatively unusual at sites in the north and west of Britain, but are commonly associated with those in lowland England. Yeavering is a case in point. In contrast to many projects in which the site is stripped by machine. Hope-Taylor (1977, 32) says that the topsoil over and around the timber buildings was removed by hand; a later account of the project suggests that this was not entirely true (Miket 2013, 158, note 12). Even so, it is unlikely that many items were missed during this process. In combination with the structural evidence it implies that these places were exceptional.

Most of the locations selected for Great Halls shared a distinctive history. The medieval buildings were commonly established amidst the remains of prehistoric structures: earthworks or arrangements of standing stones. Something similar may apply to the Neolithic building at Crathes. Here people must have observed a line of partly filled pits dating from the Mesolithic period, as these features were reopened. This may be a unique case, but half the complexes established or used during the seventh century AD retained traces of earlier activities: round barrows, round cairns, cursus monuments, monoliths or stone circles. Sometimes it was simply their presence that mattered, but at Yeavering the principal alignment of medieval buildings extended between the positions of two Neolithic or Bronze Age monuments (Blair 2018, fig. 30). Elsewhere the sequence could run in the opposite direction. The new dates for Doon Hill suggest that its importance in the Neolithic period was recalled during subsequent phases. The same site included a Middle Bronze Age cremation cemetery, a small square enclosure of later date, and two hillforts attributed to the Iron Age. Although Ian Ralston (2019) suggests that there might have been an early cairn on the site, the evidence is limited and it may be the distinctive character of certain locations that explains why they enjoyed more than one period of significance. In any case it would be wrong to imagine that their histories could be remembered in detail over an extended period. Perhaps the names of these places lasted longer than other elements. In that case their roles in the remote past would need to be reinvented. A good example is provided by Yeavering which Bede refers to as 'Ad Gefrin' (Hope-Taylor 1977, 15). The name survives in a modern form – the initial letter G would be pronounced like a Y (John Blair pers. comm.) – but nothing was known about its distinctive buildings until their outlines were recognised from the air.

Another case of mistaken identity illustrates the same points.

Ireland: the influence of Tara, Navan and Knockaulin

The rectangular buildings of the Neolithic and medieval periods contrast with a series of circular structures established in Ireland during the Iron Age. In this case a protracted history is suggested by archaeological and written sources, but their integration has created problems. These structures combine distinctive earthworks with enormous timber buildings and are usually described as 'royal sites' or 'royal centres'. That is because their names feature in early literature. Like the Great Halls of the neighbouring island, they can be found in places with concentrations of older structures (Newman 1997; Waterman 1997; Johnston & Wailes 2007; Waddell *et al.* 2009). The most extensively investigated sites are Knockaulin (Dún Ailinne), Navan Fort (Emain Macha), Rathcroghan (Crúachain) and Tara (Teamhair). Again their names have proved remarkably tenacious and in three cases they are echoed in the modern landscape.

Most of these sites share common features (Bradley 2013b). They are on low hills with views in all directions and are generally bounded by circular enclosures with an external bank and an internal ditch; an alternative was a wooden palisade. Some of the buildings inside them were approached by 'avenues', roads, or formal entranceways and could be identified as rings of posts. Due to the sheer size of these structures their excavators could not decide whether they were roofed. The dating evidence shows that the main period of use was from the second and first centuries BC, although sites like Navan Fort were established before that time. They feature in literary texts written down many years later.

For a while these distinctive monuments posed a problem because their forms were so like those of Neolithic henges in Britain, the largest of which were established in the third millennium BC. They certainly shared the same elements: circular earthwork enclosures with an internal ditch; formal approaches that provided access to the interior; and enormous wooden buildings. So striking were the similarities between them that it seemed possible that they conformed to a single style of architecture (A. Gibson 2000). If so, it must have been used for a very long time. Neolithic henges were already documented in Ireland, although they had seen little fieldwork. It was only in 1998 that the outermost earthwork at Navan Fort was investigated and shown to date from the late pre-Roman Iron Age (Mallory 2000). Until then it had been reasonable to think that it was older (Simpson 1989).

The similarities between Neolithic and Iron Age monuments were undoubtedly striking, but they had not been documented in much detail before the 1960s. It was then that two important monuments were excavated. They were the Irish 'royal centre' at Knockaulin (Johnston & Wailes 2007), and Durrington Walls close to Stonehenge (Wainwright & Longworth 1971). These sites shared several features (Fig. 3). The principal earthwork at Durrington was roughly circular and about 500 m in diameter. New fieldwork shows that it replaced a palisade which followed the same course. The outer perimeter of Knockaulin was roughly the same size and measured 500 m by 420 m. Part of it overlay another circuit about 390 m in diameter; a smaller enclosure on the same site was associated with a kind of forecourt and a large circular building. The latest earthworks at Durrrington and Knockaulin had an external bank, but their boundaries were built on different scales and the ditch of the Neolithic monument was larger than that of its Irish counterpart and wider than its equivalent

Durrington Walls

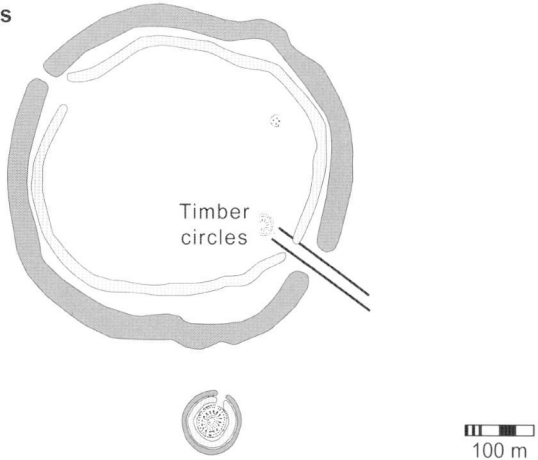

Knockaulin

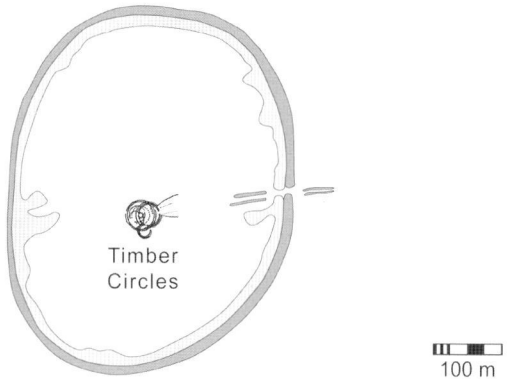

Fig. 3 Outline plans of the earthwork enclosures, avenues and excavated structures at Durrington Walls and Knockaulin. Information from Wainwright and Longworth (1971) and Johnston and Wailes (2007).

at Navan Fort. The principal timber buildings inside them were of similar dimensions. The largest structure at Knockaulin was 43 m in diameter; the equivalent figure at Navan was 40 m, at Durrington it was 38 m, and at Tara it was about 30 m. One of the principal structures at Knockaulin was approached by a roadway. So was the outer earthwork at Durrington Walls where the avenue led from the River Avon.

Most of the same elements are repeated at other sites in Ireland. The diameter of the outer earthwork at Navan Fort was 290 m, and again it had the same ground plan. A comparable enclosure at Rathcroghan was bounded by a palisade. In the centre of Navan Fort a gigantic circular building was erected in 95 BC: a precise date is provided by dendrochronology. It was buried beneath a considerable mound. There was another at Rathcroghan where remote sensing shows that a circular building 32 m in diameter was erected on its summit or embedded in its construction. It would have been up to twenty-five times the size of a small Iron Age roundhouse. Huge edifices of this kind differ from the Neolithic buildings in England because they were commonly replaced in the same positions. Individual structures may not have stood for long periods, and need not have been in continuous use.

There were circular structures of similar proportions inside some of the Neolithic henges in southern England. The largest examples in Wessex are the same size as the biggest buildings in Ireland (Fig. 4). Thus that at Mount Pleasant was 38 m in diameter (Wainwright 1979), the Sanctuary at Avebury had a diameter of 39 m (Pollard 1992), and Woodhenge – an oval setting of posts just outside Durrington Walls – had a maximum dimension of 43 m (Cunnington 1929). The Northern Circle at Durrington Walls was conceived on a comparable scale. It is hardly surprising that they had been attributed to the same tradition. If they had roofs – a point that has never been resolved – their construction must have approached the limits of what could be built at the time. They would share that characteristic with the earliest halls.

Other features are shared by monument complexes on either side of the Irish Sea. A notable feature of recent surveys at Rathcroghan and Tara is how often less conspicuous monuments have been identified around the principal structures – smaller circular enclosures, rings of posts, avenues, fences, and mounds. Little is known about them and it is uncertain when they were built. Those associated with Rathcroghan

Woodhenge

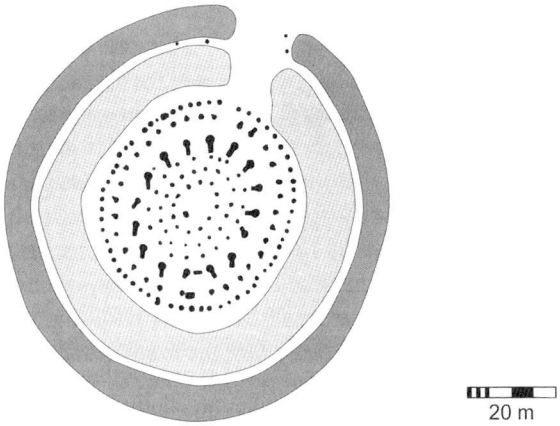

Knockaulin

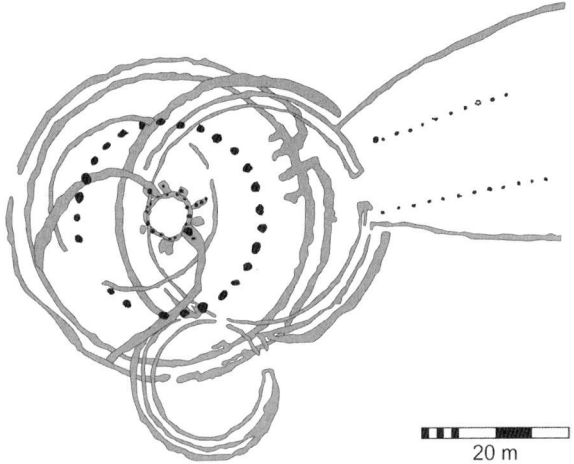

Fig. 4 Circular timber structures at Woodhenge and Knockaulin. Information from Cunnington (1929) and Johnston and Wailes (2007).

and Tara extended across much of the surrounding landscape. Fewer features were associated with the main monuments at Knockaulin and Navan Fort, but none of these constructions was built in isolation.

The same is true of Neolithic henges which were seldom self-contained. Whether they were enclosed by earthworks or palisades, they rarely appeared singly and often featured smaller monuments inside them. Others are found in the surrounding area. Durrington Walls illustrates both points as the interior of the site contains the enormous post circle considered earlier, as well as smaller buildings enclosed by a bank and ditch. The same applies to the surrounding area where another massive structure, Woodhenge, was just outside the monument. Not far away was a still more famous site. It seems likely that the largest wooden building at Durrington was established at the same time as the main setting of monoliths at Stonehenge. Both places were linked by earthwork avenues connecting them to the River Avon. Once the original structures had been abandoned or were going out of use, burial mounds proliferated in the vicinity (Pollard *et al.* 2017).

Another feature is shared between British henges and Irish royal centres, for they were built amidst the remains of older monuments. This is certainly true of the examples considered here. The Neolithic earthwork at Mount Pleasant was located near an older enclosure as well as an elongated long barrow. Further along the same ridge was a substantial palisade and a henge delimited by a circle of shafts. Similarly, Durrington Walls and Woodhenge were close to the terminal of a Middle Neolithic cursus, near to a number of long barrows, and not far from a recently discovered causewayed enclosure.

There were even closer links with the past at two of the Irish sites. The great timber buildings at Knockaulin were superimposed on the remains of what might have been a round barrow associated with Early Neolithic pottery. The excavation found numerous artefacts dating from this period, although most of them had been disturbed by later structures. The palisade or ditch that predated the earthwork perimeter is known from geophysical survey but seems to have been organised in discontinuous segments, raising the possibility that this was a causewayed enclosure (Johnston *et al.* 2009). Other examples have been identified during recent fieldwork in Ireland (W. O'Brien & O'Driscoll 2017).

The evidence from the Hill of Tara is much more clearly defined. Here the first major monument was a decorated passage tomb, again of Neolithic date. It was reused during the Early Bronze Age when it became one of the principal cremation cemeteries in Ireland (M. O'Sullivan 2005). It is relevant to this account as its position influenced the planning of the Iron Age monuments. The main palisaded enclosure – the Rath na Rioch – included the remains of the tomb on its perimeter. As seems to have happened at Knockaulin, features surviving from the past were invested with a new significance.

Origins, affinities and afterlives

So far this chapter has made two comparisons. One was between Neolithic structures in northern Britain and the Great Halls of the early medieval period; and the other between large timber structures associated with Late Neolithic henges and those in Iron Age Ireland. It has focused on the identification of monumental architecture and highlighted several features that they shared in common. On the other hand, it rejected any direct connections between them. Are there other ways of thinking about their origins?

Archaeological evidence

Two features are particularly informative: the relationship between these extraordinary structures and the domestic architecture of the same phases; and the possibility that their prototypes can be found in mainland Europe. The first question is relevant to all the buildings mentioned so far, but the second need not apply to the evidence from the 'royal centres' which seem to be peculiar to Ireland.

These issues are closely related to one another. The Neolithic halls share several characteristics with the houses of the same period. They were built using the same construction methods and materials, and, like those buildings, were commonly set on fire. The monumental structures observe similar proportions to well-documented dwellings in Ireland and again they could be divided into separate rooms (Smyth 2014). Apart from their size and extravagant use of timber, the main distinction is that they contain more subdivisions (Debert 2016). Another difference is that they are seldom associated with significant collections of artefacts apart from pottery.

In the absence of an accurate chronology it would be easy to claim that the first Neolithic houses in Ireland provided the prototypes for these impressive constructions, but in fact they were contemporary with one another; the second, smaller example on Doon Hill resembles some of these structures. More likely sources of inspiration for both groups of buildings are dwellings around the coast of Northwest Europe. They share their dimensions and rectangular ground plans, but few are recorded in detail, and the closest parallels date from a later phase, between 3500 and 3100 BC (Müller 2011). There were much longer buildings inside the enclosure at Mairy in the Ardennes (Laurelut 2011); they are discussed in detail in Chapter Five. They share the general character of the Scottish halls and in this case they were built during the period when farmers first settled these islands. It seems possible that the forms of the most massive constructions in Britain referred to connections with the Continent and the past in the way that is more often used to explain the appearance of long barrows (J. Thomas 2015).

The Great Halls of the early medieval period also make wider references. Again their layout recalls the domestic buildings of this period, some of which have been identified nearby. Here the contrast is mainly one of size. The origins of their distinctive rectangular ground plans have often been discussed. Were they inspired by insular Roman prototypes, or, as seems more likely, did they recall established architectural traditions in Scandinavia, northern Germany and the Low Countries: the regions from which eastern England was settled? Hamerow's (2012, 18–22) review of the evidence shows that similar structures are common on both sides of the North Sea. If the forms of Great Halls in Britain were influenced by those of domestic buildings, they may have referred to an ancestral homeland across the water, for enormous wooden buildings are found there although their architecture is different. Nevertheless it is on the basis of such comparisons that Anglo-Saxon buildings have been compared with the mead-hall described in *Beowulf*: an epic poem that was written in Old English but set in what is now Denmark. It seems likely that the original setting was Lejre, near to the later capital at Roskilde. Here enormous timber structures have been found by excavation (Christensen 2015); the site is discussed in Chapters Two and Seven.

By contrast, the huge buildings associated with Irish royal centres do not refer to distant prototypes, although similar features have occasionally been identified in Britain. Instead their characteristic architecture must have been influenced by the forms of insular round-houses of a kind that may even have been present at the same sites. Katharina Becker (2019) has shown that they were constructed using the same techniques as the largest structures of the Iron Age, and for that reason it is useful to think of these monuments as 'Great Houses': a term that is normally used in New World archaeology (DeBoer 1997). It is best to interpret them in relation to local developments.

Literary sources

Another perspective is suggested by literary sources of later date. Two are especially relevant here. The circular buildings in Ireland feature in the heroic tales that make up the Ulster Cycle. In the same way an early medieval hall called Heorot plays an important part in the epic poem *Beowulf*, but no purpose is served by taking their contents literally and these texts must be treated with caution. On the other hand, they do reflect some *themes* which are directly relevant to this chapter.

There is little prospect of resolving the problems. There are differences of opinion on when these texts were first written down, although it is clear that *Beowulf* was closer in time to the halls at Yeavering than the Ulster Cycle was to the Iron Age. Different scholars have favoured a date for *Beowulf* at various points between the seventh century and AD 1000 (the date attributed to the only manuscript copy), although an older text seems to have existed in the early eighth century AD (Lapidge 2000). Apart from purely linguistic considerations, the debate focuses on two issues (Hills 1997; Niles & Osborn 2007; Hines 2011). The events it describes feature a number of elements that can be identified in early medieval archaeology. The use of a Great Hall is only one of them. Others were elaborate public funerals including the practice of ship burial, the giving of lavish gifts, the deposition of treasure, and a variety of identifiable weapons. One problem is whether the sources of inspiration were in Denmark, the ostensible setting of the story, or in Britain where the poem was written down. At the same time it seems possible that the text of *Beowulf* was assembled from a variety of sources, some of them significantly earlier than the others; they even contain echoes of the Old Testament. The texts may have undergone significant changes in the course of oral transmission. That may be why it was difficult to integrate the pagan and Christian elements in the story. The final version provided a moral lesson which may not have been part of the original conception.

There are similar problems with the Irish sources which are even more disparate. If they referred to events in the Iron Age, they were in the distant past when they were recorded (Mallory 2016). Here there is a special problem for three of the royal sites that feature in these texts – Emain Macha, Crúachain and Teamhair – can be identified on the ground. As Jim Mallory has shown, there are problems in matching the ornaments, weapons, fortifications and dwellings described in early accounts with those documented in the Irish Iron Age. Instead their closest equivalents date from the later first millennium AD, and that may indicate when the tales assumed their current form. Of course they could have drawn on older sources, but it can never be proved.

On both sides of the Irish Sea integration of archaeological and literary sources is problematical, and the same applies to any direct comparisons between Britain and South Scandinavia. One possibility is that most of these texts were codified after the period of Viking settlement. Scribes working in monasteries in Britain and Ireland could have assembled this material, but that does not explain why they were preserved. Apart from their Neolithic counterparts, all the buildings considered in this chapter play a role in these accounts. What is more surprising is that they are described in comparable terms although their prototypes were so different from one another. Although they did not share a common origin, the literary accounts of them converge. Undoubtedly these structures were extraordinary pieces of architecture, but they may also have been treated as an archetype.

Beowulf

According to Seamus Heaney's (1999) translation, Heorot was 'a great mead-hall meant to be a wonder of the world for ever … the hall of halls … [It] towered, its gables wide and high'. As the hero and his companions approached it, 'the timbered hall rose before them, radiant with gold. Nobody on earth knew of another building like it. Majesty dwelt there, its light shone over many lands'. It was a 'dazzling stronghold'. Heorot was probably decorated with antlers or animal skulls (its name is the word for 'stag') and was 'handsomely structured, a sturdy frame braced with the best of blacksmith's work inside and out'. The hall contained two high seats – one of them the king's throne – and a series of gilded benches which could be taken away when a party of warriors slept there. There was a central hearth and the walls were embellished with tapestries. 'Gold thread shone in the wall-hangings, woven scenes that attracted and held the eye's attention'. The floor was also a distinctive colour. Several ancillary buildings are mentioned in the poem, and the entrance to the main structure was approached by a paved road. The door was secured by iron hinges and was wide and high enough to admit eight horses introduced as a gift for the hero. John Niles's (Niles & Osborn 2007, 177) comment on this description of Heorot is thought-provoking and apt:

> We see its true nature, as pertaining to the real world as augmented by imagination … The hall's dimensions are as they should be, in this larger-than-life heroic drama. Heorot is to any actual hall as the hero Beowulf is to any ordinary human being. The hall overshadows all other material things mentioned in the poem. It serves as the radiant centre of the hero's social world.

Most of the elements mentioned in the text are consistent with the results of excavation. The evidence of massive posts has been discussed already and Hope-Taylor's work at Yeavering even identified traces of the iron frame that reinforced the timbers. The internal fittings of a Great Hall could be represented by post holes although they can be difficult to interpret, while the 'brightly coloured' floor probably consisted of a distinctive kind of plaster favoured during the Roman period (G. Thomas 2018). These elements emphasise the scale and magnificence of Heorot, yet the poet indulged in hyperbole. The interior was supposedly decorated with ivory and there is a still more intriguing reference to a 'lofty roof of shining gold'. This feature is mentioned more than once and here he employs a literary device for which there are several precedents. According to Karl Wentersdorf (2007), golden buildings feature in early German literature and in the Prose Edda. This may also have been an allusion to the profligate use of gold in the buildings of ancient Rome. The same idea featured in the poetry of Venantius Fortunatus which was popular in Anglo-Saxon England.

The Ulster Cycle

In 1957 Rosemary Cramp wrote an influential article on 'Beowulf and archaeology'. She was able to draw on the first results of Hope-Taylor's research at Yeavering. Seven years later Kenneth Jackson (1964) took a comparable approach in his book *The Oldest Irish Tradition: A Window on the Iron Age*. His account was different because he could not use the results of excavation. Although Seán O'Riordàin had already worked at Tara, the full results of his project were published posthumously, and Jackson's study appeared before fieldwork began at Knockaulin. When he gave the original lecture in 1964 the investigation of Navan Fort was at an early stage. For that reason his description of the Great Houses associated with royal centres was based on literary evidence:

> The hall seems to have been a fairly large building, made of a wooden frame with weather-boarding, and roofed with shingles; inside, the roof was held up by carved and decorated

pillars. There was a fire on the floor and a vent in the roof for the smoke. All round the walls, apparently between the pillars, was a range of what one might call compartments like a row of boxes at a theatre, raised somewhat above the level of the floor and perhaps separated from one another by partitions or curtains. In these 'boxes'…. the chief heroes sat at the feast… each with his immediate followers about him and thence he could look into the body of the hall and watch his fellow guests. Very likely they slept there too (Jackson 1964, 20–21).

Although he under-estimated the sizes of these structures, his summary contains most of the features of what Jim Mallory (2016, 162) calls the 'Standard Irish Palace Description'. It featured a massive wooden building which was usually built of oak. In an account of Crúachain it was divided into radial compartments whose occupants were of different status, although they shared the central fireplace. Another way of understanding the layout of the building was as a series of concentric rings. The entire structure might be decorated by wood carvings and could have several doors. Apart from this last feature, the scheme is broadly consistent with archaeological evidence, but, like the description of Heorot, it adds some extraordinary elements. In one account the roof of the building was breached by no fewer than twelve glass windows. The pillars in the interior were made of bronze, and the rails that might have separated the compartments were of copper and silver. Mallory suggests that these references to metal fittings were inspired by classical or Biblical sources. Even the use of pine in the construction might have been a literary conceit. That is hardly surprising as there is general agreement that the Irish epic, the Táin, was written down by monks who would have been familiar with other texts. Most were in Latin, but they might have included translations from Greek.

A user's guide

The chapter ends with some comments about terms and methods. As this book considers examples taken from different traditions in European archaeology, it is essential to use consistent terms to describe the largest buildings. The same applies to the phases in which they were built. A potential problem concerns the word 'hall', as it has different connotations on each side of the North Sea. In Britain unusual buildings dating from the first millennium AD are generally described as Great Halls. They include the monumental structures at Yeavering and similar sites, and that is the sense in which the concept is employed here; in fact the Old English word *healle* refers to special buildings like Heorot (Helena Hamerow pers. comm.). In Scandinavian sources, however, the same word 'hall' is used for the principal chamber inside one of these buildings. It was here that literary evidence says that ceremonies took place.

There is also a contrast between the chronological schemes employed in different parts of Europe. Lowland Britain was incorporated in the Roman Empire, and here the 'Iron Age' ended when that happened and an 'Early Medieval' period commenced when imperial rule collapsed. In highland areas and in Ireland it is acceptable to refer to a Roman Iron Age. By contrast, Scandinavia was never conquered, so here the same term Iron Age covers the first millennium AD. Again the period has been subdivided but it extended to the Viking Age. The local terms will be used where absolute dates do not exist, but the English terminology will be used whenever the text refers to insular examples.

The title of this book refers to the Great House in *prehistoric* Europe. Definitions of prehistory vary between the places considered here. That is not surprising as the concept depends on an absence of historical sources rather than the character of any particular society. This has obvious implications for the methods employed in research, so that the study of prehistory depends to a large extent on field archaeology. It provides the main source for this account, but there are cases in which ostensibly prehistoric buildings in one area were contemporary with those described as early medieval in another. This chapter is a case in point. Rather than conform to a limited and all-too-insular conception of the prehistoric period, the book will cross those boundaries where it is helpful to access a wider body of research. Even so, the text is weighted towards the earlier evidence, and information from the 'long Iron Age' of Scandinavia is treated mainly as a source of ideas. This account focuses on the timber architecture of Western and Northern Europe.

Lastly, these differences are illustrated by a recent book which considers some of the same evidence from the perspective of a historian, albeit a scholar with direct experience of archaeological methods. David Rollason's (2016) excellent study *The Power of Place* has the subtitle *Rulers and their Palaces, Landscapes, Cities, and Holy Places*. It is based on first-hand knowledge of a large number of monumental buildings in medieval Europe, combined with documentary sources. It does consider a few of the same sites as this account – Yeavering, Tara, and Jelling – but its main concern is with surviving stone buildings instead of the more exiguous traces of wooden structures. It also covers the Classical and early medieval periods rather than earlier phases. For that reason the two volumes complement one another geographically and chronologically. The fact that they deal with different kinds of evidence does not present a problem, and anyone interested in what is said here should read what Rollason writes about the same subjects.

CHAPTER 2

From Anatolia to Zealand: an A to Z of Great Houses

The first chapter compared the forms of buildings of different ages and highlighted some striking resemblances in the ways in which they were conceived. But it did not say much about how they were used. Some of these issues are addressed here. Having started with material that will be familiar to readers in Britain and Ireland, Chapter Two extends much further across time and space, exploring similar issues from the era of the last hunter gatherers to the medieval period, and from Göbekli Tepe in western Asia to Lejre in South Scandinavia. Despite so much diversity they share a surprising number of elements.

Göbekli Tepe

In 2019 the Turkish government instituted the 'Year of Göbekli Tepe', following a successful 'Year of Troy' which had increased the number of visitors to the site. Now the same policy was extended to an earlier monument which was already on the UNESCO World Heritage List. Tourists could inspect the remains of 'the oldest temple in the world': a group of enigmatic structures dating between 10,000 and 8000 BC (Schmidt 2006; 2011; Dietrich 2011). On any account they were among the most significant discoveries of the late twentieth century.

The claim that this was the site of the world's oldest temple was a measured statement compared with some of the accounts circulating on the internet. That is no reflection on the high quality of the research at Göbekli Tepe, but its interpretation has given rise to much discussion. For the excavators, who are still working there, it possesses some exceptional features.

Several large walled enclosures were set deeply in the ground (Fig. 5). Geophysical survey suggests there were 20 of these circular buildings, but it is not clear how many were used simultaneously; they may have been constructed in sequence. The walls of the enclosures were renewed and extended more than once so that the floor area of each structure became progressively smaller over time. A row of benches extended around the perimeter and faced the central area.

There were settings of stone pillars within these enclosures, embellished with reliefs of wild animals, birds of prey, and snakes. They could be combined with features of the human body such as arms or

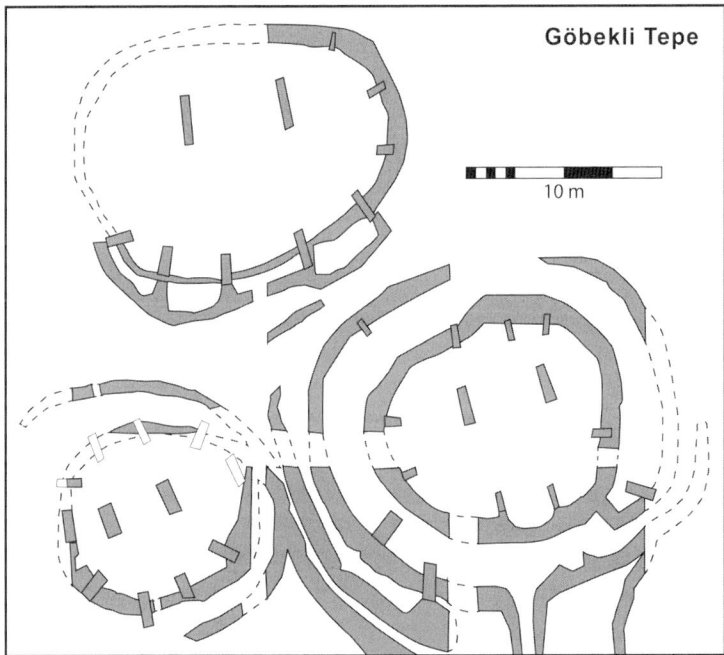

Fig. 5 The main group of excavated buildings at Göbekli Tepe. Information from Schmidt (2011).

hands and even with indications of clothing; it is obvious that they were meant to be anthropomorphic. The tallest were up to 7 m high and could weigh 50 metric tons. They were located towards the centres of the enclosures while the others were arranged along the inside wall. All the monoliths had been quarried a short distance away. Some were reused in the construction of later buildings, but even then there could have been 200 of them.

Each enclosure was filled with a mixture of artefacts, food remains and rubble. It seems to have been deposited episodically and it buried the monument once it went out of use. There were large quantities of wild animal bones, but no remains of domesticates. The proportions of different species were not the same as those depicted on the pillars which emphasised the importance of raptors, snakes and predators. Fragments of human bone were extremely rare and so far no burials have been found at Göbekli Tepe. After the remains had been covered over, a conspicuous mound accumulated so that only the tops of the tallest pillars could be seen. The site was reused, perhaps without an interval, by smaller rectangular buildings whose architecture shared some of the same features.

The early date of this complex is remarkable (Dietrich 2011). Although it was used at a time when people were making the first experiments with domesticates, the monumental structures at Göbekli Tepe seem to have been built and used by hunter gatherers. They were on top of a ridge 100 m high and were situated in a marginal area accessible from the surrounding country. Wild cereals were available here, and a recent study suggests that when the site was used there was more vegetation and a greater depth of soil (Knitter *et al.* 2019). Soon this complex was interpreted as a specialised ritual centre, a 'hill sanctuary' visited by people from the wider region. The deposits inside the enclosures were the remains of feasts provided for the teams who constructed and maintained the buildings. Others must have been consumed by visitors. The meat was entirely from wild animals, principally gazelle but also aurochs, sheep and/or goat, red deer and boar, and the bones were smashed in order to extract the marrow. There are indications that alcohol was consumed (Dietrich *et al.* 2012).

During its earliest phases the site need not have been a settlement (although the excavators have recognised some evidence of domestic activities) and in any case few people may have lived there over long periods of time. No hearths, fire pits or ovens have been discovered, nor is there is any evidence of food storage.

The excavators' interpretation was challenged by Ted Banning in 2011. His article appeared in *Current Anthropology* and, following the journal's usual procedure, it was accompanied by a discussion featuring researchers in the same field. The title of his paper ('So fair a house') is a quotation from Shakespeare's play *Macbeth* and reflects Banning's contention that the structures at Göbekli Tepe were not temples but domestic dwellings. Of course they were exceptionally elaborate and their unusual forms must have had a special significance, but it was wrong to make a categorical distinction between the rituals undertaken at a sanctuary and those connected with a house. Banning argued that the contents of the separate enclosures accumulated in the course of everyday activities and that these structures shared features with those known at villages of the same date. If simple houses had not been recorded in the earliest phase of Göbekli Tepe, it was because a limited area had been excavated. There was no reason why these buildings might not have been associated with a settlement.

Most of the commentators agreed with Banning's argument that ritual should not be treated as a self-contained sphere of activity and that the occupation of houses may not have been a purely mundane activity. The term 'temple' was probably an anachronism and more appropriate to the institutions of the state. Several responses criticised Banning's reliance on ethnographic analogy, but most accepted his comparisons with domestic sites in Anatolia. The curvilinear ground plan could be matched at early settlements where circular dwellings were succeeded by rectangular buildings. Walled enclosures were also recessed into the ground, with benches around their perimeter. Here there were more T-shaped pillars, some of which were embellished with arms and hands; even the carved reliefs at Göbekli Tepe had wider parallels. The one important difference is that these distinctive features occupied only part of a larger settlement in which the inhabitants seem to have distinguished between public and private space. Again there is evidence that their houses were formally closed when they went out of use.

Where the commentators differed from Banning their reservations were practical rather than theoretical. The excavated structures at Göbekli Tepe were much larger than the domestic dwellings on the sites with which they were compared. It would have taken a considerable effort to build them, and the quarrying, preparation and erection of the decorated pillars would have been especially demanding. It must have required considerably more work than other structures of the same date. Although Banning provided estimates of the amount of labour needed, some of the authors felt that his figures did not reflect the sheer scale of the task. The filling – effectively the burial – of the separate buildings when they went out of use was equally demanding. Assembling and transporting the material posed a particular challenge, even though its original sources had not been identified. One possibility is that the rubble was brought from abandoned quarries nearby.

Another important question remained unanswered. Were these structures really open enclosures, examples of which could be found at early Neolithic sites, or were those at Göbekli Tepe originally covered? Again smaller buildings elsewhere in Anatolia provided a source of comparison. If the massive structures did have roofs, how were they built? Banning and some of the colleagues who commented on his article suggested that they were supported by the pillars, but a programme of controlled experiments would be needed to substantiate this idea and the architectural reconstruction offered in the article is not entirely convincing. That is because it was necessary to span such a large area.

Comparison with the structures considered in Chapter One suggests a possible solution. Perhaps the forms of these monumental buildings made an explicit reference to the organisation of space in the settlements of the same date but were conceived on an altogether larger scale. In a sense they can be thought of as 'exploded' houses: houses that had been opened out to a wider world. If the rituals associated with the design and use of domestic structures extended to this site, they might have been conducted by more people and in a more formal manner. The organisation of the enclosures at Göbekli Tepe has an obvious air of theatricality. If nothing else, they would have provided an ideal setting for public performances. If, as Banning contends, these buildings must be described as houses, an apt comparison is with the Great Houses considered earlier. They have less in common with the temples that were built in other places and during later periods.

Nebelivka

Nebelivka is a 'mega-site' belonging to the Trypillia or Tripolye tradition of Ukraine (Gaydarska 2020; Gaydarska *et al.* 2020). Radiocarbon dating shows that it was used for about two centuries, between about 3975 and 3775 BC. These complexes include so many houses that they have been characterised as low-density urban settlements. They have been the subject of much discussion in recent years and have been studied by geophysical survey and excavation.

They share a number of characteristics which are illustrated by the plan of Nebelivka (Fig. 6). It features two concentric circuits of rectangular houses bounded by an external ditch, with additional buildings in the interior where they were organised along radial alignments beside a series of roads. In the centre was an open area 65 ha in extent which was kept entirely free of dwellings. There were many more buildings than are found at ordinary settlements. Similar structures have been discovered there, but they amount to no more than 10% of the totals on the largest sites. Nebelivka covered more than 200 ha and contained an estimated 1445 houses, although there is nothing to indicate how long they were occupied or how many of them were used at the same time. At Majdanetske the positions of nearly 3000 examples have been identified. Pottery kilns are associated with the mega-sites and are generally found close to these buildings or by the earthwork perimeter. Their positions avoid the empty space in the centre.

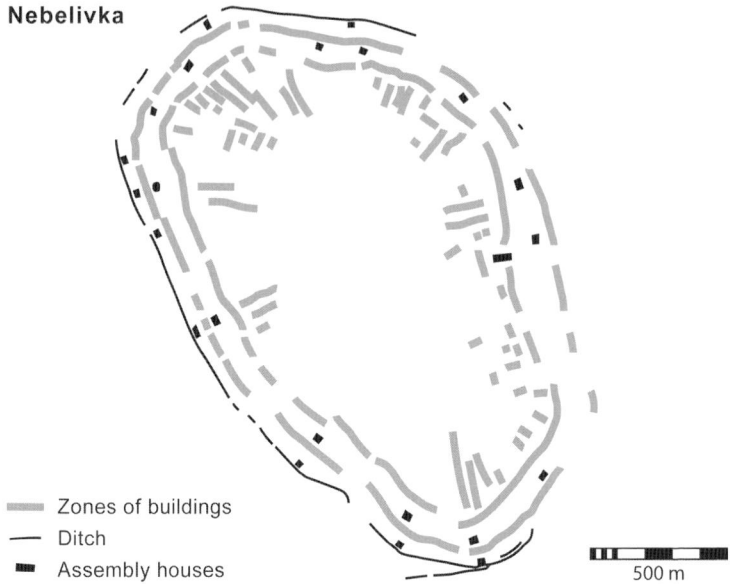

Fig. 6 Outline plan of the Trypillia mega-site at Nebelivka. Information from Gaydarska (2020).

The existence of such sites poses practical and theoretical problems which have yet to be resolved (Gaydarska *et al.* 2020). This account of Nebelivka focuses on two of its characteristics. The first is that many of the buildings were destroyed by fire. It is because this process resulted in such large concentrations of burnt daub that it was possible to map the sites by geophysical survey; the sheer size of these complexes precludes large scale excavation. The same practice of burning abandoned structures was not restricted to the mega-sites and is documented at other kinds of settlement. A second feature of Nebelivka is that the mega-site was only 250 m from a valley containing deposits suitable for pollen analysis. This allowed researchers to study a lengthy sequence which began before the Trypillia complex was established and continued after it had gone out of use. Unexpectedly, it showed that people exerted only a limited impact on the environment.

Despite the presence of so many buildings, the vegetation remained little changed. Perhaps the site was not used as intensively as many researchers had supposed.

The surveys identified a few unusually large constructions within the mega-sites. They are generally characterised as 'special' buildings. Their positions are most distinctive. There were not many examples at Nebelivka – 1.6 % of the structures identified by geophysics – but they were strategically placed for access along the routes leading towards the centre. Either they were located in between the two circuits of buildings, or between the outer ring of houses and the ditch that marked the limit of the complex. These exceptional structures were associated with each group of dwellings.

They shared some distinctive characteristics. Remote sensing showed that the largest example at Nebelivka was a rectangular construction 66 m long and 22 m wide. It had two main components. One half was defined by faint traces in the subsoil and the other part by a mass of burnt daub. There were three such buildings in the entire complex, and they appear to be the largest structures associated with any of the Trypillia mega-sites. One of them has now been excavated (Chapman *et al.* 2014; Gaydarska 2020).

The work was shared between two teams who employed rather different methods in the field. Each group used the techniques with which they were already familiar and their observations would have been influenced by their experience of other projects. The authors of the report make it clear where their interpretations are not the same, but these details have little bearing on the theme of this chapter. Their views diverge on several points: whether the 'assembly house' had been one continuous building; whether parts of it were a multi-storey construction; and whether particular areas were left open to the elements. There were more minor differences concerning the character of the features inside them: what they describe as a 'podium', areas of raised flooring, a fired clay bin, hearths, and possible altars. In addition, it was not clear whether the building had been abandoned before its remains were set on fire. The artefacts that were found raised further problems as it was not always obvious whether they were deposited during the life of the structure or whether some of them were put there after it had been destroyed. But none of these differences of interpretation affect the most distinctive features of this building: its enormous extent; its strategic location in relation to the layout of the site; and the large amount of fuel required to burn it down.

The finds from the excavation did not shed much light on the original function of the mega-structure as they were hardly different from those associated with less specialised constructions of the same date. Although there was a group of ceramic vessels, lithic artefacts were surprisingly sparsely represented. There was little to distinguish them from the assemblage associated with a house. This was no more a temple than the stone buildings at Göbekli Tepe, and neither of those sites included obvious concentrations of offerings.

Instead the excavators emphasise the extent to which the form of the mega-structure at Nebelivka shared its characteristics with the domestic architecture of the same phase. The main differences were its scale and the number of people it could accommodate. Although the excavation teams favoured different reconstructions of the building and different conceptions of how space inside it was used, their account shares a number of elements with the discussion of Göbekli Tepe:

> Several principal features … of the mega-structure are similar to features well known from Trypillia houses … but the Nebelivka examples are much larger … and more numerous …. The fired clay bin, the largest raised area and [the] podium are the largest examples of their type so far known in the Trypillia culture. It would appear that the basic elements of the … house have been borrowed and adapted to fit the great size of what remains a public building, but one without the depositional characteristics of a ritual or administrative centre … The mega-structure would have been a monumental building visible from several kilometres (Chapman *et al.* 2014, 1651–52).

This structure shared many of the characteristics of the Great Houses described in Chapter One, but there are other elements to consider. Despite the enormous effort that went into building and destroying the structures, their spacing across the site did not conform very closely to the overall design. There was much more fluidity than some interpretations have allowed and the mega-sites may have come into being episodically. Then there is another clue. It is clear that the use of this complex did not have a significant impact on the local environment. Perhaps the settlement was never inhabited continuously. Of course there must have been times when Nebelivka hosted large numbers of people, but there is nothing to indicate how long they spent there, nor is there any indication of how the site was used. Pottery was made in these places, but less is known about food production. Like Göbekli Tepe, they may have provided the settings for feasts, yet the details remain elusive. It has even been suggested that people congregated in the mega-sites at times of danger, but their earthwork perimeters were too slight to offer any protection.

Whatever model is favoured for the creation of these extraordinary complexes, it seems likely that they were visited and used over limited periods of time and were among the locations where public and private transactions were performed. The excavators' term 'assembly house' is appropriate here, for mysterious buildings like the excavated example at Nebelivka may have been among the places where communal life was organised.

Bronze Age round barrows and longhouses

This section has a narrower focus than its predecessors as it is concerned with individual buildings rather than larger groups of monuments. Each was paired with a richly furnished burial. The first part considers an Early Bronze Age building at Dermsdorf in Germany, and the second discusses similar evidence from Skrydstrup in Denmark.

Dermsdorf

The first example comes from the Únětice Culture of Central Europe (Meller 2019). It has long been known for its burials and hoards of metalwork, but domestic buildings have been found more recently. The most famous graves are the barrow burials at Helmsdorf and Leubingen which date to about 1840 and 1940 BC respectively. A third example, destroyed over a hundred years ago, has been identified at Bornhöck and is attributed to the same period. At all three sites unburnt bodies were laid out in wooden chambers beneath a cairn covered by a prominent mound. The monument at Leubingen was nearly 50 m in diameter and over 8 m high when it was investigated. It included a variety of gold and bronze objects including a series of weapons: a halberd and three small daggers or knives.

Within sight of Leubingen and only 3.6 km away was a large three-aisled timber building 44 m long and 11 m wide (Meller 2019). It was apparently isolated and was over 2 km from the nearest known settlement. Its siting was especially significant as the structure extended up to a small round barrow. This mound had been built in the Corded Ware phase and was reused for two further graves, the first in the Bell Beaker period and the other during the Early Bronze Age; the site must have remained significant for over 500 years. The orientation of the building was especially revealing as it followed an axis from northeast to southwest: the directions of the midsummer sunrise and the midwinter sunset respectively. Not only did it incorporate the earlier mound, it pointed towards the barrow at Leubingen. The long axis of the house diverged from a strict alignment between these mounds, but only by a few degrees. Had it had been constructed exactly in line with both the monuments, its layout could not have referenced the positions of the solstices; its placing involved a compromise between these different factors. The strongest connection between the building at Dermsdorf and the burial at Leubingen was a remarkable deposit of metalwork buried in a post socket at one end of the structure. It included no fewer than 98 axeheads. There were also the blanks for making two halberds, like the example found at Leubingen. It is striking that the opposite ends of this building were marked by the burial of a distinctive hoard and the remains of a mound. These features must have given it a particular significance.

Harald Meller (2019), who has studied similar deposits, puts forward two interpretations. The rich collections of artefacts indicate the presence of a social elite with contacts in distant regions. Perhaps they owed their power to control over the movement of metals and managed the import of amber coming from the north. These need not have been peaceful transactions and he interprets the numerous axes as weapons rather than tools. They were obviously important as their characteristic form was copied in gold. Meller suggests that the enormous collections of metalwork were the equipment of war bands, and compares them with the representation of different kinds of weapons in the Iron Age sacrificial deposit at Hjortspring in Denmark (Randsborg 1995). The association between the unusual longhouse at Dermsdorf and such a distinctive collection of grave goods suggests that the building played a part in the politics of the Early Bronze Age. He compares it with the 'men's houses' documented in the ethnographic record and suggests that it was associated with a group of warriors who served a leader at Leubingen. Structures of this kind are reviewed by Kent Flannery and Joyce Marcus (2014, 110–52) who consider that their use marks an important threshold in the development of complex societies.

The longhouse at Dermsdorf has structural parallels at other Únětice sites (Donat 2018, 13–34), but it also has unusual features. At 44 m it is longer than most buildings of the same period whose lengths are generally between 20 m and 35 m, and it is exceptionally wide. Few structures were equipped with three aisles throughout the interior and this example was especially distinctive because it did not form part of a larger settlement. These features would attract attention in their own right, but in this case the building was related to two already-established round barrows and a remarkable hoard of artefacts.

Skrydstrup

The building at Dermsdorf can be compared with a longhouse in Denmark which was built six centuries later. Like that at Dermsdorf it was a three-aisled structure of exceptional size. In fact it was even longer than its German counterpart – 50 m compared with 44 m – and again it was unusually wide. It was the largest of the buildings on the site and had three rooms, one of them a byre (Fig. 7). The interior contained stone fireplaces and two large storage pits or cellars (Ethelberg *et al.* 2000). It was probably related to a round barrow constructed of turves, which formed part of a small group 600 m away. One of the largest mounds covered an oak coffin containing the body of a young woman whose clothes still survived. She was wearing spiral gold rings. The grave is dated by radiocarbon to the period between 1300 and 1100 BC. Detailed scientific analysis suggests that she had come to Denmark as a young adult not very long before she died (Frei *et al.* 2019). This was a period when there were extensive contacts between Scandinavia and other regions and her presence provides a reminder of the importance of long-distance alliances. So does the large amount of metalwork circulating at the time, as none of the raw material was of local origin and all of it had to be imported. Both the barrow and the longhouse were exceptional and, taken together, they must have played a special role.

This question has been investigated in more detail in another part of Jutland where substantial barrows and three-aisled longhouses are found in exceptional numbers over the same period. Their construction made considerable demands on human labour and had a serious

Skrydstrup

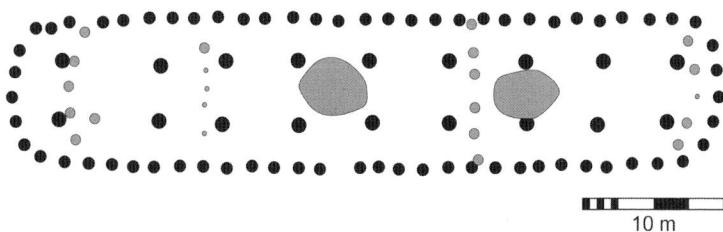

10 m

Fig. 7 Plan of the Bronze Age longhouse at Skrydstrup. Information from Ethelberg et al. *(2000).*

impact on the local ecosystem (Holst *et al.* 2013). In Denmark there was a dramatic peak in barrow construction during the later second millennium BC, and much of the clearest evidence comes from research in this part of the country. Like many other mounds, that at Skrydstrup was constructed out of turves, although the edge of the monument had a stone retaining wall. Excavation of a similar structure at Skelhøj shows that these structures were carefully designed and were the work of different groups of people who brought some of the building material from separate parts of the surrounding area. The project showed that it would have been necessary to sacrifice large amounts of grazing land in order to provide sufficient sods even for a single barrow. In fact such mounds were built in enormous numbers.

The same approach applies to the wooden longhouses, of which the example at Skrydstrup is perhaps the biggest. Each required a large amount of timber. In fact their construction made such severe demands that construction methods eventually changed. Their walls made greater use of planks and daub, and, still more important, during the following phase these buildings became substantially smaller. This was a trend that applied to all the longhouses, and exceptional structures like that at Skrydstrup were no longer built.

How were these elements related to one another? A clue may lie in an increasing dependence on imported metalwork, the supply of which reached a peak during the same period. In order to obtain this material, long-distance networks intensified and new alliances must have been formed. People may have travelled further and more often between different regions – the young woman from Skrydstrup was not an isolated case, as recent studies of human remains and their associations have shown (Frei *et al.* 2019). All three media facilitated a programme of conspicuous consumption which only came to an end as the pressures it placed on natural resources became unsustainable. That process is clearly documented by environmental evidence, in particular pollen analysis.

These features introduce new elements to the archaeology of monumental buildings. So in a very different way do the Iron Age structures at two exceptional sites.

Mont Lassois and Silchester

Mont Lassois

Again there may have been a direct connection between a Great House and an unusually rich burial. This time they were only a kilometre apart and dated from the late sixth century BC. The barrow covered the richly furnished burial of the woman who has become known as the Princess of Vix (Rolley 2003). It included personal jewellery, the remains of a wooden vehicle, a *krater* for mixing wine imported from the Mediterranean, and other equipment associated with the Classical symposium. The *krater* must have come in separate segments to be assembled at the site. In the same way a large building inside the hillfort contained fine pottery brought from Greece (Chaume & Mordant 2011).

The main part of that hillfort was organised on a grid and was divided into a series of rectilinear enclosures. Geophysical survey shows that two of them contained large apsidal buildings. There were five in all. They shared the same alignment, but only the most extensive structure has been excavated (Fig. 8). It had a kind of portico facing the rising sun, and a monumental apse in the deepest space. In its final form the structure was 34 m long and 22 m wide. The interior was partitioned by a sequence of wooden screens. A 'colonnade' extended around the outside wall. It was originally quite narrow but was rebuilt on a more generous scale during a later phase. The walls of the building seem to have been painted. Its architecture poses many problems, but most authorities agree that it would have been difficult to construct. It was replaced on the same footprint after a fire, the cause of which is not known.

The site occupied by this structure had obviously been important before and a distinctive 'ceramic hoard' was buried there during the Late Bronze Age. In the Iron Age one focus for activities seems to have been a hearth located on the long axis of the building. Another was the apse at its western end, and this was where most of the painted pottery was found. Apart from a few sherds of Attic vessels, the finds associated with this structure were unremarkable but they did include small personal ornaments. There was evidence for metal production

Mont Lassois

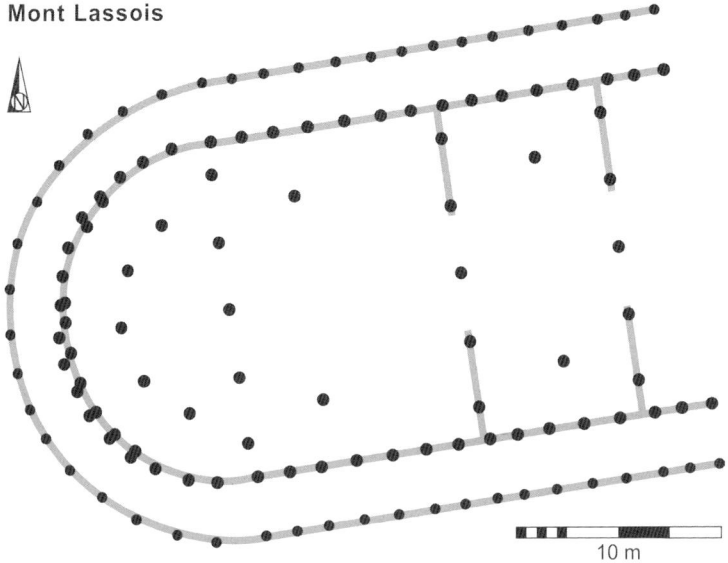

Fig. 8 The monumental timber building inside the hillfort of Mont Lassois. Information from Chaume and Mordant (2011).

and the preparation of food. The faunal remains were dominated by pig bones and the site was surely associated with feasts at which large amounts of pork were consumed. The group of apsidal structures has been interpreted as the site of a palace. The mound at Vix was not the only barrow in the vicinity of Mont Lassois and open-air sanctuaries have also been identified nearby. So have votive deposits associated with the source of the River Douix (Erdman & Chaume 2019).

Like the great barrow of Vix, the hillfort was one of a group of monuments erected during a period of contact between communities in the Mediterranean and those beyond the Alps (Cunliffe 2018, chapter 5). It was perfectly located to benefit from long-distance connections. It overlooked the headwaters of the Seine running northwards across France and was less than 100 km from the Rhone which led down to the coast near Marseilles. Both axes have been considered in discussions of the great timber building, but detailed comparisons have been inconclusive. There was another apsidal building beside the river at Vix, but structures of similar size and proportions have been difficult to identify elsewhere in France. Those quoted in a recent study date from the Early and Middle Bronze Ages and so they are irrelevant (Buchsenschutz & Motsch 2018). The only Iron Age houses provided with apses had less-regular plans and were very much smaller. They bear little resemblance to the building at Mont Lassois.

There are similar problems in looking for Mediterranean parallels. An unusual structure at Lefkandi in Greece shares its characteristic layout and seems to have played an equally restricted role, but again it is much too early for this comparison to be helpful; it is dated between 1000 and 950 BC, making it five hundred years older than the Great House at Mont Lassois (Popham *et al.* 1993). A closer comparison is with the Bouleuterion, a public building at the sanctuary of Olympia. It was of about the same age, but the only characteristic they share is the presence of an apse (Kondis 1975). All the main buildings on Mont Lassois seem to have had this feature. The simplest solution is to interpret the Great House inside the Iron Age hillfort as an ideal-ised reference to a foreign style of architecture. A crucial distinction is the choice of raw material, for timber was used at Mont Lassois and masonry in Southern Europe; there must have been problems in changing between these media. Nevertheless the construction of such a distinctive building 500 km inland from the coast could refer to a distant world and its practices. In much the same way, the layout of the nearby grave at Vix presented a version of the Classical symposium.

Silchester

The Late Iron Age oppidum at Silchester (*Calleva*) occupies a low promontory 14 km south of the River Thames (Fulford *et al.* 2018). At different times it was bounded by a substantial ditch and a series of linear earthworks. The entire complex was replaced by a major Roman town whose construction obscured some of the evidence for earlier activities on the site. Even so, artefacts and structures predating the Roman Conquest have been identified during large scale excavations at two points inside the enclosure. Its interior seems to have been divided between different compounds bounded by roads laid out on an informal grid (Fig. 9). Within them were the traces of a series of timber buildings which included both roundhouses and rectilinear

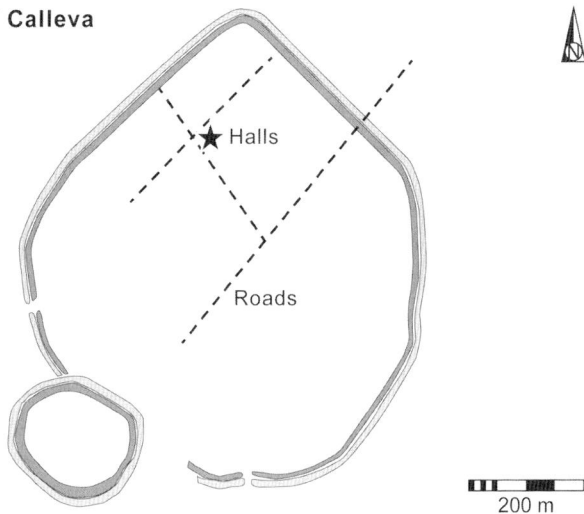

Silchester / Calleva

★ Halls

Roads

200 m

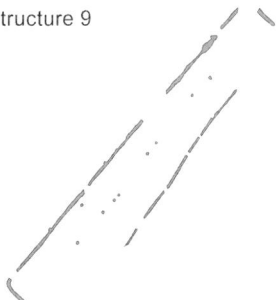

Structure 9

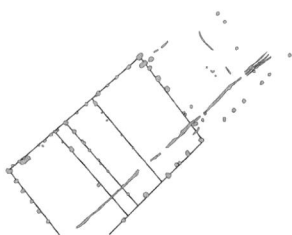

Structure 10

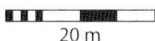

20 m

Fig. 9 Outline plan of Silchester/Calleva in the Late Iron Age, with details of the timber buildings interpreted as halls. Information from Fulford et al. *(2018).*

structures. Although it was once supposed that the circular buildings would have been replaced by this new style of architecture, it was not necessarily the case.

Inside one of the complexes was a remarkable trapezoidal structure interpreted as a hall, with a length of 47.5 m, and a width of 8.7 m at its broader end. As so often, it extended from northeast to southwest, so that its orientation acknowledged the position of the sunrise and sunset at the turning points of the year. It shares this feature with the other pre-Conquest structures at Calleva; the layout of the Roman town, on the other hand, was based on the cardinal points. This particular structure was defined by a bedding trench which was deeper on one side than the other. A row of posts extended along the centre of the building. When it was built the body of a small dog was deposited in its foundations. The original form of this structure remains uncertain, but it was replaced on almost the same footprint by a more robust building that was 12.6 m wide: an unusual width for a rectangular hall in any period. It was at least 22.5 m long. The earlier structure is dated between AD 10 and 40. Its replacement may also have been erected and used before the Roman invasion of AD 43. Nearby was another wooden building interpreted as a small temple.

The site is very unusual. It is away from the main concentration of settlements along the Thames and its tributaries and seems to have been established at a location that had hardly been used before. Although there is some evidence of agricultural production in the vicinity, the first activity at *Calleva* might have been seasonal. The clearest evidence from recent excavations is for trade and exchange, craft production and the consumption of food and drink. It is possible that different activities took place in different compounds, and they may have involved separate groups of people who travelled there for the purpose. The ceramic evidence includes fine pottery imported from the European mainland. There were containers for wine, and the plant remains from Iron Age Silchester are particularly interesting as they feature a series of exotic foods, suggesting that the people who came to the site enjoyed a different diet from those in ordinary settlements. There was a particular emphasis on culinary practices associated with Gaul and the Mediterranean. Coins were minted on the site which is usually interpreted as the royal capital of the Atrebates. That is the implication of its Roman name: *Calleva Atrebatum*.

Although the earlier 'hall' lacks obvious parallels, the character of the other structures resembles those in Gaul rather than the dwellings found at pre-Roman settlements in southern England. The same applies to the layout of the site. Not only does it seem to have been established rapidly and in an area which had not been settled on a large scale, its character was strongly influenced by the forms of high status sites on the Continent (Villard-Le Tec 2018). The same applies to the activities that happened there. The large pre-Conquest buildings that have been discovered by excavation drew on non-local sources of inspiration. That was one way in which the people who used the site – whether as inhabitants or visitors – could share in its distinctiveness. In doing so they demonstrated their special status. Silchester had many features in common with Mont Lassois.

Lejre

For a long time it was believed that this site was a central place in the early medieval (Late Iron Age) landscape of Zealand and the location of Heorot, the Great Hall described in *Beowulf*. It was associated with the Scyldings, who feature as the kings of Lejre in twelfth century Danish chronicles (Niles & Osborn 2007). There were some conspicuous remains – a series of mounds (some Neolithic and Bronze Age), and a large round barrow beside an important ship setting – but no trace of any monumental buildings had been found beneath the modern settlement. Between 1986 and 2009, however, excavation identified two groups of timber halls whose chronology extended between AD 450 and 1000 (Christensen 2015). They were identified on separate sites, 500 m from one another. The scale of the most impressive structures recalls the poet's description of Heorot (Fig. 10). Although literary scholars do not agree quite when the poem was composed, the buildings at Lejre took almost the same forms over a long period of time.

Lejre

Earlier Phase

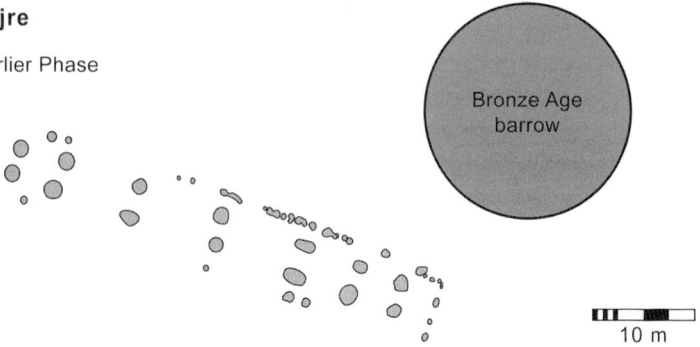

Bronze Age
barrow

10 m

Later phase

Successive
halls

Palisaded
annexe

20 m

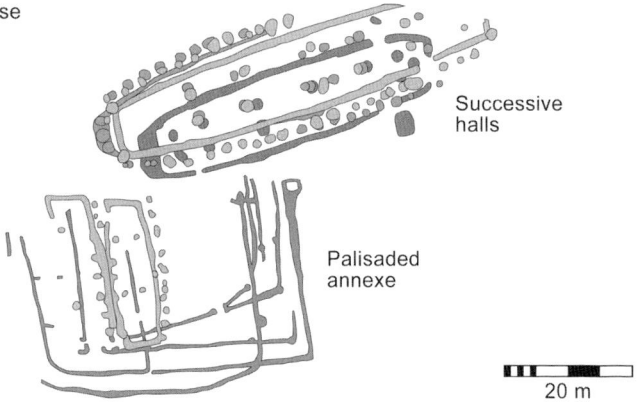

*Fig. 10 Plans of timber buildings and associated structures in the
successive complexes at Lejre. Information from Christensen (2015).*

The earlier settlement is associated with radiocarbon dates between
about AD 450 and 600. It also included diagnostic artefacts of fifth
century to early seventh century types. Its main feature was a large
timber building up to 48 m long and 7.2 m wide. There was little to
show its internal organisation, but it was accompanied by several
more structures, the biggest of which was practically the same length.
The remainder were considerably smaller, but one of them does stand

out. Compared with the others, it was built on a massive scale. It could have played a specialised role as it was aligned on a Bronze Age burial mound located beside the principal hall. Elsewhere in the excavated area there was a group of pits. Fires had been lit inside them and they contained large deposits of animal bones. Similar material was associated with decorated metalwork, glass beads, glass drinking vessels and small pieces of gold. There was also a considerable accumulation of burnt stones.

Many of the same elements are repeated in the later complex at Lejre which was more extensive than its predecessor and was used for a longer time: between about AD 700 and 1000. There may have been an interval between activities at these locations and it was then that a considerable round barrow was constructed. Again there were massive timber halls, several of which had been erected in sequence. They occupied the same positions and even employed some of the same postholes as their predecessors. The best-defined structure was 48 m long – the same length as its counterpart on the older site – but in this case it had a significantly larger floor area, for its maximum width was 11.5 m. Like its neighbours, it did not include a byre. Its entrance provided access to the largest room which might have served as a public space. Several other buildings were a little smaller, but they were replaced so often that it is difficult to decide how many of the large halls were used together. The excavator, Tom Christensen, identifies six phases of activity, during which there were between one and three such buildings. Virtually all of them conformed to the same east–west axis. Unlike those at the older site, they had slightly bowed side walls. Throughout the sequence these structures were situated inside a rectilinear enclosure. That feature was not identified in the earlier complex at Lejre.

Again ancillary buildings were associated with the largest halls and may have played a special role. One of them was within a fenced annexe and was reconstructed several times (Fig. 10). Just outside this enclosure were four graves. Thirty metres away but beside the same boundary, there was the main concentration of metalwork in the excavated area. It included ingots, weights, coins, and a range of jewellery and personal ornaments. This was not the only case in which a longhouse was paired with a smaller structure. In both instances the ancillary building was laid out at right angles to a larger hall and might have played a specialised role.

There was evidence of craft activity at Lejre, including the working of metals, wood, bone and antler. Textiles were also produced there. The site played a significant role in exchange, and the fieldwork recovered scales, weights, hacksilver, and coins. The finds from both main sites illustrate a range of contacts with distant regions. They extended into Norway, and to the south to the kingdom of the Franks. There were imported ceramics from the southern Baltic, gold bracteates, and even an Islamic coin which had been made into a pendant. The excavator suggests that some of these objects were deposited as votive offerings. Drawing on literary evidence, he believes that the accumulations of burnt stone might have been treated as 'altars'. In the case of the earlier site:

> It seems natural to connect the heated stones, the innumerable animal bones from the pits and the culture layer, plus the peculiar material objects … and to interpret this part of the settlement area as the place where heathen acts of sacrifice took place (Christensen in Niles & Osborn 2007, 123).

The finds of animal bone certainly suggest the importance of feasting at Lejre and there is evidence for the consumption of pork.

Lejre was an important cemetery in its later phases. There is no evidence that the Bronze Age barrow in the older complex was reused, but a new circular mound was built beside a series of ship settings, 500 m from the halls. It was an exceptional structure. The barrow seems to have been 5 m high and was the largest in the region. It covered a cremation burial associated with a costume with gold decoration. There are two radiocarbon dates between AD 540 and 690. The two surviving ship settings were originally part of a group of four, the largest of which must have been 70 m long and contained a number of Viking inhumation burials. There were other graves inside the later settlement. Three occupied the position of a particularly large hall, but only one of the bodies was complete. It dated from the ninth century AD. It was in the centre of the building and shared its orientation. A second group included three intact inhumations and one partial deposit. They dated from the same period. The graves were just outside the fence enclosing an ancillary building associated with this hall. They lend weight to the suggestion that the smaller structure was some kind of cult house. Their presence adds a further dimension to the archaeology of this site.

Common characteristics

The examples considered so far had a feature in common with those discussed in Britain and Ireland and were chosen because of this connection. All the buildings were exceptionally large but shared elements of their distinctive architecture with domestic dwellings. That is why they have been described as Great Halls or Great Houses. At the same time certain themes link the studies of these structures. Some apply to all of them, but others are limited to a smaller number of instances. As later chapters will show, they are by no means restricted to these particular cases.

The links with domestic dwellings took very different forms. At Göbekli Tepe the special buildings contained some of the same elements as houses, but they deployed them in a distinctive configuration. They shared their circular ground plan and on some sites they also made use of benches, pillars, and floors recessed into the subsoil. Here the main difference was one of size and mass, and the walled enclosures may never have had roofs. Similarly, the assembly houses at Nebelivka had many features in common with the other buildings on that site but again they were constructed on a more monumental scale. A similar argument applies to the Early Bronze Age longhouse at Dermsdorf which was significantly bigger than was usual in Únětice settlements. From the outside it might have looked like other buildings, but it was exceptionally large and its interior was organised in a different way. The same was the case with the enormous longhouse at Skrydstrup. In the early medieval period there was a comparable relationship between the different structures in the successive settlements at Lejre. The British examples illustrate the same point. Early Neolithic halls in Britain drew on the architecture of domestic houses but reproduced their features on a far more impressive scale. The same pattern extends to the interplay between Iron Age roundhouses and the principal structures at the royal centres of Ireland.

Some of the buildings interpreted as Great Houses formed only parts of a more extensive layout. This can be seen at several different sites. It is not clear how many structures were used together at Göbekli Tepe but the results of geophysical survey suggest that they could have been located according to one overall scheme. That was certainly the case on the Trypillia mega-sites, of which Nebelivka is an outstanding example, but here there was a certain tension between the ideal layout of the complex and the ways in which it developed on the ground. Individual elements did not conform to this design, and in any case not all the houses need have been occupied together. By contrast, the interior of the hillfort at Mont Lassois was used intensively and was subdivided between several ditched enclosures with the large apsidal buildings in a dominant position. The oppidum at Silchester also had a formal layout and the interior of the main enclosure contained a series of separate compounds. On both shores of the North Sea early medieval complexes containing Great Halls were planned with even greater formality and the entrances of separate buildings were aligned on one another. Lejre is a typical example.

In most cases there were problems distinguishing between the roles of these buildings. The problem was especially obvious in the Late Iron Age of Scandinavia where some of the Great Halls may have been associated with smaller temples or shrines. The same problem applies to Trypillia assembly houses and to the Únětice building at Dermsdorf which was related to both a burial mound and an unusual hoard of metalwork. It may also extend to the largest structure on Mont Lassois. It could have had many different functions but its unusual architecture surely evoked that of a Classical sanctuary. In the same way there may have been a small temple next to the excavated hall at Silchester. The same might have happened at Lejre. Again it would be misleading to distinguish between the sacred and profane uses of these places.

A common element is the importance of feasting. The evidence takes several forms: large or unusual accumulations of animal bones, a preference for species exploited for their meat, and evidence of ceramic vessels suitable for serving food and drink. These features are widely distributed, although it is not easy to interpret them. Faunal remains are especially common at Göbekli Tepe but for some reason they have been viewed as evidence of work feasts. It was obviously important to sustain the labour force that was building the monuments, but these remains could be related even more closely to the pilgrims who visited the completed structures. In this case all the meat was supplied by wild fauna, but at four well-documented monuments – the Neolithic henge of Durrington Walls, the Iron Age hillfort at Mont Lassois, and the early medieval complexes at Lejre and Lyminge – large quantities of pork were consumed. A mass of burnt animal bones, dominated by cattle and pigs, was spread across the site of the last timber building at the Irish royal centre at Knockaulin. Similarly, exceptional numbers of cattle bones were associated with the excavated areas at Silchester and the Great Halls at Yeavering. The occupants of Silchester enjoyed a special cuisine based on imported delicacies. Wine was imported from the Mediterranean to Vix and Mont Lassois, and the same happened at *Calleva*. There are even claims that alcohol was consumed at Göbekli Tepe.

Another feature was shared between a number of the buildings known from archaeological and literary sources. This is the evidence that they were occupied by groups of warriors. Whatever their historical accuracy, this feature is shared between the texts of *Beowulf* and the Ulster Cycle. Meller (2019) interprets the Early Bronze Age longhouse at Dermsdorf in similar terms and considers that the hoard of metalwork buried beneath one of the wall posts was actually a collection of weapons. He compares this building with the 'men's houses' documented in the ethnographic record. This idea is impossible to prove, but a distant analogy may be with the epic poem *Beowulf* in which the Great Hall was occupied by armed men, while a second building at the same site was inhabited by the women of the community. This would be especially relevant if Lejre really was the site of Heorot.

Another comparison is with a structure that has not featured so far in this account. It is the aptly-named Garrison in the Viking trading town of Birka in Sweden (Holmquist 2016). During the tenth century AD this part of the site was connected to the defensive circuit and contained a series of terraces on which timber buildings were erected. None was as large as those considered so far, but that may have been because space was limited by the local topography. The principal building was a three-aisled longhouse, 19 m in length and 9 m wide, with curving side walls. Its dimensions were by no means exceptional, but when it was investigated its unusual character soon became clear. It seems as if weapons and tools were stored together in one room, but the opposite end of the building contained a wider variety of artefacts and even included finds that had been brought from distant areas. They included glass vessels, distinctive mounts and a Byzantine coin. Their presence emphasises the exceptional status and connections of the occupants of Birka; in fact a cemetery of richly furnished graves was found nearby. Excavation of The Garrison found a remarkable quantity of weapons and pieces of armour (four hundred in all), some of which must have been intended as offerings. The deposits at Birka included a chape, numerous spearheads, and a distinctive artefact called a Thor's hammer. Like so many of the structures considered in this chapter, the hall itself was destroyed by fire and never rebuilt. Again it might have functioned as a 'men's house', although that need not have been its only role. Lena Holmquist (2016) suggests that it was originally dedicated to Odin, the god of warriors, and might have retained its significance as a sacred site after the building was abandoned.

Taken together, the evidence from these different places is both complex and confusing, but despite their different chronologies they do share a series of common elements. It seems as though buildings that resembled one another superficially might have been used in comparable ways. They show unexpected similarities that extend between the beginning of the Neolithic period and the Viking Age. If these observations have any value, they suggest that a widespread phenomenon needs to be investigated by archaeologists. But that project should not be contained within conventional period divisions; these structures have been well researched on their own terms but they have not been compared with one another over long periods of time. That is unfortunate as a comparative study might shed light on the circumstances in which they were built. This book will consider how that might be achieved, but in order to make any progress it is important to review some of the other ways in which such distinctive constructions have been studied. The principal themes of this research are discussed in Part Two. Together with what has been said already, they provide a background to the interpretations put forward in the final part of this book.

Part Two

Dream houses

CHAPTER 3

From the foundations

Part Two considers the ways in which prehistoric buildings, and in particular Great Houses, have been interpreted and extends from their physical fabric to their significance in the past. Thus it considers both practical issues and questions of archaeological theory. It begins with the most tangible elements – their foundations – and ends with more abstract constructions that might prove to be castles in the air.

Chapters One and Two suffered from a limitation, for they were based on the plans of buildings that survived as subsoil features. There were some exceptions – the stone enclosures dug into the bedrock at Göbekli Tepe, the concentrations of burnt daub at Nebelivka – but in most cases their character was shown by the foundations. They were generally represented by post holes or the trenches that held up the walls. Nothing remained of the superstructure. Of course the sheer scale of Great Houses did provide certain indications. Where they were unusually wide the roofs must have been supported by rafters of exceptional length. They would also have been particularly high. These constructions must have been unusually robust and there were occasional clues to the forms of their doorways, walls and floors. But such traces could hardly match the literary accounts of a hall like Heorot or the circular building at Crúachain. There were obvious limits to what could be inferred.

Reconstructing ancient buildings

The problem has been considered by students of ancient architecture, some of whom have ventured into the field of experimental reconstruction. There is no doubt that such projects offer plausible solutions, and in certain cases the results of this work are compelling. Such exercises test the assumptions made in the field and alert excavators to possibilities they may have overlooked. They inspire new methods of analysis, often using the methods of environmental science, and in that sense they contribute to 'middle range theory', but this emphasis on the physical character of the evidence cannot shed much light on the significance of particular buildings in the past (Townend 2007). The reconstructions may be more informative for the public than they are for archaeologists, as their presentation is so often influenced by the nineteenth century idea of the open air museum. An article on the reconstruction of the largest Viking hall in Norway includes a photograph with the revealing caption 'The chieftain's farm at Borg, entrance building comprising ticket-office, the museum shop, coffee-shop and toilets' (Jakhelln 2005, fig. 2).

Most of these projects have concerned the smaller constructions. This has happened for good reasons. Of course they were more frequent than Great Houses and more typical of the pattern of settlement. Such ventures also cost less since some of the materials have to be purchased. A roundhouse at the Butser Ancient Farm suffered in bad weather because it was simply too expensive to buy sufficient material for the roof.

Numerous projects have reconstructed circular buildings on the ground. The best example is a study of the Iron Age roundhouse at Pimperne which was led by Peter Reynolds (Harding *et al.* 1993). His account of the work provides details of the raw materials required and the amount of labour necessary for the task. It was modelled on one of the larger structures of its date in southern England, but its size was not exceptional (Harding 2009). It had a prominent porch and an outer ring of posts 12.8 m in diameter (Fig. 11).

The main components of the reconstructed house came from 36 mature oak trees, 65 young oaks, and 50 hazel stools. The rafters which supported the roof were 10 or even 11 m long; elm and ash were used in the experiment. Each weighed between 750 and 1000 kg. One person should be able to lift about 70 kg, suggesting that these could have been installed by between 10 and 14 individuals.

Pimperne

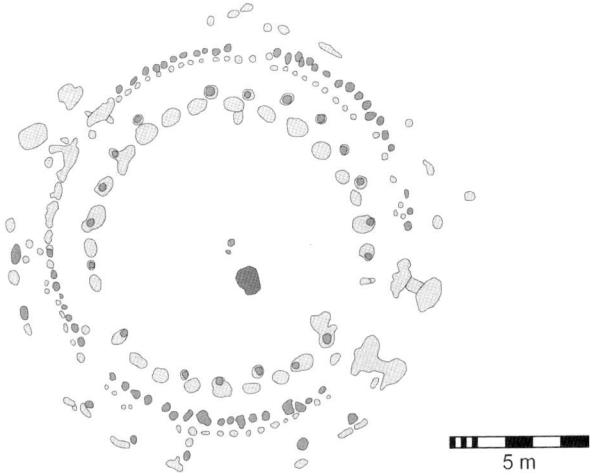

5 m

Elsloo

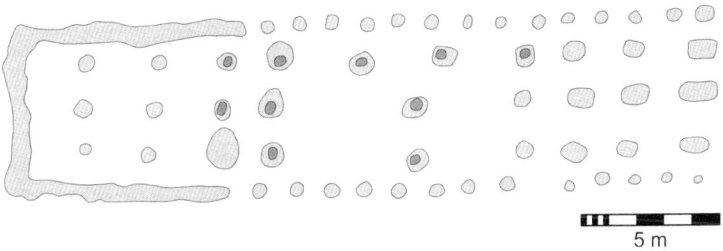

5 m

Fig. 11 Plans of the Iron Age roundhouse at Pimperne and the Neolithic longhouse at Elsloo. Information from Harding et al. *(1993) and Startin (1978).*

The roof itself required 20 tonnes of straw. With one exception, the amount of labour was less than Reynolds had anticipated, but it took a significant effort to coat the outside wall with daub. It would have been possible for the occupants of a typical Iron Age settlement to construct a building of this size. Its creation need not have imposed a special burden.

That exercise was conducted on the ground and resulted in a building which remained intact until it was dismantled after 14 years. Similar projects have involved the construction of longhouses. One of the most influential accounts is based on experimental evidence as well as nineteenth century manuals and was written by an archaeologist, Bill Startin (1978), who had trained as an engineer. What was required to build a Neolithic longhouse? The example chosen was a Linearbandkeramik structure at Elsloo in the Netherlands (Fig. 11). Again the same considerations were important. How much building material was needed, and how many people were required for the task?

In this case the house in question was 26 m long and 6 m wide and the main structural timbers consisted of oak. Startin (1978, 154) estimated the sources of the timber as:

> Three trees at 60 cm diameter, 15 trees at 30 cm, and perhaps 60 trees at 15 cm diameter or less … 10 cubic metres of daub would have been required … In addition, 350 square metres of wattle and 250 square metres of thatch would have been needed … About 60 cubic metres of soil would have been excavated for the footings.

The most demanding task was probably lifting the ridge purlin for the central part of the longhouse. A freshly felled oak timber of the right length would have weighed 840 kg, meaning that it might have taken a dozen people to raise it. It is not known how long people spent collecting suitable materials, but Startin estimates the total amount of labour invested in a building of this size at 2200 worker hours. The figure is surprisingly low and suggests that the erection of a new house was well within the capacity of the inhabitants of a settlement. The result is not unlike that for the reconstructed roundhouse, although the method of analysis was different.

The value of these two projects is that they establish a baseline from which to assess the requirements of other buildings. The early Iron Age roundhouse at Pimperne was one of the larger examples of its type in southern England, but its construction was still within the capacity of a single community. By the late pre-Roman period much larger edifices appear, most obviously at the Irish 'royal centres'. The same approach should apply to longhouses. The example studied by Startin was a typical size for a Linearbandkeramik structure, but a few were considerably larger (Hofmann & Lenneis 2017). Although the building at Elsloo was 26 m long, they reached lengths of 40 m or more, and one at Bylany was 45 m long. It was considered in his article. He estimates that its construction would have taken roughly 4000 worker hours. To put this figure in perspective, it is under 60% of Startin's estimate for the construction of Fussell's Lodge long barrow in southern England which its excavator thought was modelled on the form of a much older house.

Understandably, the sheer scale of the largest buildings means that most are reconstructed on paper. The point applies to both longhouses and roundhouses. Again two examples are helpful (Fig. 12). The latest building at Navan Fort in the north of Ireland was three times the diameter of the roundhouse built by Peter Reynolds. It was 38 m across, with an enormous post in its centre that might have stood 10 m high (Waterman 1997). It was difficult to decide whether the building had a roof, and related structures at Dun Ailinne were interpreted as open enclosures (Johnston & Wailes 2007). It would be challenging to erect a full-size replica, but a combination of favourable preservation and excellent fieldwork supplied a plausible answer. The posts of the outer wall had obviously sunk in the ground sometime *after* they were erected. Further timbers were added to provide more support, showing that they must have carried a considerable weight. As Chris Lynn (2003, 30) observed:

> We do not hear of fence posts or even telegraph poles sinking into the ground of their own accord .... It is clear that the sinking was caused by the weight the posts were carrying. That can only have been a roof, or a superstructure of some sort.

The range of variation is still greater among the longhouses of the first millennium AD. A rather different perspective comes from the largest reconstruction of a Viking building. This was at Borg in

Navan Fort

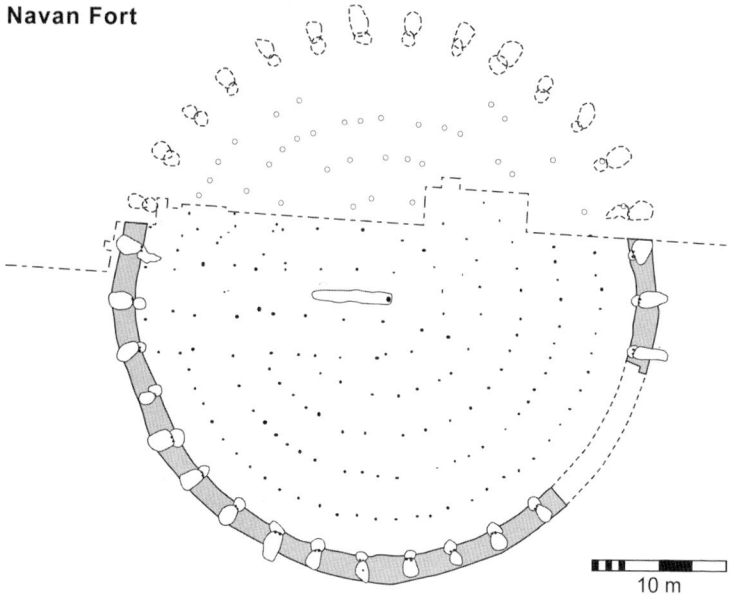

Borg

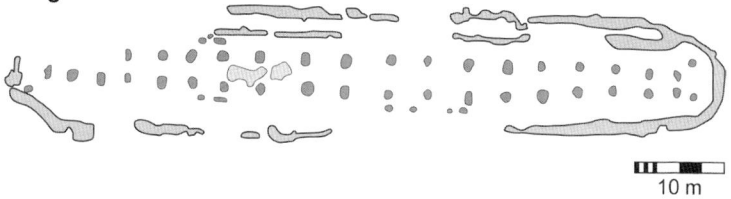

Fig. 12 Plans of the exceptionally large timber buildings at Navan Fort and Borg. Information from Waterman (1997) and Munch et al. (2003).

Lofoten in northern Norway where an extraordinary timber structure 83 m long and 9.5 m wide has been excavated (Munch *et al.* 2003). Its footprint was the basis for an impressive full-size copy which is now a public museum. It was the work of the architect Gisle Jakhelln who is a well-known expert on Nordic vernacular architecture and an advocate for the conservation of ancient buildings. The new structure was erected beside the original hall, which meant that it had to be on top of a ridge. This modern copy used well-established techniques of timber construction. In this case a different lesson can be learned, for it collapsed during a winter storm and its wooden frame needed to be reinforced with steel. This is no reflection on the quality of the project but it emphasises a point which can easily be overlooked. During the Viking Age in Norway the largest buildings were placed in the most prominent positions, even though it made them vulnerable to bad weather and gales (Eriksen 2019, 124–48). This was not an isolated instance. In parts of Scandinavia the orientations of longhouses conformed to local norms and in many cases were directed towards the cardinal points. Their positions took no account of prevailing winds (Eriksen 2019, 128–34).

In fact the Great Hall at Borg shares a striking characteristic with the circular building at Navan. Both these structures were vulnerable, but in different ways. The roundhouse started to sink under its own weight and could have become unstable. That is why posts were added to reinforce the outer wall. It is uncertain whether this would have solved the problem because the interior was soon packed with rubble and set on fire. The original structure at Borg was rebuilt, but here a potential problem was created by its size and exposed location. Such a massive edifice was vulnerable to powerful winds and the replica designed by an experienced architect collapsed. Both structures must have approached the limits of what was possible when they were built.

The same point is illustrated by other features. Experimental reconstruction shows that one of the limiting factors of early buildings was the size of their rafters. In both circular and rectangular structures it was difficult to employ timbers of more than a certain length; that was normally about 10 m. It set limits on the dimensions of these structures. Few roundhouses were much larger than the example reconstructed by Reynolds. In the same way the problems of spanning a large space meant that longhouses were rarely more than 7 m wide (Bradley 2013a). That limitation applied for a long period of time, from the earliest examples in the Neolithic to those of the Viking

Age. When structures went beyond that limit complex construction methods must have been employed. An unusually wide building like that on Mont Lassois was altogether unusual. This approach provides a basis for deciding which structures made extreme demands and identifies them as worth studying in their own right.

Experiments have also indicated the size of posts necessary to support a stable structure. Occasionally, there is archaeological evidence that these thresholds were ignored. As a result a house might have appeared disproportionately massive or tall. In a recent study Anna Beck showed that in most of the buildings at the Viking settlement of Strøby Toftgård in Denmark the diameters of the roof supports were directly related to the overall lengths of these structures; the entire range was between 10 m and 40 m (A. Beck 2017, 198). There were 60 buildings in all, and this observation applied to 80% of them. But nine examples employed significantly larger posts than the rest – perhaps they carried the weight of an upper floor. Some of these houses were between 10 m and 20 m long and similar in size to the other structures in the settlement. The remainder were between 35 m and 40 m in length and were among the biggest of all. Again that might have given them a special character.

The significance of wood

Whether they were designed as experiments or as visitor attractions, these reconstructions were of *wooden* buildings. In fact it is true of almost all the examples described as Great Houses. The preference for timber architecture is consistent with excavated evidence, but it presents an obstacle to a more ambitious analysis because so little survives. It also raises a question that is seldom asked. Why were dwellings constructed of this material where building stone was available?

At first sight practical considerations seem to have been paramount. Timber was readily available and must have been easy to obtain as areas of forest were cleared. The process extended from the Neolithic period to the Middle Ages. The opening of the landscape released quantities of potential building material, and the experience of removing trees equipped past communities with a knowledge of the properties of different kinds of wood and the best ways of working them. The answer to the question seems self-evident.

That may not be true. In fact there are two objections to the argument. The first is that during the Neolithic phase stone provided an alternative material, yet it was restricted to certain contexts. When wood was available in the same place, it was used for houses, but this restriction did not apply to tombs. Both timber and stone were deployed in monuments for the dead, sometimes in combination and less often in sequence. There are cases in which wooden structures were replaced by megaliths (Bradley 2019, 50–62). That is evident in Britain, Ireland and Northern Europe. They may have been built with different expectations of how long they would last.

A second case in which practical arguments fail is in the early medieval period when people lived among the ruins of Roman buildings. The remains could have offered an immediate source of raw material, yet it was rarely used. Instead timber dwellings were constructed, although obtaining and working the wood might have made greater demands. Other considerations must have been important. There were parts of Europe in which masonry structures were unfamiliar. That was true outside the imperial frontier, so that when migrants crossed the North Sea to Britain they were confronted by a new kind of architecture. On the other hand, indigenous communities would not have faced the same predicament. They must have made a conscious decision to reject Roman ways of building. Was that why so many towns were abandoned?

The argument has an important corollary. Early Christian buildings are an exception to the pattern. Some were of wood, but others did use stone, much of it taken from the remains of older structures. That is not surprising since the church acknowledged a close relationship with the Roman world. It was not the only context in which such material was recycled, but the choice must have been deliberate (Shapland 2013). In Anglo-Saxon England stone was appropriate for sacred architecture, but timber was preferred in other spheres. Again it is easy to suggest a prosaic reason. Perhaps ecclesiastical buildings were meant to outlast secular constructions, but that overlooks their wider associations. If masonry buildings evoked connections with the Church of Rome, timber was connected with traditions that went back to the Iron Age (Shapland 2013).

Wood was significant in many other ways. Medieval people considered rocks to be the work of giants, but Anglo-Saxon texts suggest that people and trees had a common origin. Both were alive and their qualities overlapped. Wooden objects could share that characteristic; a good example was the Christian cross. Place names indicate that certain trees were holy. At the same time individual species had specific associations. Oak, ash and yew were valued, but elder was a source of evil (Hooke 2013).

There is similar evidence from Northern Europe. According to an origin myth Odin and his brothers created humans from logs found by the sea. *Askr*, the first man, was formed from oak, and a woman, *Embla*, probably from elm (Hultgård 2006; Price 2020, 1–2). Bryony Coles (1998) suggests that some of these ideas were expressed by wooden figures found in Britain and Ireland. Male images were made of oak, but those of mixed gender were carved from yew. Perhaps the masculine images referred to Thor, while Odin, who was believed to change gender, was represented by yew or pine. Different species had their own associations but in every case they were connected with living beings. These wood sculptures are few in number, and the clearest evidence comes from the Bronze and Iron Ages. The comparisons draw on later sources of information.

Three excavated examples

The same issues arise in the archaeology of earlier periods.

At Crathes in northeast Scotland an Early Neolithic hall was erected near the River Dee. It is always difficult to reconstruct wooden buildings from subsoil features, but the excavators proposed a subtle and convincing interpretation (Murray *et al.* 2009). The earliest components were probably a pair of large posts which they describe as 'totems', set in the ground 17 m apart. They were between 30 cm and 50 cm in diameter and the sockets that supported them were a metre deep. They established the alignment of the hall which seems to have been fitted around them. Both timbers were recovered shortly before that structure was destroyed and its remains were set on fire. This was not an easy task and there was stratigraphic evidence that one of the uprights was removed immediately before the building was burnt. These particular posts must have been important; perhaps they were painted or carved. By contrast, the stumps left by the walls remained in the ground and decayed.

Similar considerations were important in the construction of Early and Middle Neolithic barrows. For a long time British prehistorians debated the relationship between two kinds of monument associated with human remains. There were chambered cairns, and mounds where deposits of human bone were placed in massive wooden containers. Did this distinction reflect a western axis with connections to the Atlantic, and an eastern zone associated with the Channel and the North Sea? Or were similar structures favoured in both regions, but built from the most accessible materials: stone towards the west, and timber to the east? Today the wooden structures are treated as the counterparts of megalithic chambers. Excavation shows that they took a distinctive form. They were large boxes or chests, closed at either end by a split tree trunk. There were similar structures in Denmark, and archaeologists came to the conclusion that the dead were placed *inside* the remains of an oak tree (Evans & Hodder 2005). There was an obvious parallel between the dissolution of human bodies and the decay of the wood. Certain trees, or certain kinds of tree, seem to have been special and their histories might have been compared with those of people. Some species of wood lasted longer than others and this could have been compared with the human lifespan. Dwellings built of these materials, particularly oak, may have shared their significance. Even their sources assumed a new importance, and recent research has shown that the holes left by windfalls can include deposits of artefacts (Evans *et al.* 1999; Lamdin-Whymark 2008). Perhaps they were left as offerings to the trees themselves. No wonder Gordon Noble's (2017) book on Neolithic woodland is subtitled *The Forest as Ancestor*.

Oak was equally significant during the Early Bronze Age in Britain. The clearest demonstration of this point is the waterlogged timber structure known as Seahenge, dated by dendrochronology to 2049 BC (Brennand & Taylor 2003). The monument had two components: the bole of an inverted oak set on the ground with its root system uppermost, and a circular fence broken by a single entrance. Its posts had been arranged with their bark facing outwards so that the entire construction resembled an exploded tree. It was the work of many people as there were scars left by more than 50 axes. Again the evidence emphasises the special importance of this particular species.

Giving life

The treatment of timber in these contexts provides a clue to the special connotations of this material. So far the account has been restricted to archaeological evidence. Can any lessons be taken from ethnography? One of the most useful sources is a book edited by Janet Carsten and Stephen Hugh-Jones (1995) with the title *About the House*. Several contributors to the volume share the same perspective. There are societies in which domestic structures are treated as if they are living beings. The point is made in the editors' introduction:

> Natural processes normally associated with people, animals or plants may also apply to the house. Houses may be said to be born, to grow, to mature and die (Carsten & Hugh-Jones 1995, 42).

That could be one reason why so many are constructed of a living substance and why domestic dwellings are embellished with anthropomorphic imagery. Their plans can even mirror the human form. A good example is provided by the Maori meeting house (van Meijil 1993). It is so famous for its wood carvings that its deeper significance can easily be overlooked. It is laid out on an axis that refers to the passage of time; the past is represented by the front part of the structure, and the future by the back of the building. Thus it involves its current occupants as well as previous generations. It is where the bodies of the dead are displayed before their funerals, and in time the building will include images of the deceased.

The entire construction takes the shape of an ancestral being, whose face is represented by the veranda and the eaves. The porch of the structure is the brain and the interior is its chest. The roof is equally significant. The ridge pole is considered as the spine of the house and the rafters are described as its ribs. The sequence in which they are introduced traces the line of descent from an original founder. Where they join the walls there are carved panels, with images that explain the origins of different sections of the community. The building is considered as a living creature, yet it performs some practical roles. It is used to commemorate the dead, but it is also a council house where their descendants conduct their business. It is a status symbol and is usually attached to a plaza where groups of people can assemble. They provide the ideal audience for the lavishly decorated exterior.

Another example comes from South Sulawesi in the Pacific where wooden houses play an equally important function. Although more monumental structures are found elsewhere on the island, Thomas Gibson (1995) describes the rituals associated with the creation of a domestic dwelling.

The first stage in the process concerns the selection of building material. Before any timber is felled a ritual specialist must consult the tree spirits to obtain their cooperation. He also decides where the posts should be placed within the building. It is most important that they are set in the ground the right way up so that they appear to be growing. A crucial distinction is between a male post and a female post; both should come from the same tree. Before the male post is set in the ground its position is marked by a piece of metal and a ceramic vessel. They are accompanied by an offering of food which is believed to share the same elements as the human body. Then the central uprights are clothed as if they are living men or women, and they are joined together as the dwelling is built.

After that, the house spirits have to be fed. Offerings of food are placed by the male and female house posts and also in the attic of the building. Others are buried beneath the house: at its centre and in each of the corners. Again distinctions of gender are very important and different provisions are associated with the male and female posts. Finally, a more elaborate ritual involves the entire structure of the building but it does not happen until the founding couple have had three children; they should include both a girl and a boy. The entire family circles the house, moving anti-clockwise around the building to protect its resident spirit. Gibson's informant related the children taking part in the ritual to the separate house posts: the male post, the female post and the peripheral posts belonging to the structure.

Again the house is indistinguishable from its occupants, and its components are explicitly related to the tree out of which it was built.

Marianne Hem Eriksen (2019, 146) quotes linguistic evidence which suggests that ancient buildings in Northern Europe had some of the same attributes:

> The etymology of Old Norse words may underpin the corporeal qualities of the Iron Age and Viking Age longhouses …. The short-end of the house, [its] 'gable', Old Norse, is related to proto-Germanic *geblan*, meaning 'head, skull' … The word for 'window', Old Norse *vindauge*, means 'wind-eye', and probably described ventilation openings constituting 'eyes' where the wind passed though the wall … And even though the etymology is unclear, many Germanic languages indicate a relationship between words for roof-supporting posts (Old Norse *stafr*) and verbs and nouns relating to 'walk forwards', 'footprint' … indicating that the posts may be the 'legs' of the house. Thus, in the words used for different constructional elements of the house, a homology between bodies and houses is … embedded.

Again the house might have been considered as a living being. Is that idea supported by archaeological evidence? The discussion starts by treating ancient houses as a general phenomenon before asking whether special considerations applied to the largest structures.

Offerings associated with buildings

If certain buildings were considered as animate they could have received offerings. It might have been how their wellbeing was sustained. No distinction was necessary between the physical fabric of a house and the people who lived inside it. Several writers have suggested that these structures had biographies like those of the communities who built them, and their histories were punctuated by rituals during which particular items were deposited. Again the model was influenced by ethnographic evidence, but its clearest exposition in European archaeology was by Fokke Gerrritsen writing in 1999. He wanted to explain two common characteristics of later prehistoric settlements. There were regions in which wooden houses were used for comparatively short periods. Although they could have been repaired, they were rarely replaced in the same positions. Instead they conformed to a model of 'wandering settlement'. He suggested that their histories were linked to those of the occupants, so that important thresholds – constructing a new dwelling or ending the use of an old one – reflected important stages in the domestic cycle. Like their inhabitants, those houses eventually died.

His approach has been influential, but it has also been questioned and it should not be treated as a new orthodoxy. That was never Gerritsen's intention. The model is relevant to certain areas and not others, and its application changed over time. His original research was on Iron Age settlements in the southern Netherlands and, as he acknowledged, it did not apply to those in France and large parts of Germany where groups of prehistoric dwellings took a different form and longhouses did not figure so widely. Nor was it especially useful in studies of an earlier phase in the northern Netherlands where formal deposits of artefacts and animal remains were associated with farmyards rather than dwellings (Arnoldussen 2008).

There are other problems (Arnoldussen 2009). At present it is not clear how long the fabric of individual structures remained intact – that can only be established by dendrochronology – and it is impossible to compare the lifespans of particular houses with the births and deaths of their occupants. The histories of domestic dwellings may have been affected by other, less predictable events, and some allowance has to be made for environmental factors, including natural disasters and disease. It is not always apparent whether the building material was recycled or if it was left to decay. On the other hand, the strongest point in favour of Gerritsen's case is the striking contrast he identities between the evidence from earlier settlements and those of the Roman Iron Age when buildings became more robust and were frequently replaced in the same positions.

The metaphor of a house 'biography' extends to the distinctive deposits associated with these buildings, and for two decades now they have been the focus of research. Some groups of artefacts, animal bones and food remains seem to be associated with the *construction* of domestic dwellings, and others with their *abandonment*. Such features shed new light on the character of particular houses and the ways in which they were treated, but it is important to acknowledge that these processes did not happen at every settlement, and even less at every building.

Evidence from the Netherlands

In Gerritsen's study (2003), foundation deposits were identified on the sites of 16 houses. Three were dated to the Late Bronze Age/Early Iron Age, and two more to the Middle Iron Age. The remainder dated from the Late Iron Age, or the period of Roman influence. Most of these deposits had been placed in sockets for the walls or roof supports, but there were others in the bedding trenches used to construct the buildings. Just one was in a doorway. The collections included intact pottery vessels, animal skulls and a human femur. The only metal objects were an iron ploughshare, and a knife. There was also a quern. Similar material was found in ancillary buildings, ditches, wells, and pits belonging to the same settlements. Here it included chisels, loom weights, human remains, and burnt grain.

In the area studied by Gerrritsen other deposits were associated with the abandonment of houses. He considered a total of 12 sites. A few offerings were in the sockets from which posts had been withdrawn, or the spaces left behind where they had rotted or were destroyed by fire. The majority occupied substantial pits excavated through the interior of the building or dug across the line of its outer wall. They had a restricted currency as nearly all of them dated between the end of the Late Bronze Age and the middle of the Iron Age. Their chronology does not match the peak of foundation deposits, which have later dates, but that is not surprising. By that time more buildings were replaced in the same positions, so there was less reason to commemorate the abandonment of a house. In this instance the material was more diverse and included complete and fragmentary ceramic vessels, loom weights, spindle whorls, and a whetstone.

Evidence from Northern Europe
There is compelling evidence that offerings were made in and around houses over a much longer period. Those in a large part of South Scandinavia have been studied by Anne Carlie (2004) whose research extended from the Neolithic period to the Viking Age. At the time she was preparing her monograph Leo Webley (2008) was investigating domestic buildings in western Denmark dated between 500 BC and AD 200. Understandably, there is no cross reference between these publications, although the study areas overlapped and their principal findings agree with one another. Since then Marianne Hem Eriksen (2019) has analysed the evidence from Norway between AD 550 and 1050. During that period both houses and their surroundings include human and animal skulls (Eriksen 2020).

The settlements studied by Carlie must be set in a wider context. When she was working there were fewer house offerings in Sweden than are known today and the main group dated from the Iron Age. Earlier examples have been identified since then; the same is true in Denmark. Stone axes had been found in association with Neolithic buildings, but metal objects of any kind were uncommon in excavated houses before the late first millennium BC. The results of these surveys can easily be misunderstood. During certain periods artefacts of these kinds were deposited elsewhere in the landscape. There they have been found in considerable numbers as single finds and hoards.

It means that some artefacts might not have been related to the domestic domain; instead they were set apart from it.

On the other hand, there are cases in which the chronological distribution of house offerings can be related to those in the wider landscape. Most of the pots associated with buildings in Denmark date from the Iron Age. This was the time when vessels containing food were placed in peat bogs (Becker 1971). The same applies to the querns buried in domestic buildings. They recall the agricultural tools deposited in marginal environments; the most obvious examples are wooden ploughs (Glob 1951). Otherwise the clearest pattern is a steady increase in groups of animal bones between the Late Bronze Age and the Viking Age.

Carlie divides house offerings into three separate categories: those connected with agricultural production; items which might have been used in magic; and an assemblage composed of weapons and sacred objects. Each had a distinctive chronology. Deposits connected with farming extended across the entire sequence, but the collections she links with magic did not feature before the Iron Age. By contrast, those with weapons and religious symbols were restricted to the first millennium AD when they first appeared with any frequency in the sixth and seventh centuries. No doubt their proportions will have altered since her book was published in 2004, but Eriksen's recent research shows that they are unlikely to have changed significantly.

Each category is explored in detail. How were these deposits organised in relation to the structure of the buildings? They were generally in the living area (the central section of the longhouse) where their positions emphasised the corners and the hearth. Others were beneath the roof supports. They were less common in the remaining parts, where livestock were kept and tools and provisions were stored. During the Iron Age offerings associated with the construction of a dwelling consisted of ceramic vessels, querns, and the remains of slaughtered animals. Strikingly similar material was connected with its abandonment and demolition. Pots were particularly common. The situation changed after the Roman Iron Age and at some of the settlements of the Migration and Viking periods such deposits were associated with ancillary buildings used for metalworking and textile production.

In the Iron Age of western Denmark particular kinds of artefacts were found in particular parts of the house (Webley 2008). The smallest ceramic vessels were deposited under the posts of the principal room and the entrance. Others were associated with the hearth and could be buried beneath it. Larger vessels could also be placed below the floor, and a few horse bones were associated with the byre. The entrance was important, but the hearth was equally significant. In well-preserved houses it was decorated with non-figurative designs which became increasingly frequent during the Roman Iron Age.

If most deposits were connected with the foundation and abandonment of a longhouse, others might have referred to the concerns of its occupants. These are the collections that Carlie associates with magic. They include a mixture of natural items and artefacts: fossil sea urchins, cattle horns, and tools made of metal and stone. She notes that these artefacts were usually pointed or sharp, for they included scissors, knives, needles, and a scythe. Like the foundation deposits, they had a distinctive distribution. It included the living area but extended to the byre. The frequency of these deposits increased during the course of the Iron Age, although it is not clear why that happened.

The distinction between these groups is likely to have been significant. The deposits associated with the construction and abandonment of the dwelling emphasised the importance of farming and fertility. In Denmark the most common components were ceramic vessels of different sizes. These pots could have contained offerings of food, as they did in the well-preserved collections from bogs. Querns made an equally obvious reference to the significance of grain, while the bones or entire bodies of animals might have been offerings of meat. In favourable circumstances concentrations of cereals have been recognised in the same contexts. This material may have included the remains of meals consumed by the occupants, but it in the light of the ethnographic evidence assembled by Carsten and Hugh-Jones (1995) it could have been buried in order to sustain the house when it was built, or to celebrate its history when it was eventually abandoned.

The assemblage that Carlie associates with the performance of magic has a different character. It is helpful to draw on European folklore in looking for an explanation. The emphasis on sharp objects recalls well-documented deposits intended to ward off evil, disease and lightning strikes. They remained important into recent centuries and have been studied in particular detail in Finland where they protected people and their animals from the threat of witchcraft (Hukantaival 2016). That might explain why the inhabitants of Iron Age buildings paid so much attention to the entrance and the byre, as both provided access to the interior. These deposits were protective or apotropaic and were directed towards the world outside. In contrast to the others, they were never meant as gifts to the house.

Offerings associated with monumental buildings

Did the same factors apply to Great Halls? Here some background is necessary. The longhouses in western Denmark increased in size from the Roman Iron Age onwards and seem to have been constructed using larger posts. The last examples in Northern Europe, which are dated to the Viking Age, provided more room for storage and could have housed a greater number of animals (Eriksen 2019). Others, including some of the largest examples, did not have byres, and here a large part of the interior was a single open space. In Norway the buildings were less standardised. This applies to the materials used to construct them, and also to their ground plans, for more of them were bow-sided longhouses. Some structures were used over a single phase, but those of higher status were rebuilt in the same positions. In that case they could be precisely superimposed.

Certain deposits still recorded the creation and abandonment of buildings. The commonest were iron knives and sickles whose sharp edges might have warded off danger, but there were almost as many querns and ceramic vessels. These items were often associated with the roof supports, but others were in the doorways, the side walls and the hearth. The clearest associations were with the initial construction of the building and, in the case of hearth deposits, perhaps with its period of use (Eriksen 2019, 165–78). They may have been put there to ensure the wellbeing of the occupants. The number of wealth items increased from the end of the second century AD onwards. Over the same period deposits of ceramic vessels became less common. Gold objects featured after AD 500 and weapons could be associated with important buildings; the collection from The Garrison at Birka is the outstanding example (Holmquist 2016). There were finds of metalwork, together with glass drinking vessels. There is evidence that elaborate artefacts were made on these sites, and literary sources suggest that their production might have involved special rituals. The most distinctive artefacts of all are the miniature gold plaques called *Guldgubbar* which depict figures who can be identified from Norse mythology. Their distributions within the largest buildings emphasise the position of the high seat. Others might have been fixed to the roof supports. The deposits also included human remains and coins.

It is unlikely that there ever was a complete break with the past, for the largest buildings were monumental versions of simpler long-houses, and the practice of making offerings continued for a long time. If the earlier dwellings were considered as living beings there seems no reason to reject the same interpretation for the Great Halls erected during the first millennium AD. Indeed there is literary evidence that they became the symbols of entire communities (Carstens 2015; Price 2020, 96). Although Carlie (2004) concluded that house offerings played different roles during the Viking Age, the Norwegian evidence studied by Eriksen (2019) shows few signs of any radical change. It is true that new elements appeared, but it is likely that special deposits were still used to animate and protect the buildings. The biographies of these dwellings and their occupants were as closely intertwined as they had been in the past.

Summary

This discussion has covered a wide range of topics and has drawn on the results of many different studies – from modern reconstructions of ancient buildings to the provision of 'house offerings' at different times and places in the past. The evidence is so abundant and so varied that it may be helpful to summarise the main points before embarking on new topics in the chapter that follows.

A common element is the distinction between domestic buildings normally associated with settlements and the unusually monumental structures described as Great Houses or Great Halls. The physical character of these buildings was comparatively easy to define as experimental evidence showed that they must have made exceptional demands on labour and raw materials. Sometimes their construction approached the limits of what could be achieved at the time. Like the first Gothic cathedrals (Helena Hamerow pers. comm.), the largest structures were in danger of collapse. The risk must have been recognised at the time.

One reason why they were so vulnerable was an obvious preference for building in timber even when stone was available and more accessible. The choice can hardly be explained in practical terms and this account quoted evidence from a variety of sources to suggest that wood was treated as a living substance and not simply as 'raw' material. The argument was supported by ethnographic sources which showed that houses themselves can be thought of as animate; they have their own histories of origins, inhabitation and abandonment. All these stages in the biography of a building can be marked by the provision of offerings intended to sustain the dwelling. They also ensure the wellbeing of its occupants.

Such offerings varied over time and space but they shared the basic feature that the houses themselves were imbued with life. They were never inert, and their biographies were caught up in those of the people who used them. Again there was an important distinction between dwellings in most of the settlements and the monumental structures identified as Great Houses. Their contents were much more distinctive and these buildings were associated with a wider variety of artefacts.

Many of the same issues will play a part in Chapter Four.

CHAPTER 4

Castles in the air

Commemorating abandoned buildings

What was the lifespan of a prehistoric house? Did it end when the building was abandoned? Or did it continue afterwards in another form? How, if at all, was its history remembered? This chapter considers these questions. It also introduces Claude Lévi-Strauss's concept of the House Society and discusses its use in archaeology.

Domestic dwellings were inhabited for very different lengths of time even when they were established in similar settings. The Neolithic settlements preserved by Alpine lakes provide an instructive example because their durations can be measured by dendrochronology. In the later fifth millennium BC they lasted for no more than 20 years, but after 3500 BC the figure had risen to a century (Whittle 2003, 143–50; Hofmann 2013). Since these buildings shared the same environment and materials, a practical explanation for the difference is unlikely. Older structures must have been abandoned more than once during a person's lifetime and there is little to suggest that the remains of older habitations were treated with much respect.

This was not true in other areas. Even when houses went out of commission after a few years, attention was paid to what was left behind. The process took many different forms. One possibility is that material was retrieved from an abandoned building and reused in the structure that took its place. It could have happened for pragmatic reasons, but this practice created a link between successive buildings, and that may have been intended. It can only be demonstrated where the timbers themselves are preserved, but this happened at the Iron Age settlements of the Assendelver Polder in the Netherlands (Therkorn 1987). In other cases, especially in Northern Europe, newly built houses were constructed on exactly the same footprints as their predecessors. That was the case at Lejre.

In Late Bronze Age and Iron Age Britain, the positions of successive buildings cut across one another without the same emphasis on the outline of the older structure. The sites of roundhouses overlapped even where ample space was available for new constructions. This relationship can hardly have come about by chance, since it would have been impossible to start work on the later house until all trace of its predecessor had been removed. On sites like those at Reading Business Park in the Late Bronze Age (Brossler *et al.* 2004), or Crick in the middle of the Iron Age (Hughes *et al.* 2015), this process extended to a whole sequence of houses. A more distinctive practice can be recognised in other cases. This is where a later building abutted an older structure or incorporated part of its wall. The original construction may have gone out of use, but it was obviously important to connect their histories. Again it happened at sites where vacant plots were available and even when this process threatened the stability of the later building. Tanja Romankiewicz has recognised this practice at two Scottish Iron Age sites, Old and New Kinord (Romankiewicz *et al.* 2020). An interesting variant has been identified by Leo Webley (2007) in a study of the use and abandonment of roundhouses in lowland England. Here one length of the wall was preserved when the rest of the structure was removed.

There were other ways of responding to older dwellings. The longhouses of the Linearbandkeramik Culture provide a well-known example. They had several unusual characteristics (Coudart 1998; Bradley 2020). All the houses in a settlement shared the same alignment and some of them may have been organised in rows. They were flanked by borrow pits which provided the material for the walls. These massive buildings were seldom replaced in the same positions. Some were extended or repaired, but in most cases they seem to have been abandoned after a fairly short period of use. When that happened, a few houses were burnt down, but in most cases their remains were left to decay *in situ* and there is little to suggest that the timbers were retrieved. As a result the settlements had a distinctive character, for at any one time, structures that were inhabited were spaced at equal intervals with the remains of deserted buildings. The positions of older longhouses could have been indicated in several ways: by their wooden shells; by the low mounds that accumulated as the covering of the wall collapsed; and by hollows left by the borrow pits dug beside them. The houses of the past (which were probably the dwellings of the dead) coexisted with those occupied by the living community, and both groups conformed to a single layout.

Just as the positions of those older buildings were respected, the borrow pits rarely filled completely, nor were they overlain by other structures. They were filled with domestic refuse that accumulated during the life of the adjacent building. This material would have been particularly fertile. The longhouses employed an exceptional number of wooden posts, but now their place was taken by patches of luxuriant vegetation. It was as if structures formed from a living substance went back to their original state. Although a few groups of buildings were enclosed by a bank and ditch, just as often a collection of abandoned dwellings was commemorated in this way. Like the pits beside the houses, these earthworks featured human remains.

A few structures were commemorated by mounds or cairns, but it was comparatively rare. This pattern has been identified by excavation at Neolithic sites in northern Germany and Denmark (Andersen 2019), but the remains of the houses can be so ephemeral that they have been difficult to identify and it is not clear whether it was a particularly common practice (Fig. 13). Domestic buildings were covered by both rectangular and circular monuments and it is obvious that there was no consistent relationship between the plans of the dwellings and those of the tombs that took their place (Bradley 2012, 76–88). Later houses were also buried beneath Danish mounds, but in this case there was a more striking relationship between the footprint of the building and the layout of the barrow that covered it (Bradley 2012, 86–88 & 169–72; Mikkelsen 2019; Overgaard 2019). The position and orientation of the main grave reflected the axis of the building and the location of its porch. At Trappendal the principal burial was on the site of the central room. So many barrows have been

Rastorf

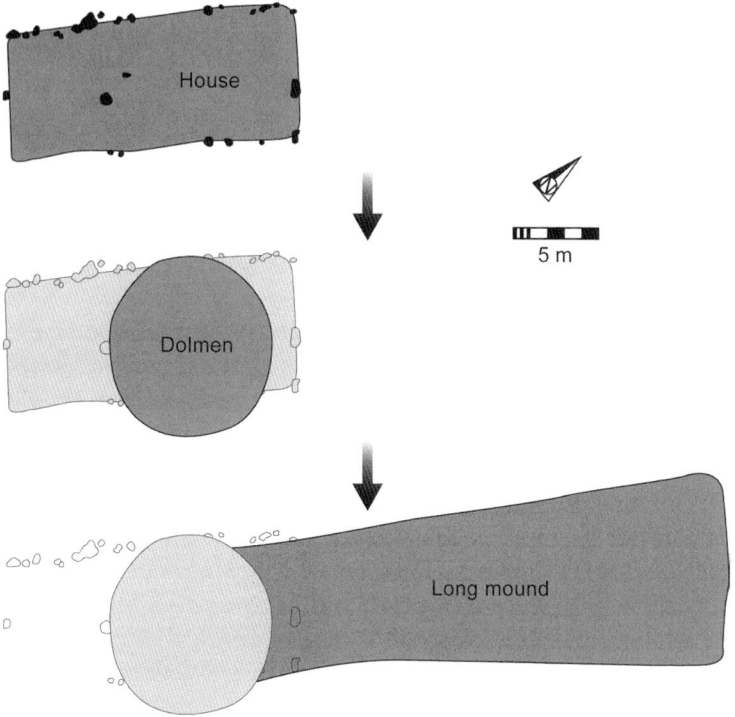

*Fig. 13 Outline plan of the Neolithic house at Rastorf which was overlain
by a circular monument and then commemorated by a long mound.
Information from Müller (2018).*

investigated and published that it is obvious that this relationship was
quite unusual, but it is documented at 20 sites in Denmark dating
from the earlier second millennium BC (Nielsen 2019, 23–34). It may
have happened in special circumstances as at least two of the dwellings
commemorated by a prominent mound had been destroyed by fire.

A similar practice is evidenced during the first millennium AD in
Scandinavia but again it was not especially frequent (Fig. 14). Mounds
or cairns were erected over the positions of older dwellings (Eriksen

Tastarustå   **Jarlsberg**

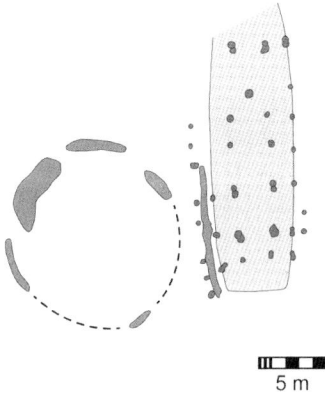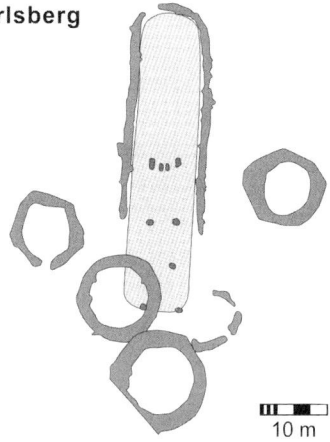

5 m   10 m

Fig. 14 Two Viking longhouses whose sites are associated with round barrows. Information from Eriksen (2016).

2016). Not all the burials were particularly rich, and some of these sites did not include human remains. This relationship is documented over a large area, and one common element is that the structures themselves were destroyed by fire. It is known that some were erected long after these houses had gone out of use. In such cases it seems possible that the monuments recalled *exceptional events* rather than *exceptional buildings*.

One kind of settlement encapsulates almost all these practices (Kienlin & Blanco-González 2020). In parts of Eastern and Central Europe houses, and even whole settlements, were burnt down at regular intervals and then rebuilt in exactly the same positions. In time the accumulation of building material formed a conspicuous mound or *tell*. The structures seem to have been destroyed when they were abandoned, yet the burnt material of which they were composed was recycled in the construction of the buildings that took their place. As the tell become higher, the history of the inhabitants was put on show. One sign of continuity was the presence of human remains in these deposits. It is possible that they were incorporated in the new constructions in order to give them life. Similar practices were discussed in Chapter Three.

Commemorating Great Houses

Houses could be commemorated in many other ways. The massive stone-lined hearth of a Late Neolithic building at Barnhouse in Orkney was removed when the structure was abandoned and, according to Colin Richards (2005, 125–26), it may have been installed at another site nearby. When the principal timber circle at Durrington Walls went out of use its location was marked by digging pits where posts had rotted or had been removed (J. Thomas 2007). These features included a selection of artefacts. At a similar structure at Ballynahatty in Northern Ireland the locations of the timbers were commemorated by small cairns (Hartwell 1998). A comparable process is evidenced on later sites. The remains of the Great Hall at Gamla Uppsala in Sweden were sealed by deposits containing a distinctive group of objects. The excavators concluded that its remains received a formal burial comparable to a funeral rite (Ljundqvist & Frölund 2015). In the same way, at Yeavering in northeast England a stone setting was built over the remains of a hall that had been destroyed by fire (Hope-Taylor 1977, fig. 47). It was interpreted as a roundhouse but it is more likely to have been a platform or cairn.

In other cases the positions of wooden buildings might be indicated by a setting of standing stones. It happened at Late Neolithic sites in Britain, like the timber structures at Temple Wood (Scott 1989) and Machrie Moor (Haggarty 1991), both of which were replaced by stone circles which shared the same outline. It also happened on a related site at Croftmoraig where two successive settings of monoliths date from the Early and Middle Bronze Ages respectively (Bradley 2016). A small timber structure, whose ground plan was exactly like that of a roundhouse, was erected inside one such circle. After a period in which this building had been repaired it seems to have been demolished and the second setting of upright stones was erected on the same footprint. In this case the timber structure was not as impressive as the stone settings associated with it, but the relationship between them was the same.

If the positions of monumental houses were marked or concealed, others were set on fire. Several examples have featured in this account, but the evidence requires careful handling. Timber buildings must have been particularly vulnerable as they could be easy to ignite. The evidence has to be considered a case at a time. At one extreme are the Trypillia mega-sites where virtually every building was burnt down (Gaydarska *et al.* 2020). Practical experiment has shown that this would require a significant amount of fuel, meaning that the process needed careful planning. It was a common practice in Eastern Europe and in this case it must have happened when buildings were abandoned. The same practice was followed at many other sites. For similar reasons the burning of Neolithic halls in northern Britain is unlikely to have occurred by chance as a variety of structures of similar date were treated in exactly the same way. They included domestic dwellings, long barrows and timber cursus monuments (Noble 2006).

The same argument would apply to three exceptionally elaborate roundhouses in the Early Iron Age settlement at Longbridge Deverill in Wessex (Hawkes & Hawkes 2012). They are thought to have been built and occupied in sequence. At the end of its period of use each structure was burnt to the ground. This happened with some formality as all these buildings had been filled with fine pottery before it happened. The excavators compare this with a funeral ceremony, even though the buildings themselves were not associated with human remains. Their treatment and contents are strikingly similar to the evidence from Neolithic halls in Britain.

Finally, there is an interpretation which is specific to the Great Halls of Scandinavia. Lydia Carstens (2015) records that some of the burnt halls contained human bones. It seems particularly significant that their remains were left undisturbed. One might argue that the regularity with which these buildings were targeted is a sign of unsettled conditions, but the same evidence could result from a ritual when important buildings went out of use; the death of the local leader might have provided an occasion. The question is considered again in Chapter Seven.

The Great House as monument and model

The use of the house as a symbol extended to several media. Its form was copied by different kinds of monuments between the Neolithic period and the Viking Age. In order to keep the argument within limits it is restricted to just three phases. The first example is the interplay between Neolithic longhouses and long barrows. A second discusses the relationship between roundhouses in Britain and Ireland and a variety of enclosures and hillforts whose chronology extends from the Bronze Age to the early medieval period. The final part considers the cross references between boat-shaped longhouses in Northern Europe and the large ship settings of the late first millennium AD. Sometimes Great Houses were chosen as the prototypes for stone and earthwork monuments, but in other cases less impressive buildings provided the inspiration for larger structures.

Early Neolithic houses and mounds

This is a familiar topic on which interpretations have changed during recent years. The initial argument has a history that goes back more than seven decades to the work of Gordon Childe (1949). Before radiocarbon dates were widely available, it was based on typology and depended on visual similarities between the plans of Linearbandkeramik longhouses and those of Neolithic mounds. It originally applied to monuments in Northern and Central Europe, but more recently similar ideas have been considered in French archaeology. Since these broad-brush interpretations were first proposed there have been new programmes of excavation and dating, and some of the early interpretations have been called into question.

Most Linearbandkeramik longhouses were rectangular, although their successors could be trapezoidal. Their plans have been compared with those of long barrows. Other monuments adopted a circular outline and were associated with passage graves. In their initial manifestations these two groups had little in common apart from the presence of human bones (and they were not evidenced at every site). Any links between them formed during a subsequent phase when long barrows could be superimposed on round mounds, as was commonly the case in Northwest Europe.

Today the connections between longhouses and long mounds must be studied on a local basis and in regions where reliable dates are available. That reduces the options considerably. In fact there are only two parts of Europe in which a more direct relationship between houses and mounds is plausible. One is in Poland, and the other in northern and western France. At present there is no evidence of links between these areas.

The Polish sequence is especially complicated. According to Joanna Pyzel (2020) it began with the construction and use of Linearbandkeramik longhouses which lasted until 4750 BC, but during the following phase they went of use; little is known about the settlement pattern that succeeded them. The construction of longhouses resumed during the Brześć Kujawski Culture from about 4350 BC, but this time the buildings took a different form and trapezoidal structures appeared. There were flat graves among these dwellings, but they were not covered by mounds. The new generation of longhouses remained important after their counterparts in other parts of Europe had been abandoned. It was only when they finally went out of use in Poland that mounds of similar shape were constructed there. The interval between the last longhouses and the earliest long barrows is uncertain but their relationship to one another is likely to be significant (Midgley 2005).

The past must have been important, as the sites of the oldest longhouses were treated in special ways. This did not depend on the preservation of memories, for the positions of these buildings could have been indicated by low earthworks and concentrations of debris. On the other hand offerings and human burials were deposited on the sites of LBK houses many years after those buildings had gone out of use. It seems as though the importance of the original houses was acknowledged. If so, that process continued for even longer and the forms of the last monumental dwellings provided the model for the first long barrows.

The same interpretation is plausible in the French example, but in this case the morphological argument is weaker because the long-houses were strictly rectilinear while some of the earthwork mon-uments were oval or round. The interval between them could have extended for a century or more until 4700 BC, but their locations were not far apart and the sites of older structures might have been identified on the ground. At Balloy two of these earthworks overlay the remains of older houses, but this relationship has not been rec-ognised anywhere else.

Again connections with the past do seem likely. Phillippe Cham-bon argues that the sites of ancient buildings could have left mounds of debris; the hollows marking infilled pits might have been equally visible. These features were not necessarily recognised as the remains of dwellings:

> It is a matter of remembrance, or how people recalled what happened before and the way they positioned themselves in [relation to] the past. Did they pay attention to the real iden-tification of features such as houses, or were they satisfied with the mere knowledge of the overall location of a former village? In the Paris Basin [older] burials existed within villages. [Then] the pattern shifted … By this time and afterwards, some places seem to have been dedicated to the dead or religious purposes (Chambon 2020, 54).

Here any relationship between domestic architecture and monuments to the dead was at a very general level.

Other possibilities have to be considered. Once the practice of building long mounds was established, those earthworks could pro-vide a model for later constructions; they need not have been con-ceived as copies of a domestic dwelling (Whittle 2020). Perhaps it was at this stage that mounds or cairns were adopted over a wider area. Another possibility is that the long mounds did refer to houses of the same date, but these were the small rectangular structures that were occasionally buried beneath them. It happened in Northern Europe, Britain and Ireland. In those cases the barrow might have represented the house but on a much larger scale.

Later prehistoric houses and enclosures

So far the main part of this discussion has been concerned with long barrows and longhouses and little has been said about the circular buildings which represent a long-lived tradition along the western coastline of Europe (Bradley 2012). They influenced Neolithic monumental architecture, but the main period in which roundhouses were significant was during the Bronze and Iron Ages. Outside the Roman Empire they remained important up to the Viking Age. How was their importance acknowledged in other media?

British and Irish roundhouses shared a number of characteristics: their size, their internal organisation, and the placing of the entrance. For the reasons mentioned earlier they rarely exceeded the dimensions of the building at Pimperne. Where that limit was passed they were distinctly unusual, and never more so than at the 'royal centres' in Ireland. In the same way, nearly all these buildings faced approximately southeast. Less is known of how the interior of a wooden roundhouse was used, but where equivalent structures in Scotland were built of stone it seems as if the central space was occupied by a hearth and the periphery by smaller rooms. The scheme is similar to that described in Irish literary sources.

The larger roundhouses are seldom found in isolation. They tend to be associated with ditched or palisaded enclosures. This was particularly evident during the Late Bronze Age in Britain and Ireland where these monuments are sometimes called ringworks (Bradley 2019, 240–43). Most of them were circular and in that case there was a direct link between the house and the perimeter. Although there are exceptions, the main structure was in the centre and was placed in line with the entrance. The importance of this axis was emphasised by occasional deposits of metalwork or the moulds for making artefacts.

The doorway of the roundhouse faced the morning sun which would have illuminated the interior, but it does not explain why the enclosure shared the same alignment. The earthwork and the roundhouse were mirror images of one another. The artefacts associated with ringworks suggest that they were more specialised than other settlements. In particular, they provide evidence of metallurgy and feasting.

Some of the same features can be identified in Iron Age Britain when they extended along a continuum from simple enclosures to hillforts. The earliest sites might contain an unusually large roundhouse (or possibly more than one), and the principal structure could be placed in line with the entrance; the building at Pimperne conformed to this pattern. But that convention soon broke down and it was more common for a hillfort to feature a series of smaller houses of approximately uniform size (Sharples 2010, 215–20; Bradley 2019, 286–94). No one structure was dominant, and these sites included other buildings suitable for keeping grain. In many areas, but not all, the defensive perimeter followed a curvilinear outline. Another feature shared with the ringworks is that the entrance had the same orientation as the houses. Only when additional space was required was the original conception abandoned. If Late Bronze Age earthworks had copied the plan of the principal house, now the idea applied to the dwellings of a whole community. Perhaps the hillfort was treated as a single 'house' by the people who lived there. It does not matter whether they were permanently resident or whether these places were used on an occasional basis.

The Irish evidence has a different contribution to make. Roundhouses and circular enclosures were built in great numbers in Ireland during the first millennium AD. That is revealing because such sites feature in law tracts dating from the eighth century (Edwards 1990, 33; Stout 1997, 11–15). They are relevant to the discussion because they emphasise the wider significance of domestic buildings and earthwork enclosures. They may record an ideal conception rather than actual practice, but this information is important. The largest buildings, which share characteristics with Great Houses, were meant to be those of 'young lords' and needed to be 11 m or more in diameter. In lower status houses the equivalent figure ought to be 5 m, which would have

Mullaghglass

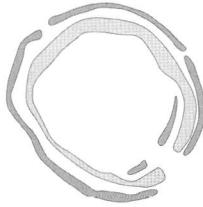

50 m

Kittyblane

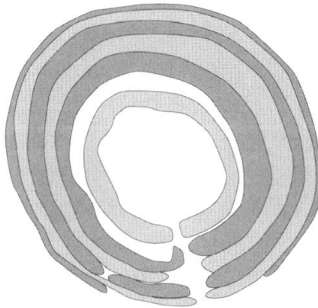

50 m

Fig. 15 Plans of two Irish ringforts which shared the same orientations and enclosed the same amount of space. They were defined by earthwork perimeters of different widths. Information from Bradley (2013a).

allowed them only 20 % of the floor area of the other buildings. It is revealing that a similar distinction applied to earthwork enclosures. The boundary of a high-status site had to be over four times the width of that at an ordinary settlement. The distinction was obvious because these places were enclosed by several concentric ramparts (Fig. 15). If the scale of the principal building was a mark of distinction, the boundary conveyed the same message. Again many of these earthworks reproduced the form of the principal roundhouse, and again their entrances faced the rising sun.

Boat-shaped longhouses in the Viking Age

It is revealing that the structures that were once called 'boat-shaped' houses are increasingly described as 'bow-sided' or 'convex' buildings

(Eriksen 2019). They are best known in the Viking Age, when some of them assumed considerable proportions, although the basic form was not entirely new. It has always been acknowledged that buildings with curving side walls dated from the same period as stone settings in the form of a boat. They can even be found on the same sites, for example the excavated complexes at Lejre and Jelling (Fig. 16). But the change of terminology betrays a certain unease. Comparing the plans of these buildings to the shape of a sea-going vessel seems to be a step too far. Rather than indulging in speculation, most scholars have sought practical explanations for this distinctive form.

It was Brian Hope-Taylor, the excavator of Yeavering, who objected most vehemently to any link between houses and ships. Discussing a recently excavated example of this kind of building, he concluded that its form was aerodynamic (Hope-Taylor 1962). Like a sports

Lejre

Hall

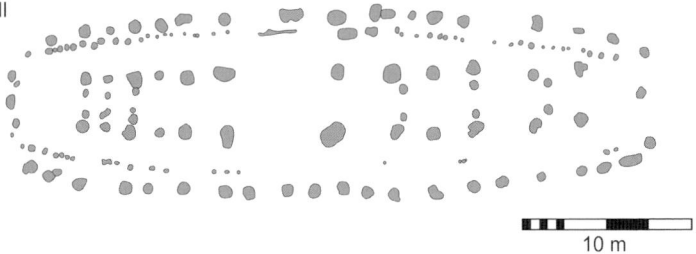

10 m

Ship setting

10 m

Fig. 16 Outline plans of a timber hall and a nearby ship setting at Lejre. Information from Christensen (2015).

car (Hope-Taylor drove one himself), it would deflect strong winds, allowing a massive structure to remain intact in bad weather. Its pitched roof achieved a similar effect, and that is why its appearance was compared with that of an upturned boat. More recently Frands Herschend (1998, 43) has argued that this design allowed people to construct higher structures and to increase the amount of space around the hearth.

There are problems with practical explanations of this kind, although they would have had some influence. One is directly related to Hope-Taylor's argument. If this was the ideal form for a large building it should have been adopted more widely. Depending on the layout of individual settlements, the wind would have exerted the same pressure on every structure, yet the proportion of boat-shaped houses varied from one site to another; they were not adopted universally. In any case some of these structures may have had a special status and even contained an unusual array of objects. At the same time the idea that this design was aerodynamic is at odds with the evidence from Norway where such buildings were particularly common. Here they were laid out on cardinal alignments which took no account of the directions of the prevailing winds (Eriksen 2019, 128–34). Purely functional considerations are insufficient.

Although Herschend discussed the advantages of building in this style, he also proposed a new interpretation of the ship burial at Oseberg in Norway. He suggested that its interior had been organised like the dwelling of a high-status woman. Its overall layout was similar to that of one of the Great Halls at Lejre and different assemblages were found in the separate rooms. Herschend (2000) characterised the Oseberg vessel and its contents as a 'house metaphor'. They were simultaneously a grave, a house and a ship. In another publication he took the same approach to a ship burial in the Swedish cemetery of Valsgärde, but it this case it represented the hall of a leading man and was provided with weapons and the equipment for a feast (Herschend 2001, 69–91).

Herschend's interpretation breaks down the distinction between watercraft and halls and goes beyond the superficial similarity between their plans. Is it possible to apply the same idea to the ship settings of the same period? They were open enclosures rather than burial mounds and the largest examples included sufficient space to accommodate a significant number of people; the same was true of the principal chamber in a Great Hall. Alexandra Sanmark's (2019) research shows that these monuments can be found at Viking assembly sites in Scandinavia where they occur together with burial mounds, cooking pits and lines of upright posts. Like the halls, these places played an important part in political and judicial administration.

The links between Great Halls and ship settings should not be over-emphasised, but they do recall a contrast discussed in Chapters Two and Three. Boat-shaped houses were built of wood but ship settings were defined by monoliths. At Lejre they are found in close proximity to one another. The contrast between stone and timber was important from the Neolithic period onwards. The connections between structures dating from the Viking Age provide a further example.

Summary

These cases are taken from three separate periods and from different parts of Europe. In every case houses provided a source of inspiration for other kinds of monuments. Their character varied, from burial mounds to hillforts and from ringworks to stone settings, but in each instance domestic buildings gained an added significance as parts of a network of associations, or even as the models for later constructions. The importance of individual structures was enhanced because they formed part of a still wider set of references. Here a good example is the complicated relationship between longhouses and ship settings. In the light of what has been said so far, how should the study of Great Houses proceed?

Sociétés à maison: house societies

An important influence has been the work of Claude Lévi-Strauss who introduced the concept of House Societies towards the end of his career (Lévi-Strauss 1975). It was never developed in any detail and some of its defining features are documented in lecture notes.

Even so his ideas have had an important influence in archaeology and anthropology and entire books have been devoted to an approach that he set out only briefly (Carsten & Hugh-Jones 1995; Joyce & Gillespie 2000; R. Beck 2007a; 2007b).

Terminology can be revealing and in this case it is much more than a question of translation. Lévi-Strauss discussed what he called '*sociétés à maison*': the character of a *society* is emphasised instead of the house itself. The English the term is 'house society', but here the emphasis is reversed and the importance of domestic buildings is highlighted. Lévi-Strauss's concern was with alliance and descent and in his conception the 'house' referred to a group of people. That is why it is sometimes capitalised as House. His discussion continued a line of thought which had found its fullest expression is his boo*k The Elementary Structures of Kinship* published more than 30 years before (Lévi-Strauss 1949). Commentaries on his work place more emphasis on the house as a *physical* structure and sometimes as a kind of monument. That is how the concept has been used by archaeologists. At times it is helpful to maintain the distinction between the French and English language terms.

Lévi-Strauss's definition makes no concessions to the reader. In *sociétés à maison* the House is:

> A moral person, keeper of a domain composed simultaneously of material and immaterial possessions, which perpetuates itself by the transmission of its name, of fortune and of its titles in a real or fictive line considered legitimate on the sole condition that this continuity can express itself in the language of kinship or alliance, and, most often, both (translation by Gillespie 2000, 27).

House Societies depart from the norms defined in his earlier work, and that is how he came to recognise this distinctive phenomenon. It is not just that certain communities diverge from the schemes he had identified; there are instances in which people describe themselves as members of a 'house'. He thought that *sociétés á maison* are established as traditional organisation breaks down and new divisions emerge.

House Societies represent an evolutionary stage between communities based on kinship and less egalitarian structures. Sometimes the members of a House do occupy a large building, but this is a secondary consideration. The concept can extend to a whole village and even to a royal domain. As Susan Gillespie (2000) says in an important review, it does not refer to a structure in which people live. Although *sociétés à maison* may feature impressive buildings, they do not need to so do. This may not pose problems for the anthropologist, but it makes the concept difficult for archaeologists to use.

Responses in social anthropology

There have been two responses to an analysis that Lévi-Strauss never presented in detail. One was in social anthropology, where traditional approaches to kinship were already being questioned. Ethnographers found it difficult to reconcile abstract models of alliance and kinship with their own experience on the ground. Instead of strictly defined notions, there was more concern with *relatedness*: with the connections between people that could actually be observed. They might be expressed in the language of kinship, but it was a social construction which had little to do with biological descent. The critique is summarised in Marshall Sahlins's (2013) book *What kinship is – and is not*. It has just two chapters: 'What kinship is – culture'; and 'What kinship is not – biology'. Instead of the traditional definition Sahlins uses the term 'mutuality of being'. But revisionist accounts have not gone unchallenged, and Bradley Ensor considers that that the traditional models of descent theory had more application in the past than they do in the ethnographic present. In his view 'the claim that people rarely, or never, practice their normative rules of marriage, post-martial residence, and descent are based on synchronic views of societies that have actually undergone dramatic transformations' (Ensor 2011, 204).

Lévi-Strauss's approach drew a mixed response from anthropologists. Although there have been attempts to employ his framework, it has also been treated with reserve. This is because his original definition was so opaque. Their ambivalence is obvious in commentaries on his work. It certainly provided a stimulus for new research, but it also had a major limitation. His use of the term House was a major weakness for he did not show enough interest in the very buildings from which this concept took its name.

That has now been remedied, and Robin Beck (2007b, 10–11) offers a useful summary of current thinking:

> The moral personhood of the house is literally personified in the body of its estate. The material substance of the house – its fields, its architecture, the bodies and icons of its ancestors, its place of origin and its carefully crafted heirlooms – is thus a living body in which creation is birth, use history is life, and destruction and re-creation are death and rebirth … The embodiment of a house's architecture – its rendering as a human body – clearly elaborates a metaphorical transfer of … social life from house members to [its] physical structure.

The original account of *sociétés à maison* was a dialogue that Lévi-Strauss was having with his earlier work, and it exercised less influence on the thinking of other anthropologists. Either the conception was modified, or it was defended because it maintained the importance of studying kinship.

Responses in archaeology

It has never been easy for archaeologists to study the same question. As Ensor (2011) says, few methods have been available and all of them are vulnerable to criticism. One approach was to investigate the transmission of craft traditions between different communities (on the questionable assumption that pottery was always made by women). Another was to conduct cross-cultural analyses employing data from the Human Relations Area Files (https://hraf.yale.edu). Cemeteries have been studied to identify the burials of men and women dressed in non-local costumes; these people may have been introduced from other areas. Such evidence was never common.

Much more information comes from the isotopes preserved in human bones and from ancient DNA. The most useful studies consider whole cemeteries like those of the Linearbandkeramik, but it is too soon to say how far the results of the new work will support long-established models of social organisation (Bickle & Whittle 2013; Knipper *et al.* 2017). The success of this research requires a secure connection between an individual settlement and a group of associated graves.

If archaeologists were wary of kinship studies, they were attracted by studies of houses because these structures left a physical trace behind. The buildings were constructed on very different scales, but some were truly massive. They also shared features in common with monuments of the kinds considered in this chapter. Soon House Societies were being claimed in many periods and regions. Most of the elements shared between these accounts are listed by Alfredo González-Ruibal and Marisa Ruiz-Gálvez (2016). Although they are concerned with the communities in the Mediterranean, the same features can be identified in the archaeology of a wider area. The most obvious are:

> Houses as key symbolic elements. [T]his can be seen in the presence of shrines … [There were] houses imbued with religious or cosmic symbolism (decoration, ritual offerings in the house or the vicinity); and the transformation of an ancient house or its remains into a social symbol or a ritual space.
>
> A strong material investment in the house itself [which] can be in size, complexity, monumentality or decoration … Spaces of material and immaterial wealth can be integrated in a single multi-room building, or aggregate domestic compounds or house clusters.
>
> A strong concern with the past; repeated occupation of the same ancestral grounds by the same house, heirlooms, and ancestor cults … Religious spaces are often built on top of earlier houses, revealing both a genealogical intent and the sacred connotations of the house (González-Ruibal & Ruiz-Gálvez 2016, 387–88).

Nearly all these elements can be inferred from excavated evidence. These authors also refer to literary or historical sources concerning the status of the occupants.

Discussion

Is this concept helpful? And, if it does raise problems, how can they be addressed?

The first point to make is the House Society is an ethnographic category, created to address a specific problem in anthropological theory. Its creation was really a private matter, more relevant to the development of Lévi-Strauss's ideas than the current concerns of his discipline. Its real importance has always been to the study of kinship rather than the investigation of buildings, whether they existed in the past or are in use today. The defining feature of a House Society is a kind of social organisation which cannot be addressed directly by archaeological methods, although scientific analysis of human remains may make a contribution in the future. Still more important, the status of '*sociétés à maison*' remains a controversial subject within anthropology and for that reason it would be ill advised for archaeologists to borrow the concept uncritically.

The second point considers the societies that have already been interpreted in this way. The catalogue is extremely varied. Archaeological examples range from the pit houses of coastal hunter gatherers in Finland around 2000 BC (Vaneeckhout 2010) to Mycenaean palaces (González-Ruibal & Ruiz-Gálvez 2016). Historical examples are still more varied, including the monumental buildings associated with the royal dynasties of early modern Europe whose very names are significant: the House of Bourbon, and the House of Hapsburg. Less extreme examples include camps of rustic cabins in New Hampshire (Brereton 2005). There are some structures that have already featured in this account: Early Neolithic halls in northern Britain (J. Thomas 2015 & 2016), and Maori meeting houses in New Zealand (Sissons 2010). There are also the buildings that attracted Lévi-Strauss's attention in the first place. They were shared between South America and

Southeast Asia. He considered that the House as an institution exists at every level from the family to the state, but the category includes examples which have so little in common that its value is greatly reduced. Like the chiefdoms that have been so popular among prehistorians, a term borrowed from social anthropology has already been applied too widely and may be losing its value. If House Societies were so numerous and so diverse, the concept is better avoided by archaeologists. These ideal structures really are castles in the air.

A third observation is still more troubling. Lévi-Strauss argued that Houses appear at a quite specific juncture, as communities organised according to kinship change and new differences of status emerge. He has been criticised for using an evolutionary framework, but this misses an important point. The significance of House Societies may have been exaggerated, but most of the ideal types adopted in archaeology are based on ethnographic examples. They need to be considered in the contexts in which they were originally recorded. The problem was discussed by Matthew Spriggs (2008) in an article with the provocative title 'Ethnographic parallels and the denial of history'. As he observed, the most influential sources of information date from a period *after* colonial contact when it was safe for anthropologists to live in particular societies. Although his paper concerned the misuse of Melanesian evidence, it has the same implication for models drawn from other regions. Where these sources are confronted with the sequences documented by archaeology it is clear that the 'ethnographic present' was no more than that: it was only an episode in a longer and more varied history. That is why Ensor (2011, 204) suggests that revisionist accounts of kinship 'are based on synchronic views of societies that have actually undergone dramatic transformations'. That may well be true of *sociétés à maison*. It is also why Gillespie (2007) asks the pertinent question '*When* is a House?' Perhaps its characteristic features were not the result of gradual internal processes but a specific response to outside pressures.

In fact her question is directly relevant an ethnographic example quoted earlier. The Maori meeting house has been discussed by Jeffrey Sissons (2010). It is known that these buildings assumed their special roles after European contact, although their forms recalled those of earlier structures which were both the dwellings of chiefs and where their warriors slept. Not only did they celebrate the ancestors of the community, they became symbols of independent identities in a colonial world. Here genealogies were recited and narratives were performed. They assumed these roles when warfare was proscribed and developed in parallel with changes of land tenure. Sissons (2010, 383) concludes that:

> Anthropologists … entering a rural Maori community unaware of the historical processes in which meeting houses have participated have been inclined to view these buildings as symbols of enduring descent groups because this is how they are represented by the people who live with, in, and around them … [T]his was probably not the case… They were built by communities in order to host large political gatherings and/or symbolise alliances between groups in opposition to the colonial government.

Although the organisation of these building has points in common with Great Houses in ancient Europe, their historical context is important and may be directly relevant to such comparisons. Ethnographic examples can be valuable as sources of ideas (the next chapter takes one as its point of departure), but they can be no more than that and should not invested with a degree of authority that they do not possess.

Spriggs advocates a completely different approach. Not only are such accounts based on short periods of observation within a lengthy history, it can be wrong to invest them with seemingly timeless qualities. They have to be viewed in relation to a longer expanse of time. Thus the roles of Maori meeting houses must be explained by the politics of the colonial era. Spriggs's solution is simple. It is more productive to compare long term developments with one another. In most cases that is only possible using the methods of field archaeology. A good example is a recent article comparing society in Late Bronze Age Scandinavia with developments during the Viking Age (Ling *et al.* 2018). Although it cites descriptions of other communities, the emphasis on *sequence* is paramount. This is the element that frees researchers from the limitations of ethnographic comparisons taken out of context.

A way forward

This chapter has been concerned with the archaeology of monumental buildings and has drawn on both ethnographic and archaeological examples. The following chapters will follow Matthew Spriggs's lead by comparing the *sequences* that led to the construction and use of Great Houses in several areas of Europe. It is concerned with their historical contexts and does not look for evidence of an ideal social type. Chapter Five treats Neolithic buildings in Britain, Ireland and France. Chapter Six focuses on monumental structures of the late pre-Roman and Roman Iron Ages on both sides of the Irish Sea. Then Chapter Seven compares the Great Halls built in Britain and Scandinavia during the first millennium AD and contrasts their development with the reinvention of royal centres in Ireland. This sequence encapsulates many of the developments studied in the book. Finally, Chapter Eight offers a brief summary of the findings of this project.

Part Three

Setting the house in order

CHAPTER 5

On a larger scale

Introduction

The previous section emphasised two important points. The forms of monumental buildings did not exist in isolation. Their significance could be established by comparing them with domestic structures, but it was at least as informative to relate them to other kinds of public architecture, including enclosures and mounds. At the same time, it was necessary to investigate the circumstances in which these buildings were made and used. Models derived from anthropology might be less helpful than the sequences documented by archaeology. This chapter investigates these issues in relation to three groups of Neolithic (and Chalcolithic) structures in Britain, Ireland and France, dating from the fourth and third millennia BC. The first group comprises enormous timber buildings in Scotland and southern England. The second extends across northern and western France, while the third covers most parts of Britain and Ireland.

From Colombia to Crathes

For all the caution expressed in Part One, ethnographic studies can still inspire home-grown examples. This discussion begins by comparing an influential account of longhouses in South America with two of the Neolithic halls introduced at the beginning of this book. Their juxtaposition is not fortuitous. Christine Hugh-Jones, whose monograph *From the Milk River* studied life in a Colombian longhouse, also contributed to a volume on prehistoric buildings in Europe (Hugh-Jones 1979 & 2002). It is ironic that the most apt comparison with her case study is a timber hall which was excavated more than ten years after the article was published. It was at Crathes on the River Dee in northeast Scotland (Murray *et al.* 2009). This building has already featured in the first chapter, but its most remarkable feature is that it was one of a pair. The famous site of Balbridie was on the opposite riverbank only a kilometre away (Fig. 17).

Hugh-Jones's book documented the organisation of a longhouse in the New World and the ways in which it was used. She discussed its strategic placing in relation to the social, physical and cosmological landscapes around it. She acknowledged that her research took place after the lives of the inhabitants had been affected by contacts with traders and missionaries. Such buildings were no longer as large as their predecessors, but their layout remained the same. Several observations are particularly relevant here.

Like the structures at Crathes and Balbridie, the Colombian longhouse was beside a river and the movement of the current was reflected by its plan. The occupants believed that the first settlers had travelled up the river in the past, and the axis of the building illustrated that idea. It distinguished between an area of origin in one direction, and the dangerous unsettled forest, in the other. As if to emphasise this distinction, there was a door at either end.

Her account recalls Shannon Fraser's comments on the hall at Crathes:

> The positioning of the building … would seem chosen to accentuate its mass and monumentality … The near east-west orientation of the building – which it shares with the hall at Balbridie – may be tied in to a wider world … The sun and moon traverse the sky each day, from east to west, from the sea to the mountains … Just a few minutes' walk away the River Dee flows from its source in the west, eastwards to the sea … Salmon and sea trout … travel westwards to its high reaches and back down to the sea through spring, summer and autumn (Murray *et al.* 2009, 67).

The name of the river comes from an early root *deua* which suggests that at one time it was considered as a female divinity.

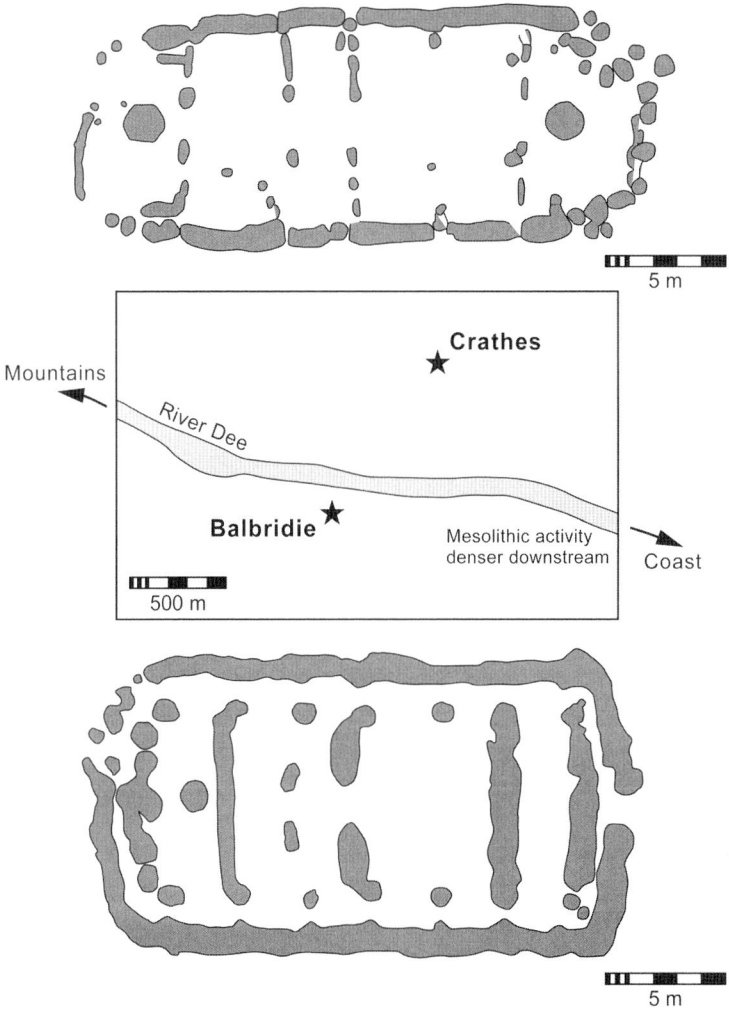

Fig. 17 The locations and plans of the Neolithic halls on opposite banks of the River Dee at Crathes and Balbridie. Information from Murray et al. (2009) and Fairweather and Ralston (1993).

The pairing of Neolithic buildings on either side of a river is not found anywhere else. Their positions are important and recall another part of Hugh-Jones's analysis. They were located midway between the coast which was settled at the time and high ground in the interior where there is less sign of Neolithic activity. These structures also occupied an important point in relation to the past. Northeast Scotland was one of the first areas colonised by farmers in Britain (Whittle *et al.* 2011, fig. 15.8) and it is likely that settlement extended along the valley from the sea. That direction was emphasised by the doorways of both buildings. The hall at Crathes was used for no more than 50 years, and probably during the 38th century BC. That is as early as any dated monument in Scotland.

The past was important in yet another way. This area already had a special significance and the placing of the halls may have acknowledged that history. As Shannon Fraser says, the Dee is an important salmon river. Excavation at Crathes established that the site was already important during the Mesolithic phase when a line of substantial pits was excavated 150 m from the position of the hall. They were much older than the building, but their positions could still be recognised as they were recut during the later period. This phenomenon has not been identified in other parts of Britain. Still more unusual are the dense concentrations of Mesolithic artefacts beside the river. They accumulated over a long time but their use extended into the fifth millennium BC.

One of them was very close to the hall at Crathes. It followed the course of the river for 2 km, and even small-scale excavation (it covered just over 100 m^2) found 30,000 pieces of worked flint (Wickham-Jones *et al.* 2016). Surface survey has located further findspots upstream, although they seem to be less frequent. In the opposite direction, recent excavation at Miltimber 12 km from the halls found a second group of Mesolithic pits. Again they were recut during the Early Neolithic period; the same process has been recognised on the coastal plain. Miltimber was another place where a large collection of artefacts was recovered near the Dee (Dingwall *et al.* 2019, 33–48 & 89–122).

The distributions of Mesolithic and Neolithic activities overlapped. Indigenous communities had followed the river into the mountains although the most intensive occupation was nearer to the coast. How were their occupation sites related to those of the following period? A new excavation on the high ground towards the source of the river has identified activity contemporary with the timber halls, but here it was associated with artefacts of Mesolithic character (Wickham-Jones *et al.* 2020). Downstream to the east it is obvious that there was an explicit concern with the past. Here older pits were reopened, but it may be equally significant that the halls were erected at a point where occupation had been particularly intense. It is not clear whether the change happened rapidly and whether the indigenous population was displaced. These are difficult questions because the Neolithic dates from Crathes and Balbridie are among the earliest in Scotland (Sheridan 2013).

Team building

The siting of these two buildings suggests some new concerns. One interpretation can be discounted. There is nothing to suggest direct continuity between the Mesolithic and Neolithic phases on Deeside. Both halls were associated with finds of cereals, and with fine pottery in a style introduced from Continental Europe. Their ground plans resemble a series of timber buildings within the Michelsberg enclosure at Mairy in the Ardennes which should date from the same period (Laurelut 2011). Their appearance in northeast Scotland is consistent with the evidence from other sites which suggests that the region was settled by farmers early in the fourth millennium BC. If the inhabitants of the river valley continued to live off wild resources, there is no evidence to show this. It seems more likely that they were assimilated into a new community.

Crathes and Balbridie have the same characteristics as other halls that featured in Chapter One. Like those sites, they date from the very beginning of the Neolithic period. They share their unusual dimensions and exceptional ground plans. They are associated with cereals and ceramics but for the most part they lack the more diverse assemblages found in settlements of the same date. For example, excavation of the hall at Crathes found 50 pots and 50 lithic artefacts. A small domestic building 20 km away at Garthdee produced a smaller number of vessels (only 34), but eight times as many pieces of worked stone (Murray & Murray 2014).

The early halls have other characteristics in common. As Chapter One has shown, they were exceptionally large and their construction must have made exceptional demands. In most cases they approached the maximum width for a roofed building of their type. At the same time they share two features with monuments of similar date. Their massive gables resemble the wooden facades of burial mounds like that at Lochill; this was recognised during the excavation of Balbridie (Fairweather & Ralston 1993). These halls are also divided into a series of small rooms. In some respects they resemble the internal divisions in Early Neolithic houses, but the presence of so many partitions must have impeded movement around the building. It would have been especially difficult at Balbridie and Claish (unless the excavated features were of more than a single phase). These spaces may have performed different roles, and one of them could be larger than the others. At the same time they bear a striking resemblance to the arrangement of internal divisions within the fabric of long mounds and long cairns where they seem to have distinguished the contributions of different teams building the monument (McFadyen 2007). Perhaps the rooms inside the halls were used by separate parts of the community. Fraser observed that the buildings on opposite sides of the Dee shared roughly the same alignment. It could have referred to the course of the river, but an east–west orientation was very common among barrows and megalithic tombs. Indeed Julian Thomas (2015 & 2016) has suggested that the halls were a source of inspiration for these monuments.

Alison Sheridan (2013) favours a more practical interpretation for the halls. They date from the first phase of Neolithic colonisation and were where immigrant farmers lived together in the same building before they settled larger areas of land. After that initial phase domestic sites became smaller and more dispersed. This would be consistent with the sizes and early dates of the Scottish halls, but it does not explain why they were so elaborate.

Another perspective is suggested by the site of Mairy with which they have been compared (Laurelut 2011). Here a much wider range of evidence is available. As many as 30 buildings were identified in the excavated part of an enclosure defined by a ditch and five palisades (Fig. 18). The smallest structures were the same size as some of the domestic buildings in Ireland, but the biggest was 60 m long and 13 m wide; there was another group with lengths between 42 m and 45 m. Many of these structures were larger than their counterparts in Britain where the longest, the hall at Carnoustie, extended for 35 m. Those at Mairy had up to five separate rooms: the same number as the building at Crathes. Not only did the excavated area contain an unparalleled number of buildings, it included more than 200 pits. Their interpretation has a bearing on how the site was used. They contained intact ceramic vessels and collections of animal bones which

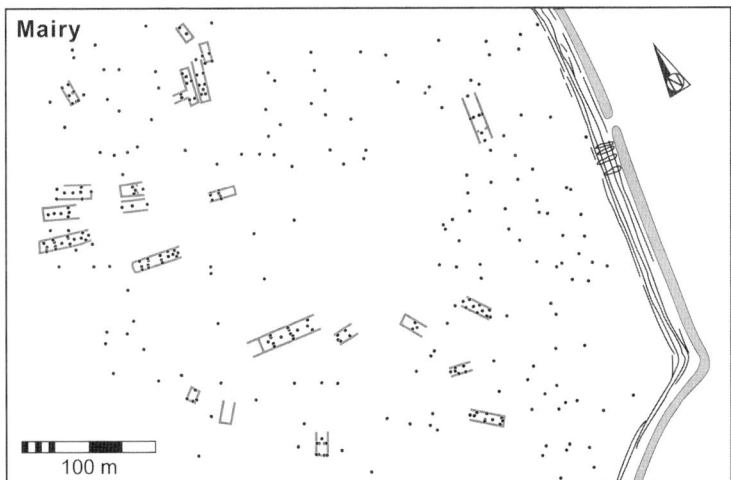

Fig. 18 Timber buildings inside the excavated part of the Neolithic enclosure at Mairy. Information from Laurelut (2011).

are interpreted as the remains of sacrificial offerings and feasts. They had been placed in the ground with some formality. The site contained large quantities of pottery which could be dated to three successive phases. An interesting feature is that throughout the entire sequence the ceramic assemblage combined the attributes of two different regional traditions. It seems possible that Mairy was where people from separate communities met on special occasions. That makes it even less likely that the buildings were normal dwellings, and they remain unparalleled on the Continent. Could the same interpretation apply to their British counterparts?

An alternative to Alison Sheridan's approach is also based on the chronology of timber halls in Scotland, but takes into account the sophistication of these structures and their contents. Again there was an obvious reference to domesticity of a kind that is not in evidence among late Mesolithic foragers. Chapter One suggested that these buildings shared the attributes of excavated houses and expressed them on an extravagant scale. The evidence from Balbridie and Crathes is revealing because their surroundings had already played a significant part during an earlier period. How can the evidence be interpreted?

One way of considering the striking juxtaposition between the Mesolithic settlements and the halls is to envisage a confrontation between two different ways of life, but there are problems with this approach. Much of the Mesolithic evidence dates from an earlier period than the Neolithic buildings, and at the moment it is not clear whether the traditional use of the river and its resources extended as late as 4000 BC, except on the highest ground. That remains to be established. What is evident is that the positions of older pits – whatever their original functions – could still be identified on the ground. Their significance may not have been remembered, but people would be able to recognise their earthworks. They would also be aware of the unusual amount of worked flint on the surface. The pits at Crathes, and others downriver at Miltimber, were reopened during the Early Neolithic phase. It could have been an attempt by recent settlers to integrate traces of past activity into a new way of life. The siting of the halls might have had the same effect.

Could these halls have played a part in establishing a new order? The argument would apply not only to the buildings in Northern Britain but to three exceptionally large timber structures in southern England: those at Penhale Round, Yarnton and Whitehorse Stone. Like the Scottish examples, they date from a time when land use changed completely and there is the first evidence of agriculture. Two contained very few artefacts, but in this case they lacked the links with the past seen at sites on Deeside.

The oldest of the three was at Whitehorse Stone in southeast England and dates from the 41st or 40th centuries BC: the very beginning of the insular Neolithic period (Booth *et al.* 2011, 63–118). It might have been used for up to 350 years (although this seems unlikely as not many posts were replaced). The structure itself was isolated, but a smaller building of the usual size for a house of this period was identified 280 m away and had almost the same alignment. The hall was 17.5 m long and 7 m wide and was defined by rows of posts as well as a foundation trench. It was the smallest of the English examples and only slightly longer than the largest houses of the same date in Ireland. It was associated with burnt grain but contained very few artefacts. Its ground plan is distinctive as it resembles that of two square buildings built end to end. The hall at Whitehorse Stone had not been set on fire. It was near to two, or possibly three, megalithic tombs. They have not been dated, but an example at Coldrum 10 km away was probably erected in the 39th century BC (Wysocki *et al.* 2013). The site of the larger building at Whitehorse Stone was reused by two small circular structures. One replaced the other, and the earlier of the pair was associated with Late Neolithic Grooved Ware.

A second example at Yarnton, in the upper Thames valley, was rather later and was probably constructed in the 38th century BC. Unlike its counterpart at Whitehorse Stone, it was defined entirely by postholes (Hey *et al.* 2016, 51–62). It was larger and measured 20.5 m by 10.5 m and again it could be composed of two square modules, each of the same size. This time it was in an area with other evidence of early activity (although that may reflect the large scale of the excavation), but it produced exceptionally few finds apart from evidence of cereals. On the other hand, there were human remains in the postholes. There was a small circular building of the same date 450 m away. During the Late Neolithic period a pit containing sherds of Grooved Ware was dug on the long axis of the building, suggesting that its position could still be recognised. The sequence at Whitehorse Stone was very similar.

Finally, the biggest of these structures was at Penhale Round in southwest England. It had been damaged by later occupation on the site, but excavation identified a rectangular post-built structure about 25 m in length and 7 m wide. It was defined by spaced posts rather than a foundation trench and contained a hearth (Nowakowski & Johns 2015, 22–66). In contrast to the others, it was associated with a significant number of sherds and stone tools, as well as cereals. The ceramics were of Early Neolithic type and radiocarbon dates on short-lived samples suggest that this structure was used for a brief period, at some stage between 3950 and 3700 BC. That places it towards the beginning of Neolithic activity in this part of Britain (Whittle *et al.* 2011, fig. 15.8) Again the building had not been burnt. Around it were other Neolithic features, including a circular stake-built structure only 4.3 m in diameter which can be compared with an even smaller example of similar shape at Yarnton.

Discussion

Taken together, Crathes and Balbridie suggest a distinctive role for Early Neolithic halls during an important period of transition in Scotland. Perhaps they were not domestic dwellings shared by arrivals from other regions, but monuments whose very construction brought people together to participate in a common task. They were used on an occasional basis and helped to establish new social groups at a time of unparalleled social and economic change. If so, they were public architecture of a special kind, and through their reference to the forms of more modest buildings they became the Great Houses of a larger population. But their effect was to establish new communities rather than provide a home for one that already existed. Just as they incorporated the remains of a past in a new setting, they incorporated people in the present and helped them to engage with an unfamiliar world. Their construction was part of a process by which new lineages formed and their place in society was assured.

The English evidence is slightly different. Unlike the sites in Scotland, the large buildings were not built at the same times, nor were they set on fire. On the other hand, their dates do reflect the first agricultural settlement in the regions where they were constructed, so that Whitehorse Stone is the earliest example: a result that compares with other dated contexts in southeast England (Whittle *et al.* 2011, fig. 15.8). Again all three structures were associated with carbonised grain. They also date from a period when human remains were assuming a special significance, perhaps indicating a new concern with the past. The structure at Yarnton included fragments of cremated and unburnt bone, and Whitehorse Stone was close to at least two megalithic tombs.

In the light of this information a final point needs making. Not only were all the Neolithic halls constructed at the very beginning of this period, they lacked any obvious precedent within Britain or Ireland. They appeared suddenly, along with novel resources, unfamiliar practices and a new material culture. The earliest monuments are also found in this phase. But unlike those mounds or cairns, and the enclosures that were built afterwards, the periods of use of these buildings were comparatively brief. Like the domestic dwellings of the same period, they had a finite chronology and it was soon at an end. These halls were a short-lived phenomenon and one that occurred in a particular historical setting. In that respect they were very different from the buildings in France considered in the following section.

French connections

The discovery of Late Neolithic and Chalcolithic Great Houses in France followed a similar course to the British research summarised in Part One, and the first examples were found by the same methods. The most important was excavation, followed by radiocarbon dating.

An especially influential project took place at Antran in the west of the country where a large rectangular structure was investigated. Since it was located in an area with Late Bronze Age and Iron Age burials it was natural to date this building to the same period; monuments of similar proportions had already been identified in later prehistoric cemeteries. As had happened with Balbridie, the radiocarbon dates from Antran came as a surprise (Pautreau 1994). Contrary to expectations, they were two thousand years older than expected: between 2880 and 2500 BC.

This particular structure was defined by a foundation trench as well as a setting of posts. The point was important as related buildings could sometimes be recognised from the air. In common with earlier sites in Scotland, the existence of a continuous perimeter made them easier to identify. It was more difficult to establish their contexts. They did not resemble Linearbandkeramik longhouses in France and some of the crop mark sites along the Atlantic coast were outside their distribution altogether. Another source of comparison might have been the structures at Mairy close to the border with Belgium, but, as this chapter has shown, they dated from an earlier period.

The combination of excavation and aerial reconnaissance shows that related structures were unusually diverse. This applies to their distribution which was bounded by Flanders, Brittany, the Dordogne and Languedoc (Louboutin *et al.* 1994; Fouéré 1998; Joseph *et al.* 2011). Following the work of Luc Laporte (2012), the main distinction is between an eastern (or northeastern) tradition of architecture and a western style. There could have been differences of chronology between them but they are not clearly defined. Buildings of these kinds may have been used from the end of the fourth millennium BC to the middle of the third. Their forms were just as varied (Fig. 19). Although they shared the basic outline of a longhouse, they were built on very different scales. In the northeast of France the smaller examples could be between 10 m and 20 m long and between 5 m and 8 m wide. They had two aisles and apsidal ends, and were defined by spaced postholes which made them difficult to identify by remote sensing. By contrast, most of the larger structures had foundation

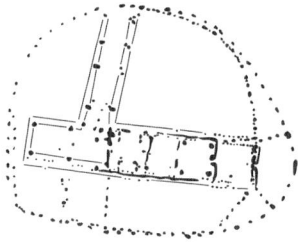

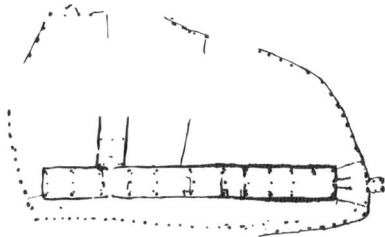

Fig. 19 Plans of monumental Late Neolithic buildings at three sites in
northern and western France. Information from Joseph et al. (2011)
and Tinévez and Nicolas (2004).

trenches and were about 25 m in length and as much as 10 m wide.
One exceptional structure, Building B at Houplin-Ancoisne, was
almost twice that size (Praud *et al.* 2007).

Those in the west of France were even less homogenous, but again
they had two aisles. Their lengths were usually between 10 and 20
m and their widths were generally similar to those of structures in
the north, but about 30% of them were between about 40 and 100 m

long and up to 15 m wide. The most monumental of all were at Les Chavis, Vouillé, where two enormous longhouses were accompanied by smaller examples, and one at Pléchâtel, La Hersonnais which was succeeded by three other buildings (Tinévez & Nicolas 2004; Tinévez 2005; Nicolas *et al.* 2019). Again the larger structures had continuous foundation trenches, but they lacked the apsidal ends found in the northern group.

Despite these differences, the longhouses of northeast France share important features with examples closer to the Atlantic (Scarre 2011, 262–66). Those in Pas-de-Calais and the Somme contained as many as four separate rooms, although this was not always the case. To the west, where some of the buildings were larger, there might be more subdivisions, with a total of 11 compartments inside the earliest of the successive structures at Pléchâtel, La Hersonnais. The orientations of these longhouses are interesting, too. Those south of the River Loire extended between northeast and southwest, and the buildings to its north reversed this pattern and were aligned from northwest to southeast; the same was true of most of the well-preserved structures in the other group. The plans of these buildings acknowledged the directions of the midsummer and midwinter solstices.

It is more difficult to fix their chronology. Nearly all the dates are between 3000/2900 and 2500 BC, but Houplin-Ancoisne could have been earlier (this point is disputed). In the western group the sequence may have begun with the construction of small buildings before that phase. The monumental longhouses were usually a later development. There are cases in which individual buildings were replaced, and at Pléchâtel, La Hersonnais there is evidence that they had been burnt down. There is even more variation at individual sites and the larger examples were sometimes associated with fenced enclosures. The sequence is not always clear. Sometimes they abutted the side wall of the longhouse, but in other cases these buildings were at the centre of a more extensive compound. In one case the main range of compartments was supplemented by a separate wing which provided access to a side entrance (Tinévez & Nicolas 2004).

The sites with several small buildings may very well have been settlements, but this interpretation can hardly extend to the largest structures. Like the Neolithic halls in Scotland, they reproduced the features of domestic dwellings on a monumental scale, yet remarkably few artefacts are associated with certain of these sites. Where they are found, they include fine blades and daggers made of Grand Pressigny flint, arrowheads, and pottery. A 60 m long structure at Challignac included four copper beads and an unusual proportion of decorated ceramic vessels (Burnez 2010). It provided striking evidence for the consumption of pork. The assemblage from Pléchâtel, La Hersonnais is equally informative (Tinévez & Nicolas 2004). It contained nearly 3000 sherds, but only 100 pieces of worked flint. The other stone tools might have been used to dig the foundation trenches and were reused as packing for the walls. There was also an obsidian bead, imported from an unknown source. The structures in the northeastern group of longhouses contained loom weights and spindle whorls associated with textile production (Joseph *et al.* 2011).

The plans of the larger buildings have another characteristic (Laporte & Tinévez 2004). They resemble those of three different kinds of Neolithic tomb in the same areas of France: megalithic *allées couvertes* and angled passage graves to the west, and, to the north, *allées sépulcrales* which were set into the ground and constructed of timber. Although their sizes differ from those of the wooden buildings, they have strikingly similar plans and, like the longhouses, these monuments feature a series of distinct compartments, separated from one another by thresholds or internal subdivisions (Peek 1975). It is not a new idea to suggest that the organisation of mortuary monuments was influenced by the layout of domestic dwellings (the notion was considered briefly in Chapter Four) but in this case there is a chronological problem. As Chris Scarre has pointed out, these tombs date from the end of the fourth millennium BC, but most of the longhouses that share similar features were built several centuries later. The conventional relationship has to be reversed and the tombs, most of which would have remained accessible long after they were built, must have provided the prototypes for these timber structures.

If so, this has implications for how the longhouses are understood:

> The inevitable conclusion is that these massive buildings incorporating elements of the funerary domain are more likely to have been for ceremonial performances, connected perhaps with feasting and commemoration of the dead, rather than domestic structures of everyday life … The third millennium 'great houses' of western and northern France were not models for the tombs but modelled upon them (Scarre 2011, 265).

These comparisons concern both the principal groups of large timber buildings. The key site in the western tradition is Pléchâtel, La Hersonnais where four exceptionally massive structures were built in sequence (Tinévez & Nicolas 2004). Their positions overlapped and three of them were associated with palisaded enclosures whose outlines have been compared with those of Neolithic mounds or cairns. In the same way, the stone compartments associated with such structures have been compared with the organisation of separate rooms inside the longhouse. Sometimes the comparison is even more detailed and extends to the placing and forms of the entrances, and the restrictions placed on free movement within both groups of buildings. The similarities even extend to the distributions of pottery and other artefacts inside them (Laporte 2012). The one limitation to this exercise is that bone does not survive on such acid soils. A similar exercise connects the buildings in northeast France with *allées sépulcrales* which were excavated into the subsoil (Peek 1975). Both groups featured the same range of small compartments. The largest longhouse, Houplin-Ancoisne, plays a prominent role in these comparisons (Praud *et al.* 2007). The placing of subdivisions within both groups of structures is much the same, but in this case human remains survive.

The links between these different structures are most apparent in plan, but they were built on very different scales. The most impressive longhouses were between three and five times the sizes of their apparent prototypes. That is most obvious in the western group. It is important to remember this when their plans are juxtaposed on the printed page. At the same time the distributions of timber halls and monuments to the dead did not always coincide, with the result that the tradition represented by Houplin-Ancoisne hardly overlapped with the main concentration of *allées sépulcrales*. That may be due to the accidents of discovery – the longhouses themselves were identified relatively recently – but it makes their interpretation more complicated.

Laporte (2012) has raised the possibility that because of these connections structures like Pléchâtel, La Hersonnais were dedicated to the dead. That might be consistent with the evidence from western France where human bones rarely remain, but it would not explain the situation in the northeast of the country, where they are associated with specialised tombs but not with the above-ground buildings. Another problem is that the largest longhouses can be accompanied by smaller structures of the kind that feature in settlements: they are really aggrandised versions of domestic dwellings. Perhaps the strongest implication of the links between longhouse and *allées sépulcrales* is that the burial chambers contained the remains of large numbers of people. Analogy with the main building at Houplin-Ancoisne raises the possibility that it was associated with living groups of similar or even greater size.

The chronology of these longhouses has another implication. The development of increasingly massive buildings, especially in Atlantic regions, happened over the same period as the development of an important exchange network based on the circulation of Grand Pressigny flint from Touraine in the west of France (Mallet *et al.* 2012). As the scale of production and distribution grew, so did the sizes of these buildings. If it was a gradual development, that was not true of its end. The peak of stone working happened shortly before the adoption of Bell Beakers along the west coast of Europe, but there are associations between the two phenomena (Ihuel *et al.* 2015) and by the end of the Chalcolithic period one network had almost entirely supplanted the other. Architectural traditions changed more rapidly, however, and the tradition of building longhouses lapsed in the middle of the third millennium BC. Even the smaller examples went of use and were replaced by new kinds of dwellings (Nicolas *et al.* 2019).

That is most relevant to the archaeology of western France. How were these developments related to the sequence across a wider area? Research by Nicole Mallet and her colleagues has shed new light on this question (Mallet *et al.* 2012). Based on a corpus of 6000 finds, they document significant changes in the significance of Grand Pressigny flint. This is important as earlier work had placed more emphasis on how the material was worked. These authors showed that its history could be divided into four phases, during which the character of the products changed, the scale of extraction increased, and the artefacts themselves circulated over larger areas. At first their distribution extended from its source as far as Brittany. This phase was dated between 3300 and 3100 BC. Then between about 3100 and 3000 BC Grand Pressigny flint travelled to the Paris Basin and southwest to the foothills of the Alps. By 2900 BC it covered even more of the interior of the country, but it was not until a final phase between 2800 and 2400 BC that it reached the Netherlands and the Mediterranean. By this stage some of these artefacts were taken 1000 km from their source. They have never been found in Britain or Ireland.

There were important changes over this period. The first products were less standardised than the later ones and were generally smaller. When the network reached its fullest extent fine flint blades and daggers were made with enormous skill and exported from western France. The daggers account for 90% of the artefacts. Grand Pressigny flint was seldom used for other objects and at the peak of production between 2650 and 2450 BC it was probably worked by specialists. There is no evidence that the process was tightly controlled and extraction of the stone was not restricted to a single location. Diagnostic artefacts were made in enormous numbers. Between 2800 and 2400 BC it is estimated that 10,000 to 20,000 artefacts were produced every year.

The special value of Grand Pressigny products is clear from their use as grave goods over a wide area. Their contexts range from megalithic tombs in Atlantic Europe to single burials associated with Corded Ware and Bell Beakers. They account for about 25% of the discoveries with good records. The objects themselves were usually in fine condition, but microscopic analysis suggests that they might have been used as sickles rather than weapons (Plisson *et al.* 2002). Another possibility worth considering is that the edge wear was caused by contact with an organic container. They might have been removed for display on special occasions: a feature that has already been recognised with Neolithic axeheads in the Netherlands (Wentink 2006). In contrast to the undamaged examples associated with the dead, those found in settlements include tools made out of broken objects. Grand Pressigny flint also occurs in hoards and on fortified sites of the same date.

It can hardly be a coincidence that the chronology of monumental longhouses ran in parallel with the production of these artefacts. Their distributions also coincide. These buildings were most complex between 2900 and 2500 BC, and that is when artefact production was at its height and required the greatest skill. In the same way, the northern group of longhouses, which reaches as far as Flanders, dates from the period when the distribution of these objects extended over the largest area. It is no surprise that they have been found on those sites. These two developments must have been related to one another, and both processes changed with the adoption of Maritime Bell Beakers that circulated along the Atlantic between the Iberian Peninsula, to the south, and Britain and Ireland, to the north (Nicolas *et al.* 2019). During the same phase sources of metal near the coast became increasingly important. This is not to deny that there were Beaker graves with Grand Pressigny artefacts (Ihuel *et al.* 2015), or that pottery in the new tradition was present in small quantities at longhouses in the Atlantic group where they have been assigned to the latest phase. In the same way, the decorated ceramics associated with great buildings like that at Challignac copied designs in the Beaker repertoire. More important than stylistic connections was the movement of people that must have brought them about (Olalde *et al.* 2018).

How should the largest buildings be interpreted? There is no reason to choose a single answer. Three observations are especially important. Like the Neolithic halls in Scotland, their architecture was based on the features of domestic dwellings but reproduced them on a monumental scale. A second, much less predictable source of inspiration was provided by three kinds of chambered tombs which were obviously associated with death and the supernatural. The link between those domains was the presence of Grand Pressigny flint in settlements as well as graves.

The large structures coexisted with smaller buildings of a related form, and sometimes both kinds can be found on the same sites. It is clear that their roles were not the same in every case. The small quantity of artefacts associated with a monumental longhouse like that at Pléchâtel, La Hersonnais suggests that it might have played a specialised role. So does the unusual assemblage from Challignac with its evidence of decorated pottery and feasting. Surely these were public buildings, and there is little to imply that they were the dwellings of any kind. On the other hand, the connection between the erection of these buildings and the movement of Grand Pressigny flint might mean that they were where important artefacts changed hands. Daggers made of this distinctive material also appear in burials where their presence could have been related to the identity of the dead person. Mallet and her colleagues believe that these artefacts enjoyed a special status, suggesting that they were the prerogative of particular individuals, but even here there are problems. If 10,000 or more blades of Grand Pressigny flint were made every year, they would not have been especially rare. In any case there is evidence that broken daggers were reworked as a source of material for making ordinary tools. It is unlikely that one interpretation will apply in every case. Exactly the same problems arise in Bronze Age archaeology where intact objects feature in special deposits like those in rivers, while broken fragments of the same types could be recycled as scrap metal. Perhaps the *histories* of individual objects were more important than their forms (Bradley 2017, 50–54).

A feature that does stand out is the close relationship between the establishment of long-distance contacts and the construction of the most elaborate buildings. Another is the way in which this system changed with the emergence of a new network associated with the adoption of metals. There is scientific evidence of population move-ments at this time, but the relationship between these elements has still to be worked out in detail. That will require a more exact chro-nology, but it is interesting that very similar problems arise in another region where monumental buildings were erected during the third millennium BC. There are lessons to be learned from comparing these sequences with one another. The following section considers a network that developed on the other side of the Channel. It extended between Britain and Ireland and connected regions as far apart as Orkney and Wessex. But so far there is nothing to indicate any con-nections with France.

From Stenness to Stonehenge

Between 3000 and 2400 BC most parts of Britain and Ireland were connected by a single network. It may have originated a century or two before that time and in some areas it seems to have continued into the Chalcolithic (Bell Beaker) period. Unlike the French example, it was based on shared beliefs rather than the movement of portable artefacts. Although individual objects did travel over long distances, the strongest links are illustrated by the forms of domestic buildings, those of stone and earthwork monuments, and a common visual culture (Sheridan 2004; Bradley 2019, 108–43).

   This network probably developed first in Orkney and on the east coast of Ireland which were in close contact by about 3300 BC. At its fullest extent it included both islands and reached from northern Scotland to southwest England. It is best evidenced in areas with con-centrations of monuments, but is represented in other regions by the assemblages buried in pits. In different areas this network was associ-ated with a range of exceptional structures including passage graves, henges, stone circles and palisaded enclosures. It was also typified by a distinctive kind of oblong or circular house. These different types of structure were associated with a style of pottery, Grooved Ware, which originated in the north and shared its decoration with domestic buildings, tombs and portable artefacts (J. Thomas 2010; Carlin 2017).

While objects made from distinctive materials did circulate between different regions, they were much less common than Grand Pressigny products on the Continent (Jones & Diaz-Guardamino 2019). Flint mines were established in East Anglia and northeast Scotland, but it has been difficult to establish the distribution of their products. Most stone axe quarries in Britain and Ireland were used during an earlier phase, but activity continued at a few of these sites.

The sharing of beliefs seems to have been more important than the circulation of non-local artefacts and materials (Bradley 2019, chapter 3). They seem to have focused on a solar cosmology, and some of the largest monuments were orientated on the solstices (Prendergast *et al.* 2017): a feature that developed independently in the Grand Pressigny network on the Continent. In Britain and Ireland the largest timber and earthwork monuments were closely associated with springs and watercourses, including the head of one of the principal rivers at Avebury. In Ireland, prominent hills and mountains could be selected for the construction of passage graves. One of these locations, Loughcrew, featured rock outcrops embellished in a style that overlapped with the decoration of megalithic tombs (Shee Twohig *et al.* 2010).

The strongest links were between communities around the Irish Sea and there is genetic evidence of a close relationship between the people buried in passage graves in different parts of Ireland (Cassidy *et al.* 2020). In Britain the northern limit of this network is illustrated by the structures on the Stenness peninsula in Orkney. Its southern counterpart is the concentration of monuments around Avebury and Stonehenge.

The growth of Late Neolithic buildings

The Grooved Ware network featured more than one type of domestic building, but only the commonest form is considered here. It was also the most widely distributed. The best preserved of these structures were in Orkney where they were built of stone; they may have included the earliest examples. There was a striking contrast between their external and internal appearances. Seen from outside, they were generally oblong or circular (although they occurred on a few sites with long oval structures). The interior was usually rectilinear, with a square central hearth and a series of recesses set into the wall. The entrance was generally towards the southeast and faced the rising sun (Richards 2005; Richards & Jones 2016).

If Grooved Ware houses in Orkney were built from local sandstone, their counterparts in other regions were usually constructed of timber. This reflected the quality and availability of the most suitable material. The characteristic layout of the dwellings at sites like Barnhouse and Skara Brae was also rendered in wood. The hearth itself rarely survives, but the central part of the building is represented by a square or rectangular setting of posts, while the outer wall can be identified as a circular or oblong arrangement of postholes or stakeholes. Reconstruction of a roundhouse of this kind at Greenbogs showed that it was comparatively easy to build and that the central setting helped to support the roof (Noble *et al.* 2012). Such buildings were usually smaller than those of the later Bronze Age and Iron Age. Late Neolithic examples could be associated with pits containing formal deposits of artefacts and animal bones, but these comparatively slight buildings are so uncommon that it is difficult to decide if this was a general pattern.

Their characteristic form was reproduced at a variety of scales, and in a range of different contexts, from settlements to ceremonial centres. Their relationship to one another is obscured by the current terminology, so that the smaller examples are described as 'houses' and the largest as 'timber circles' (A. Gibson 2005; Pollard 2009). In fact there is a continuum from ephemeral domestic buildings to the largest buildings inside henge monuments. In between those two extremes there were impressive examples like those at Ballynahatty (Hartwell 1998), Armalughey (Carlin 2018, 137–44), and Machrie Moor (Haggarty 1991). The first of these was inside a palisaded enclosure, but the others were freestanding (Fig. 20). Their associations varied from site to site. They were constructed around the exterior of the passage grave at Newgrange (Brindley 1999, fig. 3.6) and in front of the entrance to

Greenbogs

Machrie Moor

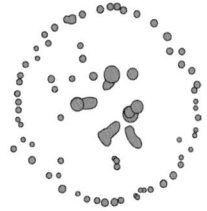

Ballynahatty

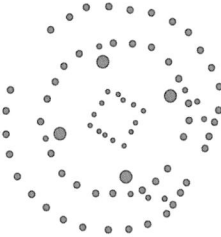

10 m

Armalughey

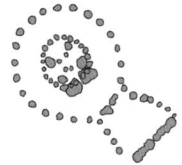

Fig. 20 Four timber buildings with similar plans, each of which was associated with Grooved Ware. Information from Bradley (2019) and Carlin (2018).

the tomb at Knowth where the building was associated with carefully placed deposits of artefacts (Eogan & Roche 1997, 101–201).

Excavations at Durrington Walls illustrate the wide range of contexts in which such buildings appear, as the site featured wooden structures of two different sizes (Parker Pearson 2007; J. Thomas 2007). They shared the same basic plan. The smallest were a series of houses whose remains survived because they had been buried beneath the bank of the henge. They were associated with Grooved Ware, and the excavator compares their layout with the stone structures at Skara Brae. By contrast, the large timber settings for which the site is best known were conceived on such a large scale that it is uncertain whether they could have been roofed. They were roughly eight times the diameter of the smaller buildings on the same site. Outside one entrance at Durrington was the massive structure of Woodhenge (Cunnington 1929). The largest buildings in Britain and Ireland had several features in common. They were defined by concentric rings of posts; as many as nine are indicated by geophysical survey at Stanton Drew in southwest England (David *et al.* 2004). They could be surrounded by circular earthworks or palisades, but it is not always clear whether these enclosures were later constructions. Again they were not only associated with decorated pottery. They could include large quantities of faunal remains, which might be the residue of feasts; and as so often happened on the sites of Great Houses, the remains were dominated by pig bones. Despite the different scales on which these structures were built, all of them contained selected groups of artefacts.

A still more striking pattern has been identified by Alex Gibson (2005) who has shown that timber buildings of this kind became considerably larger over time and that the biggest examples of all were erected in the middle of the third millennium BC. The same almost certainly applies to stone circles, which will be considered in due course. Solstical alignments are clearly documented and were important at several of the sites, including Durrington Walls and Woodhenge. If these places were used for communal feasts at the turning points of the year – Durrrington was used at midwinter – it is interesting that isotopic analysis of the animal bones found in excavation suggest that people travelled long distances to participate in those events (Craig *et al.* 2015; Madgwick *et al.* 2019b). Again the most striking characteristic of the Late Neolithic structures is they were enormously enlarged copies of the domestic dwellings in which the visitors might have lived at other times. Later timber circles became progressively smaller and less impressive until they were about the same size as domestic dwellings. In northern Britain that process extended until the middle of the Bronze Age, a thousand years later.

The forms of Late Neolithic monuments

Just as the house provided a source of reference for later monuments, including Iron Age hillforts and Viking ship settings, the dwellings associated with Grooved Ware influenced the forms of other structures. Although there was a wide range of variation, they were of two main kinds. Some connections were with chambered tombs, while others were with settings of upright stones.

The connection between domestic buildings and passage graves is clearly evidenced in Orkney although there may have been a more general association between circular houses and megalithic tombs in Atlantic Europe (Bradley 2012). This idea is based on a very small number of instances, and it is only in the Northern Isles that it can be developed in detail. The relationship between these traditions of architecture is evidenced in several ways. The case is most convincing at Howe where a chambered tomb was superimposed on the site of a building with a similar plan to the dwellings at Barnhouse and Skara Brae (Ballin Smith 1984). It has been interpreted as a 'mortuary house', but it may be unnecessary to make this assumption.

The resemblance between these buildings can be seen in other ways. The circular or oblong houses associated with Grooved Ware in Orkney have a distinctive layout, with a large central space around a square stone-lined hearth and a series of recesses set in the interior wall. These small compartments are like the side-chambers of passage tombs, and their plans are remarkably similar to one another. Like the domestic buildings, local passage tombs can have rectilinear chambers, but the covering mound is often circular. Important thresholds within these monuments were marked by incised motifs like those recorded in the settlement at Skara Brae (Richards 2005; Richards & Jones 2016). They are known in greater numbers in the buildings on the Ness of Brodgar where excavation is currently taking place (Towers *et al.* 2017; Card 2018; Edmonds 2019, 250–77). They are also found on pottery and other portable artefacts (A. Thomas 2016).

Those connections could have been peculiar to Orkney, but the evidence may be biased because these buildings are better preserved than their counterparts in other regions where they were generally of wood. The largest examples have been considered already and seem to have made an explicit reference to the layout of the house. It is possible that most examples were covered by a roof. Other monuments shared the same ground plan but were built partly, or entirely, of stone. The familiar design of a square inside a circle was executed in different media. Sometimes the entire plan was laid out as a setting of monoliths. In other cases stone structures could have replaced ones made of wood. Occasionally there were composite monuments that utilised both materials.

A useful point of departure is provided by two monuments on the Scottish mainland (Fig. 21). At Balbirnie a stone circle 14 m in diameter was associated with cremation burials which dated from about 3000 BC. In its centre was a stone platform similar to the hearths found in Orcadian houses (Ritchie 1974; A. Gibson 2010). In this case

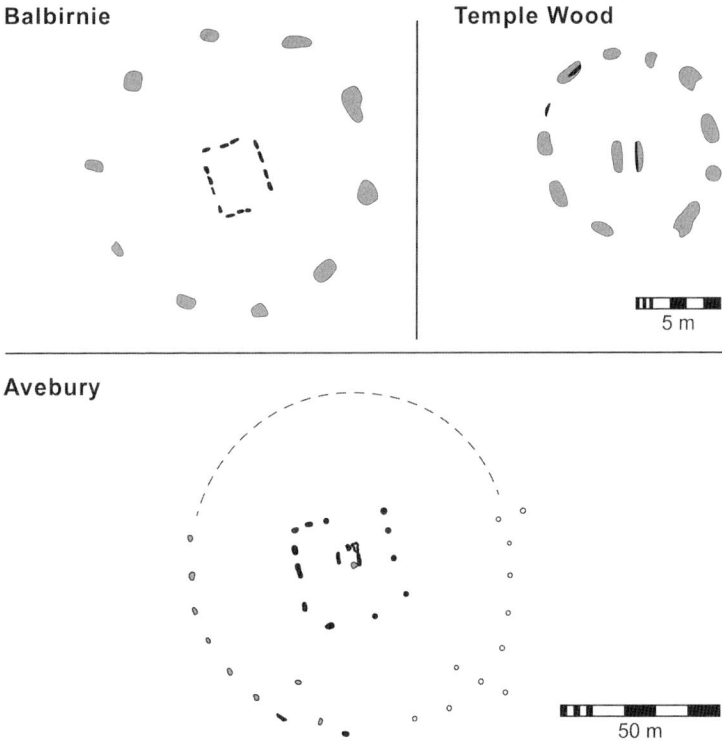

Fig. 21 Three stone settings comprising a square within a circle. Information from Ritchie (1974), Scott (1989) and Gillings et al. (2019).

it was 3 m square. A second example is the northeast stone circle at Temple Wood which replaced a timber setting on the same footprint (Scott 1989). In the equivalent position to the platform at Balbirnie there were two slots defining a rectangular feature. This time the monument was rather smaller and is not so closely dated. Here the ring of monoliths was only 10 m in diameter.

The same development from a timber structure to a stone setting has been identified on Machrie Moor on the Isle of Arran, off the west coast of Scotland (Haggarty 1991), and has sometimes been treated as a general development in Neolithic Britain. New dates cast doubt on this assumption and one of the best-known monuments in southern England was almost certainly a composite structure constructed from both materials. It was located inside the large henge monument at Mount Pleasant where a smaller enclosure contained a remarkable building consisting of five concentric rings of posts. Four corridors aligned on the cardinal points converged on a central area bounded by a rectilinear setting of monoliths (Wainwright 1979). In accordance with the chronology favoured at the time the excavator assigned this feature to a later phase and identified it as a kind of freestanding monument called a 'cove'; the term was often applied to oval, square or semi-circular stone settings (Burl 1988). At Mount Pleasant this feature was the equivalent of the arrangement of posts in the middle of a Late Neolithic dwelling and there is no reason to accept the sequence proposed by Wainwright. Again the circular structure could be interpreted as an enormous house. It was 38 m in diameter and was associated with decorated pottery and evidence of meat consumption (Greaney *et al.* 2020).

Stone circles could also have square settings in the centre, but little is known about them. The largest example has been identified inside the henge at Avebury, where part of it was excavated before its full extent was revealed by geophysical survey (Fig. 21). Although the basic layout was a square within a circle, the evidence is actually more complex. The basic layout was a ring of monoliths 100 m in diameter (the Southern Circle), with a setting of equally large standing stones defining a 30 m square at its centre. In the middle were the slots for a much smaller setting, most probably of wood, measuring 6.9 m by 6.8 m (Gillings *et al.* 2019). Although it has been interpreted as the position of a house, it might have been the innermost part of a composite stone and timber monument. It has the same outline as Late Neolithic timber buildings – a square enclosed by a circle – but its size is unprecedented and exceeds that of even the largest of those structures. The clearest example, at Mount Pleasant, was 38 m in diameter, but the stone structure inside Avebury was two and a half times that size. Its position was eventually marked by the 'Obelisk', the tallest stone on the site. It may be no accident that it is the largest structure to conform to this characteristic layout and that it should be positioned inside an enormous henge.

This particular structure is a new discovery but the ultimate expressions of the same template were already well known, although they had not been interpreted in quite these terms. They are found towards the opposite ends of the distribution of Late Neolithic Grooved Ware. One is Maeshowe – the greatest passage tomb in Orkney – and the other is Stonehenge (Fig. 22). Maeshowe probably dates from about 3000 BC, while Stonehenge assumed its characteristic form between 2620 and 2480 BC. In a recent paper Tim Darvill (2016) compares its layout with that of other buildings of this date. Maeshowe and Stonehenge were among the most impressive Neolithic monuments anywhere in Britain.

Maeshowe is different in several ways from the other passage tombs in Orkney (Richards 2005, chapter 9). It occupies a circular platform surrounded by a ditch; and the chamber and passage were framed by enormous slabs of sandstone, very like the monoliths inside a nearby henge. In fact they are so similar in size and shape that Colin Richards suggests that they may have been taken from a dismantled circle. Four of them were employed in the entrance passage, while another four stood 3 m high at the corners of the square central chamber. There were also side chambers which resembled the recesses set into the house walls at Skara Brae.

The monoliths built into the chamber of Maeshowe may have been placed there for aesthetic reasons as they do not support the roof. On

Maeshowe

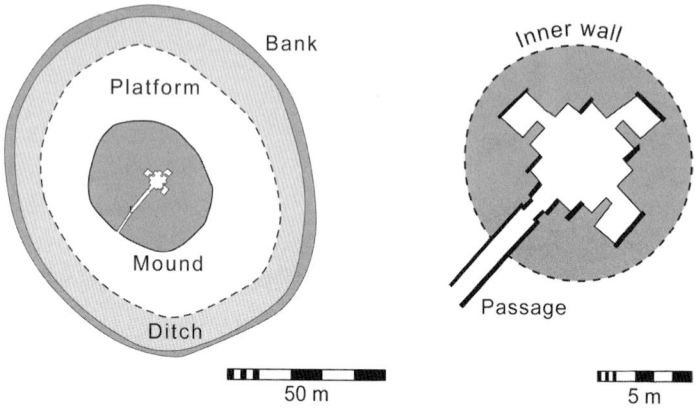

Stonehenge

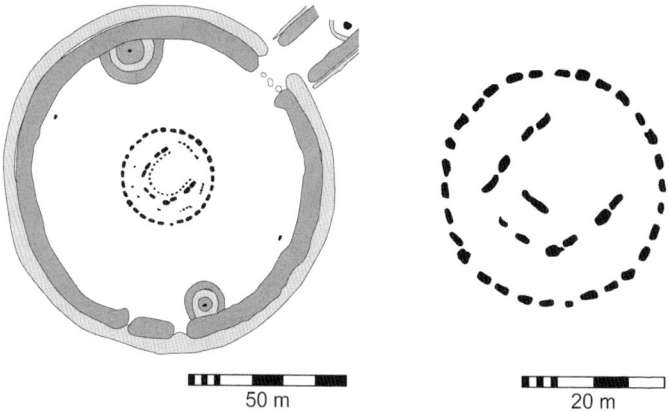

Fig. 22 Square (or approximately square) structures enclosed by circular monuments at Maeshowe and Stonehenge. Information from Bradley (2019) and Darvill (2016).

the other hand, practical considerations mean that they must have been erected before this part of the monument was built; there would have been a time when they were effectively freestanding. One possibility is that the pillars that became the corners of the chamber were originally a square setting in their own right, enclosed by a circular earthwork and perhaps by a ring of uprights. When the monument was reconstructed, those in its centre remained intact while others were reused. A few of them defined the limits of the entrance passage, but the remainder could have been re-erected at the Stones of Stenness not far away. This hypothesis is impossible to prove, but Maeshowe illustrates the familiar layout of a square in the centre of a circle.

The archaeology of Stonehenge illustrates a familiar problem in Neolithic archaeology, for its component parts have often been interpreted separately, as if the structure was simply an amalgam of different classes of monument. The outer ditch has been compared with that of a causewayed enclosure, and the lintels joining the orthostats with the techniques of timber architecture. The innermost setting of uprights was classified as another 'cove'. Darvill's new analysis simplifies this outline, just as small-scale excavation has simplified the structural sequence on the site (Cleal *et al.* 1995; Darvill *et al.* 2012; Darvill 2016). The central setting is not exactly rectilinear, nor is it the oval that the term *cove* implies; on the other hand, its outline was reinforced by a more regular horseshoe of stones recycled from an older monument. The simplest way of characterising this structure is as a rectangle enclosed within a circle. The comparison is strengthened by comparison with the plans of wooden monuments, including one of the post settings at Durrington Walls nearby. The use of lintels and carpentry joints at Stonehenge emphasises its links with wooden buildings (A. Gibson 2005). In a curious way it also resembles the exploded houses at Göbekli Tepe, and again there have been implausible reconstructions that interpret the structure as the skeleton of a building whose roof was supported on the standing stones (Crampton 1967).

A question of timing

The buildings considered in this chapter might have been used in similar ways but they originated in very different contexts. The first examples date from one of the principal transitions in prehistoric

Britain: the settlement of the earliest farmers, some of whom were colonising an unfamiliar landscape. This development had an impact on the natural environment and marked the first appearance of domesticated cereals and livestock. Almost every feature associated with indigenous hunter gatherers disappears from the archaeological record. The new way of life must have made unprecedented demands. It encouraged a novel perception of time influenced by the nurturing of crops and domesticated animals from year to year, and this could account for an increasing concern with the history of the community and its dead. The performance of important tasks required the pooling of labour for clearing land, sowing and harvesting grain, and the construction of monuments. Social relations would have changed with the development of sedentism, and the building and use of Great Halls provided a crucial focus for new kinds of collective identities and a focus for events in which local groups could participate. The most obvious occasions were feasts at which the new kinds of food were consumed. The House symbolised those links and strengthened the bonds between different groups of people at a time when the taking and farming of new land were making unprecedented demands. Afterwards collective projects changed from the construction of halls to the creation of mounds and enclosures, which left more lasting traces behind and remained significant for longer. Viewed in that perspective, timber halls were comparatively short-lived, but for a limited period at the beginning of the Neolithic phase the use of such structures was crucial.

The Great Houses of Late Neolithic Britain were quite different. They were broadly contemporary with those in France and their histories must have followed a similar trajectory, with a gradual increase in the sizes of these structures. Yet there is no sign of any connections between the people who erected them. Grand Pressigny flint has never been found in these islands, and the two groups of timber buildings are linked with different styles of megalithic tombs. Although rectangular buildings of the right date have been identified in Orkney and the Boyne Valley, they are only now being excavated and it is too soon to consider their wider affinities (Card 2018; Leigh *et al.* 2019). On the other hand, both the sequences considered here do have points in common. They document extensive networks linking different areas, and in each case their geographical extent increased over time. Even more striking, they were affected – sometimes drastically – by the expansion of a different network, associated with the use of Bell Beakers and metal artefacts. There is scientific evidence of population change, although its rapidity and scale remain to be established (Olalde *et al.* 2018; Parker Pearson *et al.* 2019). At the same time there was an obvious contrast between these sequences. In France the impressive buildings that developed in parallel with the circulation of Grand Pressigny blades changed with the adoption of Beaker pottery and metalwork, although a few sherds in the new style were associated with these structures. Artefacts made from this kind of flint also appeared in Beaker graves. Even so, it seems as if the longhouses went out of use quite rapidly and were replaced by smaller buildings of an entirely different form.

In Britain, however, the first appearance of settlers from Continental Europe had a different impact and in regions as far apart as Wessex and Orkney the largest henges, stone settings and timber monuments were built at just this time. The synchronism between different areas is striking and extends to the dates for monuments as far apart from one another as Stonehenge, Mount Pleasant and the Ring of Brodgar. So is the evidence that enormous structures like those at Durrington Walls were used for less than 50 years. It is possible that the indigenous population reinforced its traditional beliefs by constructing ceremonial centres on a grander scale than ever before. It happened as the power of traditional practices was threatened from outside (Greaney *et al.* 2020). In this case such structures did not disappear completely, but it was in southern England where the largest examples had been built that the most radical changes happened. Further to the north and west, established forms of monuments were still constructed and used, but on a smaller scale.

The revised dating of Stonehenge emphasises this point. As long as it was believed to be an Early Bronze Age monument it could be considered as the focal point of a Wessex Culture with connections reaching as far as Brittany, Central Europe and the Aegean. Now that its basic structure has been back-dated to the Late Neolithic period it must be reconsidered. Today it looks more like a last-ditch attempt to reinforce traditional norms during a period of uncertainty and change. Its construction did not achieve that aim. By the time that rich burials clustered around it, its heyday had long passed and it was respected as an ancient monument.

The two sequences ran in parallel, but they were very different even though local societies were facing similar pressures. In one case enormous monuments were built; in the other case, they were abandoned. There would be similar developments in Britain and Ireland 2000 years later, and people reacted to them in equally distinctive ways. They included the reappearance of enormous houses whose forms were inspired by those of domestic buildings, but any direct connection between these developments is most unlikely and the evidence needs to be studied on its own terms. Chapter Six compares the archaeology of two regions where it is possible to study the circumstances in which these structures were established.

CHAPTER 6

Social distances

The last trumpet

In 1798 workmen made a curious discovery beside a lake in the north of Ireland. According to an account written at the time:

> Four brazen trumpets were found in boggy land on the borders of Loughnashade … Near the trumpets were found human skulls and other bones (Lynn 2003, 70–71).

In 1819 another source recorded that:

> The tradition of the place is that a mighty battle was fought there, and that some King of Ulster had his palace not far distant … One of [the instruments was] … sounded by a trumpeter belonging to the 23rd Regiment of Dragoons and … could be heard for miles (Lynn 2003, 70–71).

Three of the trumpets (more correctly, horns) are lost, but the one survivor is displayed in the National Museum of Ireland. It has been dated to the pre-Roman Iron Age. It is made of sheet bronze and is decorated in the same style as the sword scabbards of the same period (Raftery 1984).

Loughnashade is important for three reasons and its archaeology illustrates some of the unusual features of Iron Age Ireland.

The lake was only 300 m from the perimeter of the royal centre of Navan Fort, which overlooks the site. That is why the 1819 account refers to the 'palace' of a 'King of Ulster'. The link between these sites is especially close as tree ring dating has shown that its enclosure ditch was excavated at the beginning of the first century BC. A great timber building in its centre dates from the same period. It replaced a series of older structures, meaning that the use of the hilltop must have overlapped with the deposit at Loughnashade (Waterman 1997).

Secondly, the surviving horn is decorated in an insular version of the La Tène style of Celtic Art which is found across large areas of Europe from the early fifth century BC. It is usually dated according to stylistic criteria, but British artefacts made in this tradition have radiocarbon dates beginning in the late fifth or fourth centuries BC (Garrow *et al.* 2009). Those from cemeteries in northeast England have been compared with the Irish metalwork (Raftery 1984). In other regions of Britain similar types can be associated with hillforts, open settlements, pre-Roman temples and hoards (Garrow & Gosden 2012). But here there is a striking contrast, for few of the Irish examples came from similar contexts, and nearly all of them were in rivers, bogs and lakes.

Lastly, Loughnashade has been investigated by pollen analysis, which showed that the local landscape became increasingly wooded around 200 BC, suggesting that the area was not intensively settled at the time when the largest monuments were erected (Weir 1994).

It was these problems that led Barry Raftery (1994) to write of the 'invisible people' of late pre-Roman Ireland. Fewer settlements have been identified than those of the early first millennium BC, and, even where they are located, the structural evidence is meagre (K. Becker 2009; Corlett & Potterton 2012). Pottery was no longer in use, and the most striking evidence comes from sites where iron was worked. Otherwise there were chance finds of bronze artefacts, and the hand mills known as querns. Objects decorated in the La Tène style occur in the same parts of the country as the royal centres and, like them, they are effectively absent from the southwest. The same distinction is illustrated by the querns. The simplest examples, saddle querns, are recorded in regions in which elaborate artefacts are absent, but the distribution of rotary querns coincides with that of fine metalwork, and a few examples were decorated in the same style. Rotary querns could process more grain than other types.

Perhaps this provides indirect evidence for the importance of feasts (Bradley 2019, 32–33).

Navan Fort and its counterparts

Navan Fort is one of a small group of timber and earthwork monuments identified in the early Middle Ages as 'royal capitals' (Mallory 2016). It was the ultimate successor of a triple-ditched Late Bronze Age hillfort (Haughey's Fort) a kilometre to its west (Mallory and Baban 2014). The two locations may have been separated by a linear earthwork of the same date, but most of the excavated features at Navan date from the Iron Age. There is an important link between these places. Two hundred metres from Haughey's Fort was an artificial pool, the King's Stables, which contained sword moulds contemporary with the hillfort, together with animal bones and a human skull (Lynn 1977). It might have been the counterpart of Loughnashade where similar remains were associated with the horns deposited a thousand years later.

Navan Fort was identified in later sources as Emain Macha, the capital of Ulster. Its counterparts in other regions were Tara, Knockaulin, Rathcroghan, the Rock of Cashel and possibly Uisneach. With the exception of Cashel which may not have played a special role until later, these complexes share several features. It would be anachronistic to discuss pre-Roman Iron Age structures in terms of a scheme invented many years afterwards (Newman 1997; Waddell 2014; Mallory 2016). Instead this account deals with their early histories.

These complexes have a number of elements. The earthworks include large circular enclosures with an external bank and an internal ditch, considerable mounds, and smaller structures described as ring barrows. Linear land boundaries have been identified near to Navan. There were also timber structures: curvilinear palisades, wooden buildings laid out as a figure-of-eight, and, most striking of all, the huge monuments described in Chapter One as Great Houses. Like the conjoined circular constructions, they were inside the principal enclosures.

The Great Houses

Impressive timber buildings are recorded at four of these sites: Navan Fort (Waterman 1997), the Hill of Tara (Grogan 2008), Knockaulin (Johnston & Wailes 2007), and Rathcroghan (Waddell *et al.* 2009). They are known from large scale excavation at Navan and Knockaulin and from more fragmentary remains at Tara. At Rathcroghan they have been recognised by non-invasive surveys.

These structures took two forms. The best known is the massive circular building beneath the mound at Navan. It was defined by five concentric rings of posts and an exterior wall. The entire structure was just under 40 m in diameter and had an upright post at its centre. The interior was crossed by three parallel aisles leading from the west, but there was no sign of a formal entrance. The orientation of the building was exceptional as roundhouses were usually entered from the east and faced the direction of the rising sun. Its remains were well-preserved and it had other unusual features. There was no sign of a floor or a central hearth. After an interval during which the structure was reinforced, it was packed with rubble and set on fire. Then its remains were covered by the mound.

A similar structure has been identified by geophysical survey on the unexcavated site of Rathcroghan, but less is known about the sequence there. It shared important elements with its counterpart at Navan Fort. Its footprint was rather smaller – the wooden building was 32 m in diameter compared with 38 m – and it may have been modified on more than one occasion. In this case it is not clear whether the timber building was erected on top of an existing mound or whether it was encapsulated in its construction. Again there are indications that it was entered from the west. The summit of the mound was approximately level and about 65 m in diameter; at Navan Fort the equivalent figure was 50 m. The mound at Rathcroghan was accessed by ramps facing east and west. Again the project found evidence of intensive burning, but it is not known when it happened.

These buildings shared several features. Both were exactly circular and were defined by concentric rings of posts: at least three on the basis of geophysical survey at Rathcroghan, and five at Navan Fort where they were found by excavation. In each case their main (or only) entrance was to the west. Both were associated with conspicuous round mounds and may have been set on fire. It is possible that a smaller structure of the same form was built beside the mound at Rathcroghan, but the evidence is more difficult to interpret.

At Knockaulin there was a structure of almost the same size as the large building at Navan. It was defined by two palisade trenches, with a concentric setting of uprights inside them. This post circle was 20 m in diameter, but the diameter of the outer perimeter was 43 m. In contrast to the interpretation of Navan Fort, the excavator interpreted it as an open enclosure. In the centre was another ring of posts only 6 m in diameter. It lacked an entrance and was interpreted as the foundations of a tower. But it may not have formed part of the same design, and the nature of this monument still remains in doubt.

The second type of timber structure poses even greater problems, although their traces are easy to identify because their plan is a figure-of-eight (Fig. 23). They have been identified by excavation at Navan Fort, Knockaulin and Tara. Their sizes and proportions vary from site to site.

Where sufficient evidence survives, the structures had similar outlines. They shared the same basic plans and orientations. They conformed to a cardinal alignment and the larger ring was always to the north. The biggest were Circles A and C at Navan Fort and a similar pair of buildings in the centre of a large enclosure at Knockaulin. In each case one component had a diameter of 30 m while the diameter of the other part was 20 m. At both sites the northern section of the monument was accessed by a timber entranceway leading from the east: the opposite of the orientation of the biggest buildings at Navan and Rathcroghan. Both halves were rebuilt, but their respective wall lines did not cut across one another. At Knockaulin a subsidiary entrance communicated between these features.

There were smaller examples of the same type. The buildings on the Hill of Tara were badly disturbed but the northern of the pair seem to have been 18 m to 20 m in diameter, and their counterparts had diameters between 10 m and 14 m (again they were rebuilt on more

Navan Fort

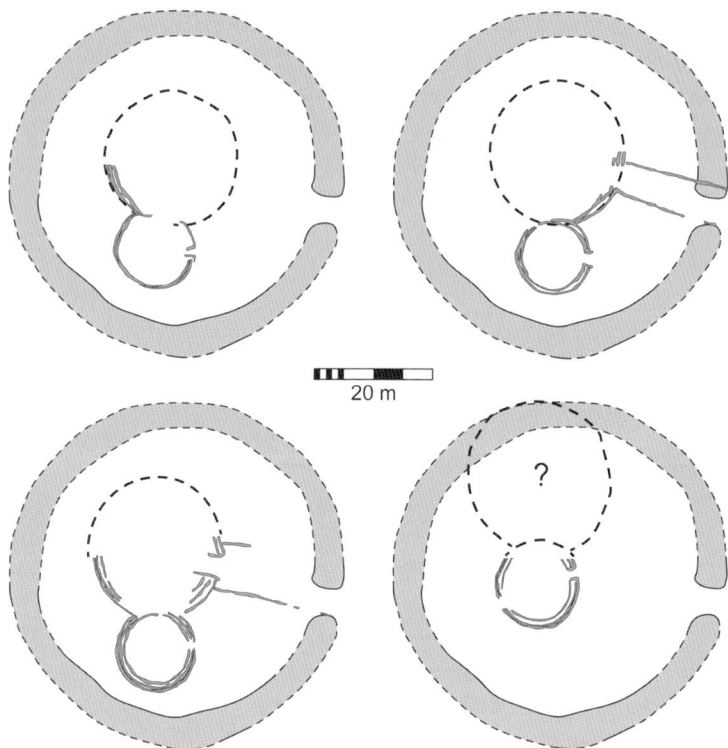

Fig. 23 Successive figure-of-eight structures sealed by the great mound at Navan Fort. They are shown in relation to the outline of an earlier earthwork on the same site. Information from Waterman (1997) and Gleeson (2020).

than one occasion). The larger enclosure was defined by a foundation trench, but there was an internal setting of posts which may have formed part of the same structure. Even smaller were the figure-of-eight buildings preserved beneath the mound at Navan. Like the other examples, both halves were different sizes, but in this case their diameters were between 10 m and 13.5 m. Again they were entered from the east, and the northern section may have been approached through a forecourt screened by fences. The structures were rebuilt on several occasions, and in this case the perimeter of the northern component cut across the boundary of the other part. In some phases there was no obvious access between them.

There is a little evidence of sequence. On Site B at Navan Fort the figure-of-eight structures were replaced by the huge circular building. There was a strikingly similar development at Knockaulin where the two conjoined structures were replaced by the large monument described earlier. It was about the same size as the great roundhouse at Navan Fort. Thereafter the sequences diverged. Activity continued at Knockaulin and only an insubstantial mound was built there.

There are differences of opinion concerning the figure-of-eight structures. Did both parts have a roof, or should they be interpreted as roundhouses with a yard or annexe? Were both of them fenced enclosures? These questions are addressed by Katharina Becker (2019) in a recent article. She makes three important points. The paired foundation trenches that define so many of these structures might have supported the inner and outer faces of a load-bearing wall; the same technique is documented at a number of settlements. She observes that some of those at Irish royal centres had drainage gullies, suggesting that they were substantial buildings. The presence of hearths inside the structures at Navan supports the comparison with domestic dwellings. The case cannot be proved, but there seems every reason to interpret these features as 'houses' of a special kind. Becker argues that the architecture of the royal centres should not be treated separately from that of other sites. The same techniques gained an added emphasis when they were used in these monuments.

Dating evidence

It is difficult to date them. There are many reasons why this poses a challenge. The results of O'Riordàin's excavation at Tara were not published until many years after his death. Those of work at Knockaulin were also delayed and improvements to radiocarbon dating meant that some of the samples obtained during the original work now seem less suitable for analysis (Bayliss & Grogan 2013). At the same time the long sequence of building and rebuilding at both sites meant that the deposits were often disturbed and some of the most significant contexts might have contained residual material. There was also the problem that the Irish Iron Age was aceramic, meaning that sherds originally attributed to that phase might actually be Late Bronze Age (Raftery 1995). It was a problem at Navan where there was typical Bronze Age and pre-Roman Iron Age metalwork from the excavation. Both Iron Age and Roman objects were found at Tara and Knockaulin, but seldom in reliable contexts.

Dendrochronology was employed at Navan. It dated the largest timber structure and the ditch bounding the hilltop. It also extended to linear earthworks in the vicinity, suggesting a major phase of construction during the first century BC. It is more difficult to study the local landscape, but an unusual enclosure at the nearby site of Lismullin was probably built during the fourth century BC (O'Connell 2013). The structural sequence at Navan Fort was even longer and may have begun with a circular ditched enclosure associated with a ring of posts dated to the Late Bronze Age. It could have been the source of the pottery found in later deposits. More relevant to this account are the radiocarbon dates associated with figure-of-eight buildings there. The earliest are likely to date from the second century BC and the entire sequence of structures lasted no more than a hundred years. An interval followed before the construction of the enormous roundhouse.

At Tara the most recent excavation suggests that a large internally-ditched enclosure, the Rath na Rioch, dates from the first century BC (Roche 2002). Figure-of-eight structures were identified beneath the Rath of the Synods. Their history extended over the first and second centuries AD (Grogan 2008). The evidence from Knockaulin is less precise as most of the dates came from a laboratory whose results appear to be too young. At present they suggest that the main timber structures were contemporary with those at Tara, but the most diagnostic artefacts from the excavation are older and span the third or second centuries BC to the first century AD (Johnston & Wailes 2007).

To sum up, the main elements of the royal centres originated by the second and first centuries BC. The evidence from Lismullin suggests that palisaded enclosures, fenced avenues and rings of posts were established 200 years before. The clearest evidence of a substantial circular building comes from Navan Fort where it dates from the beginning of the first century BC. It provides a *terminus ante quem* for a series of figure-of-eight structures on the same site, but similar buildings were still constructed at Tara during the second century AD. Two of the large earthwork enclosures have satisfactory dates. Like the ditch bounding Navan Fort, the Rath na Rioch at Tara was built during the first century BC. Thus the royal centres were established well before the first Roman impact on Ireland and continued in use after the conquest of the neighbouring island.

Leading separate lives

Why were they constructed at this time, and how can they be interpreted? The evidence is paradoxical. On one level the island was closely linked to other parts of Atlantic Europe; that is clear from linguistic evidence (Sims-Williams 2020) and the presence of La Tène metalwork (Raftery 1984). On another, its archaeology is idiosyncratic.

There is an obvious contrast between the situation in the Bronze Age and the period when the royal centres were built. During the late second and early first millennia BC Ireland had played an important role in the Atlantic Bronze Age and received distinctive artefacts from regions as far apart as Iberia and Scandinavia (Waddell 2010, chapters 6 & 7). The production of gold ornaments was at its peak and local communities participated in the long-distance movements of swords, spears, jewellery, and the cauldrons and flesh hooks used at feasts. Recent excavations have identified enclosed settlements as well as hillforts (O'Brien & O'Driscoll 2017). One of them, Rathgall, was associated with a particularly large number of artefacts, including imports from the Continent. Haughey's Fort, close to Navan, contained another exceptional assemblage. There is widespread evidence for metalworking, and even the inhabitants of Dún Aonghasa in a remote setting in the Aran Islands were making weapons in an international style. The results of pollen analysis show a significant impact on the landscape.

That changed between 900 and 750 BC. These dates are significant as they are consistent with a reduction in the circulation of foreign metalwork. Less information is available between that time and the fourth century BC, which is when the monument at Lismullin was built. Barry Raftery (1984) concluded that the La Tène style first appeared in Ireland around 300 BC. Writers in the Mediterranean were well aware of voyages along the Atlantic, and Ptolemy mapped the Irish coastline in the second century AD, basing his information on the accounts of traders who travelled there by sea. It seems as if relations with the European mainland had resumed on a significant scale. Yet there remains a problem.

In some respects the Irish Iron Age documents a similar process to the sequence in other parts of Northwest Europe where the number of settlements increased and certain sites assumed a dominant role. Those on the Continent included large hillforts and *oppida*. There was an increase in the production and exchange of special artefacts. Some of them were deposited at sanctuaries, while others were buried with the dead (Cunliffe 2018, 273–309). That did not happen in Ireland where events took a different course. Hillforts went out of use by the end of the Bronze Age and sacred sites took a distinctive local form. The same applies to burials (McGarry 2009). Long-distance connections did not lapse, but their character seems to have changed. This point is illustrated in three ways.

Irish La Tène metalwork

Despite the number of weapons, ornaments and regalia deposited in the Iron Age landscape, sanctuaries like those in Gaul and England have never been found in Ireland. The deposit at Loughnashade is consistent with a pattern that may go back to the Bronze Age when exceptional objects had been associated with major hillforts. More often La Tène metalwork lacks obvious associations. Rectangular structures found with inhumation graves at Marnhill and Kilmainham have been compared with shrines in Britain and France, but both sites date from a later period (Walsh 2012). The burials that were contemporary with the metal finds contain very few items apart from beads, brooches, and pieces of decorated bone (McGarry 2009). They were associated with small round mounds or ring ditches of a kind that was used throughout the first millennium BC. The finest artefacts are not represented. This contrasts with graves in northeast England, the richest of which contain decorated items very like those in Ireland. They date from the late third and second centuries BC. In this case they were associated with square barrows of a form found in Continental Europe (Giles 2012).

In another way the Irish finds are consistent with a wider pattern. Artefacts with La Tène decoration are discovered in rivers, lakes and bogs on the European mainland. Another comparison is with the finds from Llyn Cerrig Bach by the northwest coast of Wales. Radiocarbon dating shows that they were deposited at intervals between the fourth or third centuries BC and the mid first century AD (Macdonald 2007). Like the horns from Loughnashade, they were associated with the bones of animals and possibly people. In this respect the Irish material conformed to a wider pattern. The difference, and it is an important one, is that it rarely comes from dry land.

The finest metalwork in Ireland had a distinctive character. Barry Raftery (1984) suggested that its closest parallels were in Gaul, but it was made in an insular style and there are few direct imports from the Continent. Its repertoire was extremely varied: small personal items made of bronze and gold, including necklaces, pins and decorated mounts; and more elaborate pieces like torcs and ostentatious headgear. It included swords, spears and shields. Horses must have been particularly important and the metalwork featured harnesses, bridle bits, yokes and the fittings for wheeled vehicles. The same style of decoration extended to a small number of standing stones and the rotary querns mentioned earlier.

Much of this equipment was associated with display and personal appearance, but it was not necessarily the prerogative of a ruling elite, although this remains a possibility. It is equally likely that Celtic Art had a religious significance (Megaw & Megaw 2001). Irish artefacts lack the associations of Continental and British material because so many of them were deposited in water rather than graves. For that reason it is impossible to relate these objects to the status of particular people.

The ambiguous relationship between Ireland and the wider world is best expressed by a collection of metalwork from Broighter (Waddell 2010, 206–09). It was found on the edge of Lough Foyle which provides an important natural harbour. Its contents were remarkable: a lavishly decorated gold torc, two others made of twisted gold, and a pair of wire necklaces. With them were models of a cauldron and a boat, both of the same material. The vessel was equipped with a mast and oars and is dated to the first century BC. The large torc is decorated in the La Tène style and has parallels in Britain and on the Continent – the connection with other areas is aptly symbolised by the model boat – yet the setting was appropriate for deposits of insular metalwork like that at Loughnashade. The Broighter hoard shows the same mixture of the exotic and local that characterises the Irish Iron Age as a whole. That is made even clearer by the royal centres that flourished at the same time.

Royal centres in Ireland – and elsewhere?

If the deposition of fine metalwork conformed to a longer history in Ireland, the earthworks and buildings have few counterparts in other regions. The large circular enclosures have been compared with the Goloring near Koblenz in western Germany which has an external bank and a platform in the interior. In its centre was a feature interpreted as a deep post socket. It might have supported a wooden statue like those identified in recent years (Fernández Götz 2016, 171–72). Although the earthwork resembles some of the Irish monuments, it is poorly dated and is probably earlier than those sites (Raftery in Waterman 1997, 221–24). In the same way, the figure-of-eight structures of the Irish Iron Age have been compared with houses in the north of Scotland, but they were built during a much later period and the resemblance between their plans is not particularly strong

(Harding 2017, 318–21); they also feature in Ireland in the seventh and eighth centuries AD (A. O'Sullivan *et al.* 2014, 11). A much better comparison is with two conjoined buildings at Moss Carr in northeast England. An Iron Age enclosure on the same site was approached through a funnel-shaped entrance similar to those at Knockaulin and Rathcroghan (K. Becker 2019). It is not far outside the distribution of burials associated with metalwork like that in Ireland.

There might have been another link between those regions. Excavations at Stanwick, little more than 60 km from Moss Carr, identified the sites of two successive roundhouses that were explicitly compared with the enormous Irish buildings (Haselgrove 2016, 411–14). They dated between about 30 BC and AD 40, meaning that their use could have overlapped with their counterparts at the royal centres. Only parts of these structures could be investigated, but they were defined by substantial post pits and might have stood 9 m high. They were not associated with an exceptional collection of artefacts, but Stanwick was an unusually rich site, with contacts that extended into Continental Europe before the Roman Conquest.

A closer comparison may be with a group of timber buildings at Thetford in East Anglia (Fig. 24). Here two rectilinear enclosures were built in sequence at what was already an important settlement, cemetery and production site (Gregory 1991). The first earthwork was associated with a massive roundhouse, 14 m in diameter. It was modified in the succeeding phase when two buildings of the same type were erected beside it. All three were particularly substantial and may have risen to an exceptional height. Their entrances faced west as well as east (the first construction was rebuilt to conform to this arrangement). Both the structures added to the original design were flanked by smaller circular enclosures which may have lacked a roof. This arrangement recalls the figure-of-eight design favoured in Ireland.

Their dates are similar, and the buildings and enclosures at Thetford were in use between approximately AD 40 and 70. The timing is revealing. Like the largest structures at Stanwick, the monumental roundhouses conformed to a long-established insular tradition. This is surely significant as they were in an area of resistance to Roman rule, with one documented rebellion in AD 47, followed by Boudicca's

Knockaulin   **Thetford**

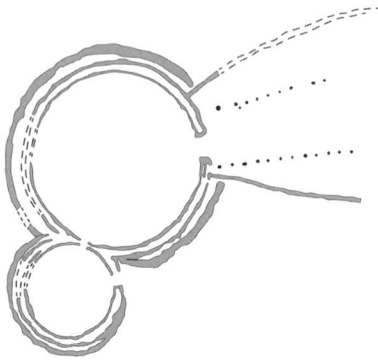 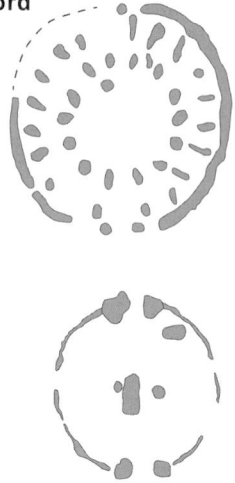

20 m   5 m

Fig. 24 Paired structures at the Iron Age sites of Knockaulin and Thetford. Information from Johnston and Wailes (2007) and Gregory (1991).

uprising 13 years later. Their construction in a defiantly insular form could have been a political statement, and it is not surprising that they were dismantled after the violence had ended. There have been suggestions that this was a royal residence, but the excavator favoured a different interpretation:

> The extraordinary investment of resources in the construction of the … enclosure led to the initial hypothesis of a tribal centre …: the 'Boudicca's Palace' theory. But the absence of domestic activity and the scarcity of imported luxury goods … soon rendered this untenable. … [It was] a largely ceremonial or religious site (Gregory 1991, 197).

This section has considered analogies for the Irish evidence, but these are the only examples that can be compared with the Iron Age royal sites. In no case are the parallels exact. Either they present chronological problems, or the structures are unusual, even in their local contexts. Otherwise the buildings found at places like Navan and Tara were peculiar to Ireland and did not occur anywhere else.

Associations with older monuments

The most obvious features dating from the Irish Iron Age were directly linked with the remains of ancient monuments. Some examples are so well known that their peculiar character can be overlooked.

Those Neolithic and Bronze Age monuments were integrated into the plans of several of the royal centres, and other ancient structures were reused during the pre-Roman and Roman periods. The practice was so widespread that it became one of the chief characteristics of the Iron Age. The features that were incorporated in these complexes would have been highly visible; there is no reason to suppose that their original significance was remembered. There is convincing evidence from four of the sites. The clearest example was on the Hill of Tara where a Neolithic passage grave, the Mound of the Hostages, provided the focal point for both the principal enclosures (M. O'Sullivan 2005). It was not the first time that it had been reused. It had already been one of the largest cremation cemeteries of the Early Bronze Age, and a small round barrow or ring ditch was constructed beside it, most probably during the Late Bronze Age.

There may have been a circular barrow of Neolithic date in the middle of the Iron Age complex at Knockaulin (Johnston & Wailes 2007). The timber structures were built over its remains and Chapter One suggested that the earthwork perimeter of the entire site might have followed the course of a causewayed enclosure. Roseanne Schot's geophysical survey at Uisneach has identified a ditched enclosure 200 m in diameter with a prominent mound at its centre. The barrow was supposedly the findspot of a Bronze Age cist. Elsewhere on the same site the remains of a megalithic tomb were bounded by a circular palisade (Schot 2011).

Navan Fort conforms to the same pattern and the buildings in its centre were superimposed on the remains of a circular enclosure dating from the Late Bronze Age. It was 45 m in diameter and was defined by a shallow ditch (Waterman 1997). On its inner edge was a ring of substantial posts. Although it was probably later than the occupation of Haughey's Fort, comparable features were found there (Mallory & Baban 2014).

Iron Age reuse of prominent monuments was not restricted to the royal centres and has been recognised in other places. Perhaps the best known are Neolithic monuments: the main passage grave at Knowth, another mound at Kiltierney, and a cemetery at Lough-crew. The largest monument at Knowth was surrounded by a series of inhumations, some of which were associated with beads, bronze rings, bone dice and gaming pieces. They are no different from the burials found with prehistoric ring ditches. Five of the graves have radiocarbon dates between 40 BC and AD 200 (Eogan 2012, 689–94). The burials can be compared with a group of low mounds around the edge of the monument at Kiltierney. They included cremated bone, brooches and glass beads. The one unusual item was the handle of a bronze mirror. The cemetery is associated with two dates spanning the second and first centuries BC (McHugh & Scott 2014, 126). The reuse of the chambered tombs at Loughcrew took place at the same time. Cairns H and L contained deposits of bone slips, some of which were decorated with similar designs to La Tène metalwork. Two dates were obtained by Mara Vejby (2016) and extend between 200 and 40 BC. Again they fall in the same period as the royal centres.

The organisation of Tara in the Iron Age

The clearest example of this connection with the past comes from Tara. Patrick Gleeson (2012) distinguishes between the initial layout of the site and the features associated with its reuse as a royal site during the later first millennium AD. The largest of the early structures were the Rath na Rioch, which was defined by an earthwork and palisade, and an enclosure discovered by geophysical survey known as the 'Ditched Pit Circle'. They were about the same size as one another and their boundaries overlapped on either side of the Mound of the Hos-tages. Each enclosure had another structure at its centre. Inside the

Rath na Rioch was a prominent mound, An Forrad, which has never been excavated. In the middle of the other monument was the Rath of the Synods which overlay a circular earthwork of uncertain date and character. It had been levelled by the time the figure-of-eight structures were erected there. Remote sensing has identified yet another enclosure surrounding An Forrad (Schot *et al.* 2016). It was rather smaller than the Rath na Rioch and abutted the Ditched Pit Circle (Fig. 25). The passage grave was incorporated in its perimeter. The

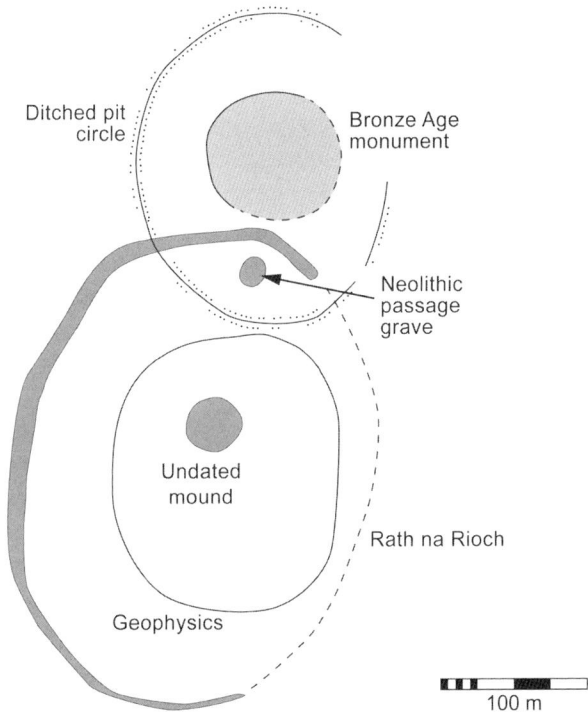

Hill of Tara

Ditched pit circle

Bronze Age monument

Neolithic passage grave

Undated mound

Rath na Rioch

Geophysics

100 m

Fig. 25 *The principal monuments on the Hill of Tara, comprising two conjoined enclosures, each with a circular earthwork in its centre. The sequence of construction remains to be established. There was a Neolithic passage grave where their perimeters converged. Information from Schot* et al. *(2016).*

effect was to create an enormous figure-of eight, linking an alignment of two or, possibly three, circular mounds. As Gleeson suggests, the form of the Iron Age buildings was reproduced on a greater scale and extended over much of the hilltop. The diameters of the enclosures at Tara were about 550 m and 400 m. Those of the excavated buildings at Navan Fort were 30 m and 20 m respectively, but geophysical survey has identified an even larger figure-of-eight structure of some kind there (O'Driscoll *et al.* 2020).

A splendid isolation

How were the features of the Irish Iron Age related to one another?

Most accounts of this period on the European mainland emphasise the importance of long-distance connections and the movement of luxury goods. They describe the emulation of foreign practices and exotic types of architecture (Cunliffe 2018). That was surely the case at Mont Lassois and Silchester which were considered in Chapter Two, and it is why Celtic Art is often thought of as a fusion of indigenous ideas and Classical prototypes. In the same way, the development of complex societies in Western Europe might have been precipitated by contacts with people in the Mediterranean: first, the Greeks, and then Etruscans and Romans. But this approach has little to offer to studies of pre-Roman Ireland. It is clear that, like other regions, it did have long-distance contacts, yet the only serious evidence of outside influence is the adoption of La Tène metalwork.

Perhaps too much emphasis is placed on the impact of the Roman world on insular developments. That is because literary sources say that an invasion from the neighbouring island was planned or possibly took place. Even if it did happen, its impact was extremely limited (Cahill Wilson 2014). But the most persuasive dating evidence suggests that most, if not all, of the royal centres developed in the second and first centuries BC. That is long before the Roman world extended any closer than Spain and up to 150 years before Caesar conquered Gaul. Events in Britain would have had even less impact, and its western seaboard was outside the area in which the pattern of settlement changed significantly during the early first century AD.

Instead of conforming to the expected pattern, the inhabitants of Ireland went their own way. They had their links with a wider world but expressed them with circumspection. They shared a widespread belief system documented by deposits of valuables in water, but there is no evidence of any dryland sanctuaries, rich burials, or large defended settlements that can be compared with those on the Continent. Nor was there any attempt to emulate foreign styles of architecture. Instead the public buildings of this period, like the huge roundhouse and the figure-of-eight structures at Navan, have an explicitly local character. It seems as if the inhabitants of the island shared a powerful sense of their separate identity and expressed it in a way that would have been immediately apparent to travellers from other places. The contrast with wider traditions was deliberate, explicit and pervasive. The Great Houses considered in this chapter took a form with its roots in a local tradition. At the end of the first millennium BC communities living in Ireland returned to impressive but enigmatic monuments that had been built many years before, and they gave them new life. These processes were directly linked to one another. Not only did people eschew most of the references to distant areas favoured in other regions of Europe, they identified closely with an insular past. More than anything else, it was the resource on which social and religious authority was built.

The problem is to take the interpretation further once researchers distance themselves from literary sources which refer to a later period. Their dilemma is well expressed by Conor Newman (1998, 131):

> The existence of central authority, sacred or secular, local, regional or national, in Iron Age Ireland can only be inferred from analysis of the archaeological evidence. It is clear from the scale of the monuments at the 'royal' sites that concerted and co-ordinated labour was required in their construction, large numbers of people were rallied and organised and, when it was ritual monuments that were being built, inspiration for the designs would have come from the religious quarter even if the workforce was mobilised by a secular authority …

> [I]t is probable that there was both sacred and secular authority in late prehistoric Ireland: but were they embodied in one and the same institution, one and the same person?

Developments in the Roman period

The basic layout of the royal centres was established up to 200 years before the Christian era, and there is little evidence that they maintained their original significance beyond the second century AD. Great Houses were not used after that time. Their sites seem to have lost some of their significance and their components may have been less monumental; this is certainly suggested by Conor Newman's (1998, 133–34) own excavation at Raffin Fort where the final layout of the site is dated between the early fourth and late sixth centuries AD; in the same way a circular building, 16 m in diameter, on Site A at Navan seems to date between AD 400 and 700 (O'Driscoll *et al.* 2020). The 'royal' sites were conceived on a smaller scale until their roles were re-invented from the eighth century AD: a process which is considered in Chapter Seven. Newman's study emphasises the course of events. It seems that the Irish landscape was increasingly divided between local kingdoms. He suggests that the breakdown of the late pre-Roman system happened after the conquest of Britain. Far from being a distant threat to insular communities, Rome was now a neighbour and it was no longer possible for the inhabitants of Ireland to distance themselves in the way that had happened until then. In fact there are occasional burials of settlers who had crossed the Irish Sea. There are also finds of Roman coins and artefacts, and even hoards of metalwork (Cahill Wilson 2014). A site like Tara was not necessarily abandoned, but it was no longer the focus of ambitious building projects. Without any obvious military intervention, the Imperial power changed the course of local politics.

These developments are most obvious at three sites where Roman artefacts are documented in detail: Newgrange, Freestone Hill, and Tara, all of which are not far from the east coast where most of the imports are found.

Like Knowth, the Neolithic passage grave at Newgrange assumed a new importance at this time. Michael and Myles Gibbons (2016) suggest that the rings, gaming pieces and a glass bead found outside the monument might have been associated with graves, like those around the nearby tomb of Knowth where similar items are recorded. John Ó Néill (2013) even suggests that the mound at Newgrange was rebuilt. There were other items whose chronology extended into the third and fourth centuries AD. They had a more distinctive character (Carson & O'Kelly 1977). Where their locations are documented, they seem to have been placed around three standing stones in front of the entrance to the tomb (although its position might not have been known at the time). They included coins (some were made of gold and others were converted into medallions), gold and silver finger rings, brooches, a bronze bracelet, a necklace, a bridle bit, and the chape for a scabbard. The most unusual item was the terminal of a Middle Bronze Age gold torc bearing a Roman inscription. Ó Néill interprets its message as a dedication to the dead. Most authorities accept that Newgrange was treated as a sacred site and that these artefacts were meant as offerings (Carson & C. O'Kelly 1977; M. O'Kelly 1982, 47–48).

The same interpretation is favoured for the Roman objects from Freestone Hill, most of which date to the fourth century AD (Raftery 1969). Again there was an obvious reference to the insular past, and the principal monuments on the site were an Early Bronze Age ring cairn associated with 15 burials, and a Late Bronze Age hillfort. The older structure was surrounded by a walled enclosure. It was approximately circular and measured 36 m by 30 m, with an entrance to the southeast and a hearth in the centre. There were no other buildings during this phase. The artefacts recovered by excavation resemble those from Newgrange, although the collection was not so rich. In this case they included bronze rings, bracelets, toilet instruments, and a decorated mount. There were also glass bracelets, beads and a Roman coin issued between AD 337 and 340. Animal bones were abundant and were mainly those of cattle and pigs. Many of the pigs were young, suggesting that they were raised to provide meat for feasts.

The third site is the Rath of the Synods at Tara. It should have been the most informative of this group, but its archaeology has suffered. Between 1898 and 1901 it was the scene of a misguided attempt to find the Ark of the Covenant. A Roman coin hoard does seem to have been discovered, but half the deposits were removed without any record. In 1952 and 1953 a proper excavation did take place, but its director, Sean O'Riordàin, died not long afterwards. By the time that his records were studied, a few had gone missing and some of the plans had disintegrated. The present account is based on what survives (Grogan 2008).

The enclosure was circular and was defined by three or four concentric earthworks. There were areas of paving and postholes in the interior, but they have been difficult to interpret. Any buildings might have been of wood as iron nails survived, but enough remained undisturbed to show that they could not have included a roundhouse of any size. During its Roman phase the main feature was a prominent earthwork rather than a monumental building.

The finds from the Rath of the Synods resemble those from Newgrange and Freestone Hill, but they featured other elements. In common with those sites there were bronze rings, brooches, pins and a bracelet; and there were the usual glass beads. But the excavation also found the chape for a dagger, part of a mirror, and fragments of glass vessels and high-quality ceramics imported to serve food and drink. Coarse wares were entirely absent. The finds span the second to fourth centuries AD but most of the diagnostic material dates from the later part of this period. The animal bones were listed and no longer survive, but the dominant species were the same as those at Freestone Hill. The enclosure has been described as a 'residential' site, but it occupied a place with an extraordinary history. To judge from its pivotal location on the Hill of Tara, it could have been used by special people and might have played a special role. Their activities emphasised the existing importance of feasting and personal appearance, but they were conducted using unfamiliar kinds of artefacts. In some ways this was a new departure, and by the late Roman period the inhabitants of Ireland finally acknowledged the impact of the wider world. In this setting Great Houses were no longer an important as a connection to the past.

On the frontier

In an important contribution to a conference on the significance of Tara, Ian Armit (2013) compared the representation of Roman artefacts in Ireland with their contexts in Scotland. In this case they were associated with monumental houses of an unusual kind.

The drystone architecture of Iron Age Scotland raises many issues, few of which have so far been resolved. Fortunately, the problems are simplified because the assemblages that share most features with those in Ireland are associated with a distinctive group of structures around the Antonine Wall (Macinnes 1984). They are usually characterised as 'lowland brochs' (Armit 2003, 119–32). Two features are especially important: the character and chronology of these buildings; and the kinds of artefacts found there.

Stone houses and their chronologies

The term broch applies to tall circular buildings – effectively towers – which were used as domestic dwellings in the Scottish Iron Age, and particularly in the Northern and Western Isles and in Caithness (Fig. 26). A few of them attained heights of 10 m or more. They are related to other monuments which reproduce the forms of domestic dwellings in stone (Romankiewicz 2011; Sharples 2019). Perhaps the principal feature of brochs is that they had more than one floor. The height and mass of these buildings are their most impressive features and they could be erected in conspicuous positions: on local prominences, cliffs and small islands. It is likely that they enjoyed a special status (although it would be wrong to assume that all brochs had the same significance). There are two reasons for taking this view. The first is their structural complexity and the labour needed to build them (Sharples 2019). It is not clear whether their erection was managed by specialists, but there is an obvious contrast with the

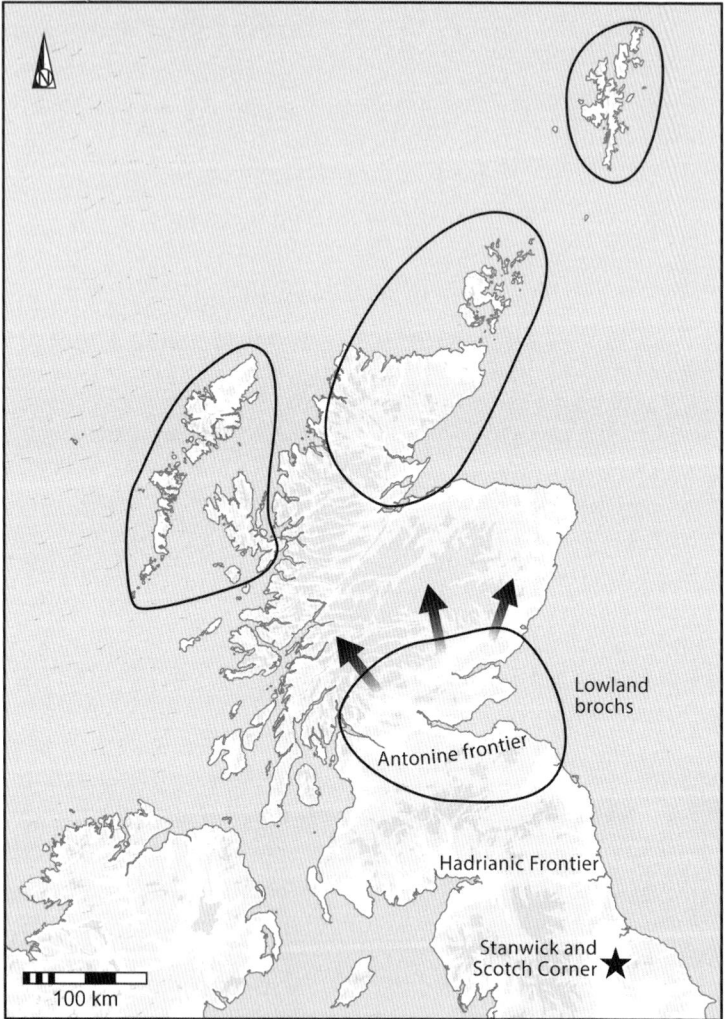

Fig. 26 The distributions of four regional groups of brochs in relation to the successive Roman frontiers and the positions of the rich Late Iron Age sites at Stanwick and Scotch Corner. The lowland brochs shared elements with structures further to the north. Information from Armit (2013) and Harding (2017).

evidence of roundhouses in southern England which could have been built by the inhabitants of a single settlement. Brochs made significantly greater demands and Ian Armit (2003, 76) estimates that an average structure of this kind might have taken 10,000 worker-days: '10 people labouring for nearly three years, or 100 people labouring for nearly three months'. At the same time these buildings might have accommodated more people than an ordinary dwelling. Most of the simpler buildings in England had a single floor and were well under 10 m in diameter. The interior of a broch can be the same size, but greater space was available because they had upper storeys. A difficulty with the argument that they were high status dwellings is that it presupposes the existence of lesser buildings in the same areas. They have been difficult to find.

In fact many brochs seem to be isolated, but they could be defended by a ditch, a rampart or a wall. They are also found at the centre of groups of domestic buildings, some of which were enclosed. These arrangements vary from region to region (Harding 2017). It is hard to demonstrate that brochs were coeval with the structures built around them, but there are examples in which all the components conform to a single design. In that case the tower is the dominant feature. It is more difficult to compare the organisation of these structures with the plan of a simpler roundhouse, but that is because the main accommodation may not have been at ground level, but, where it was the case, both groups were laid out according to the same principles. There was an open area around a central hearth and a series of compartments against the inside wall. There seems little doubt that brochs were grandiose versions of a traditional dwelling. That argument is supported by excavated evidence that suggests that their original prototypes were roundhouses with unusually thick walls. They may have existed as early as 600 BC and over time they increased in size and mass.

These buildings cannot be considered in isolation as there is evidence that other structures underwent the same elaboration (Harding 2017). That applies to large domestic structures, small walled enclosures (*duns*), and even the underground cellars known as souterrains. If the brochs were the most prominent features in Orkney, Shetland,

Caithness and the Western Isles, parallel developments were happening close to the North Sea, around the Moray Firth, and on Deeside and Tayside. The same process was represented in the southwest of the country. They can also be recognised among timber buildings, including some unusually large roundhouses and crannogs.

It is not certain when and where brochs first developed, but there is increasing evidence that they originated in the north where the site of Old Scatness in Shetland is particularly well dated. There a broch was constructed between 390 and 200 BC (Dockrill *et al.* 2015). It is less clear when the same methods of building were adopted in other regions but again it is most likely to have happened during the first centuries BC and AD. There are problems in excavating these structures. The remains of brochs can be masked by deep deposits in their interiors which make them difficult and expensive to investigate. In some cases only the later levels are recorded.

Lowland brochs

In spite of all these problems, it is easy to appreciate the distinctive character of the lowland brochs (Romankiewicz 2011, 39–72 & 454–93). They are organised according to a radial plan which resembles the arrangement in Caithness and the Northern Isles rather than structures along the west coast. The sizes of their interiors are unusually diverse, and in this case they vary across the distribution of these buildings, with the smaller examples towards the west and the larger ones to the east; an important consideration was the availability of timber to support the roof and upper floors. An important distinction is illustrated by the positions of their entrances. The western group of lowland brochs have the same orientations of those in Skye and the Western Isles, and the central and eastern groups follow the same pattern as Caithness and Orkney. They even occupy similar positions in the landscape. Sometimes two structures are so similar that they are described as 'twins' (Romankiewicz 2011, 59–61). This applies to Edin's Hall near the North Sea and East Burray in Orkney, 350 km away. Another feature is shared between different parts of their distribution. Edin's Hall in the eastern group and Fairy's Knowe in the central cluster seem to have been unusually conspicuous monuments. Estimates of their height place them among the tallest buildings in Iron Age Scotland.

On a more local level their distribution is deceptive as the three main groups appear to cluster on either side of the Antonine Wall, but their chronology rules out a direct relationship between them and the Roman frontier. Fraser Hunter's (in press) work has shown that the six sites with satisfactory dating evidence were built before the Wall was constructed in the 140s AD. Some of the brochs had already been demolished by then. Other relationships may be more informative. Several lowland brochs overlay timber roundhouses (one inside a palisaded enclosure), and three were within existing hillforts.

Six sites were occupied during the period of Flavian military activity in Scotland between about AD 77 and 87. Another three excavated brochs did not include any Roman artefacts and may have gone out of use before that time. The radiocarbon dates from Leckie are important as they suggest that the broch was constructed between the middle of the first century BC and the mid first century AD (MacKie 2016). Although the sites are associated with Roman artefacts, their presence need not show when those structures were built, and the lowland brochs could well have originated some time before the invasion of Scotland.

The character of the associated artefacts

Although their dates hardly overlapped, the finds associated with lowland brochs were like those considered in Ireland. Although the contexts of those artefacts were very different, the people who used them shared a similar lifestyle. Fraser Hunter found that seven Scottish sites contained an unusually wide variety of artefacts dating from this period. One of them was a crannog, another was a hillfort, but all the remaining five were lowland brochs. Their contents were strikingly similar to one another. They included Samian pottery, amphorae, mortaria, glass vessels, bronze vessels, beads, brooches and coins. Again the emphasis was on personal appearance and the consumption of food and drink, but, unlike the evidence from Tara, these collections also included coarse pottery, suggesting their use as settlements. The artefacts from Fairy Knowe are particularly informative as the structure was well preserved and its contents are documented in detail (Main 1998). Among the most notable items were the handle of a tankard, glass bottles for keeping liquids, finger rings (one of them with enamelled decoration) and amber beads. Animal bones were poorly preserved but were predominantly those of cattle. The large collection from Leckie is similar but it adds other elements, the most striking of which were a glass bowl, a glass jar, a bronze bowl, a bronze mirror, a fine enamelled chain brooch and an iron fitting for a chariot (MacKie 2016).

North and south

The contents of lowland brochs suggest a link with the Roman world to the south, but the architecture of these buildings evokes connections with regions further north. That could be explained as long as their occupation was associated with the Antonine frontier, but closer attention to their chronology appears to rule this out (Macinnes 1984; Hunter in press). They are more directly linked with the Flavian advance into Scotland, which happened 70 years before and lasted only a decade. There are indications that such buildings might have been constructed before that happened. There were sites which lacked Roman finds (they were rare in any part of the country until the Flavian advance), and it is certainly the implication of the radiocarbon dates from Leckie. The use of more elaborate buildings had started by the first century BC, and the building of lowland brochs was only part of a more general development. If so, the status of the occupants cannot have resulted from their contacts with the invading power. It must have developed earlier. The unusual artefacts from the lowland brochs provided a new medium for displaying *existing* social distinctions. Another one was architecture.

This group of monumental roundhouses occupied an intermediate position between two different worlds. Despite the similarities between structures in separate regions, the lowland brochs were nearly 200 km away from the nearest buildings of the same kind (Fig. 26). Some of the same architectural devices did occur elsewhere, most obviously at duns, but the links with Ian Armit's 'Towers in the North' are too striking to be ignored (Armit 2003). They suggest connections with Caithness and Orkney on the east coast, and with Skye and the Hebrides to the west. The fact that these buildings drew on more than one source of inspiration is not consistent with an episode of settlement from highland areas. In any case the prototypes for the lowland brochs were on opposite sides of the country from one another.

To the south, and slightly closer, was an extraordinary site which has already played a part in this chapter. Although it featured two monumental roundhouses, Stanwick had entirely different connections from the Scottish monuments, yet their chronologies could have overlapped. The excavator's Period 4 is dated between 30 BC and AD 40. It was when those timber buildings were erected, but it was also when the inhabitants obtained a wide range of luxury goods from southern England and the Continent (Haselgrove 2016). In the south drastic social and political changes happened between Caesar's expeditions to Britain in the mid-first century BC and the Claudian invasion a hundred years later. The people who lived at Stanwick, or at Scotch Corner 6 km away (Fell 2020), benefitted from their contacts with other areas, but the inhabitants of lowland Scotland did not do so. Instead they emphasised their affinities with communities living much further to the north. They adopted the specialised style of architecture associated with a distant elite. It must have been a conscious decision. Of course they did have links with northern England – that is shown by their characteristic metalwork (MacGregor 1976; Hunter 1999) – but these building projects were entirely their own. The lowland brochs in Scotland occupied a debateable land in between separate communities, and their subsequent histories emphasised the vulnerability of that position.

When the conquering army entered that region it brought with it a new material culture. It was no longer possible for people to keep a distance from the new world to the south. It seems likely that some of the occupants of lowland brochs joined the invading force, for there are a few pieces of military equipment among the finds from these sites, and swords made in an indigenous style have even been discovered in Roman forts (Hunter in press). More important, by allying themselves with the invaders and emulating their way of life, local leaders gained access to a range of items through which they could display their status. They may well have controlled the supply of such artefacts to other people (Macinnes 1984). They maintained their traditional concerns with personal appearance and feasting, but now they had new ways of expressing them.

It was a difficult balance to sustain. Certain communities allied themselves with their new rulers, but they still lived in monumental buildings which were copies of structures in regions that would never form part of the Roman province. The positions of these people must have been increasingly dependent on the presence of the occupying power. After a decade or so, the military forces withdrew and early in the second century AD a frontier was established 150 km to the south where Hadrian's Wall was built. There would be further incursions into Scotland and for a while a new boundary was created – the short-lived Antonine Wall – but by that stage most of the lowland brochs had already been abandoned and five or six of these structures had been destroyed (Hunter in press). Their demolition has been attributed to the Roman forces (MacKie 2016), but it seems just as likely that their use came to an end during a period of *internal* conflict after the army had left. *In contrast to the situation in regions further to the north, few of these sites were reused.* Their significance was short-lived and now it came to a sudden and dramatic end.

Architectures and identities

This chapter has considered the strategic use of Great Houses at about the same time in two neighbouring countries, Ireland and Scotland.

It has also discussed the relationships between the people who built them and the expansion of Roman power.

The title, 'Social Distances', is not just a reference to the conditions in which this discussion was written; it also refers to the ways in which ancient architecture was used to emphasise some relationships and to reject or contain others. In the Irish case the key relationship was with the surviving fabric of the past and with particular kinds of building that had an extended history. They provided a vital resource at a time when the inhabitants of Iron Age Ireland were exposed to outside influences that they may have wished to keep in check. As it became harder to maintain their separate identities, they deployed traditional architectural forms on an exaggerated scale. That was an effective method during the pre-Roman period, but when the neighbouring island was incorporated into the Empire this stance was increasingly difficult to maintain. Great Houses may have gone out of use, but Roman objects were treated with circumspection and deposited in specialised contexts, like the votive deposits at Newgrange, Freestone Hill and Tara. At the same time those artefacts may have been selected because they were compatible with an established lifestyle that emphasised personal appearance and the importance of feasts. The same concerns had been expressed by the use of La Tène metalwork.

The Scottish sequence illustrates another kind of social distancing. It also shows its limitations as a strategy. Again the construction of monumental houses played a pivotal role, but in this case there was much less emphasis on the past. Although the lowland brochs might be constructed on sites that had already achieved some importance – timber roundhouses, a palisaded enclosure, and several hillforts – the stone buildings that eventually took their place did not refer to that history. Instead their forms were an explicit reference to an architectural style that had developed in a distant region and which may well have been the prerogative of a restricted section of society. In doing so, the people who built them were expressing their affinities with communities in the north of Scotland and resisting other influences coming from the south. That applies to the late pre-Roman period as well as the developments leading to the Flavian occupation.

In this case the monumental roundhouses did not go out of use, but now they were inhabited by people who owed a new allegiance to Rome. In contrast to the finds from Irish sites (with the possible exception of Tara where the structural evidence is poor), the artefacts associated with lowland brochs were deposited in the course of domestic occupation rather than rituals. On the other hand, these collections owed much of their survival to the rapid destruction of these buildings. After a brief period in which they provided the setting for feasts using Roman material culture and drawing on Roman culinary practices, these places were no longer credible symbols of local distinctiveness; their occupants were compromised. It was probably for that reason that most of the lowland brochs were levelled, abandoned and never replaced. At the same time their associations were completely repudiated. It was only in the areas that did not fall under Roman control that brochs and the structures that succeeded them would have a longer history. In those regions their use extended into the post-Roman period and lasted until the Viking Age (Harding 2017). Some of the problems of the later first millennium AD will be considered in Chapter Seven.

CHAPTER 7

Halls of residence and Halls of Fame

Great Houses in Iron Age Scandinavia and Anglo-Saxon England

So far this book has confronted some difficult issues. The available evidence can be ambiguous, poorly recorded or fragmentary, but in principle the situation ought to improve in studying the monumental houses of the first millennium AD. They have seen large-scale excavations; there are the first useful documentary sources; and Great Halls feature in the earliest heroic literature. But that may be too optimistic. Writing about the period in Northern Europe – the region with the most impressive timber buildings – the historian Chris Wickham (2016, 80) says this:

> In [AD] 500 the border of the Roman empire divided the known from the unknown in Europe. North of the border, what we have is archaeology, which tells us about many things but by no means all – plus the views of Roman observers looking northwards, which were … usually ill-informed … using the 'barbarians' as a mirror to reflect critiques of Roman society itself.

Even the literature of Britain, Ireland and Northern Europe raises serious problems. It was written down long after the events it described; its historical accuracy has been disputed; and its original character may have been altered to provide a Christian moral. As Chapter One has shown, the main source of information for Anglo-Saxon buildings in England, *Beowulf*, was actually set in Denmark (Niles & Osborn

2007). Similarly, the most detailed information on Old Norse religion comes from the sagas written down in Iceland after the Conversion (Andrén 2014).

Fortunately all these questions have been considered by other writers. So has the character of settlements with monumental halls. A different approach may be helpful here. This chapter has two objectives: to review the main explanations for the adoption of Great Houses in Scandinavia; and to compare them with the approaches taken to analogous buildings in Anglo-Saxon England and early medieval Ireland. The archaeological evidence has been summarised already, with accounts of sites like Lejre, Yeavering and Tara, but there is more to say about the circumstances in which they came into being, and the ways in which they were used.

This analysis is by no means comprehensive and is primarily concerned with *two traditions of research* rather than a wider phenomenon which extended well beyond the areas considered here. That is why excavated halls in Northern Germany and the Low Countries are not discussed, although those regions were among the principal sources of the people who settled Britain during the post-Roman period. *Beowulf* can be used to illustrate the links between England and South Scandinavia, but the strength of that connection should not be overemphasised. Their histories certainly overlapped, but the differences between their monumental buildings were at least as important as the points they had in common. Again it is useful to contrast the sequences documented by field archaeology.

South Scandinavia

This account begins with Scandinavia. The archaeological and historical evidence is so complex that it could easily occupy a volume on its own, but it contains four main strands which are considered here.

The organisation of domestic buildings

There was an essential continuity between the plans of earlier Iron Age dwellings and those of the Great Houses, but the change was not just one of size. Although the scale of major structures certainly increased, their internal organisation was modified (Hamerow 2002, 12–26). Throughout the first millennium BC Scandinavian longhouses had been provided with three aisles and stalls for livestock. That arrangement persisted throughout the long Iron Age, but there were new developments. Certain buildings became significantly larger and more robust than the others. At the same time the biggest structures dispensed with stalls altogether and used a central space as the principal room. This was a characteristic of the most prosperous farms, for these buildings were associated with a wider range of artefacts. Frands Herschend (1993) suggests that the room was used as a hall by people who did not live there. The development took place from the third century AD and marked the beginning of a process by which some major longhouses became public buildings. This must have been an initiative of the most successful farmers and it reflected their increasing status. For that reason such settlements have been described as 'magnate farms' or 'central places' (the latter term was borrowed from geography but was used as a metaphor).

Another influence came from regions further to the south where masonry structures had been a common feature; some of them remained in use after the collapse of the Roman administration. They included elite residences, villas, forts, temples, palaces and churches. Anders Andrén (2014, 105–15) argues that Roman military architecture provided a source of inspiration for the stone forts of Öland, but the halls in Scandinavia were usually built of wood. The presence of massive buildings across the imperial frontier can hardly have gone unnoticed and might have suggested the construction of monumental dwellings in neighbouring regions. But there would always be a difference of scale. Even if the largest example at Lejre provided the prototype for Heorot, it enclosed only 45% of the space occupied by the Great Hall of Charlemagne's palace at Aachen (Rollason 2016, 273–89). Both these structures were impressive in their own terms. Their histories overlapped, yet they belonged in different worlds.

This summary is too simple. Lars Jørgensen (2004, 132–39) has shown that there were two 'generations' of monumental buildings.

The earliest examples originated in the third century AD, while others began life in the sixth and seventh centuries and also included examples dating from the eighth and ninth centuries. The first group includes those at Gudme, Uppåkra, Helgö and Sort Mulde. The other category covers Tissö, and a site which has already featured here: the larger group of buildings at Lejre. Current research shows that Gamla Uppsala in Sweden can be added to the list. Most sites were used for a long period and their character could have changed over the course of time. They might move to nearby locations, as in fact happened at Lejre (A.S. Beck 2017, 262).

In Jørgensen's analysis the first generation of sites was characterised by 'an accumulation of craftsman's farms or dwellings grouped around an elite residence – a structure and organisation they retained over subsequent centuries'. Their successors were rather different. 'Compared with the first-generation sites, the structure and organisation changed in the later places … Permanent farms with craft activities do not appear… [and] they seem to have been superseded by seasonal market places' (Jørgensen 2004, 132). These sites show greater signs of formal planning and important structures were sometimes situated within substantial rectilinear enclosures. More of the successive buildings were superimposed. To different extents these developments are illustrated by excavations at Tissö, Jelling and the second group of halls at Lejre. They contrast with the dispersed pattern in the previous phase and suggest that by now social conventions were generally accepted or imposed.

Long-distance trade and exchange

Another important factor was participation in trade and the acquisition of wealth from overseas (Ludowici 2010; Jørgensen 2010). Two of the principal sources were the late Roman Empire and the kingdom of the Franks, although these international contacts could extend much further. The best evidence comes from places where valuable artefacts were accumulated and made.

For many years researchers had focused on imported artefacts, from personal ornaments to feasting equipment, and from weapons to coins. Although their distributions varied over the course of time, they extended across the Roman frontier and were found throughout Denmark, where they were best represented in Zealand, Jutland and Funen. Other examples were in southern Sweden and on the Baltic islands of Öland and Gotland. Some were simply chance finds, and others were associated with burials. These discoveries seemed to document the emergence of local elites, but much of this research was restricted to portable artefacts. The point is made by Birger Storgaard (2003, 106):

> The archaeological finds … testify to a considerable Roman interest in the southern Scandinavian area … More than a thousand Roman-made silver, bronze and glass vessels, along with a large number of Roman coins, bronze statuettes, glass beads and other jewellery … are known from southern Scandinavia and northern Germany … from … the first to fourth centuries AD.

The earliest central places were well placed to capitalise on maritime contacts. Helgö was an island in Lake Mälaren and was directly accessible by sea (Clarke & Lamm 2017). Sort Mulde was 2 km from a harbour (Adamsen 2009), and Gudme was 4 km from the shore of Funen (Nielsen *et al.* 1994). Uppåkra was further away, but it was only 8 km inland (Larsson 2019). The major complex at Gudme was linked to the coastal settlement of Lundeborg where there is evidence of craft production and another concentration of imports. Jorgensen makes the point that such complexes included a series of separate farms, workshops, cemeteries and sacred places. But at their heart there were monumental halls.

Gudme is perhaps the most extensively investigated and achieved its greatest importance between the fourth and sixth centuries AD (Nielsen *et al.* 1994). The area had long been known for finds of foreign artefacts, some of which were of particularly fine quality. They featured caches of raw material, coins, collections of personal jewellery, and hoards containing necklaces, arm-rings and the mounts for decorated scabbards. There were also by-products from working metals. Six thousand objects have been found there, among them the contents of five silver hoards and six gold hoards.

The main timber structure was one of the earliest halls in Scandinavia. It was accompanied by two smaller buildings and was associated with fragments of Roman silver, coins, neck-rings, bronze artefacts, figurines and glass. The building was exceptionally robust, with huge posts bedded deeply in the ground, and could have had an upper storey. It was 50 m long and 10 m wide. This structure was erected during the third century BC and remained in use for roughly a hundred years. It was as monumental as any of the Great Houses considered in this book.

How were these elements combined? Charlotte Fabech and Ulf Näsman (2013) bring together an analysis of the settlement hierarchy and a classification of the objects associated with these sites. 'Central places' that were important within their own regions included the normal range of items associated with domestic occupation: pottery, tools, querns, equipment for textile production, brooches and beads. These places also featured more distinctive artefacts: Roman coins, the medallions known as bracteates, figures of gold foil, weapons, glass, crucibles, ingots and moulds. They shared these specialised types with the most important sites which also contained helmets, gold objects of foreign origin, and pieces 'with high artistic value'. Clearly, access to exotic materials and objects played a major role. That was especially important as lavish displays of grave goods became less important at the end of the Roman Iron Age. It seems as if control over the circulation of valuables played an increasing part when the largest halls were built. The text of *Beowulf* shows the significance of giving and receiving gifts.

Warfare
One of the most striking features of North European archaeology is the discovery of damaged weapons in bogs and lakes. Influenced by the writings of Roman authors, archaeologists interpret them as the belongings of defeated armies, sacrificed by the victors after a battle. Such deposits form part of a long tradition and this practice

is documented at Iron Age sanctuaries in Gaul which also include human bodies (Løvschal & Holst 2018). The deposits found in Scandinavia are generally later in date and the majority were used (often on more than one occasion) between AD 200 and 600, with a peak in the third century. Excavation at Alken Enge in Jutland has shown that the members of the defeated army were also sacrificed, but in this case their bodies were deposited in a separate location from their possessions (Løvschal *et al.* 2019). The remains of the victims were not far from the weapon deposit at Illerup. On the other hand, the bodies at Alken Enge were earlier than most of the collections of war gear.

The chronology of these deposits is informative in other ways, for it is clear that some of them were in places with a long-established significance. Vimose, for example, received offerings associated with natural fertility before the first of eight collections of weapons was discarded there (Pauli Jensen 2009). In northern France the major collections of arms and human remains at sanctuaries predate Caesar's conquest of Gaul (Løvschal & Holst 2018). Although deposits like those at Vimose and Illerup belonged to a later period, their locations were well outside the Roman frontier. Here there is evidence of repeated acts of violence. Some of the weapons were of non-local types (they even include Roman swords) and may have been brought by raiders coming from Germany, Poland, Gotland and Norway. If the immediate sources of these war bands were outside the frontier, the expansion of the Roman world would have displaced local people. Raiding provided a new way of achieving political power and Scandinavian warriors might have been recruited as mercenaries. There was added instability in the earlier sixth century AD when parts of Northern Europe were badly affected by environmental changes caused by volcanic eruptions (Price 2020, 74–77).

One indication of unsettled conditions is the building of defences. In Denmark linear earthworks were constructed to control land routes, and other barriers prevented incursions by sea (Norgård Jørgensen 2003). The land boundaries were established during the second and third centuries AD and their creation seems to have been influenced by Roman models. Most of the underwater barrages were later and date from the mid-third to early fifth centuries AD. It was a period when entire boats were deposited together with damaged weapons; at Nydam this happened on three occasions during the third and fourth centuries AD.

The clearest evidence of conflict is the treatment of Great Houses which were commonly destroyed by fire. They were often rebuilt in exactly the same positions. It is possible that a structure of this kind presented such a powerful image that burning it amounted to a political act. According to Lotte Hedeager (2011, 147):

> The hall was the centre of the human micro-cosmos, the symbol of stability and good leadership. The hall was also the location where communal drinking took place, which had the purpose of creating bonds of loyalty … The hall … served as [a] geographical and ideological centre … As the literature tells us, earls and kings could oppress and ruin each other by simply destroying their opponent's hall.

The same practices were followed so often that they took on the character of a ritual. This is consistent with the idea that such structures had lives of their own and were indistinguishable from the people who built and used them. By destroying the fabric of the hall their enemies cast doubt on the social bonds on which its existence depended. That might explain why all trace of a burnt hall could be concealed by covering it with stones or other deposits.

Unearthly powers

Attitudes to the supernatural and the past were as important as access to new kinds of wealth, and again they were sources of power. Fabech and Näsman (2013) provide an influential account of the changing roles of sacred places. Their interpretation helps to resolve a problem posed by early texts which use the terms *harg* and *havn* to refer to the places used for rituals. Some authorities had interpreted them as natural features, including bogs, lakes, springs, islands, forests, rocks and hills. Deposits of artefacts and animal bones were recorded from all these locations. Other researchers believed that the words referred to special buildings: temples or shrines. There is an apparent contradiction, but the problem would be resolved if these places played comparable roles during different phases. This is what Fabech and Näsman propose. The significance of these technical terms might have changed. For example, '*Harg* originally meant 'elevation' or 'height' but was later used to name prominent farmsteads, as well as sacred buildings with idols' (Fabech & Näsman 2003, 82).

Their approach helps to explain the growing importance of halls during the first millennium AD. That might well apply to Gudme where three hills have names that refer to their sacred character: *Offerbjerget* (the sacrificial hill), *Gudernes bjerg* (the hill of the gods), and *Helligdomsbjerget* (the sacred hill). Similarly the name Helgö means a holy island. Another example comes from the fort of Eketorp which was occupied between the fifth and seventh centuries AD. The site included a spring where pig and horse skulls were deposited from the Roman Iron Age to the Viking period. It was just outside the entrance of the fortress, but it is clear that activity began before it was built and continued after its abandonment. Most of the bones dated from the seventh century AD. The site contained an important deposit of gold figures similar to those found in halls, suggesting that more formal rituals happened there. Fabech and Näsman suggest that such sites took over some of the roles of older sanctuaries. That development would have strengthened the authority of a new elite.

A similar process involved the remains of the past, especially the earthworks associated with earlier generations (Lund & Arwill-Norbladh 2016). The clearest example was at Lejre where the halls were built near to four ship settings and a series of ancient mounds. The most striking relationship was between a conspicuous round barrow (the findspot of a Bronze Age sword) and a massive Iron Age longhouse which was erected beside it (Christensen 2015). In other cases new monuments could have copied the appearance of older ones in the vicinity. This was probably the case at Jelling where two enormous mounds covered the largest ship setting in Scandinavia (Fig. 27; Randsborg 2008; Holst *et al.* 2000; Jessen *et al.* 2014). It must have applied to the great round barrows at Gamla Uppsala which were

Jelling

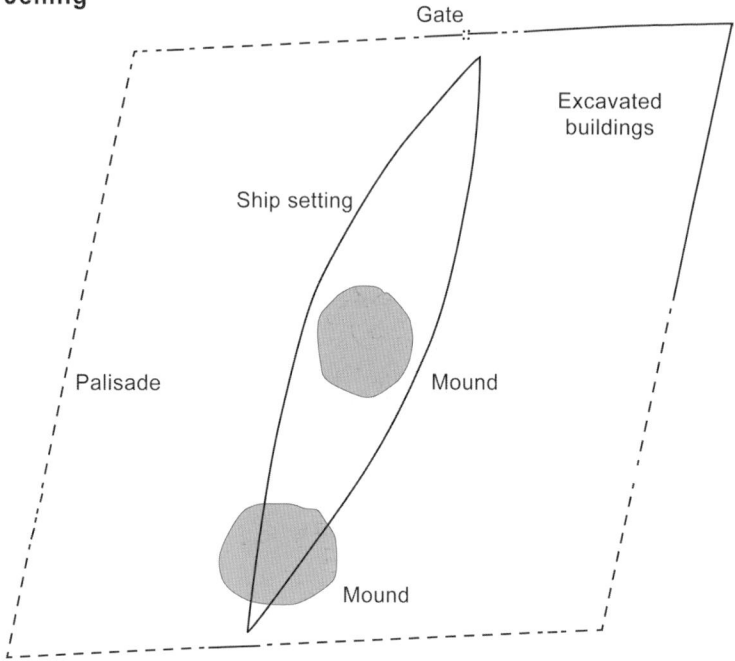

Fig. 27 Outline plan of the royal complex at Jelling, showing the positions of two monumental mounds and an enormous ship setting. Information from Holst et al. *(2000).*

built during the sixth and seventh centuries AD. Only 8 km away at Håga there was a tumulus of similar proportions. It dated from the Late Bronze Age, but became known as King Bjorn's Mound because it was so similar to those monuments (Kaliff & Oestergaard 2018). It was excavated by Oscar Almgren on the mistaken assumption that it would date from the first millennium AD.

These are not the only examples of a widespread practice. Timber structures were established beside groups of older Iron Age graves, as happened at Toftum Ness (A.S. Beck 2017, 274). The positions of these burials might have been marked, and the builders clearly intended to establish a connection between them. There were even earlier burials close to the halls at Tissö. The people who constructed them could have linked their fortunes to powerful places in the landscape.

The roles of Great Houses in Scandinavia

There has been a long-running discussion in Scandinavian archaeology. Were special buildings dedicated to the gods during the first millennium AD, or were rituals performed together with secular activities inside the dwellings of local leaders? Were these structures simply prosperous farms, or were they 'aristocratic residences' and even military bases?

At first linguists considered the meanings of the terms used in early texts. Like those discussed in Chapter One, they were recorded during a later period, but they certainly described the places where ceremonies occurred. How were they related to features on the ground? Perhaps these sources referred to temples, but that interpretation went out of fashion and most authorities concluded that rituals were conducted in other locations. The idea held sway until settlement excavations raised yet another possibility. People might have engaged with the supernatural within specific parts of buildings that played other roles. Particular rooms might have been employed on an occasional basis (Herschend 1993). Great Houses could have combined the roles of elite residences, feasting halls and temples, but each of these functions was fulfilled on a different occasion. Projects like the excavation at Lejre show that some of these structures were paired with small buildings which contained unusual deposits. In the light of this research it is even more important to know how to interpret the halls. Did they always combine sacred with secular roles, or were those functions discharged in separate structures?

Two important sites in Sweden illustrate these different perspectives and epitomise nearly all the features that have figured in this account. One is Gamla Uppsala (Old Uppsala), and the other is Uppåkra, outside Lund, 650 km to the south.

Gamla Uppsala and Uppåkra

If the earliest literary texts presented problems for archaeologists interpreting Late Iron Age buildings, the same was true of an account of Gamla Uppsala composed by the missionary Adam of Bremen in the eleventh century AD (Price 2020, 211–13). In his words the existence of a pagan temple on the site was 'the final hindrance opposing the victory of Christianity'. He wrote about:

> A very famous temple called Uppsala … In this temple, entirely decked out in gold, the people worship the statues of three gods in such wise that the mightiest of them, Thor, occupies a throne in the middle of the room intended for ceremonial banquets. [Odin] and [Freyr] have places on either side … The people also worship heroes made gods, whom they endow with immortality because of their remarkable exploits …. A gold chain goes round the temple [and] hangs over the gable of the building … The shrine stands on level ground with mountains all about it like a theatre …. Near the temple stands a very large tree with wide spreading branches, always green winter and summer. What kind it is nobody knows. There is also a spring at which pagans are accustomed to make their sacrifices, and into it to plunge a live man (translation Sundqvist 2016, 110–11).

Olof Sundqvist (2016, 125) considers the implications of his account:

> Adam was referring to a multifunctional hall building … [which] was not only intended for religious rituals and symbols, but also for other purposes, such as a dining room at banquets, a room for political-judicial meetings and a gathering place for the *hird* [a group of professional warriors].

In that respect it resembles the 'men's houses' considered in Chapter Two. Such rooms were a special feature of bow-sided longhouses, the main feature of which was a continuous space where a large number of people could gather. It is no accident that the name Uppsala means 'the high halls' (Price 2020, 98).

So much seems clear, but Adam's text raises difficult questions. They concern his intentions and his reliance on literary sources, and both have been disputed. He wanted to emphasise the disturbing side of paganism and described the human sacrifices conducted at the site. At the same time he emphasised the unnatural character of this region, where the human population coexisted with Amazons, Cyclops and creatures who stood on one foot and fed on human flesh. The influence of Greek and Roman mythology is obvious and, like the description of Heorot in *Beowulf,* his statement that the temple was 'entirely decked out in gold' may have been influenced by Classical literature. Another source was the Biblical account of Solomon's temple. There are dangers in taking any part of Adam's description literally as his aim was not to inform but to promote the Christian message. Although he claimed to have talked to people with first-hand experience of how the place was used, this might have been a rhetorical device to convince an audience of the urgency of his mission. The building of a cathedral on the site shows that the project succeeded.

The evidence provided by archaeology is equally confusing. At first sight most of the key elements are present at Gamla Uppsala (Fig. 28). It features enormous round barrows like that at Lejre (they could have been the 'mountains' mentioned in Adam's account). There were smaller burial mounds and a series of earthwork terraces on which timber halls were constructed. The graves associated with the 'royal mounds' date from the sixth and seventh centuries AD, although less impressive cemeteries were still being used in the Viking Age. At the same time excavation has identified the remains of a massive bow-sided hall, 50 m long and up to 12 m wide, as well as two smaller buildings used as workshops for metal production and for making jewellery (Ljundqvist & Frölund 2015). The Great House was burnt down around AD 800 when its remains were covered over in a ritual that the excavators compare with a cremation burial. Its special character is obvious, but this evidence presents a problem, for the demise of the hall *predates Adam's account of Gamla Uppsala by 250 years.* At present there is not much archaeological evidence from the period in which he was writing. Did his account represent the situation at Old Uppsala as it existed during the eleventh century AD, or did he describe a mythical past in order to justify his mission?

Other possibilities are worth taking seriously. If his account is to be believed, the hall he described still awaits discovery. One idea is that the building at Gamla Uppsala simply changed location and that it occupied the same site as the later cathedral. There is no evidence of this, but something similar happened over the same period at Lejre, Tissø and Järrestad where in each case new structures were erected about 500 m from their predecessors (A.S. Beck 2017, 262). Adam's description does not shed any light on this question. On the other hand, what is clear is that at some time, when he was writing or in the distant past, the roles of halls and temples were combined.

Uppåkra was very different (Larsson 2019). This site was occupied between the first century BC and the tenth century AD and may have been used for even longer. It extended over 40 hectares and contained deposits of cultural material up to 2 m thick. No fewer than 14,000 artefacts were recovered by metal detector survey. The highest part of the occupied area included four burial mounds, two of which are still recognisable as earthworks. They are located near a church of uncertain date, although the earliest Christian burial there dates from AD 900. There is a dense concentration of surface finds in the same part of the site, which is also the centre of the complex. Given the sheer range of artefacts, it was chosen for excavation.

The work identified a sequence of timber buildings, two of them substantial halls, with a smaller rectilinear structure nearby, which the excavators describe as an 'enigmatic house' and compare with the architecture of a Scandinavian stave church (Fig. 28; Larsson 2004). Although it occupied a limited area, it was especially massive and must have been an exceptionally tall building. It was used for a very long period and was rebuilt on six occasions between AD 200 and 950. Pigs' jaws were buried beneath two of the roof supports which may have been embellished with miniature figures made of gold similar to those at Eketorp. Around AD 500 a gilded bronze beaker and an ornate glass vessel were buried beneath the floor. Despite its lengthy history, this structure remained undamaged when both the neighbouring halls were set on fire.

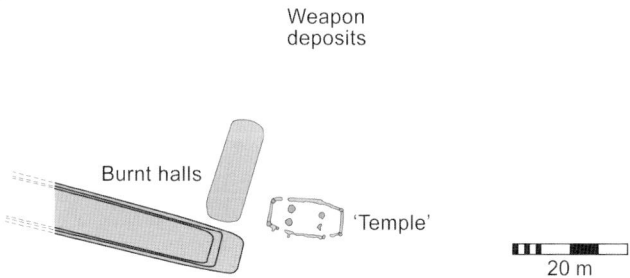

Fig. 28 Outline plans of the excavated complexes at Gamla Uppsala and Uppåkra. Information from Ljundqvist and Frölund (2015) and Larsson (2019).

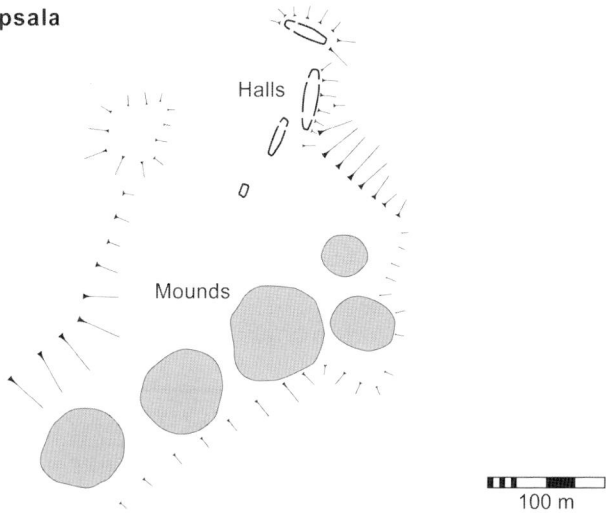

Those buildings were also used for a long time and the larger hall was destroyed on three occasions. The remains of both structures included burnt human bones, implying that they were specifically targeted in acts of violence. Not far away there were damaged weapons (mainly spears) and more human remains which date between AD

400 and 600. They resemble the war booty deposits of similar date but are unusual because they were not placed in bogs or lakes. They can be compared with the finds of later date from The Garrison at Birka (Holmquist 2016).

There was an obvious contrast between the excavated buildings at Uppåkra. Both the excavated halls were burnt down and some of the people inside them were killed. Their weapons were left lying on the ground. There were several of these episodes, but any attacks seem to have been directed towards the occupants of the halls themselves. The large quantity of cattle bones suggest that they gathered there for feasts.

By contrast, the adjacent building survived and remained intact for 700 years. It was associated with a series of distinctive deposits: bronze and glass vessels, and gold figures decorated with images which included the gods Odin and Thor. Lars Larsson (2019) compares this structure with Odin's mythical hall Valhöll (Valhalla) where spears were used for the rafters (Price 2020, 261–62); the Birka Garrison may have been similar. There seems to have been an obvious distinction between the Great Houses at Uppåkra and the temple built beside them, and that contrast is reinforced by their different histories. Their separate roles had been established from the outset and remained unchanged until people converted to Christianity.

The field archaeology of Uppåkra spans a longer period than the excavated buildings at Gamla Uppsala. The documentary history, which includes the testimony of Adam of Bremen, tells another story. It is surprisingly difficult to reconcile these sources of information. What was the relationship between Great Houses and temples? At Old Uppsala Adam says that they were combined and there is no reason to doubt this part of his account, but at Uppåkra they were divided between separate structures. There never was a single relationship between those elements, but there is similar evidence from Lejre, Tissö and other sites in Scandinavia.

How do the halls compare with structures of similar date in England? Did they have similar origins, and were all of them built for the same reasons?

Anglo-Saxon England

Until Rosemary Cramp (1957) compared the literary account of Heorot with the evidence from Yeavering, Anglo-Saxon buildings in Britain had seemed quite different from the large structures on the Continent. What was entirely new was the size of the halls at Yeavering. She compared the text of *Beowulf* with the information from that site and showed that they had features in common. The recognition of similar sites has added weight to her argument. Large scale excavations have followed in two of these places: Cowdery's Down (Millett & James 1983) and Lyminge (G. Thomas 2013). Rendlesham has been investigated by field survey (Scull *et al.* 2016), and other examples are documented by smaller projects, geophysics and air photographs. Outside the areas of Anglo-Saxon settlement – in northern and western Britain – a few large wooden buildings have been identified, suggesting the importance of other kinds of monumental architecture (Carver 2019, chapter 3). The most convincing examples are those inside three fortified sites: the reused fort of Birdoswald on Hadrian's Wall (Wilmott 1997, chapter 10), the hillfort at South Cadbury (Alcock 1995, 30–43), and a defended enclosure at Rhynie in northeast Scotland (Noble *et al.* 2019).

Cramp's article considered that the structures recently identified at Yeavering were most like buildings in Northern Europe.

Similarities with Northern Europe

During the first millennium AD the halls in both regions had features in common, although the links between them no longer seem so direct. Perhaps they are more relevant to questions of interpretation (Hamerow 2010).

In both traditions the Great Houses occupied one end of a continuum. The most complex buildings can be found together with simpler examples, but there are indications of increasingly ambitious and specialised projects. Groups of smaller houses can be found close to the complexes with Great Halls. Examples include the relationship between the elaborate structures at Yeavering and Milfield, on the one hand, and the settlement at Thirlings, on the other (C. O'Brien & Miket 1991).

Most of the Great Halls in Britain date from the seventh century AD, but some places were occupied before then. They were surrounded by zones in which specialised activities were undertaken: the working of silver, gold, bronze, iron and glass, textile production, and the making of jewellery. They are harder to identify than their Scandinavian counterparts, but this is because the excavations have been on a smaller scale. Only one site, Rendlesham, has seen systematic survey. Otherwise these patterns have to be inferred from the distribution of chance finds. The excavation of Yeavering, for instance, targeted the buildings identified from air photographs rather than the areas in between them; the most important evidence of metalworking was found in excavating a Neolithic monument nearby (Tinniswood & Harding 1991). The same applies to the discovery of cemeteries close to the halls. They have been located by accident, and there are cases in which groups of graves were known long before any major buildings were identified. A good example is Long Wittenham in the upper Thames valley (Hamerow & McBride 2018).

There are striking contrasts among the artefact collections from Great Hall complexes in Britain, two of which, Rendlesham and Lyminge, were exceptionally rich, while others, notably Yeavering, have produced very few finds. The difference is essentially regional. The most productive sites are towards the south and east, and the poorest to the west and north. Again one factor could have been maritime trade. Rendlesham is by the River Deben which leads to the southern North Sea. Lyminge was connected to the Middle Saxon port of Sandtun on the Channel coast. In this case the link is shown by archaeological and documentary evidence. It recalls the relationship between Gudme and Lundeborg. The same connections did not extend to sites a long way inland which had few imported artefacts; the Thames Valley may have been an exception.

Other features influenced the locations of these complexes. The past and its associations were especially important. Just as the buildings at Lejre referenced a series of ancient monuments, so did those at Yeavering where an alignment of halls and other structures extended between earlier prehistoric monuments. The older structures were probably a stone circle, two round barrows and a henge. At Sutton Courtenay the principal features were a cursus and a series of Bronze Age burial mounds. This relationship is not found everywhere. Adam McBride discusses 18 groups of halls. Eight acknowledged the positions of older monuments (usually circular earthworks of some kind), but similar evidence is absent from another eight sets of buildings; in the two remaining cases the evidence is ambiguous (McBride 2020, 66–72).

If Anglo-Saxon buildings reused the sites of older monuments, so did single graves and cemeteries. They have been studied by Howard Williams (1998) and their chronology is particularly relevant here. The frequency of reused monuments increased through the late fifth and sixth centuries AD, but it was during the seventh century, the period of the Great Halls, that it reached its peak. Most of these burials contained a simpler assemblage than their predecessors, but there was a significant exception. Some very rich graves were associated with reused or newly-built round barrows. These 'princely' burials had the same chronology as the buildings and shared a similar distribution (Blair 2018, fig. 29).

There were references to the Roman world just as there were in Northern Europe, but the sites of older towns in England were almost deserted by this time. Four features call for comment. The poet's account of Heorot described its coloured floor. This could be a reference to the use of the material known as *opus signinum*, and fragments, reddened by pieces of ground brick or tile, were found in the early medieval halls at Lyminge and Dover (G. Thomas 2018); an alternative might be mosaic floors (John Blair pers. comm.) There are other references to Roman structures. *Beowulf* describes the metalled or paved road leading to Heorot. This kind of construction would be familiar in England, but not in Denmark where the poem was set. Another link is the wooden 'grandstand' at Yeavering. Its distinctive architecture resembled that of a Roman amphitheatre, an example of which has been identified at Newstead, 40 km away (Clark & Wyse 1999). Another link with the ancient world was the way in which settlements, including Great Hall complexes, could be organised on a grid, employing similar techniques to Roman surveyors (Blair *et al.* 2020). Yeavering supplies a good example.

An important theme links the largest buildings in Britain and South Scandinavia. They were regularly demolished and rebuilt in the same positions. Sometimes the new construction was different from its predecessor, but the later structure was usually of the same type. In Northern Europe many of the halls were burnt down. There is less evidence of this from English sites, but there have been fewer excavations. It seems as if other buildings were replaced before they needed repairing. New buildings took the place of older ones so rapidly and so often that it may not have happened by chance. They were intended for special occasions. As John Blair (2018, 123) says:

> Magnificent theatres though they were, the great halls complexes were not built to last … The frequency with which these massive seventh-century complexes were rebuilt is startling … Rather than dwellings in the normal sense, these complexes look like assertions of their owners' dominance over domestic space, spiritual power, and communal ritual. Although presumably built to last longer than a single year, it is easy to imagine the halls as settings for feasts, ceremonies and high points in the calendar rather than day-to-day life.

Lastly, another problem is shared by archaeologists working on both sides of the North Sea. This account has discussed the confusing relationship between elite dwellings and structures interpreted as cult houses or temples. The question is not restricted to Scandinavia and raises problems in Anglo-Saxon studies. Small square buildings were attached to the Great Halls at Yeavering and Cowdery's Down and might have been used as shrines, but there is little to show it. The main exceptions are at Yeavering where one of them was superimposed on a prehistoric monument and contained a series of human burials. Another structure was associated with a deposit of cattle skulls. These interpretations are reasonable, but the excavator believed that a pagan shrine was reused as a Christian church. Again it was associated with a cemetery, but he based this claim on purely historical grounds. Bede recorded that King Edwin and his followers were converted to the new religion when St Paulinus visited Yeavering. There is no reason to question the documentary record, but there is nothing in the field evidence to show why this particular building must have been a church. That is the problem. Sacred and secular buildings may look alike in excavation, and so may those dedicated to different beliefs. In England the problem is especially serious as there is evidence that more rulers converted to Christianity during the Anglo-Saxon period and that elite settlements were sometimes transferred to the church and became religious institutions (G. Thomas 2013). Their architecture may not have changed and there are problems distinguishing between them. The point is made particularly clearly by John Blair (2005, 204–12).

Differences from Northern Europe
At the same time there were contrasts.

The most striking concern the chronologies of these buildings. The Great Halls of Northern Europe were built between the third and tenth centuries AD, meaning that their use extended between the Roman Iron Age and the Viking period. Their Anglo-Saxon counterparts are not precisely dated, but most of the evidence from artefacts and radiocarbon suggests that they were a feature of the seventh century. That is consistent with the few documentary references to these sites, especially Bede's account of the conversion of King Edwin. It is obvious that they were comparatively short-lived.

There were significant differences between these complexes. The most obvious is the lack of byres in Anglo-Saxon structures. This is surprising since their architecture is clearly related to that of ordinary longhouses in Northern Europe where this feature had been important since the Bronze Age. On the other hand, the smaller buildings in settlements around the North Sea are indistinguishable from one another (Hamerow 2012, 18–22). The absence of stalls on the English sites remains an unsolved problem; perhaps animals were kept in the open. There were other ways in which buildings in Britain differed from those in Scandinavia. They lack the curving side walls of their

Northern counterparts, although a few Anglo-Saxon buildings can be described as 'angle-sided' (Gardiner 2013, 63–69). It seems unlikely that aerodynamic structures were widely adopted in one part of Europe and largely rejected in another. A different explanation for this distinction must be found.

A still more obvious contrast concerns the sizes of these buildings. The largest stand out in the settlements of Britain and Scandinavia, but they hardly compare with one another. The biggest Anglo-Saxon buildings were little over 20 m long (the excavated hall at Sutton Courtenay, with a length of 30 m, was altogether exceptional). More considerable buildings are recorded in Northern Europe. This applies to the early hall at Gudme as well as the main building at Gamla Uppsala which was constructed almost 500 years later. In fact they were the same length; both were 50 m long. The principal room inside such a building provided almost as much space as the entire structure of an Anglo-Saxon Great Hall.

Other differences extend to the areas around these structures. At first sight they did have features in common. There is some evidence of workshops in which special artefacts were made. This pattern is well known in Scandinavia and has been identified by fieldwork at Rendlesham and probably Sutton Courtenay. It has also been traced through the distribution of chance finds around Great Halls in the upper Thames valley. McBride's (2020, 73–78) recent study suggests further examples of this arrangement. Although this recalls the evidence from a complex like Gudme, there is a problem in comparing the evidence from Northern Europe with that in Anglo-Saxon England. According to Jørgensen (2004 & 2009) it was a feature of the 'first generation' of magnate farms in Denmark and Sweden. Later sites were used less intensively and were superseded by 'seasonal market places'. This raises a chronological issue. The evidence of large-scale craft production in Northern Europe dates between the third and sixth centuries AD. A different model describes the situation between the seventh and ninth centuries. It means that superficially similar arrangements were followed at different times in Scandinavia and Britain.

In any case sites like Gudme, Helgö and Sort Mulde were in locations close to the sea, allowing their inhabitants to engage in long-distance trade. The same would apply to Rendlesham and Lyminge (and possibly to sites in the Thames valley), but it does not explain the distribution of other Anglo-Saxon Great Halls. They are found around the periphery of the most densely settled regions and cannot be described as 'central' places like their Scandinavian counterparts. They were accessible from their local hinterland (Austin 2017) but were poorly equipped to exercise control over a wider system of exchange. It seems more likely that they achieved their initial importance because they were where assemblies took place. They owed some of their power to the presence of older monuments.

The clearest evidence comes from Yeavering. According to Bede's account it was a royal site, yet it contained a series of buildings that were organised around a series of prehistoric structures that were still visible in the seventh century AD. The early medieval layout was based on an alignment of large posts which extended between two Bronze Age monuments (Fig. 29). There is more than one way of interpreting the excavated evidence, but most accounts agree that the

Yeavering

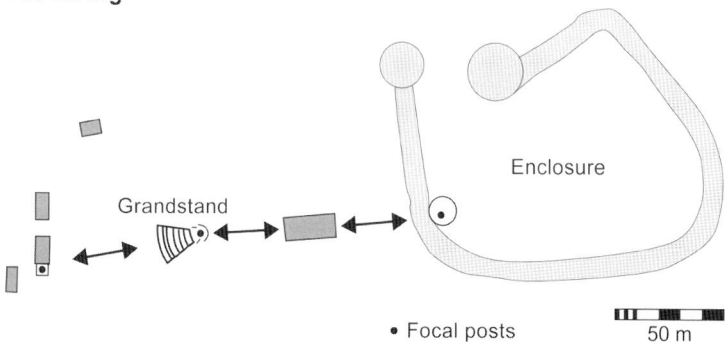

• Focal posts   50 m

Fig. 29 *The alignment of timber buildings, the 'grandstand' and three massive posts in an early phase at Yeavering. The posts at either end of the alignment reused the positions of prehistoric monuments. Information from Hope-Taylor (1977), Blair (2018) and McBride (2020).*

earliest timber buildings were comparatively small and that during the first phases the main structure was a timber theatre or 'grandstand' which conformed to the same axis (Hope-Taylor 1977). The Great Halls were built afterwards, and this distinctive structure eventually went out of use. A building that was ideally suited for assemblies was replaced by a group of monumental structures which is sometimes interpreted as a palace.

It is difficult to establish the order in which buildings were used unless their positions were superimposed. Despite that problem McBride (2020) identifies important changes in the later uses of these sites. The halls were subdivided and they were sometimes separated from one another by a network of enclosures. At the same time the later structures were less substantial than their predecessors and less effort went into building them. This was particularly true at Yeavering where a 'theatre' suitable for open air assemblies sems to have been abandoned and there was more emphasis on the interiors of the halls. Access to certain areas was controlled and the balance between public and private spaces may have changed. It will be important to decide whether this development was peculiar to this particular site or whether it reflected a wider trend. At present too much rests on the evidence of air photographs and new excavations are needed.

Discussion

The account of Scandinavian structures was organised around four themes. Do the same ideas apply to the Great Houses in Anglo-Saxon Britain?

There were some striking similarities, but there were also differences which make any direct comparison problematical. There seems no doubt that the monumental buildings in both regions drew on simpler domestic buildings for their prototypes. Although they might have made occasional references to the Roman world, their models were more local, and for that reason their detailed designs did not have very much in common. The features that they did share – their elongated ground plans and unusual scale – were outweighed by the contrasts between them. Both groups were occupied by an elite and might have been used (at least on some occasions) as public buildings. They may even have been employed in similar ways, but they represent a *common concept* rather than a single *type* (Walker 2010). That is why the account of Heorot would have been comprehensible to an Anglo-Saxon audience, no matter where *Beowulf* was set, or when it was composed.

Two themes have more application to the Scandinavian sites than their British counterparts. One is warfare. Apart from the Staffordshire Hoard (Fern *et al.* 2020), there is no collection of Anglo-Saxon metalwork that compares with the deposits of war booty in Northern Europe. While John Naylor (2015) shows that there were weapons in British rivers, they occur in smaller numbers than those of the Bronze Age and Iron Age. In the same way, although battles are documented in historical sources, the people buried with swords, spears, and shields show surprisingly few injuries inflicted in combat and Heinrich Härke (1990) argues that it may be wrong to identify them as 'warriors'; the symbolism of military conflict could have been as important as its practice. It is not clear how many Anglo-Saxon halls were set on fire, but it seems to have happened at Yeavering.

This account also considered control over long-distance trade, but in this case the most compelling evidence comes from sites near the English coast. That is not to say that this process was unimportant – its significance is clearly shown by the contents of Anglo-Saxon graves – but it seems to have had little influence on the development of Great Halls, some of which were outside the regions with much portable wealth. Of course, there is a famous exception that proves the rule, for the complex at Rendlesham was close to the barrow cemetery at Sutton Hoo (Carver 2005). The same relationship is present in the upper Thames valley (McBride 2020) but it may not have extended into the north and west.

The strongest link between the Anglo-Saxon and Scandinavian traditions was the significance attached to the past. It is most evident in the attention paid to older monuments, whose siting influenced the layout of later buildings and even the decision to erect them in a particular place. Ancient burial mounds seem to have been especially important and their forms may have been copied in building earthworks of the same type. At Lejre one group of halls incorporated a Bronze Age barrow and others were erected near a newly constructed mound. If the use of ancient features recalls the organisation of Yeavering or Sutton Courtenay, there was an important difference between the sequences in Britain and Scandinavia. In Northern Europe, Great Halls assumed the roles of other sacred locations, but there is less evidence of votive deposits in the Anglo-Saxon landscape. Here the *physical* traces of the past exercised more influence over later generations.

Exactly the same was true in Ireland.

Epilogue: the reinvention of Irish royal centres

It is worth returning to some of the sites introduced in previous chapters. Their field archaeology is well documented by excavation, survey and remote sensing, but it has been difficult to relate the results to the literary sources that refer to these places. Much of the fieldwork indicates a context in the pre-Roman and Roman Iron Ages, but the historical evidence suggests an active role in the later first millennium AD.

Whatever the circumstances in which they were written down, these texts include elements that cannot refer to the period established by excavation. They were influenced by Classical sources which were not accessible until later, and they also reveal a knowledge of the Bible. Similarly, the descriptions found in these accounts do not refer to the artefacts of the Irish Iron Age (Mallory 2016, 229–53). Instead they describe elements that can only be matched in early medieval contexts. As Chapter One has indicated, the one significant exception is the presence of enormous roundhouses which flourished from the second century BC and went out of use during the Roman Iron Age. Even then, the size of domestic dwellings was a measure of social position in the laws of the eighth century AD.

It is worth considering when the historical sources first appeared. According to Patrick Gleeson (2012 & 2020) the texts were composed or written down when Ireland was emerging from a period of fragmentation. During the first century BC the landscape had been dominated by a limited number of large and distinctive earthworks, palisaded enclosures and monumental buildings, although local centres certainly existed at the time. After the second century AD it split into petty kingdoms. There was a complex hierarchy of rulers, and many small political units. By the eighth century AD, and possibly before, a new power structure had developed and larger polities became increasingly significant. The Hill of Tara, which had played such a major part in the prehistoric period, regained its dominant position. But now it happened in a very different context.

It would be easy to suppose that all the features on that site conformed to a single layout, for this was how they were viewed by the first antiquarians. The same idea might apply to its counterparts at Knockaulin, Rathcroghan and Uisneach which include a similar range of earthworks. Fieldwork has established that some of them were already ancient by the later first millennium AD, but that does not imply that all the structures were built in the prehistoric period. Is it possible to distinguish a second generation of monuments at these sites, and could they be associated with renewed activities during an early medieval phase? That is Gleeson's contention, and it has much in its favour.

Several components have not provided any evidence of an Iron Age date, but others originated during a later period (Fig. 30). The most prominent element was the ringfort: a distinctive kind of circular enclosure that occurs in great numbers in Ireland and is usually dated between AD 600 and 850 (Stout 1997). It is generally interpreted as an independent farm whose status was displayed by its material wealth and by the width of its earthwork boundary. The histories of these monuments included a period in which glass vessels and fine pottery were brought to high status sites from mainland Europe, together with their contents which included foodstuffs, spices and wine (Campbell 2007). The same locations provide evidence of specialised metalworking. Another element identified by Gleeson (2020) is the stepped mound which could be formed by adapting an older

Hill of Tara

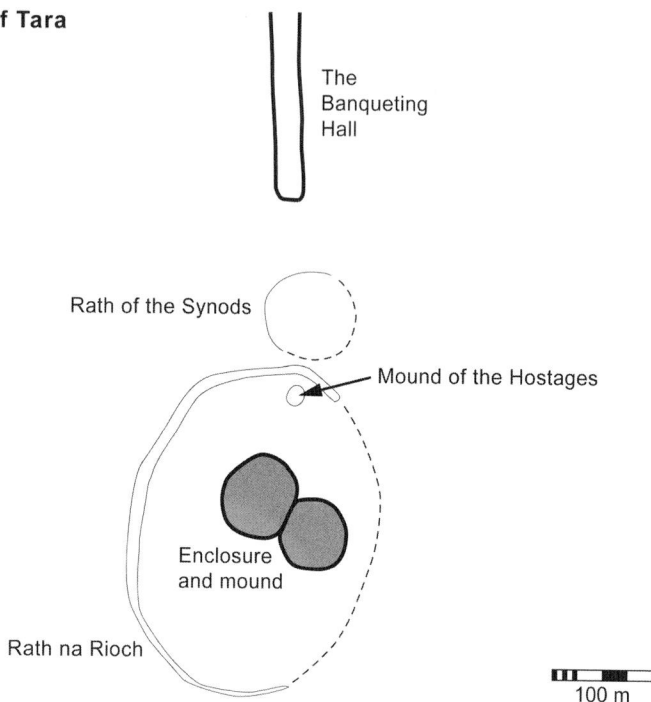

Fig. 30 The early medieval monuments on the Hill of Tara in relation to the earlier structures on the same site. Information from Schot et al. *(2016) and Gleeson (2020).*

structure. Here the clearest evidence comes from Knowth where the main chambered tomb was treated in this way. It was used for burials during the seventh and eighth centuries AD and the Neolithic entrance passages were reopened. It is documented as another royal capital (Eogan 2012).

These two elements are important as they could be combined to create a distinctive structure in which an enclosure resembling a ring-fort was joined to a prominent mound in a figure-of-eight formation. This arrangement is found at several sites. It was not exclusive to the royal centres identified in insular sources but is a conspicuous feature of the major complex at Rathcroghan (Waddell *et al.* 2009). The same configuration is found in the middle of the Rath na Rioch at Tara, where the initial structure of the mound could have been older (Gleeson 2020). A variant of this pattern is recorded at Uisneach where two conjoined enclosures at Rathnew adopted the same plan (Macalister & Praeger 1928). The combination of two kinds of earthwork recalls a design that had already been important in the Iron Age, but that need not pose a problem as the outlines of the main enclosures at Tara would still have been visible on the ground. In a sense the monument at Knowth combined these elements in a different way, for here two concentric ditches like those of a ringfort redefined the existing Neolithic mound. This was not an ordinary settlement, as the domestic buildings on its summit date from a later phase (Eogan 2012).

The Hill of Tara shared another kind of earthwork with Knockaulin and Uisneach. This is the earthwork avenue of the kind described, rather obscurely, as a 'royal droveway'. The best-known example was the 'Banqueting Hall' which was aligned on the Rath of the Synods, the Mound of the Hostages and the Rath na Rioch. It has never been dated but is similar to an earthwork with royal associations on another site, 20 km away. This feature was at Teltown and had a complex history (M. O'Brien & Waddell 2018). Although it may have originated during the prehistoric period, it achieved its final form in the ninth or tenth centuries AD. That is likely to have implications for the age of its counterpart at Tara. Similar earthworks led to other royal centres and could have been associated with their renaissance during the early medieval period.

Great mounds, ditched roadways and ringforts were the main additions to the ancient sites. Like their counterparts elsewhere in Ireland, the enclosures might have contained houses, but it is possible that they were employed on special occasions. That must be determined by excavation. Remote sensing in the Rathcroghan complex located a large structure inside a circular enclosure on top of the mound of Rathmore, but its diameter (15 m) is much less than those of the Iron Age Great Houses (Waddell *et al.* 2009, 66–79). A similar earthwork at Deer Park Farm was used between the seventh and tenth centuries

AD (Lynn & McDowell 2011), and another building 16 m in diameter has been identified inside Navan Fort and tentatively dated between AD 400 and 700 (O'Driscoll *et al.* 2020).

There is documentary evidence that the mounds were used for royal inaugurations: a practice that continued into the high medieval period. Elizabeth Fitzpatrick's (2004) study of this practice shows that it took place at prehistoric round barrows and natural features, as well as newly constructed earthworks. Many inauguration mounds were associated with other kinds of monuments. At Tara, which became associated with the High Kings of Ireland, the ceremony may have involved a procession to the hilltop from the royal crannog of Lagore 5 km away (Newman 2011). It led up the embanked avenue aligned on the Rath of the Synods. The presence of prehistoric monuments along the route emphasised the antiquity and authority of the ceremony. For the first time in their histories these 'centres' might have been truly 'royal'.

All these places feature in early Irish sources and many would have been well known from the tales of gods and heroes in the Ulster Cycle. They were set in the past but played a vital role in the politics of the early medieval period. This is not the place to discuss the details of these texts which have inspired many generations of research. Their sources and veracity remain in question and so does their relevance to the Irish Iron Age, but there is one genre that encapsulates many of these issues.

This is the *Dinnshenchas* which is sometimes defined as 'the lore of places' (Schlüter 2017). It recorded the traditions associated with Irish place names and showed how they came into being. One of the best known is an early medieval poem 'Tara noblest of hills' which described the earthworks that could be recognised on the site. It identified them with locations mentioned in the heroic tales, and it cited their names. The text referred to a series of ancient monuments and explained their relationship to one another on the ground. The details were so precise that nearly 200 years ago George Petrie (1839) was able to identify them during his survey of the site.

Why was the poem composed? Tara had long been considered as the seat of kings: a place which was used for public assemblies and the inauguration of rulers. For a while it was controlled by the southern Uí Néils, but by the eleventh century AD their influence was waning. By emphasising the significance of the hill the court poet could advance their claims to a distinguished history (Bhreathnach 1993 & 1999). The poem interpreted the remains on the Hill of Tara in relation to the narratives preserved in the ancient texts. Taken together, they provided an origin myth that combined literary sources with physical remains. By associating the Hill of Tara with the Uí Néils' political agenda, the *dinnshenchas* emphasised the age of the surviving monuments. As so often happens, the methods of field archaeology were used for political ends.

Summary

This chapter has studied some conceptions of the Great House in three different regions of Europe and considered how they varied from place to place. It also investigated developments that overlapped in time, although the local sequences contrasted with one another and were of entirely different lengths. The most extended was in Northern Europe and the briefest was in Britain. Unlike these developments, the histories of the Irish monuments were discontinuous. Similar distinctions applied to the lives of the buildings themselves. These structures were more durable in Scandinavia and short-lived in Anglo-Saxon England. Although they were frequently replaced, in Britain that process extended for only a century, while in Northern Europe it lasted for considerably longer. None of this applies to the Irish evidence where the idea of a monumental dwelling played a part in national literature many years after such structures had gone out of use. Here the Iron Age buildings were massively material and their early medieval counterparts were largely imaginary; they were a product of the 'Irish Dreamtime' (Mallory 2016). The North European halls were imposing and monumental, but when the last examples were built, their equivalents in Ireland had become the subject of legends. The only feature that all these buildings shared – a characteristic that distinguishes them from most of their successors – is that they were constructed of wood rather than stone.

Their functions were almost equally diverse. The Scandinavian examples may have played more roles than the majority of their British counterparts. They were elite residences, but they also doubled as temples and military bases. In that guise they played a role in a process of raiding and warfare, and it could be the reason why so many of them were set on fire. Less can be said about the Great Halls in Anglo-Saxon England. Perhaps they were used mainly on special occasions. Unlike their counterparts in Northern Europe, few produce large collections of artefacts. It seems likely that they were the sites of assemblies and were visited by their owners on an occasional basis. Several sites may have been gifted to the church when the Christian religion was adopted. The same model does not apply to their Scandinavian counterparts where the Conversion happened significantly later (Sanmark 2004).

In principle, the Irish sequence could have followed the same course as events in Anglo-Saxon England, for the new religion was adopted so widely that the early medieval phase is sometimes called the 'Early Christian' period. Instead, the main role of the royal sites was ceremonial and it is not clear whether many people lived there. Again assemblies were important and these sites were where new rulers began their reigns. Their authority depended on the power of myth, and that is why so many ancient monuments were reused. They were provided with a new history.

Building societies: a summary and some conclusions

Chapter Eight provides a modest restatement of the case. It does not advance any dogmatic conclusions. Instead it emphasises the main developments identified in this book and speculates on their significance.

The forms of Great Houses

The book began by describing the striking similarities between Neolithic and early medieval halls in Britain. It also considered the resemblance between other Neolithic buildings and the enormous Iron Age structures at the Irish royal centres. Although the chronological confusions have been resolved, the creation of such massive edifices still remains a problem. They resembled the domestic dwellings of the same periods, but were conceived on a monumental scale. In the absence of a more exact term, they have been characterised as Great Houses, and Chapter Two considered further examples with a wide distribution across space and time. The same sites will feature here, although they represent only a sample of an even more general phenomenon. It is obvious that they illustrate a recurrent idea in ancient Europe. Although they share structural features in common, it is surprising how many of them were employed in similar ways, and it seems possible that they were erected in comparable circumstances. Some of those developments are considered here.

Great Houses must be identified on a regional basis, for such structures often formed part of a continuum with its origins among the local domestic buildings. For instance, the Great Halls of Anglo-Saxon England have features in common with those in Northern Europe, and both were monumental versions of ordinary dwellings. But they were conceived on different scales from one another and many of the insular examples were only half the size of their Scandinavian counterparts. Similarly, the biggest circular buildings in the royal centres of Navan and Knockaulin were more than twice the diameters of the structures at Thetford and Stanwick with which they have been compared.

Subject to that qualification, all the buildings considered in the book had physical features in common. If the most obvious elements were their exceptional scale and the ways in which their forms were inspired by domestic architecture, they shared other characteristics, too. There were cases in which successive structures were precisely superimposed. The excavated evidence suggested that each of them was used for an unusually short period of time. Their internal organisation was equally distinctive and again it set them apart from their prototypes. The internal space might be rearranged in order to provide more subdivisions. Examples include Early Neolithic halls in Scotland and some of the Late Neolithic longhouses in France. Alternatively, the interior had one major room which could be considered as a hall in its own right. That was true of the largest Iron Age buildings in Scandinavia which did not include the byres associated with ordinary dwellings. Another feature was a preference for building in wood, even where suitable stone was available.

These features make it easy to recognise the distinctive nature of Great Houses, but this account leaves out some of their most striking characteristics. Several examples approached the limits of what could be achieved at the time. Their construction made exceptional demands and there was a risk that they would collapse. It also put strains on the supply of timber. They became increasingly difficult to roof, and there are cases in which it is not certain whether an excavated building was covered or left open. The same limitation applies to both round and rectangular structures, and it is why they seldom exceeded a certain size. In particular, longhouses of any date had about the same widths; where that threshold was passed they were exceptional. The same limitation did not apply to their lengths which were very varied. The sizes of the posts suggest that certain structures had an upper floor. This would have increased the amount of usable space inside them. It was also the case with Scottish brochs, but this arrangement was not so common among ordinary dwellings. There could have been a contrast between their outward appearance and their internal organisation. The isolated Únětice longhouse at Dermsdorf might have looked like those in settlements, but it had three aisles rather than the usual two.

Not all the models were local. There were cases in which prehistoric buildings were modelled on exotic prototypes. That was particularly true in the pre-Roman Iron Age when the halls at Mont Lassois drew on a Mediterranean model and the largest structures at Silchester resembled those in northern France. In other cases such influences were just as decisively rejected. Thus people in lowland Scotland modelled their most elaborate buildings on the stone towers established further to the north rather than styles of architecture associated with the expanding Roman world. The same process is illustrated by the great roundhouses at Stanwick and Thetford which were built close to the time of the Conquest, and more obviously by the enormous circular structures associated with Irish royal centres.

One feature connects a number of buildings discussed in this account. The rectangular structures were frequently aligned on the position of the sun at the turning points of the year. The commonest relationship was with the midsummer sunrise and midwinter sunset. This is illustrated by the Late Neolithic longhouses south of the River Loire, the Bronze Age longhouse at Dermsdorf, and the Iron Age layout of Silchester. North of the Loire a similar convention meant that Late Neolithic buildings acknowledged the positions of the midsummer sunset and the midwinter sunrise. An alternative was the use of cardinal alignments, and this was the practice with Viking halls in Norway. These orientations seem to have been more important than the directions of the prevailing winds. As a result the largest examples were vulnerable. Circular structures also acknowledged the direction of the sunrise, so it is revealing when their orientation was reversed.

Assuming they were roofed, the lack of light inside the enormous buildings at Navan Fort and Rathcroghan might have emphasised their special character.

Lastly, there was a contrast between Great Houses that were built in isolation and others which formed part of a more varied group of buildings. In some cases they could have been the focal point of a settlement. Examples include: Late Neolithic sites in Orkney and northern and western France; some of the royal centres in Ireland; and the largest structures of the Scandinavian Iron Age. Two additional features emphasised the distinction between them and ordinary dwellings. They could be accessed along formal entranceways like those at Durrington Walls in the Neolithic period, Knockaulin and Rathcroghan in the Iron Age, and Tara in the first millennium AD. Alternatively they might be located inside special enclosures, for instance those at Lejre and Tissö.

The uses of Great Houses

A common practice was the provision of feasts. They feature in written accounts, but the clearest evidence comes from excavated contexts containing faunal remains, special plant foods, and evidence of alcoholic drinks. The residues of feasts were deposited with some formality, and the material extends from the fillings of the subterranean buildings at Göbekli Tepe to the concentrations of burnt rocks and animal bones at Lejre.

A second was craft production. Although the activities of smiths are well documented in early literature, the archaeological evidence can be given equal weight. In this case it extends from the final working of Grand Pressigny daggers in France to the making of garnet jewellery in an excavated hall at Gamla Uppsala. The status of the products is evident from the funerary record. Artefacts of similar kinds were imported and were distributed in and around these buildings. This was a feature of the Iron Age and there is particularly striking evidence from Silchester and Gudme. The dispersed distribution of farms, workshops and sacred places around the latter site resembles the organisation of *oppida* during the late pre-Roman period (Moore & Ponroy 2014).

Historical sources document some activities in greater detail than archaeology can provide. Great Halls were used for assemblies and royal inaugurations, but the material evidence was comparatively limited. The most convincing elements were the stepped mound at Knowth and the 'grandstand' at Yeavering. People might have come from far away and there were indications that animals were introduced on special occasions; isotopic evidence has shown that some had been brought long distances. There was similar evidence from Durrington Walls in the Neolithic period and Navan Fort in the Iron Age (Madgwick *et al.* 2019a; 2019b). Another clue is provided by pollen analysis. Despite the enormous number of buildings at Nebelivka, studies of samples collected just outside its perimeter showed that the presence of these structures had little impact on the environment: the use of this place must have been occasional or short lived. That was why the excavators called the largest buildings 'assembly houses'. There was similar evidence from the royal centre at Navan, for it was established during the period when sediments in the nearby lake show a *decrease* in human activity. The site was obviously outside the main area of settlement. It seems likely that people went there on special occasions.

Another common activity was documented by excavation. This was the practice of setting wooden buildings on fire. It is unlikely to have one explanation but was a consistent feature of many of the sites considered here: from Nebelivka to Navan Fort, and from Mont Lassois to Gamla Uppsala. It may have two explanations, apart from accidents. One is that certain kinds of structure had to be burnt once their period of use was over. It applied to the domestic buildings of the Trypillia Culture as well as those at the mega-sites, and it was also true of houses and other structures in Neolithic Britain and Ireland. Although the early halls were ignited, the same process extended to long barrows and cursus monuments.

A different procedure was widely documented at the Great Halls of the first millennium AD. They were burnt down on a regular basis and certain structures experienced this treatment on several occasions. Perhaps the building was considered to embody the people who used it. The presence of burnt human remains and weapons at a site like Uppåkra suggests they were deliberately targeted. Like the sacrificial deposits of the first millennium AD, these places provide evidence of raiding and warfare. It is obvious that power centres were attacked and destroyed.

Other elements were documented at a smaller number of sites. One was the presence of *men's houses* of the kind described by Flannery and Marcus (2014). Although this is an ethnographic category, the interpretation is consistent with a number of literary sources: the epic poem *Beowulf*, the Ulster Cycle, and Adam of Bremen's account of Gamla Uppsala. The archaeological evidence is much more limited, but it might include the role of The Garrison at Birka. Meller (2019) extended the idea to the Bronze Age longhouse at Dermsdorf, but its application depends on whether the artefacts associated with the building were weapons rather than tools.

Another widespread pattern was for Great Houses to be associated with smaller structures interpreted as cult houses. Alternatively, the halls themselves served a variety of functions and the principal space inside them may have played that role. It seems to be the implication of Adam's description of Gamla Uppsala. There were several examples of large halls accompanied by ancillary buildings. There was a possible shrine beside the Iron Age example at Silchester, and during the first millennium AD this became a widespread pattern. It was commonest in Scandinavia. Those at Lejre and Uppåkra are documented in detail, and in each case the putative shrines were associated with metalwork, glass vessels and human remains. The temple at Uppåkra also contained images of Odin and Thor. There the case is unambiguous, but at Yeavering it has been difficult to distinguish between pagan and Christian buildings on the site. Similar problems have arisen elsewhere in Anglo-Saxon England. Perhaps this is not surprising as Pope Gregory instructed his missionaries to transform pagan shrines into Christian place of worship (Helena Hamerow pers. comm.).

The assemblages associated with Great Houses were often distinctive. They took two forms. Sometimes they featured fewer artefacts than the settlements of the same date. This applied to most of the Early Neolithic halls in Britain, some of their Late Neolithic equivalents in France, and a number of Anglo-Saxon examples. There was little to suggest sustained use or occupation. These assemblages had a specialised character; quantities of fine pottery were associated with Neolithic buildings that contained few lithic artefacts. By contrast, later halls could have exceptional contents, including the Attic pottery at Mont Lassois and the rich collections from Gudme, Rendlesham and Uppåkra. In South Scandinavia these collections became more common with time. It was not always possible to distinguish between items discarded during the use of these sites and offerings intended to sustain the buildings themselves. The latter assumed a growing significance during the first millennium AD and were quite different from the collections associated with other sites.

The histories of Great Houses

Some of these complexes shared a distinctive history. One of the most obvious features was the attention paid to the surviving fabric of the past. It also extended to places whose sacred character is indicated by their names; Gudme and Helgö are the most obvious examples. There were two phases in which the presence of ancient monuments was a significant factor. One was during the Irish Iron Age when the complexes described as royal centres were organised around the remains of chambered tombs and barrows. The best-known evidence comes from the Boyne Valley and the Hill of Tara. The same process was followed in the early medieval period when it took two forms. At sites like Yeavering, Lyminge and Lejre the presence of prehistoric structures influenced the layout of the buildings, but this was not a feature of every site. In Ireland, on the other hand, the sequence was even more complex. Not only were Neolithic and Bronze Age features incorporated in the early medieval layout, the same was true of the monuments erected there during the Iron Age. By the end of the first millennium AD it seems unlikely that anyone could distinguish between the different generations of structures on these sites.

Other developments were important but took place less often. Mounds might be constructed over the remains of buildings that had played a special role in the past. It happened with a small number of earlier prehistoric houses in Denmark and something similar is evidenced at Navan Fort in Ireland. During the first millennium AD the same practice was followed at a few sites in Scandinavia. It was less common in Britain where the outlines of Neolithic structures could be commemorated by settings of monoliths.

Finally, the past importance of these places was celebrated in literary sources, but they pose many problems as they were written down many years later and their accounts are anachronistic. It is clear that the Ulster Cycle was a creation of the later first millennium AD even though it referred to places whose importance was established in the Iron Age. These texts provide an invented history, recorded because it played a role in the politics of a later period. So did the Irish *dinnshenchas* which included a famous description of the monuments on the Hill of Tara. The poem added lustre to the Uí Néil dynasty at a time when its power was failing. Adam's account of Gamla Uppsala may have had a similar character, for he described the hall at Uppsala as if it was still in use. Excavation suggests that it had been destroyed long before his time. In this case his intentions were obvious, as he wished to rid the place of its pagan associations.

Palaces?

A few sites discussed in earlier chapters were explicitly described as palaces, either in historical sources or by the people who investigated them. Palaces of some kind feature in Irish texts, and have been discussed in archaeological accounts of Mont Lassois, where this view was favoured, and Gallows Hill, Thetford, where it was rejected. The term carries certain connotations, for it can imply a residence rather than a temporary power base. The archaeological evidence is frequently ambiguous. Were particular buildings inhabited, or were they reserved for use on public occasions? If someone did live there, were they occupied continuously? It is known that early medieval rulers travelled between different places, staying on an occasional basis. Even if particular structures, or groups of structures, were occupied at intervals, that idea does not exclude the possibility that other parts of the same complexes had a different history. They may have been used by a caretaker population and could have been more like ordinary settlements. That is why the distinction between isolated halls and those with lesser buildings is significant.

In any case this formulation leaves out what might have been their most important characteristic. If the presence of a local leader was one factor, another was that of the people ruled. Assemblies played an important role in ancient Europe. They were where the population gathered on an occasional basis and where communal business was carried out. Decisions were made, laws were enacted, leaders were chosen, and Irish sources show they were where rulers were inaugurated. These questions are usually studied by historians and place name scholars, but recently they have engaged the interest of archaeologists, and new kinds of research are under way (Pantos & Semple 2003). Examples include the Óenach Project in Ireland (Gleeson 2018) and two special volumes of the *Journal of the North Atlantic* (Sanmark *et al.* 2013 & 2015). It is clear that such gatherings were not restricted to monumental houses. The point is illustrated by Adam McBride's interpretation of Yeavering in which one of the first medieval structures was a wooden theatre. In his view the Great Halls were built afterwards (McBride 2020).

If certain structures were occupied as leaders journeyed from site to site, there could have been particular times of year when people would gather. They may have included midwinter and midsummer, and in Irish society they focused on the four festivals that punctuated the agricultural cycle. Their antiquity is uncertain, but such considerations must have been important during the earlier prehistoric period. Wooden buildings and other monuments were commonly used at the solstices, and the Neolithic animal bones from Durrington Walls suggest that feasts concentrated around the shortest days of the year.

Whether the main uses of Great Houses were residential or administrative, continuous or intermittent, there can be no mistaking their special status. They stand out from other buildings through their scales, their complex designs, and the amount of labour required for their construction. Sometimes the raw materials were difficult to access. The work could be dangerous and time consuming, and it needed coordination and skill. In certain cases – but by no means all – the special status of the halls was reflected by the artefacts deposited when the project began.

The management of public events might have changed its character over time. They could have been controlled by emerging elites, so that what were originally public assemblies, linked to ritual observance, were increasingly directed by special interests. Perhaps social divisions became more explicit and eventually led to conflict. This model is proposed to explain the emergence of Iron Age *oppida* (Wendling & Winger 2014; Fernández Götz 2018). In any case the adoption of monumental buildings was only one part of a wider process. Another was the provision of rich burials. It is illustrated at several places which have featured in this account: Dermsdorf, Skrydstrup, Mont Lassois, Lejre and Gamla Uppsala.

Temporary palaces

If it is too simple to describe many of these structures as 'palaces', were they temporary constructions? Where absolute dates are available, they show that certain buildings were used for surprisingly short periods. That certainly applies to the first timber halls in Scotland, which were confined at a single phase, and to the entire complex at Durrington Walls whose history spanned less than half a century. Something similar is suggested by other excavated evidence. A succession of figure-of-eight structures was preserved beneath the great mound at Navan. Fieldwork showed that at least four examples were erected in sequence over the course of a century. The replacement of halls on Scandinavian sites might have been almost as rapid and in some cases they followed one another in virtually the same positions.

At Lejre they even employed the same postholes as their predecessors. People must have accepted that timber buildings were unlikely to remain intact for long. Timber would decay and there was a risk of fires. Indeed there is plenty of evidence that they were destroyed deliberately.

The chronologies of Great Houses can show sudden peaks and troughs. Among the biggest structures were those inside henges in Britain. They date from the middle of the third millennium BC. Their precursors were considerably smaller, and the same is true of the buildings that followed them. Within the limits of radiocarbon dating, their history coincides with a short period in which other large monuments were built. This development ran in parallel with the use of enormous longhouses in the north and west of France, but here there was a striking difference. If there is little to suggest a sudden increase in their size or rate of construction, their demise was rapid. They went out of use over a short period and were replaced by small structures of a completely different kind. It would be worth investigating their chronology in more detail.

The same applies to the royal centres in Ireland, whose dating is disputed, and to the Great Halls in England which are assigned to the seventh century AD. Were their creation and abandonment equally abrupt, or might they have been spread over a longer period? Again a sustained programme of scientific dating is needed to find this out. At present one important contrast is obvious. The Anglo-Saxon buildings had a much shorter history than their Scandinavian counterparts whose chronology extended over most of the first millennium AD. If the sequences at such sites had anything in common, it was the frequency with which individual structures were erected and replaced. Another contrast may be equally informative. Great Halls in Northern Europe were increasingly robust and even took special forms (the bow-sided buildings are the obvious example). They contrast with the excavated structures at Yeavering which became less massive over time. Some of the buildings considered in this book were used on a temporary basis, but that need not apply to them all.

Reasons for building Great Houses

In what circumstances did Great Houses appear and disappear? It is surprising to find that the same elements were important in several instances and that they featured in different periods and different parts of Europe. The details of these cases were reviewed in the last three chapters and only the clearest examples are referred to here.

The most obvious factor was the exposure of local communities to influences from other regions. They could take several forms and had various consequences. These processes included phases of settlement and the adoption of different ways of producing food. They were the main features at the beginning of the Neolithic period in Britain which involved the introduction of domesticated plants to an island where their natural prototypes were absent. They also extended to the new strains of cattle and pigs and the first exploitation of sheep and goats. Still more important, new resources were introduced by settlers from the Continent along with unfamiliar beliefs and a distinctive material culture. Chapter Five suggested that the erection of Great Houses in Scotland was one of the ways in which new communities formed in an unfamiliar setting.

The most convincing evidence of settlement by immigrant farmers is provided by ancient DNA. The same method documents a phase of population change in the mid- to late third millennium BC. This was associated with Bell Beakers and the earliest metalwork. Again it saw the construction of timber buildings, but in this case the relationship between these processes was less direct. In Britain and Ireland settlement from Continental Europe impacted on a network that featured henges, stone circles and rock art; it also extended to the forms of domestic dwellings and those of timber monuments that used them as their model. As the two traditions came into contact there was a dramatic increase in the scale of buildings of an entirely insular form. They might have been intended as a restatement of indigenous beliefs. The opposite development happened in France where a tradition of enormous longhouses was abandoned in the face of similar pressures.

The same process was followed in other cases. In Ireland a different kind of network was associated with the adoption of La Tène metalwork from the Continent. The influence of these new contacts was held in check for at least 200 years as the local inhabitants asserted traditional norms by erecting roundhouses of a long-established kind. These buildings were constructed on a greater scale than before. While artefacts of exotic kinds circulated across large parts of the island, they rarely appeared in similar contexts to those in neighbouring countries; the only exceptions were the deposits placed in water. Perhaps public architecture allowed local polities to express their resistance to influences from outside. That process was maintained for some time after the Roman conquest of Britain.

These cases suggest two common scenarios. Great Houses were generally built during periods of culture contact. Some of these developments were sudden, but others were less abrupt, and only a few can be considered as crises. Either new styles of architecture were adopted rapidly, as if to acknowledge the impact of the wider world, or they were decisively rejected and traditional forms of building were constructed on a larger scale. The main exception was in Scandinavia where similar buildings were erected throughout the first millennium AD.

The clearest case in which monumental structures developed rapidly was in Early Neolithic Scotland where timber halls of considerable proportions were associated with some of the earliest finds of cereals and fine pottery. Although it is difficult to identify a single model for the new buildings, they have counterparts in Ireland and on the Continent. It is not the only case in which such a relationship can be identified. It is possible that the same approach can be taken to the introduction of Early Bronze Age metalwork to Denmark where the largest longhouses built around 2000 BC have similar features to those of the Únětice Culture in Central Europe (Nielsen 2019).

There were also Iron Age examples. The most impressive buildings on Mont Lassois were influenced by Mediterranean architecture: a connection that was emphasised by the presence of Attic pottery in the Great House, and the form and contents of the nearby burial at Vix. In the same way, the plan of Iron Age Silchester drew on sources of inspiration in France, and its inhabitants received imported artefacts, food and wine from the European mainland. These examples are quoted because they conformed to wider patterns recognised during these phases.

This perspective is equally relevant to the Roman and post-Roman Iron Ages of Scandinavia when this region participated in long-distance trade through sites like Gudme and Helgö. The scale of these connections is well known, and there is evidence that their inhabitants engaged in craft production on a significant scale. It is equally clear that massive wooden buildings were erected, but their forms raise an interesting problem. They drew on a style of architecture that extended back many years, but in some cases their scale was new. It is a moot point how much the Great Hall at the centre of the Gudme complex owed to local traditions and how far its monumental appearance was inspired by structures in the Roman world.

The same problem arises with the Great Halls of Anglo-Saxon England. Here the evidence is particularly complex. These buildings monumentalised a kind of domestic architecture introduced by settlers who had crossed the North Sea more than a century earlier; it seems to have owed less to insular Roman buildings. At the same time the *idea* of erecting structures of such size and elaboration must have been suggested by contacts during the seventh century AD when the movement of precious objects was at its height. In this case people may have emulated structures in Northern Europe, but only after they had been established there for a long time. To a traveller between these regions the difference between these monumental houses could have been as striking as their similarities.

It seems as if communities emulated exotic styles of building just as they acquired exotic artefacts. They were equally likely to maintain a distance and even to amplify the contrast between traditional practice and new beliefs and social conventions. A curious feature is that both relationships placed the same emphasis on real or invented pasts. By the early Middle Ages the Irish royal centres were organised around two series of ancient monuments: one extending from the Neolithic to the Iron Age, and the other dating from the later first millennium AD. In this case certain elements might have been long-lived: an emphasis on circular outlines and figure-of-eight constructions. In the same way the complexes at Yeavering and Lejre incorporated the remains of ancient monuments, but there was an important difference. There was nothing in common between their plans and those of the Great Halls on these sites. Newly established elites may have tried to legitimise their status by referring to a distant past – that is the lesson of the Irish literature – but these traditions were invented for the purpose.

Great Houses and Great Halls were built for many reasons.

The symbolism of the Great House

If these buildings were constructed at times of sudden change, why did people choose domestic structures as their model? Other impressive monuments were erected at the same time – burial mounds and stone settings – but the house was generally the commonest point of reference.

Another question arises. Why were such monumental houses built at such specific times? The simplest answer is also the most satisfactory. They provided an appropriate metaphor for a group of people who considered that they shared important bonds in common; that is what Marshall Sahlins (2013) meant by 'mutuality of being'. They represented themselves as a single community – a 'household' – and that explains the title of this chapter. By building Great Houses, people were also building societies. In fact they were doing two very different things. Often they were committing themselves to a common project and a new set of relationships, or they were reinforcing their existing links in the face of outside pressures. As Matthew Spriggs (2008) observed, it is not a matter of identifying social types. Much depends on comparing local sequences with one another.

It is worth recalling a model proposed by John Cherry over forty years ago, for it retains its validity. He argued that monuments were a feature of two main periods (Cherry 1978). They could be built when societies were in a formative stage. Their construction played a part in establishing a new kind of community. It engaged people in a common enterprise: one that made extraordinary demands. The metaphor of the House makes perfect sense in this context, although it is questionable whether Lévi-Strauss was right to recognise a single kind of society.

In any case Cherry's analysis identified another situation in which monumental structures were built. When established structures were threatened similar projects were organised. They were intended to reinforce links between people that were in danger of being undermined. This was not a new initiative as its object was to reassert the traditional order. Great Houses could be a feature of this phase as well, and their creation was quite different from the breakdown of established relationships postulated by Lévi-Strauss. The monumental buildings documented by field archaeology are too varied to be compared with his '*sociétés à maison*'.

For millennia Great Houses provided one of the key symbols in ancient Europe. They were also among the most impressive physical structures built there. Inevitably, their study raises more questions than it can answer, but that is the problem with archaeology. All this book can claim is that it makes a case for studying these extraordinary buildings at an appropriate scale.

Bibliography

Adamsen, C. 2009. *Sorte Muld: Wealth, Power and Religion at an Iron Age Central Settlement on Bornholm*. Rønne: Bornholms Museum.

Alcock, L. 1995. *Cadbury Castle, Somerset: The Early Medieval Archaeology*. Cardiff: University of Wales Press.

Andersen, N. 2019. House sites under burial monuments in the Sarup area of south-west Funen. In L. Sparrevohn, O. Kastholm and P.O. Nielsen (eds), *Houses for the Living: Two-aisled Houses from the Neolithic and Early Bronze Age in Denmark*, 123–34. Copenhagen: University of Southern Denmark.

Andrén, A. 2014. *Tracing Old Norse Cosmology*. Lund: Nordic Academic Press.

Armit, I. 2003. *Towers in the North: The Brochs of Scotland*. Stroud: Tempus.

Armit, I. 2013. Objects and ideas: Roman influences at Tara and beyond. In M. O'Sullivan, C. Scarre and M. Doyle (eds), *Tara from the Past to the Future*, 288–94. Dublin: Wordwell.

Arnoldussen, S. 2008. *A Living Landscape. Bronze Age Settlement Sites in the Dutch River Area*. Leiden: Sidestone Press.

Arnoldussen, S. 2009. Dutch residential mobility: A commentary on the 'wandering farmstead' model. In A. Kren-Leeb, J. Beier, E. Classen, F. Falkenstein and S. Schwenzer (eds), *Mobilität, Migration und Kommunikation in Europa während des Neolithikums und der Bronzezeit*, 147–59. Langenweissbach: Beier & Berann Archäologische Fachliteratur.

Austin, M. 2017. *Anglo-Saxon 'Great Hall Complexes'. Elite Residence and Landscapes of Power in Early England, c. AD 550–700*. PhD thesis, University of Reading.

Ballin Smith, B. 1994. *Howe: Four Millennia of Orkney Prehistory*. Edinburgh: Society of Antiquaries of Scotland.

Banning, E. 2011. So fair a house: Göbekli Tepe and the identification of temples in the Pre-Pottery Neolithic of the Near East. *Current Anthropology* 52, 135–53.

Barclay, G., Brophy, K. and MacGregor, G. 2002. Claish, Stirling: An early Neolithic structure in its context. *Proceedings of the Society of Antiquaries of Scotland* 132, 65–137.

Bayliss, A. and Grogan, E. 2013. Chronologies for Tara and comparable royal sites of the Irish Iron Age. In M. O' Sullivan, C. Scarre and M. Doyle (eds), *Tara from the Past to the Future*, 105–44. Dublin: Wordwell.

Beck, A.S. 2017. *Assembling the House, Building a Home. The Late Iron Age Longhouse (500–1000 AD)*. Aarhus: Aarhus University.

Beck, R. (ed.) 2007a. *The Durable House: House Society Models in Archaeology*. Carbondale, IL: Southern Illinois University.

Beck, R. 2007b. The durable house: Material, metaphor, and structure. In R. Beck (ed.), *The Durable House: House Society Models in Archaeology*, 3–24. Carbondale, IL: Southern Illinois University.

Becker, C. 1971. 'Mosepotter' fra Danmarks jernalder: problemer omkring mosefundne lerkar og deres tolkning. *Arbøger* 1971, 5–60.

Becker, K. 2009. Iron Age Ireland – finding an invisible people. In G. Cooney, K. Becker, J. Coles, M. Ryan and S. Sievers (eds), *Relics of Old Decency. Archaeological Studies in Later Prehistory*, 351–61. Dublin: Wordwell.

Becker, K. 2019. Irish Iron Age settlements and society: Reframing Royal Sites. *Proceedings of the Prehistoric Society* 85, 273–306.

Bhreathnach, E. 1993. The topography of Tara: The documentary evidence. *Discovery Programme Reports* 2, 68–76.

Bhreathnach, E. 1999. Authority and supremacy in Tara and its hinterland. *Discovery Programme Reports* 5, 1–23.

Bickle, P. and Whittle, A. 2013. *The First Farmers of Central Europe: Diversity in LBK Lifeways*. Oxford: Oxbow.

Blair, J. 2005. *The Church in Anglo-Saxon Society*. Oxford: Oxford University Press.

Blair, J. 2018. *Building Anglo-Saxon England*. Princeton: Princeton University Press.

Blair, J., Rippon, S. and Smart, C. 2020. *Planning in the Early Medieval Landscape*. Liverpool: Liverpool University Press.

Booth, P., Champion, T., Foreman, S., Garwood, P., Glass, H., Munby, J. and Reynolds, A. 2011. *On Track: The Archaeology of High Speed 1 Section 1 in Kent*. Oxford: Oxford Archaeology.

Bradley, R. 2012. *The Idea of Order: The Circular Archetype in Prehistoric Europe*. Oxford: Oxford University Press.

Bradley, R. 2013a. Houses of commons, houses of lords: Domestic dwellings and monumental architecture in prehistoric Europe. *Proceedings of the Prehistoric Society* 79, 1–17.

Bradley, R. 2013b. Enclosures, mounds and great houses. In M. O' Sullivan, C. Scarre and M. Doyle (eds), *Tara from the Past to the Future*, 249–55. Dublin: Wordwell.

Bradley, R. 2016. Croftmoraig: The anatomy of a stone circle. In R. Bradley and C. Nimura (eds), *The Use and Reuse of Stone Circles*, 141–51. Oxford: Oxbow.

Bradley, R. 2017. *A Geography of Offerings. Deposits of Valuables in the Landscapes of Ancient Europe.* Oxford: Oxbow.

Bradley, R. 2019. *The Prehistory of Britain and Ireland*, 2nd edition. Cambridge: Cambridge University Press.

Bradley, R. 2020. Keeping order in the Stone Age. In D. Hofmann (ed.), *Magical, Mundane or Marginal? Deposition Practices in the Early Neolithic Linearbandkeramic Culture*, 227–37. Leiden: Sidestone Press.

Brennan, N. and Hamerow, H. 2015. An Anglo-Saxon Great Hall complex at Sutton Courtenay/Drayton, Oxfordshire. A royal centre of early Wessex? *Archaeological Journal* 172, 325–50.

Brennand, M. and Taylor, M. 2003. The survey and excavation of a Bronze Age timber circle at Holme-next-the Sea, Norfolk, 1998–9. *Proceedings of the Prehistoric Society* 69, 1–84.

Brereton, D. 2005. House society and practice theories illuminate American campsteads. *Anthropological Theory* 5, 135–53.

Brindley, A. 1999. Irish Grooved Ware. In R. Cleal and A. McSween (eds), *Grooved Ware in Britain and Ireland*, 23–35. Oxford: Oxbow.

Brophy, K. 2007. From big house to cult house: Early Neolithic timber halls in Scotland. *Proceedings of the Prehistoric Society* 73, 75–96.

Brossler, A., Early, R. and Allen, C. 2004. *Green Park, Phase 2 Excavations 1995.* Oxford: Oxford Archaeology.

Buchsenschutz, O. and Motsch, A. 2018. Réflexions sur l'architecture monumentale à la fin du premier âge du Fer. In A. Villard-Le Tec (ed.), *Architectures de l'âge du Fer en Europe occidentale et centrale*, 259–71. Rennes: Presses universitaires de Rennes.

Burl, A. 1988. Coves: Structural enigmas of the Neolithic. *Wiltshire Archaeological Magazine* 82, 1–18.

Burnez, C. 2010. *Le Camp à Challignac (Charente) au IIIe millénaire av. J.-C.* Oxford: British Archaeological Reports S2165.

Cahill Wilson, J. 2014. *Late Iron Age and 'Roman' Ireland*. Dublin: Discovery Programme Reports 8.

Campbell, E. 2007. *Continental and Mediterranean Imports to Atlantic Britain and Ireland, AD 400–800.* York: Council for British Archaeology.

Card, N. 2018. The Ness of Brodgar. *Current Archaeology* 335, 20–28.

Carlie, A. 2004. *Forntida byggnadskult*. Stockholm: Riksantikvarieämbetets forlag.

Carlin, N. 2017. Getting into the groove: Exploring the relationship between Grooved Ware and developed passage tombs in Ireland c. 3000–2700 cal BC. *Proceedings of the Prehistoric Society* 83, 155–88.

Carlin, N. 2018. *The Beaker Phenomenon? Understanding the Character and Context of Social Practices in Ireland 2500–2000 BC.* Leiden: Sidestone Press.

Carson, R. and O'Kelly, C. 1977. A catalogue of the Roman coins from Newgrange, Co. Meath, and notes on the coins and related finds. *Proceedings of the Royal Irish Academy* 77C, 35–55.

Carsten, J. and Hugh-Jones, S. (eds). 1995. *About the House: Levi-Strauss and Beyond.* Cambridge: Cambridge University Press.

Carsten, J. and Hugh-Jones, S. 1995. Introduction. In J. Carsten and S. Hugh-Jones (eds), *About the House: Levi-Strauss and Beyond*, 1–46. Cambridge: Cambridge University Press.

Carstens, L. 2015. Powerful space. The Iron-Age hall and its development during the Viking Age. In M.H. Eriksen, U. Pedersen, B. Rundberget, I. Axelsen and H.L. Berg (eds), *Viking Worlds. Things, Space and Movement*, 12–27. Oxford: Oxbow.

Carver, M. 2005. *Sutton Hoo: A Seventh-century Princely Burial Ground and its Context.* London: British Museum Press.

Carver, M. 2019. *Formative Britain. An Archaeology of Britain, Fifth to Eleventh Centuries AD.* Abingdon: Routledge.

Cassidy, L., Ó Maoldúin, R., Kador, T., Lynch, A., Jones, C., Woodman, P., Murphy, E., Ramsey, G., Dowd, M., Noonan, A., Campbell, C., Jones, E., Mattiangeli, V. and Bradley, D. 2020. A dynastic elite in monumental Neolithic society. *Nature* 582, 384–88.

Chambon, P. 2020. 'Cicéron c'est Poincaré'. Dealing with geometry, Neolithic house plans and the earliest monuments. In A. Barclay, D. Field and J. Leary (eds), *Houses of the Dead?,* 47–58. Oxford: Oxbow.

Chapman, J., Yu, M., Gaydarska, B., Burdo, N. and Hale, D. 2014. Architectural differentiation on a Trypillia mega-site: Preliminary report on the excavation of a mega-structure at Nebelivka, Ukraine. *Journal of Neolithic Archaeology* 16, 135–56.

Chaume, B. and Mordant, C. (eds). 2011. *Le complexe aristocratique de Vix: nouvelles recherches sur l'habitat, le système de fortification et l'environnement du mont Lassois.* Dijon: Éditions Universitaires de Dijon.

Cherry, J. 1978. Generalisation and the archaeology of the state. In D. Green, C. Haselgrove and M. Spriggs (eds), *Social Organisation and Settlement*, 411–37. Oxford: British Archaeological Reports.

Childe, V.G. 1949.The origin of Neolithic culture in Northern Europe. *Antiquity* 23, 129–35.

Christensen, T. 2015. *Lejre bag Myten*. Moesgård: Jysk Arkaeologisk Selskab.

Clark, S. and Wyse, A. 1999. Evidence for extramural settlement north of the Roman fort of Newstead (Trimontium), Roxburghshire. *Proceedings of the Society of Antiquaries of Scotland* 129, 373–91.

Clarke, H. and Lamm, K. 2017. *Helgö Revisited: A New Look at the Excavated Evidence for Helgö, Central Sweden*. Schleswig: Verein zur Förderung des Archäologischen Landesmuseums.

Cleal, R., Walker, K. and Montague, R. 1995. *Stonehenge in its Landscape: Twentieth Century Excavations*. London: English Heritage.

Coles, B. 1998. Wood options for wooden figurines. In A. Gibson and D. Simpson (eds), *Prehistoric Ritual and Religion*, 163–73. Stroud: Sutton.

Corlett, C. and Potterton, M. (eds). 2012. *Life and Death in Iron Age Ireland in the Light of Recent Archaeological Excavations*. Dublin: Wordwell.

Coudart, A. 1998. *Architecture et société néolithique: l'unité et la variance de la maison danubienne*. Paris: Maison des sciences de l'homme.

Craig, O., Shilito, L.M., Albarella, U., Viner-Daniels, S., Chan, B., Cleal, R., Ixer, R., Jay, M., Marshall, P., Simmons, E., Wright, E. and Parker Pearson, M. 2015. Feeding Stonehenge: Cuisine and consumption at the Late Neolithic site of Durrington Walls. *Antiquity* 89, 1096–109.

Cramp, R. 1957. Beowulf and archaeology. *Medieval Archaeology* 1, 57–77.

Crampton, P. 1967. *Stonehenge of the Kings: A People Appear*. London: Baker.

Cunliffe, B. 2018. *The Ancient Celts*, 2nd edition. Oxford: Oxford University Press.

Cunnington, M. 1929. *Woodhenge*. Devizes: George Simpson.

Darvill, T. 1996. Neolithic buildings in England, Wales and the Isle of Man. In T. Darvill and J. Thomas (eds), *Neolithic Houses in Northwest Europe and Beyond*, 77–111. Oxford: Oxbow.

Darvill, T. 2016. Houses of the Holy: Architecture and meaning in the structure of Stonehenge, Wiltshire, UK. *Time and Mind* 9, 89–121.

Darvill, T., Marshall, P., Parker Pearson, M. and Wainwright, G. 2012. Stonehenge remodelled. *Antiquity* 86, 1021–40.

David, A., Cole, M., Horsley, T., Linford, N., Linford, P. and Martin, L. 2004. A rival to Stonehenge? Geophysical survey at Stanton Drew, England. *Antiquity* 78, 341–58.

Debert, J. 2016. When artefacts can't speak: Towards a new understanding of British Early Neolithic timber structures. In J. Debert, M. Larsson and J. Thomas (eds), *In Dialogue: Tradition and Interaction in the Mesolithic–Neolithic transition*, 19–26. Oxford: British Archaeological Reports.

DeBoer, W. 1997. Ceremonial centres from the Cayapas (Ecuador) to Chilli-cothe (Ohio, USA). *Cambridge Archaeological Journal* 7, 225–53.

Dietrich, O. 2011. Radiocarbon dating the first temples of mankind. Comments on 14C dates from Göbekli Tepe. *Zeitschrift für Orient-Archäologie* 4, 12–25.

Dietrich, O., Heun, M., Notroff, J., Schmidt, K. and Zarnkow, M. 2012. The role of cult and feasting in the emergence of Neolithic communities. New evidence from Göbekli Tepe, south-eastern Turkey. *Antiquity* 86, 674–95.

Dingwall, K., Ginnever, M., Tipping, R., Van Wessel, J. and Wilson, D. 2019. *'The Land was Forever': 15,000 years in North-east Scotland*. Oxford: Oxbow.

Dockrill, S., Bond, J., Turner, V., Brown, L., Bashford, D., Cussans, J. and Nicholson, R. 2015. *Excavations at Old Scatness, Shetland, Vol. 2*. Lerwick: Shetland Heritage Publications.

Donat, P. 2018. *Häuser der Bronze- und Eisenzeit im mittleren Europa*. Langenweissbach: Beir & Beran.

Edmonds, M. 2019. *Orcadia. Land, Sea and Stone in Neolithic Orkney*. London: Head of Zeus.

Edwards, N. 1990. *The Archaeology of Early Medieval Ireland*. London: Routledge.

Ensor, B. 2011. Kinship theory in archaeology: From critiques to the study of transformations. *American Antiquity* 76, 203–27

Eogan, G. 2012. *The Archaeology of Knowth in the First and Second Millennia AD*. Dublin: Royal Irish Academy.

Eogan, G. and Roche, H. 1997. *Excavations at Knowth, 2*. Dublin: Royal Irish Academy.

Erdman, K. and Chaume, B. 2019. Tracing 2000 years at the source of the Douix, Côte-d'Or, France: Water, offerings, and recurrence. *Proceedings of the Prehistoric Society* 85, 307–30.

Eriksen, M.H. 2016. Commemorating dwelling. The death and burial of houses in Iron and Viking Age Scandinavia. *European Journal of Archaeology* 19, 477–96.

Eriksen, M.H. 2019. *Architecture, Society and Ritual in Viking Age Scandinavia*. Cambridge: Cambridge University Press.

Eriksen, M.H. 2020. 'Body-objects' and personhood in the Iron and Viking Ages: Processing, curating, and depositing skulls in domestic space. *World Archaaeology* 52, 103–19.

Ethelberg, P., Jørgensen, E., Meier, D. and Robinson, D. 2000. *Det sønderjyske landbrugs historie – Sten- og bronzealder*. Haderselev: Sønderjyllands Museum.

Evans, C. and Hodder, I. 2005. *A Woodland Archaeology: The Haddenham Project, Vol. 1*. Cambridge: McDonald Institute for Archaeological Research.

Evans, C., Pollard, J. and Knight, M. 1999. Life in woods: Tree-throws, 'settlement' and forest cognition. *Oxford Journal of Archaeology* 18, 241–54.

Fabech, C. and Näsman, U. 2013. Ritual landscapes and sacral places in the first millennium AD in south Scandinavia. In S.W. Nordeide and S. Brink (eds), *Sacred Sites and Holy Places: Exploring the Sacralization of Landscape through Space and Time*, 53–109. Turnhout: Brepols.

Fairweather, A. and Ralston, I. 1993. The timber halls at Balbridie, Grampian region, Scotland: The building, the date, the plant macrofossils. *Antiquity* 67, 313–23.

Fell, D. 2020. *Contact, Concord and Conquest: Britons and Romans at Scotch Corner*. Barnards Castle: Northern Archaeological Associates.

Fern, C., Dickinson, T. and Webster, L. (eds). 2020. *The Staffordshire Hoard: An Anglo-Saxon Treasure*. London: Society of Antiquaries.

Fernández Götz, M. 2016. The power of the past: Ancestral cult and collective memory in the Central European Iron Age. In V. Sîrbu, M. Jevtić, K. Dimitrović and M. Ljŭstina (eds), *Funerary Practices in the Bronze Age and Iron Age in Central and Southeast Europe*, 165–78. Belgrade: Čačak.

Fernández Götz, M. 2018. Urbanisation in Iron Age Europe: Trajectories, patterns and social dynamics. *Journal of Archaeological Research* 26, 117–62.

Fitzpatrick, E. 2004. *Royal Inauguration in Gaelic Ireland c. 1100–1600*. Woodbridge: Boydell Press.

Flannery, K. and Marcus, J. 2014. *The Creation of Inequality*. Cambridge, MA: Harvard University Press.

Fouéré, P. 1998. Deux grands bâtiments du Néolithique final artenacien à Douchapt (Dordogne). In A. D'Anna and D. Binder (eds), *Production et identité culturelle. Actualité de la recherche*, 311–28. Antibes: Éditions Association pour la promotion et la diffusion des connaissances archéologiques.

Frei, K., Bergerbrand, S., Jorkov, M., Harvig, L., Sikora, M., Price, T.D., Frei, R. and Kristiansen, K. 2019. Mapping human mobility during the third and second millennia BC in present-day Denmark. *PLOS ONE* 14(8), e0219850.

Fulford, M., Clarke, A., Durham, E. and Pankhurst, N. 2018. *Iron Age Calleva*. Britannia Monograph 32. London: Society for the Promotion of Roman Studies.

Gardiner, M. 2013. The sophistication of Late Anglo-Saxon timber buildings. In M. Bintley and M. Shapland (eds), *Trees and Timber in the Anglo-Saxon World*, 21–77. Oxford: Oxford University Press.

Garrow, D. and Gosden, C. 2012. *Technologies of Enchantment? Exploring Celtic Art 400 BC to AD 100*. Oxford: Oxford University Press.

Garrow, D., Gosden, C., Hill, J.D. and Bronk Ramsey, C. 2009. Dating Celtic art: A major radiocarbon dating programme of Iron Age and early Roman metalwork in Britain. *Archaeological Journal* 166, 79–123.

Gaydarska, B. (ed.) 2020. *Early Urbanism in Europe. The Trypillia Megasites of the Ukrainian Forest-Steppe*. Berlin: De Gruyter.

Gaydarska, B., Nebbia, M. and Chapman, J. 2020. Trypillia megasites in context: Independent urban development in Chalcolithic Eastern Europe. *Cambridge Archaeological Journal* 30, 97–101.

Gerritsen, F. 1999. To build or to abandon. The cultural biography of late prehistoric farmsteads in the southern Netherlands. *Archaeological Dialogues* 6(2), 78–114.

Gerritsen, F. 2003. *Local Identities. Landscape and Community in the Late Prehistoric Meuse – Demer – Scheldt Region.* Amsterdam: Amsterdam University Press.

Gibbons, M. and Gibbons, M. 2016. The Brú: A Hiberno-Roman cult site at Newgrange? *Emania* 23, 67–78.

Gibson, A. 2000. Circles and henges: Reincarnation of past traditions? *Archaeology Ireland* 14, 11–14.

Gibson, A. 2005. *Stonehenge and Timber Circles*. Stroud: Tempus.

Gibson, A. 2010. Dating Balbirnie: Recent radiocarbon dates from the stone circle at Balbirnie, Fife, and a review of its place in the Balfarg/Balbirnie site sequence. *Proceedings of the Society of Antiquaries of Scotland* 140, 51–77.

Gibson, T. 1995. Having your house and eating it: Houses and siblings in Ara, south Sulawesi. In J. Carsten and C. Hugh-Jones (eds), *About the House: Levi-Strauss and Beyond*, 129–48. Cambridge: Cambridge University Press.

Giles, M. 2012. *A Forged Glamour: Landscape, Identity and Material Culture in the Iron Age*. Oxford: Windgather Press.

Gillespie, S. 2000. Lévi-Strauss: Maison and sociétés à maisons. In R. Joyce and S. Gillespie (eds), *Beyond Kinship. Social and Material Reproduction in House Societies*, 22–52. Philadelphia, PA: University of Pennsylvania Press.

Gillespie, S. 2007. When is a House? In R. Beck (ed.), *The Durable House: House Society Models in Archaeology*, 25–50. Carbondale, IL: Southern Illinois University.

Gillings, M., Pollard, J. and Strutt, K. 2019. The origins of Avebury. *Antiquity* 44, 480–99.

Gleeson, P. 2012. Constructing kingship in early medieval Ireland: Power, place and ideology. *Medieval Archaeology* 65, 1–33.

Gleeson, P. 2018. Gathering communities: Locality, governance and rulership in early medieval Ireland. *World Archaeology* 50, 100–20.

Gleeson, P. 2020. Archaeology and myth: Making the gods in early medieval Europe. *Medieval Archaeology* 64, 65–93.

Glob, P. 1951. *Ard och plov in Nordens Oldtid*. Aarhus: Aarhusuniversitetsforlaget i Aarhus.

González-Ruibal, A. and Ruiz-Gálvez, M. 2016. House-societies in the ancient Mediterranean. *Journal of World Prehistory* 29, 383–437.

Greaney, S., Hazell, Z., Barclay, A., Bronk Ramsay, C., Dunbar, E., Hadjas, I., Reimer, P., Pollard, J., Sharples, N. and Marshall, P. 2020. Tempo of a mega-henge: A new chronology for Mount Pleasant, Dorchester, Dorset. *Proceedings of the Prehistoric Society* 86, 199–236.

Gregory, T. 1991. *Excavations in Thetford 1980–1982. Fisons Way*. Norwich: East Anglian Archaeology 53.

Grogan, E. 2008. *The Rath of the Synods, Tara, Co. Meath*. Dublin: Wordwell.

Haggarty, A. 1991. Machrie Moor, Arran: Recent excavations of two stone circles. *Proceedings of the Society of Antiquaries of Scotland* 58, 51–94.

Hamerow, H. 2002. *Early Medieval Settlements*. Oxford: Oxford University Press.

Hamerow, H. 2010. Herrenhöfe in Anglo-Saxon England. *Siedlungs- und Küstenforschung im südlichen Nordseegebiet* 33, 59–67.

Hamerow, H. 2012. *Rural Settlements and Society in Anglo-Saxon England*. Oxford: Oxford University Press.

Hamerow, H. and McBride, A. 2018. A seventh-century 'great hall complex' at Long Wittenham, Oxfordshire. *Medieval Settlement Research* 33, 88–89.

Harding, D. 2009. *The Iron Age Round-house*. Oxford: Oxford University Press.

Harding, D. 2017. *The Iron Age in Northern Britain*, 2nd edition. London: Routledge.

Harding, D., Blake, I. and Reynolds, P. 1993. *An Iron Age Settlement in Dorset. Excavation and Reconstruction*. Edinburgh: Edinburgh University Department of Archaeology.

Härke, H. 1990. Warrior graves? The background of the Anglo-Saxon weapon rite. *Past and Present* 126, 22–43.

Hartwell, B. 1998. The Ballynahatty complex. In A. Gibson and D. Simpson (eds), *Prehistoric Ritual and Religion*, 32–44. Stroud: Sutton.

Haselgrove, C. (ed.) 2016. *Cartimandua's Capital?* York: Council for British Archaeology.

Hawkes, S. and Hawkes, C. 2012. *Longbridge Deverill Cow Down*. Oxford: Oxford University School of Archaeology.

Heaney, S. trans. 1999. *Beowulf*. London: Faber and Faber.

Hedeager, L. 2011. *Iron Age Myth and Materiality*. Abingdon: Routledge.

Herschend, F. 1993. The origin of the hall in Southern Scandinavia. *Tor* 25, 175–99.

Herschend, F. 1998. *The Idea of the Good in Late Iron Age Society*. Uppsala: Uppsala University.

Herschend, F. 2000. Ship grave hall passage – the Oseberg monument as compound meaning. *Proceedings of the 11th International Saga Conference*, 2–7. Sydney: Sydney University.

Herschend, F. 2001. *Journey of Civilisation. The Late Iron Age View of the Human World*. Uppsala: Uppsala University.

Hey, G., Bell, C. Dennis, C. and Robinson, M. 2016. *Yarnton: Neolithic and Bronze Age Settlement and Landscape*. Oxford: Oxford Archaeology.

Hills, C. 1997. Beowulf and archaeology. In R. Bjork and J. Niles (eds), *A Beowulf Handbook*, 291–312. Exeter: University of Exeter Press.

Hines, J. 2011. Literary sources and archaeology. In H. Hamerow, D. Hinton and S. Crawford (eds), *The Oxford Handbook of Anglo-Saxon Archaeology*, 968–85. Oxford: Oxford University Press.

Hofmann, D. 2013. Living by the lake. Domestic architecture in the Alpine Foreland. In D. Hofmann and J. Smyth (eds), *Tracking the Neolithic House in Europe*, 197–227. New York: Springer.

Hofmann, D. and Lenneis, E. 2017. Size matters? Explaining exceptional buildings in the central European early Neolithic. In P. Bickle, V. Cummings, D. Hofmann and J. Pollard (eds), *The Neolithic of Europe*, 145–58. Oxford: Oxbow.

Holmquist, L. 2016. Birka's defence works and harbour. In L. Holmquist, S. Kalmring and C. Hedenstierna-Jonson (eds), *New Aspects on Viking-age Urbanism*, 35–43. Stockholm: Stockholm University Archaeological Research Laboratory.

Holst, M.K., Jessen, M., Andersen, S. and Pedersen, A. 2000. The late Viking-Age royal construction at Jelling, central Jutland, Denmark. *Praehistorische Zeitschrift* 87, 474–504.

Holst, M.K., Rasssmussen, M., Kristiansen, K. and Bech, J-H. 2013. Bronze Age 'herostats': Ritual, political and domestic economies in Bronze Age Denmark. *Proceedings of the Prehistoric Society* 79, 265–96.

Hooke, D. 2013. Christianity and the 'sacred tree'. In M. Bintley and M. Shapland (eds), *Trees and Timber in the Anglo-Saxon World*, 228–50. Oxford: Oxford University Press.

Hope-Taylor, B. 1962. The 'boat-shaped' house in Northern Europe. *Proceedings of the Cambridge Antiquarian Society* 55, 16–22.

Hope-Taylor, B. 1977. *Yeavering. An Anglo-British Centre of Early Northumbria*. London: HMSO.

Hugh-Jones, C. 1979. *From the Milk River*. Cambridge: Cambridge University Press.

Hugh-Jones, C. 2002. Houses in the Neolithic imagination: An Amazonian example. In T. Darvill and J. Thomas (eds), *Neolithic Houses in Northwest Europe and Beyond*, 185–93. Oxford: Oxbow.

Hughes, G., Woodward, A., Barnett, S., Bashford, L. and Bredon, M. 2015. *The Iron Age and Romano-British Settlement at Crick Covert Farm*. Oxford: Archaeopress.

Hukantaival, S. 2016. *'For a Witch Cannot Cross the Threshold'. Building Concealment Traditions in Finland c. 1200–1950*. Turku: University of Turku.

Hultgård, A. 2006. The Askr and Embla myth in a comparative perspective. In A. Andrén, K. Jennbert and C. Raudvere (eds), *Old Norse Religion in Long-term Perspectives*, 58–62. Lund: Nordic Academic Press.

Hunter, F. 1999. Iron Age hoarding in Scotland and northern England. In A. Gwilt and C. Haselgrove (eds), *Reconstructing Iron Age Societies*, 108–33. Oxford: Oxbow.

Hunter, F. in press. First contacts in Scotland: A review of old and new evidence. In N. Mrđíc (ed.), *Proceedings of the 24th Limes Congress*. Belgrade: Institute of Archaeology.

Ihuel, I., Mallet, N., Pelegrin, J. and Verjux, C. 2015. The dagger phenomenon: Circulation from the Grand-Pressigny region (Frances, Indre-et-Loire) in western Europe. In M. Prieto Martínez and L. Salanova (eds), *The Beaker Tradition in Europe*, 113–26. Oxford: Oxbow.

Jakhelln, G. 2005. Høvdingsetet på Borg. Konstruksjonsspor er nødvendig, men ikke tilstrekkelig for tolkning. *AmS-Varia* 43, 137–46.

Jackson, K. 1964. *The Oldest Irish Tradition: A Window on the Iron Age*. Cambridge: Cambridge University Press.

Jessen, M., Holst, M., Lindblom, C. and Pedersen, A. 2014. A palisade fit for a king: Ideal architecture at King Harald Bluetooth's Jelling. *Norwegian Archaeological Review* 47, 42–64.

Johnston, S., Campana, D. and Crabtree, P. 2009. A geophysical survey at Dún Ailinne, County Kildare, Ireland. *Journal of Field Archaeology* 34, 385–402.

Johnston, S. and Wailes, B. 2007. *Dún Ailinne: Excavations at an Irish Royal Site 1968–1975.* Philadelphia, PA: University of Pennsylvania Museum of Archaeology and Anthropology.

Jones, A.M. and Díaz-Guardamino, M. 2019. *Making a Mark.* Oxford: Oxbow.

Jørgensen, L. 2004. Norse religion and religious sites in Scandinavia in the 6th–11th century. In H.C. Gulløv (ed.), *Northern Worlds*, 129–50. Copenhagen: National Museum.

Jørgensen, L. 2009. Pre-Christian cult at aristocratic residences and settlement complexes in southern Scandinavia in the 3rd–10th centuries AD. In U. von Freeden, H. Friesinger and E. Wamers (eds), *Glaube, Kult und Herrschaft*, 329–54. Bonn: Rudolf Habelt.

Jørgensen, L. 2010. Gudme and Tissø. Two magnate complexes in Denmark from the 3rd to the 11th century AD. In B. Ludowici (ed.), *Trade and Communication Networks of the First Millennium AD*, 273–85. Stuttgart: Niedersächsisches Landsmuseum Hannover.

Joseph, F., Julien, M., Leroy-Langelin, E., Lorin, Y. and Praud, I. 2011. L'architecture domestique des sites du IIIe millénaire avant notre ère dans le Nord de la France. *Révue Archéologique de Picardie* numéro spécial 28, 249–73.

Joyce, R. and Gillespie, S. (eds). 2000. *Beyond Kinship. Social and Material Reproduction in House Societies.* Philadelphia, PA: University of Pennsylvania Press.

Kaliff, A. and Oestergaard, T. 2018. *Bronze Age Håga and the Viking King Björn.* Uppsala: Uppsala University.

Kienlin, T. and Blanco-González, A. 2020. *Current Approaches to Tells in the Prehistoric Old World.* Oxford: Oxbow.

Kirby, M. 2011. Lockerbie Academy: Neolithic and Early Historic timber halls, a Bronze Age cemetery, an undated enclosure and a post-medieval corn-drying kiln in south-west Scotland. *Scottish Archaeological Internet Reports* 46. Available at: https://archaeologydataservice.ac.uk/archives/view/sair/contents.cfm?vol=46.

Knipper, C., Mittnik, K., Massey, C., Kucukkalipici, I., Mauss, F., Winterborn, E. Stastiewicz, J., Krause, J. and Stockhammer, P. 2017. Female exogamy and gene pool diversification in the transition from the final Neolithic to the Early Bronze Age in Central Europe. *Proceedings of the National Academy of Science* 114(38), 1–6. DOI: 10.1073/pnas.1706355114.

Knitter, D., Braun, R., Clare, L., Nykamp, M and Schütt, B. 2019. Göbekli Tepe: A brief description of the environmental development of the surroundings of the UNESCO World Heritage Site. *Land* 8, 72.

Kondis, J. 1975. Olympia. In E. Melas (ed.), *Temples and Sanctuaries of Ancient Greece*, 101–16. London: Thames and Hudson.

Lamdin-Whymark, H. 2008. *The Residue of Ritualised Action: Neolithic Depositional Practices in the Middle Thames Valley*. Oxford: British Archaeological Reports.

Lapidge, M. 2000. The archetype of *Beowulf. Anglo-Saxon England* 29, 5–41.

Laporte, L. and Tinévez, J.Y. 2004. Neolithic houses and chambered tombs of Western France. *Cambridge Archaeological Journal* 14, 217–34.

Laporte, L. 2012. Dépôts de mobilier, architectures et pratiques funéraires dans le Centre-Ouest de la France au cours du Néolithique récent et final, dans son context atlantique. In M. Sohn and J. Vaquer (eds), *Sépultures de la fin du Néolithique en Europe occidentale*, 113–45. Toulouse: Archives d'Ecologie Préhistorique.

Larsson, L. (ed.) 2004. *Continuity for Centuries. A Ceremonial Building and its Context at Uppåkra, southern Sweden*. Stockholm: Almqvist and Wiksell.

Larsson, L. 2019. Uppåkra. A central site in the south Scandinavian Iron Age. *Acta Archaeologica* 90, 13–42.

Laurelut, C. 2011. Mairy (Ardennes françaises): un site d'habitat … ou pas? Premiers éléments de réflexion sur la fonction du site. *Révue Archéologique de Picardie* numéro special 28, 139–65.

Leigh, J., Stout, G. and Stout, M. 2019. Report on the research excavation at Newgrange Farm. *Ríocht na Midh*, 15–51.

Lévi-Strauss, C. 1949. *Les structures élementaires de la parenté*. Paris: Presses universitaires de France.

Lévi-Strauss, C. 1975. *La voie des masques*. Geneva: Albert Skira.

Ling, J., Earle, T. and Kristiansen, K. 2018. Maritime mode of production: Raiding and trading in seafaring chiefdoms. *Current Anthropology* 59, 488–524.

Ljundqvist, J. and Frölund, P. 2015. Gamla Uppsala – the emergence of a centre and a magnate complex. *Journal of Archaeology and Ancient History* 16, 2–30.

Louboutin, C., Olivier, L., Constantin, C. Sidéra, I., Tresset, A. and Farrugia, J-P. 1994. La Tricherie à Beaumont (Vienne): un site d'habitat du Néolithique récent. In X. Gutherz and R. Joussaume (eds), *Le Néolithique du Centre-Ouest de la France*, 307–25. Poitiers: Association des archéologues de Poitou-Charentes.

Løvschal, M. and Holst, M. 2018. Govering martial traditions. Post-conflict ritual sites in Iron Age Northern Europe (200 BC–AD 200). *Journal of Anthropological Archaeology* 50, 27–39.

Løvschal, M., Iversen, R.B. and Holst, M.K. 2019. *De dræbte krigere i Alken Enge*. Aarhus: Jysk Arkeologisk Selskab.

Ludowici, B. (ed.) 2010. *Trade and Communication Networks of the First Millennium AD*. Stuttgart: Niedersächsisches Landesmuseum Hannover.

Lund, J. and Arwill-Nordbladh, E. 2016. Divergent ways of relating to the past in the Viking Age. *European Journal of Archaeology* 19, 415–38.

Lynn, C. and McDowell, J. 2011. *Deer Park Farms. The Excavation of a Raised Rath in the Glenarm Valley, Co. Antrim*. Belfast: Stationery Office.

Lynn, C. 1977. Trial excavations at the King's Stables, Tray Townland, County Armagh. *Ulster Journal of Archaeology* 40, 42–62.

Lynn, C. 2003. *Navan Fort. Archaeology and Myth*. Bray: Wordwell.

Macalister, R. and Praeger, R. 1928. Report on the excavation of Uisneach. *Proceedings of the Royal Irish Academy* 38C, 69–126.

Macdonald, P. 2007. *Llyn Cerrig Bach. A Study of the Copper Alloy Artefacts from the Insular La Tène Assemblage*. Cardiff: University of Wales Press.

MacGregor, M. 1976. *Early Celtic Art in North Britain*. Leicester: Leicester University Press.

Macinnes, L. 1984. Brochs and the Roman occupation of lowland Scotland. *Proceedings of the Society of Antiquaries of Scotland* 114, 235–49.

MacKie, E. 2016. *Brochs and the Empire*. Oxford: Archaeopress.

Madgwick, R., Grimes, V., Lamb, A., Nederbragt, A., Evans, J. and McCormick, F. 2019a. Feasting and mobility in Iron Age Ireland: Multi-isotope analysis reveals the vast catchment of Navan Fort, Ulster. *Nature Scientific Reports* 9, 19792.

Madgwick, R., Lamb, A., Sloane, H., Nederbragt, A., Albarella, U., Parker Pearson, M. and Evans, J. 2019b. Multi-isotope analysis reveals that feasts in the Stonehenge environs and across Wessex drew people and animals throughout Britain. *Science Advances* 5(3). DOI: 10.1126/sciadv.aau6078

Main, L. 1998. Excavation of a timber round-house and broch at the Fairy Knowe, Buchlyvie, Stirlingshire, 1975–8. *Proceedings of the Society of Antiquaries of Scotland* 128, 293–417.

Mallet, N., Ihuel, E. and Verjux, C. 2012. Le diffusion des silex du Grand-Pressigny au néolithique. *Revue archéologique du Centre de la France* Supplément 38, 131–47.

Mallory, J. 2000. Excavation of the Navan ditch. *Emania* 18, 21–35.

Mallory, J. 2016. *In Search of the Irish Dreamtime. Archaeology and Early Irish Literature*. London: Thames and Hudson.

Mallory, J. and Baban, G. 2014. Excavations in Haughey's Fort East. *Emania* 22, 13–32.

McBride, A. 2020. *The Role of Anglo-Saxon Great Hall Complexes in King-dom Formation, in Comparison, and in Context AD 500–750*. Oxford: Archaeopress.

McFadyen, L. 2007. Neolithic architecture and participation: Practices of making in early Neolithic Britain. In J. Last (ed.), *Beyond the Grave*, 22–9. Oxford: Oxbow.

McGarry, T. 2009. Irish late prehistoric burial ring-ditches. In G. Cooney, K. Becker, J. Coles, M. Ryan and S. Sievers (eds), *Relics of Old Decency: Archaeological Studies of Later Prehistory*, 413–23. Dublin: Wordwell.

McHugh, R. and Scott, B. 2014. The prehistoric archaeology of County Fer-managh. In C. Foley and R. McHugh (eds), *An Archaeological Survey of County Fermanagh*, 55–164. Belfast: Northern Ireland Environment and Heritage Service.

Megaw, V. and Megaw, R. 2001. *Celtic Art: From its Beginning to the Book of Kells*. London: Thames and Hudson.

Meller, H. 2019. Princes, arms, sanctuaries: The emergence of complex authority in the central German Únětice Culture. *Acta Archaeologica* 90, 39–79.

Midgley, M. 2005. *The Monumental Cemeteries of Prehistoric Europe*. Stroud: Tempus.

Miket, R. 2013. Understanding British/Anglo-Saxon continuity at Gefrin: Brian Hope-Taylor's excavations on Yeavering Bell. *Archaeologia Aeliana* 42, 133–60.

Mikkelsen, M. 2019. Two-aisled houses from the area around Viborg and Holstebro. In L. Sparrevohn, O. Kastholm and P.O. Nielsen (eds), *Houses for the Living: Two-aisled Houses from the Neolithic and Early Bronze Age in Denmark*, 215–36. Copenhagen: University of Southern Denmark.

Millett, M. and James, S. 1983. Excavations at Cowdery's Down, Basingstoke, Hampshire, 1978–81. *Archaeological Journal* 140, 151–279.

Moore, T. and Ponroy, C. 2014. What's in a wall? Considerations on the role of open settlements in La Tène Gaul. In H. Wendling and K. Winger (eds), *Paths to Complexity. Centralisation and Urbanisation in Iron Age Europe*, 140–55. Oxford: Oxbow.

Müller, J. 2011. *Megaliths and Funnel Beaker Societies in Change 4100–2700 BC*. Amsterdam: Kroon-Voordecht 13.

Müller, J. 2018. Social memories and site biographies: Construction and per-ception in non-literate societies. *Analecta Praehistorica Leidensia* 49, 9–17.

Munch, G.S., Johansen, O.S. and Roesdahl, E. 2003. *Borg in Lofoten. A Chief-tain's Farm in North Norway*. Trondheim: Tapir.

Murray, H. and Murray, C. 2014. Mesolithic and Early Neolithic activity along the Dee: Excavations at Garthdee Road, Aberdeen. *Proceedings of the Society of Antiquaries of Scotland* 144, 1–64.

Murray, H., Murray, C. and Fraser, S. 2009. *A Tale of Unknown Unknowns: A Mesolithic Pit Alignment and a Neolithic Timber Hall at Warren Field, Crathes, Aberdeenshire*. Oxford: Oxbow.

Naylor, J. 2015. The deposition and hoarding of non-precious metals in early medieval England. In J. Naylor and R. Bland (eds), *Hoarding and the Deposition of Metalwork from the Bronze Age to the 20th Century: A British Perspective*, 125–43. Oxford: British Archaeological Reports.

Newman, C. 1997. *Tara: An archaeological survey*. Dublin: The Discovery Programme.

Newman, C. 1998. Reflections on the making of a 'royal site' in early Ireland. *World Archaeology* 30, 127–41.

Newman, C. 2011. The sacral landscape of Tara: A preliminary exploration. In R. Schot, C. Newman and E. Bhreatnach (eds), *Landscapes of Cult and Kingship*, 22–43. Dublin: Four Courts Press.

Nicolas, C., Favrel, Q., Rousseau, L., Ard, V., Blanchet, S., Donnart, K., Fromont, N., Manceau, L. Marcigny, C., Marticorena, P., Nicolas, T., Pailler, Y. and Ripoche, J. 2019. The introduction of the Bell Beaker Culture in Atlantic France: An overview of settlements. In A. Gibson (ed.), *Bell Beaker Settlement of Europe*, 329–52. Oxford: Prehistoric Society Research Paper 9.

Nielsen, P.O. 2019. The development of two-aisled longhouses in the Neolithic and Early Bronze Age. In L. Sparrevohn, O. Kastholm and P.O. Nielsen (eds), *Houses for the Living: Two-aisled Houses from the Neolithic and Early Bronze Age in Denmark*, 9–50. Copenhagen: University of Southern Denmark.

Nielsen, P.O., Randsborg, K. and Thrane, H. (eds). 1994. *The Archaeology of Gudme and Lundeborg*. Copenhagen: Akademisk Forlag.

Niles, J. and Osborn, M. (eds). 2007. *Beowulf and Lejre*. Tempe: Medieval and Renaissance Texts and Studies 223.

Noble, G. 2006. *Neolithic Scotland: Timber, Stone, Earth and Fire*. Edinburgh: Edinburgh University Press.

Noble, G. 2017. *Woodland in the Neolithic of Northern Europe: The Forest as Ancestor*. Cambridge: Cambridge University Press.

Noble, G., Gondek, M., Campbell, E., Evans, N., Hamilton, D. and Taylor, S. 2019. A powerful place of Pictland. Interdisciplinary perspectives on a power centre of the 4th to 6th centuries AD. *Medieval Archaeology* 63, 56–94.

Noble, G., Greig, M. and Millican, K. 2012. Excavations at a multi-period site at Greenbogs, Aberdeenshire, Scotland and the four-post timber architecture tradition of Late Neolithic Britain and Ireland. *Proceedings of the Prehistoric Society* 78, 135–71.

Norgård Jørgensen, A. 2003. Fortifications and the control of land and sea traffic in the pre-Roman and Roman Iron Age. In L. Jørgensen, B. Storgaard and L. Gebauer Thomson (eds), *The Spoils of Victory. The North in the Shadow of the Roman Empire*, 194–209. Copenhagen: National Museum.

Nowakowski, J. and Johns, C. 2015. *Bypassing Indian Queens*. CD. Truro: Cornwall County Council.

O'Brien, C. and Miket, R. 1991. The early medieval settlement at Thirlings. *Durham Archaeological Journal* 7, 57–91.

O'Brien, M. and Waddell, J. 2018. Excavations at a linear earthwork at Teltown, C. Meath. *Journal of Irish Archaeology* 27, 33–56.

O'Brien, W. and O'Driscoll, J. 2017. *Hillforts, Warfare and Society in Bronze Age Ireland*. Oxford: Archaeopress.

O'Connell, A. 2013. *Harvesting the Stars: A Pagan Temple at Lismullin, Co. Meath*. Dublin: National Roads Authority.

O'Driscoll, J., Gleeson, P. and Noble, G. 2020. Re-imagining Navan Fort: New light on the evolution of a major ceremonial centre in Northern Europe. *Oxford Journal of Archaeology* 39, 247–73.

O'Kelly, M. 1982. *Newgrange: Archaeology, Art and Legend*. London: Thames and Hudson.

Olalde, I., Brace, S., Allentoft, M.E., Armit, I., Kristiansen, K., Booth, T., Rohland, N., Mallick, S., Szécsényi-Nagy, A., Mittnik, A., Altena, E., Lipson, M., Lazaridis, I., Harper, T.K., Patterson, N., Broomandkhoshbacht, N., Diekmann, Y., Faltyskova, Z., Fernandes, D., Ferry, M., Harney, E., de Knijff, P., Michel, M., Oppenheimer, J., Stewardson, K., Barclay, A., Alt, K.W., Liesau, C., Ríos, P., Blasco, C., Vega Miguel, J., Menduiña García, R., Avilés Fernández, A., Bánffy, E., Bernabò-Brea, M., Billoin, D., Bonsall, C., Bonsall, L., Allen, T., Büster, L., Carver, S., Castells Navarro, L., Craig, O.E., Cook, G.T., Cunliffe, B., Denaire, A., Dinwiddy, K.E., Dodwell, N., Ernée, M., Evans, C., Kuchařík, M., Francès Farré, J., Fowler, C., Gazenbeek, M., Garrido Pena, R., Haber-Uriarte, M., Haduch, E., Hey, G., Jowett, N., Knowles, T., Massy, K., Pfrengle, S., Lefranc, P., Lemercier, O., Lefebvre, A., Heras Martínez, C., Galera Olmo, V., Bastida Ramírez, A., Lomba Maurandi, J., Majó, T., McKinley, J.I., McSweeney, K., Balázs Gusztáv, M., Modi, A., Kulcsár, G., Kiss, V., Czene, A., Patay, R., Endródi, A., Köhler,

K., Hajdu, T., Szeniczey, T., Dani, J., Bernert, Z., Hoole, M., Cheronet, O., Keating, D., Velemínský, P., Dobeš, M., Candilio, F., Brown, F., Flores Fernández, R., Herrero-Corral, A.-M., Tusa, S., Carnieri, E., Lentini, L., Valenti, A., Zanini, A., Waddington, C., Delibes, G., Guerra-Doce, E., Neil, B., Brittain, M., Luke, M., Mortimer, R., Desideri, J., Besse, M., Brücken, G., Furmanek, M., Hałuszko, A., Mackiewicz, M., Rapiński, A., Leach, S., Soriano, I., Lillios, K.T., Cardoso, J.L., Pearson, M.P., Włodarczak, P., Price, T.D., Prieto, P., Rey, P.-J., Risch, R., Rojo Guerra, M.A., Schmitt, A., Serralongue, J., Silva, A.M., Smrčka, V., Vergnaud, L., Zilhão, J., Caramelli, D., Higham, T., Thomas, M.G., Kennett, D.J., Fokkens, H., Heyd, V., Sheridan, A., Sjögren, K.-G., Stockhammer, P.W., Krause, J., Pinhasi, R., Krause, J., Haak, W., Barnes, I., Lalueza-Fox, C. and Reich, D. 2018. The Beaker phenomenon and the genomic transformation of northwest Europe. *Nature* 555, 190–96. DOI: 10.1038/nature 25738.

Ó Néill, J. 2013. Being prehistoric in the Iron Age. In M. O' Sullivan, C. Scarre and M. Doyle (eds), *Tara from the Past to the Future*, 249–55. Dublin: Wordwell.

O'Sullivan, A., McCormick, F., Kerr, T., Harney, L. and Kinsella, J. 2014. *Early Medieval Dwellings and Settlements in Ireland, AD 4400–1100*. Oxford: British Archaeological Reports.

O'Sullivan, M. 2005. *Duma na nGiall: The Mound of the Hostages, Tara*. Bray: Wordwell.

Overgaard, K. 2019. Two-aisled longhouses from the Neolithic and Early Bronze Age in the Sikeborg area. In L. Sparrevohn, O. Kastholm and P.O. Nielsen (eds), *Houses for the Living: Two-aisled Houses from the Neolithic and Early Bronze Age in Denmark*, 287–95. Copenhagen: University of Southern Denmark.

Pantos, A. and Semple, S. (eds). 2003. *Assembly Places and Practices in Medieval Europe*. Dublin: Four Courts Press.

Parker Pearson, M. 2007. The Stonehenge Riverside Project: Excavations at the east entrance of Durrington Walls. In M. Larsson and M. Parker Pearson (eds), *From Stonehenge to the Baltic*, 125–44. Oxford: British Archaeological Reports.

Parker Pearson, M., Sheridan, A., Jay, M., Chamberlain, A., Richards, M., and Evans, J. (eds). 2019. *The Beaker People. Isotopes, Mobility and Diet in Prehistoric Britain*. Oxford: Prehistoric Society Research Paper 7.

Pauli Jensen, X. 2009. From fertility ritual to weapon sacrifices. The case of the south Scandinavian bog finds. In U. von Freeden, H. Friesinger and E. Wamers (eds), *Glaube, Kult und Herrschaft*, 53–64. Bonn: Rudolf Habelt.

Pautreau, J-P. 1994. Le grand bâtiment d'Antran (Vienne): une nouvelle attribution chronologique. *Bulletin de la Société Préhistorique Française* 91, 418–19.

Peek, J. 1975. *Inventaire des mégaliths de la France. 4: Région Parisienne.* Paris: CNRS.

Petrie, G. 1839. On the history and antiquities of Tara Hill. *Transactions of the Royal Irish Academy* 18, 25–232.

Plisson, H., Mallet, N., Bocquet, A. and Ramsmeyer, D. 2002. Utilisation et rôle des outils en silex du Grand-Pressigny dans les villages de Charavines et de Portalban (Néolithique final). *Bulletin de la Société préhistorique française* 99, 793–811.

Pollard, J. 1992. The Sanctuary, Overton Hill: A re-examination. *Proceedings of the Prehistoric Society* 58, 213–26.

Pollard, J. 2009. The materialisation of religious structures in the time of Stonehenge. *Material Religion* 5(3), 332–53.

Pollard, J., Garwood, P., Parker Pearson, M., Richards, C., Thomas, J. and Welham, K. 2017. Remembered and imagined belongings. Stonehenge in the age of the first metals. In P. Bickle, V. Cummings, D. Hofmann and J. Pollard (eds), *The Neolithic of Europe*, 279–97. Oxford: Oxbow.

Popham, M., Calligas, P. and Sackett, L. 1993. *Lefkandi II: the Protogeometric Building at Toumba, Part 2.* Oxford: British School at Athens, supplementary volume 23.

Praud, I., Bernard, V., Martial, E. and Palau, R. 2007. Un grand bâtiment du Néolithique final à Houplin-Ancoisne, 'Le marais de Santes' (Nord, France). In M. Bisse (ed.), *Sociétés néolithiques. Des faits archéologiques aux fonctionnements socio-économiques*, 445–60. Lausanne: Cahiers d'Archéologie Romande 108.

Prendergast, F., O'Sullivan, M., Williams, K. and Cooney, G. 2017. Facing the sun. *Archaeology Ireland* 31(4), 10–17.

Price, N. 2020. *The Children of Ash and Elm.* London: Allen Lane.

Pyzel, J. 2020. Houses of the living, houses of the dead: A view from the Polish lowlands. In A. Barclay, D. Field and J. Leary (eds), *Houses of the Dead?*, 39–46. Oxford: Oxbow.

Rackham, O. 1976. *Trees and Woodland in the British Landscape.* London: Dent.

Raftery, B. 1969. Freestone Hill, Co. Kilkenny: An Iron Age hillfort and Bronze Age cairn. Excavation: Gerhard Bersu 1948–1949. *Proceedings of the Royal Irish Academy* 68C, 1–108.

Raftery, B. 1984. *La Tène in Ireland: Problems of Origins and Chronology.* Marburg: Vorgeschtlichen Seminar Marburg.

Raftery, B. 1994. *Pagan Celtic Ireland*. London: Thames and Hudson.

Raftery, B. 1995. The conundrum of Irish Iron Age pottery. In B. Raftery, V. Megaw and V. Rigby (eds), *Sites and Sights of the Iron Age*, 149–56. Oxford: Oxbow.

Ralston, I. 2019. Going back in time: Reassessment of the timber halls at Doon Hill, Dunbar. *Transactions of the East Lothian Antiquarian and Field Naturalists' Society* 32, 4–27.

Randsborg, K. 1995. *Hjortspring. Warfare and Sacrifice in Early Europe*. Aarhus: Aarhus University Press.

Randsborg, K. 2008. Kings' Jelling. *Acta Archaeologica* 79, 1–23.

Richards, C. 2005. *Dwelling Among the Monuments*. Cambridge: McDonald Institute for Archaeological Research.

Richards, C. and Jones, R. (eds). 2016. *The Development of Neolithic House Societies in Orkney*. Oxford: Windgather.

Ritchie, J.N.G. 1974. Excavation of a stone circle and cairn at Balbirnie, Fife. *Archaeological Journal* 131, 1–32.

Roche, H. 2002. Excavations at the Ráith na Rig, Tara. *Discovery Programme Reports* 6, 19–165.

Rollason, D. 2016. *The Power of Place*. Princeton, NJ: Princeton University Press.

Rolley, C. (ed.) 2003. *Le tombe princière de Vix*. Paris: Picard.

Romankiewicz, T. 2011. *The Complex Roundhouses of the Scottish Iron Age*. Oxford: British Archaeological Reports.

Romankiewicz, T., Bradley, R. and Clarke, A. 2020. Old Kinord, Aberdeenshire. Excavation and survey at an Iron Age settlement on Deeside. *Proceedings of the Society of Antiquaries of Scotland* 149, 221–47.

Sahlins, M. 2013. *What Kinship Is – And Is Not*. Chicago: University of Chicago Press.

Sanmark, A. 2004. *Power and Conversion. A Comparative Study of Christianisation in Scandinavia*. Uppsala: Uppsala University.

Sanmark, A. 2019. *Viking Law and Order. Places and Rituals of Assembly in the Medieval North*. Edinburgh: Edinburgh University Press.

Sanmark, A., Semple, S., Mehler, N. and Iversen, F. (eds). 2013. Debating the *Thing* in the North, I. *Journal of the North Atlantic* special issue 5.

Sanmark, A., Iversen, F., Mehler, N. and Semple, S. (eds). 2015. Debating the *Thing* in the North, III. *Journal of the North Atlantic* special issue 8.

Scarre, C. 2011. *Landscapes of Neolithic Brittany*. Oxford: Oxford University Press.

Schlüter, D. 2017. 'Boring and elusive'? The dinnshenchas as a medieval Irish literary genre. *Journal of Literary Onomastics* 6, 22–31.

Schmidt, K. 2006. *Sie bauten die ersten Tempel*. Munich: Beck.

Schmidt, K. 2011. Göbekli Tepe: A Neolithic site in southeastern Anatolia. In G. McMahon and S. Steadman (eds), *The Oxford Handbook of Ancient Anatolia*, 917–33. Oxford: Oxford University Press.

Schot, R. 2011. From cult centre to royal centre: Monuments, myths and other revelations at Uisneach. In R. Scot, C. Newman and E. Bhreatnach (eds), *Landscapes of Cult and Kingship*, 87–113. Dublin: Four Courts Press.

Schot, R., Fenwick, J., Beusing, R. and Rassmann, K. 2016. A new programme of discovery at Tara. *Archaeology Ireland* 30, 18–21.

Scott, J. 1989. The stone circle at Temple Wood, Kilmartin, Argyll. *Glasgow Archaeological Journal* 15, 53–125.

Scull, C., Minter, F., and Plouviez, J. 2016. Social and economic complexity in early medieval England: A central place complex on the East Anglian kingdom at Rendlesham, Suffolk. *Antiquity* 90, 1594–612.

Shapland, M. 2013. Meanings of timber and stone in Anglo-Saxon building practice. In M. Bintley and M. Shapland (eds), *Trees and Timber in the Anglo-Saxon World*, 21–44. Oxford: Oxford University Press.

Sharples, N. 2010. *Social Relations in Later Prehistory: Wessex in the First Millennium BC.* Oxford: Oxford University Press.

Sharples, N. 2019. Monumentalising the domestic. House societies in Atlantic Scotland. In B. Currás and I. Sastre (eds), *Alternative Iron Ages. Social Theory from Archaeological Analysis*, 284–305. Abingdon: Routledge.

Shee Twohig, E., Roughley, C., Shell, C., O'Reilly, C., Clarke, P. and Swanton, G. 2010. Open-air rock art at Loughcrew, Co Meath. *Journal of Irish Archaeology* 19, 1–28.

Sheridan, A. 2004. Going round in circles? Understanding the Irish Grooved Ware 'complex' in its wider context. In H. Roche, E. Grogan, J. Bradley, J. Coles and B. Raftery (eds), *From Megaliths to Metals*, 26–37. Oxford: Oxbow.

Sheridan, A. 2013. Early Neolithic habitation structures in Britain and Ireland: A matter of circumstance and context. In D. Hofmann and J. Smyth (eds), *Tracking the Neolithic House in Europe*, 283–300. New York, NY: Springer.

Simpson, D. 1989. Neolithic Navan? *Emania* 6, 31–33.

Sims-Williams, P. 2020. An alternative to 'Celtic from the East' and 'Celtic from the West'. *Cambridge Archaeological Journal* 30, 511–29.

Sissons, J. 2010. Building a house society. The reorganisation of Maori communities around meeting houses. *Journal of the Royal Anthropological Institute* 16, 372–86.

Smyth, J. 2014. *Settlement in the Irish Neolithic*. Oxford: Prehistoric Society Research Paper 6.

Spriggs, M. 2008. Ethnographic parallels and the denial of history. *World Archaeology* 40, 538–52.

Startin, W. 1978. Linear Pottery Culture houses: Reconstruction and manpower. *Proceedings of the Prehistoric Society* 44, 143–59.

Storgaard, B. 2003. Cosmopolitan aristocrats. In L. Jørgensen, B. Storgaard and L. Gebauer Thomson (eds), *The Spoils of Victory. The North in the Shadow of the Roman Empire*, 106–25. Copenhagen: National Museum.

Stout, M. 1997. *The Irish Ringfort*. Dublin: Four Courts Press.

Sundqvist, O. 2016. *An Arena for Higher Powers. Ceremonial Buildings and Religious Strategies for Rulership in Late Iron Age Scandinavia*. Leiden: Brill.

Therkorn, L. 1987. The structures, mechanics and some aspects of inhabited behavior. In R. Brandt, W. Gooenmann-van-Waateringe and S. van der Leeuw (eds), *Assendelvers Polders Papers 1*, 177–224. Amsterdam: Cingula 12.

Thomas, A. 2016. *Art and Architecture in Neolithic Orkney*. Oxford: Archaeopress.

Thomas, G. 2013. Life before the minster: The social dynamics of monastic foundation at Anglo-Saxon Lyminge, Kent. *Antiquaries Journal* 93, 109–45.

Thomas, G. 2018. Mead-halls of the Oisingas: A new Kentish perspective on the Anglo-Saxon Great Halls complex phenomenon. *Medieval Archaeology* 62, 262–303.

Thomas, J. 2007. The internal features at Durrington Walls: Investigations in the Southern Circle and Western Enclosures. In M. Larsson and M. Parker Pearson (eds), *From Stonehenge to the Baltic*, 145–57. Oxford: British Archaeological Reports.

Thomas, J. 2010. The returns of the Rinyo-Claction Folk? The cultural significance of the Grooved Ware complex in Later Neolithic Britain. *Cambridge Archaeological Journal* 20, 1–15.

Thomas, J. 2015. House societies and founding ancestors in Early Neolithic Britain. In C. Renfrew, M. Boyd and I. Morley (eds), *Death Shall Have No Dominion*, 138–53. Cambridge: Cambridge University Press.

Thomas, J. 2016. House societies and the beginnings of the British Neolithic. In J. Debert, M. Larsson and J. Thomas (eds), *In Dialogue: Tradition and Interaction in the Mesolithic–Neolithic transition*, 3–10. Oxford: British Archaeological Reports.

Tinévez, J-Y. 2005. Pléchâtel (Ille-et-Vilaine), La Hersonnais: un ensemble de quatre bâtiments du Néolithique final dans le contexte des grandes architectures de l'Ouest de la France. In O. Buchsenschutz and C. Mordant (eds), *Architectures protohistoriques en Europe occidentale du Néolithique final à l'âge du Fer*, 315–29. Paris: Éditions du Comité des travaux historiques et scientifiques.

Tinévez, J-Y. and Nicolas, É. 2004. *Le site de La Hersonnais à Pléchâtel (Ille-et-Vilaine): un ensemble de bâtiments collectifs du Néolithique final.* Paris: Société Préhistorique Française.

Tinniswood, A. and Harding, A. 1991. Anglo-Saxon occupation and industrial features in the henge monument at Yeavering, Northumberland. *Durham Archaeological Journal* 7, 93–108.

Towers, R., Card, N. and Edmonds, M. 2017. *The Ness of Brodgar*. Kirkwall: Ness of Brodgar Trust.

Townend, S. 2007. What have reconstructed roundhouses ever done for us? *Proceedings of the Prehistoric Society* 73, 97–111.

Vaneeckhout, S. 2010. House societies among coastal hunter-gatherers. A case study of Stone Age Ostrobothnia, Finland. *Norwegian Archaeological Review* 43, 12–25.

Van Meijil, T. 1993. Maori meeting houses in and over time. In J. Fox (ed.), *Inside Austronesian Houses*, 194–218. Canberra: Australian National University.

Vejby, M. 2016. Radiocarbon dates from the Loughcrew Cairn H bone slips. *Oxford Journal of Archaeology* 35, 213–21.

Villard-Le Tec, A. (ed.) 2018. *Architectures de l' Âge du Fer en Europe occidentale and centrale*. Rennes: Presses Universitaires de Rennes.

Waddell, J. 2010. *The Prehistoric Archaeology of Ireland*, 2nd edition. Dublin: Wordwell.

Waddell, J. 2014. *Archaeology and Celtic Myth*. Dublin: Four Courts Press.

Waddell, J., Fenwick, J. and Barton, K. 2009. *Rathcroghan. Archaeological and Geophysical Survey in a Ritual Landscape.* Dublin: Wordwell.

Wainwright, G. 1979. *Mount Pleasant*. London: Society of Antiquaries.

Wainwright, G. and Longworth, I. 1971. *Durrington Walls: Excavations 1966–1968.* London: Society of Antiquaries.

Walker, J. 2010. In the hall. In M. Carver, A. Sanmark and S. Semple (eds), *Signals of Belief in Early England,* 83–102. Oxford: Oxbow.

Walsh, F. 2012. Iron Age sanctuary enclosure, boundary ditch and kilns at Kilmainham, Co Meath. In C. Corlett and M. Potterton (eds), *Life and Death in Iron Age Ireland in the Light of Recent Archaeological Excavations*, 303–12. Dublin: Wordwell.

Waterman, D. 1997. *Excavations at Navan Fort 1961–71.* Belfast: The Stationery Office.

Webley, L. 2007. Using and abandoning roundhouses: A reinterpretation of the evidence from Late Bronze Age–Early Iron Age Southern England. *Oxford Journal of Archaeology* 26, 127–44.

Webley, L. 2008. *Iron Age Households. Structure and Practice in Western Denmark 500 BC–AD 200*. Moesgård: Jutland Archaeological Society.

Weir, D. 1994. The environment of Emain Macha. In J. Mallory and J. Stockman (eds), *Ulidia*, 171–80. Belfast: December Publications.

Wendling, H. and Winger, K. 2014. Aspects of Iron Age urbanism at Manching. In H. Wendling, H. and K. Winger (eds), *Paths to Complexity. Centralisation and Urbanisation in Iron Age Europe*, 132–39. Oxford: Oxbow.

Wentersdorf, K. 2007. The *Beowulf*-poet's vision of Heorot. *Studies in Philology* 104, 409–26.

Wentink, K. 2006. *Ceci n'est pas une hache. Neolithic Depositions in the Northern Netherlands*. Leiden: Microweb.

Whittle, A. 2003. *The Archaeology of People. The Dimensions of Neolithic Life*. London: Routledge.

Whittle, A., Healy, F. and Bayliss, A. 2011.*Gathering Time: Dating the Early Neolithic Enclosures of Southern Britain and Ireland.* Oxford: Oxbow.

Whittle, A. 2020. The long and short of it: Memory and practice in the Early Neolithic of Britain and Ireland. In A. Barclay, D. Field and J. Leary (eds), *Houses of the Dead?*, 79–90. Oxford: Oxbow.

Wickham, C. 2016. *Medieval Europe*. New Haven, CT: Yale University Press.

Wickham-Jones, C., Kenworthy, J., Gould, A., McGregor, G. and Noble, G. 2016. Archaeological excavations at Nethermills Farm, Deeside, 1978–82. *Proceedings of the Society of Antiquaries of Scotland* 146, 7–55.

Wickham-Jones, C., Noble, G., Fraser, S., Warren, G., Tipping, R., Paterson, D., Mitchell, W., Hamilton, D. and Clarke, A. 2020. New evidence for upland occupation in the Mesolithic of Scotland. *Proceedings of the Prehistoric Society* 86, 13–42.

Williams, H. 1998. Monuments and the past in Anglo-Saxon England. *World Archaeology* 30, 90–108.

Wilmott, T. 1997. *Birdoswald. Excavations of a Roman Fort on Hadrian's Wall and its Successor Settlements*. London: English Heritage.

Wysocki, M., Griffiths, S., Hedges, R., Bayliss, A., Higham, T., Fernandez-Jalvo, Y. and Whittle, A. 2013. Dates, diet and dismemberment: Evidence from the Coldrum megalithic monument, Kent. *Proceedings of the Prehistoric Society* 79, 61–90.